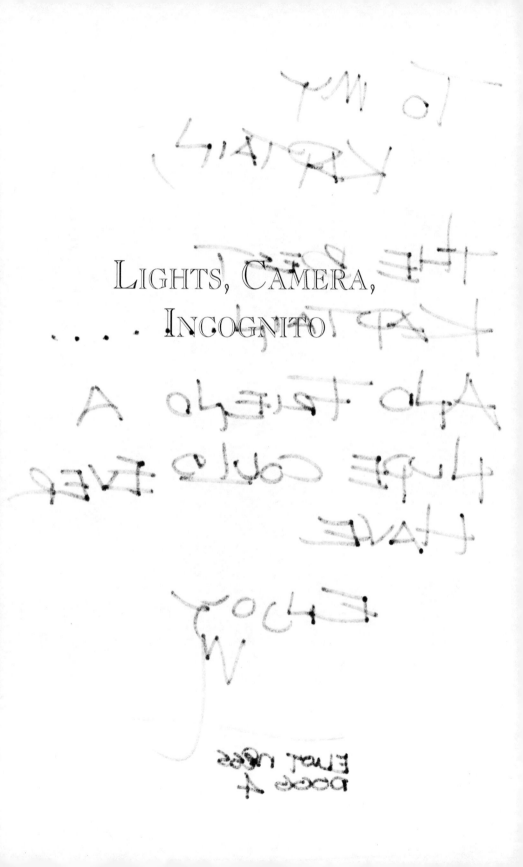

Lights, Camera,
Incognito

TO MY
KAPTAIN,

THE BEST
KAPTAIN.......
AND FRIEND A
HYPE COULD EVER
HAVE

ENJOY

ELIOT NESS
DOGG 4

Lights, Camera, Incognito

a novel by

Martin P. Travis

To order additional copies of this book, contact:
Xlibris
844-714-8691
www.Xlibris.com
Orders@Xlibris.com
827492

In memory of my wife, Geanese

To my daughters, Dana and Scarlett

Inspiration is a spirit of love

1

Summer. Night. A breeze, faint as a dying man's pulse, swirled around a badly worn old shingled roof. Dilapidated windows adorned with hairline cracks possessed the lone beam of light, that of a still burning candle staring out like a faint glimmer of a lighthouse lamp at sea.

A full moon split the midnight sky with a wide beam that leaped to the earth with the steadiness of a mountain falls stream. In the vanilla flash, the twisted weeds around the broken wood window frame slid into view as distinct and clear as a stark-colored photograph.

The landscape of predawn darkness existed all around: weeds, twigs, and mud from a day before thunderstorm. Twinlike oaks stood before the façade. A cloud covered the moon. Darkness abounded.

There was a clue of movement inside. A man paced back and forth before disappearing once more. The breeze grew stronger. An intermittent howl commenced then ceased just as quickly as it began. There was that man again. The silhouette of his head seemed flat, his arms long and muscular as he shifted back and forth. And suddenly the moon's beam appeared once more, and everything changed back.

The wind faded quickly as it appeared. The light of the moon abruptly stopped as if an executioner's switch at a penitentiary had been thrown. A rooster cock-a-doodle-dood. The birds sang. The grass wore a clinging wet cool dew like a man who wears his hat tight over his eyelids. Early-morning light slowly began to creep in, signaling the advent of one more day.

A one-story sharecropper shack stood above a grassy slope bordered with logs of wood. It was the front of the house. A chicken wire fence supposedly acted as a barricade, but the rips and holes merely made it worn looking and unsightly. The rectangle of still water from a mud puddle mirrored a sky possessing no clouds, yet it emerged into a keen brightness as the sun ascended, forming a foggy haze.

Off into the distance, a mule attempted to sample his breakfast of wild grass and discarded feed. To the mule's dismay, he was unable to enjoy the delicacy because of the persistent pestering of a floppy-eared bloodhound. The place was Tuskegee, Alabama, on a summer morning in 1927.

The man continued his slow deliberate pacing on a creaky wood and dirt floor. He was dressed in a blue collared shirt and old worn slacks. A soiled handkerchief drooped like a wilted rose from his back pocket. His navy blue suit jacket, handed down to him by his older brother, was two sizes too big.

A cast-iron pot sat in the middle of the living room, the place where last night's meal of chitterlings, beans, and corn meal were served. The photograph of a married couple sat on the cracked mantle. He was Negro, tall, rectangular lean face, brown eyes, and heavy lips. Strong wrists appear from his ragged shirtsleeves. His dark black hair was precisely parted on the left.

His name was Abel Johnson. He had returned home from Tuskegee Institute, the local Negro college. Two days earlier, he received his degree in agricultural science. Abel was part of a graduating class of three. He was once a sharecropper, taking over that family tradition from his father and older brother. They had been dead, murdered by Klansmen for allegedly staring too long at a county judge's daughter. Another older brother managed to escape this barren decadence by moving to New York City. He wanted no part of the land now. Twenty-two years old, educated, his eyes and mind were wide open with a realization and anticipation of another world existing beyond the impoverished, former slavery lands of Alabama.

"Abel? Abel, youz up already?"

In the open room in back, Abel's momma spoke softly while slowly making her way toward her son. A short, round-faced woman, she was dressed in a tattered emerald-green nightgown and a floor-length beige robe. Her jet-black hair had just a tint of gray and was cinched in a hard bun. The last fifteen years had seen Momma wearing that same hairstyle. Momma was born in Tuskegee, grew up in Tuskegee, married, and raised her three sons in Tuskegee. Momma was going to die in Tuskegee. Her grandmother operated an underground railroad of slaves through Alabama, Tennessee, Indiana, Illinois, and Canada. That was Momma. Those were her roots. Once Abel left home and Momma died, that would be the last of the Johnsons of Macon County.

"Yeah, Momma, I'm up. Just waitin' 'till it's time to catch the seven-fifteen."

Abel's momma didn't want him to leave. She knew that in all likelihood, she would never see her youngest son again. She was against him moving to New York to live with his older brother, Isaiah. In her opinion, Isaiah would never live the Christian way of life that she had worked so hard to instill in Abel.

"I'll fix you some breakfast fo' you go."

"Naw, Momma, just black coffee," replied Abel.

Abel's mind was focused on leaving. Since graduation, his bags have been packed. It pained him terribly to leave his momma lone, probably forever. Abel was never coming back to Tuskegee. He was convinced leaving to stake his fortune elsewhere benefits not only him but also Momma. Abel was smart, smart enough to realize the world beyond Tuskegee offered better than this, better than a life of sloppin' pigs, tilling fields, feeding chickens, and being called nigger in your face. Today was the day he embarked on the rest of his life, day 1. He had wanted this freedom, his liberation for so long, so badly, the actual event had become anticlimactic.

"What kind of work you hope to find up there in New York City?" asked Momma, still hoping in her own way she can convince Abel not to leave.

Abel tried not to show how perturbed he was getting toward his momma. They had been through this conversation many times before over the past months. Now he wished she would just give up and give him her blessing.

"I want to be a writer," he responded. "Isaiah says they got some sort of colored newspaper up there."

Momma called out, "Did you say just coffee?"

"Huh? Yeah, Momma." He returned to pacing the room with the determined look to leave his personal hellhole. He sat down.

"Althea be by to see youz off fo' you go."

That's exactly what Abel did not want to hear, not another futile female attempt to convince him not to leave Tuskegee. Althea's motives were strikingly different than Momma's. Althea loved Abel. Althea loved Abel like a woman who possesses the yearning of uncontrollable passion for a man. Her heart bore the ache of a love that is about to dissipate. She had loved Abel ever since they set their almond-colored eyes on each other as kids. That was when Althea's family moved to Tuskegee from Natchez, Mississippi.

Abel cared for Althea. He liked her very much. He liked her even more because they lost their virginity together. Abel was not interested in hauling a simple-thinking country woman from Alabama to New York with him. Abel didn't want a wife, a child, a home. The only thing Abel wanted to cradle was pencil and paper.

His coffee was piping hot, black as tar, just the way he liked it. A soft knock on the door turned the coffee cold as a January morning in Minnesota. All Abel could think about was one more confrontation with a woman before his bus arrived. He kept his head focused straight ahead at the wall while Momma walked by to answer the door. Althea stepped in.

"So nice you came by," Momma told Althea. "Such a pleasant surprise." Momma loved Althea because she knew Althea loved Abel.

"I wanted to visit fo' Abel left this mornin'," replied Althea in a hushed country-girl tone.

There was still consternation over seeing Althea's face again since last night's argument. For Abel, it was like gazing in a window. Althea Moore was nineteen, three years younger, but a hard life of sharecropping in the cotton fields had aged her beyond her teenage years. Still, her face Abel had seen almost as often as his own reflection.

"Reckon I'll let y'all sayz youz goodbyes," said Momma, taking her cue to slip out back to feed the chickens. While grabbing her bucket, she held on to one last ounce of hope Althea can somehow convince Abel to stay.

Abel had difficulty looking Althea in the eye.

"Momma says you ain't been sleepin' good."

Abel frowned then shrugged.

"Nervous 'bout the trip, I guess. New York City's

an awful big town." Thoughts of the unknown have Abel terrified on the inside. Having an older brother living there already eased him a bit. But he was going to New York for honest writing work, not to run policy numbers for a Negro criminal named Bumpy Johnson. His thoughts bombarded him. What if he couldn't find a writing job? What if he fail? Why was he traveling over a thousand miles to go shine some white man's shoes? Of course Abel was scared, but his momma and Althea, under no circumstances, must sense his trepidation.

"You gonna need yo' sleep."

Abel retorted emphatically back to Althea that a twenty-two-year-old man can take care of himself, "I've spent my damn life sleeping."

Althea knew he was angry now when he started spewing cuss words in Momma's Christian home.

"I'm ready to write. Be my own man. Be another Paul Robeson. He's in Harlem a lot. Maybe I can meet him." He attempted a smile. "I'm making steady progress toward that goal."

Althea was silent, never comfortable when Abel throws his Tuskegee Institute college education in her fifth-grade level face. He would miss her greatly. They knew each other all too well. The past few days, they could not spend time together without rehashing dated guilt, moments of passionate tendencies, and times of regrets. Althea knew she fought a losing battle. Their horizons were strikingly different.

Without explanation, Abel stood, walked over to the mantle where his diary of notes, thoughts, and personal writings sat. He grabbed his book and coffee and walked outside, never turning to or speaking to Althea. Althea was left behind so that her eyes may have welled up with tears.

Outside on the porch, Abel found what he had hoped to find this morning. The peacefulness outside was like a quiet room exposed in his own brain. There he could gather himself, lose himself, become fully involved with his writing. *Start from the beginning,* Abel tells himself.

He opened his diary to a blank piece of paper then pulled out a sharpened pencil from his shirt pocket. He fumbled through the diary, looking for inspiration or a thought he might want to write about. He wrote feverishly, beginning at the top of the page so that the whiteness of the paper seemed to gaze back at him. For a brief moment, there was an echo of pleasure, the excitement of creating words. Yet the self-forgetting concentration didn't lend itself to anything meaningful.

Instead it stood off in the distance. Suddenly the words didn't come when needed, and as his fingers gripped the pencil, Able saw he was not getting his thoughts right, the expression of love, the bitterness of pain, the feeling of loneliness.

He ripped the page out and started again. He was usually such a pensive writer, he didn't require much inspiration. Rather, he held thought in his head as he wrote. He forged on, writing quickly. But the thoughts, ideas, concepts were as dark as the still of night. Nothing connected.

Abel closed his eyes.

I'm stuck, he told himself.

It was not just a lack of sleep but something else that was bothersome. His world was no longer round and real but fractured and feverish as that dream of his dead father that came to him in flashes last night. He searched the darkness under his skull, hunting for the writer's block that never seemed to go away. He needed something intense and strong to distract him from the blankness. He had always been able to lose himself in work, whether late at night while Momma slept or in the fields after a long day's work tilling. Not this morning.

A brief panic set in. Would he be like this for the rest of his life?

There was a smell like a suggestion of smell, a smell caught from the corner of his nose like a man's stench. Yes, a stench of a man that has been working in the Alabama fields from the time you can't see in the morning to the time you can't see at night. He sniffed the back of his hand then the air, but it was from inside his head, another memory of the past. It faded but not before he could identify it. It was the smell of his dead father who now stood before him in spirit. He was telling Abel to leave Tuskegee, to go before some white cracker lynched him like they did his father and older brother, James.

"Get out, boy, 'fore you next," said his father's voice ringing in Abel's head.

Abel's father was a tireless worker of the fields as his father and as his. In all probability, their male African ancestors were great farmers. That's all the generations of Johnson men knew how to do. He knew that's why Isaiah left. A year or so ago, Isaiah wrote Abel to say New York City was a place where a Negro could get work and find himself. But Isaiah wasn't interested in being a janitor, waiter, or bootblack. He said the only Negroes with money were the ones involved in the numbers racket or who ran gambling and prostitution houses, those lowlives who leeched off those poor souls who left the south for greener pastures up north and now couldn't fend for themselves.

There was that voice of his father ringing inside once more. "Get out, boy. Get out."

Abel was the youngest of three sons. Being the youngest made Abel the favorite in his father's eyes. He made sure Abel stayed in school, put enough savings away to send him to the Negro college called Tuskegee Institute. Abel's father felt he represented the last opportunity for him to be a good, loving father. His older son, James, was like him, with a temper as fierce as a lion's. It was not surprising to the Negroes in Tuskegee when the both of them were found hanged and castrated together. They were always seen getting into shouting matches with the white townsfolk. When called "uppity nigger," they would yell right back, "Red-necked crackers!" The Klan did it—everyone knew it. But so what? What could you do about it? What were Momma and the two sons to do? Hire a detective to uncover the truth? Find an attorney to pressure the county prosecutor? What could they or any Negro do about it? Nothing.

Abel's father was an unloving, domineering, adulterous husband to Abel's momma. A hateful, cruel father to his older brothers. At times, he would beat James and Isaiah within an inch of their lives, but not Abel. Abel's father resented the type of life he was forced to provide for his family—a life of sharecropping, a two-room shack, and no running water. Some of Abel's early writings are about his time as a twelve-year-old boy working the fields and helping out with the chickens. Chicken was the only meat the Johnson family ever ate.

Abel wrote feverishly now. The words began to flow. His father appearing before him sent Abel into a writing tizzy. *Now this is how it's supposed to go,* he told himself. Thoughts about his father prompted Abel to write about the time he gave him a baby chick. Abel made that chick his personal pet. Gave him a name, Sonny, on account of his uncle Sonny, his father's younger brother. Abel loved Sonny, raised him over the months into a fine-looking healthy chicken.

Suddenly the thoughts and words didn't flow as easily. His memory of Sonny had become tarnished. He could only think of that painful and sad moment that happened in his life. Abel didn't want to write. He wanted to reflect, reflect on the loss of life. For a chicken? Yes, a chicken. As far as Abel was concerned, Sonny was family and was privy to any rights bestowed on all poor Negro families living in the south.

The lead of his pencil cracked. With anger, Abel threw the pencil down. But before reaching into his pocket for another one, he stopped to remember, maybe remember for the last time. Abel never forgave his father for killing Sonny, having him defeathered, and fried up for the family to eat. Abel's father wasn't thinking about the murder of a family pet. "Family gots to eat first, boy." Sonny was never spoken of from that day on.

"Get your ass to the back, nigger, and stay there."

Abel stood frozen at the front of the bus as all eyes of the white passengers were fixed on him.

"I mean now!" shouted the bus driver.

Nobody had to tell him he was supposed to sit in the back. Nobody, especially a redneck white man, had to tell any Negro where his or her place was. Just having the privilege to ride through the south on a thousand-mile journey was enough of a victory for Negroes in 1928. Be that as it may, Abel still wondered if being embarrassed and humiliated in front of a bus full of white strangers was necessary. That bus driver felt so.

"How many times I gots to tell you, boy? You hard a' hearin', nigger? Now get!"

Someone from the back of the bus shouts, "He just a dumb coon, Arch! Send him back here. We'll keep an eye on him fer you."

"Yessu."

Abel froze, his daydream over. He slowly made his way toward the back of the bus. The discerning, hateful, and judgmental eyes sliced Abel open like a hot knife to butter. The mumbling among white passengers were not loud enough to interpret. Without bringing attention to himself, Abel swerved his head around to see if there were any other Negroes on that bus. There weren't. He was all alone and possibly will be the only one all the way to New York. Abel knew he had to be careful traveling through the south. He could get off the bus only to run to the weeds and bushes to relieve himself. That would be the game plan all the way to New York. He had Momma's biscuits and butter to feed himself until he reached Isaiah's in New York.

There was the last seat in the very last row waiting for Abel. Abel sat alone. The heads now returned facing the front of the bus. The engine accelerated. The bus moved through Macon County. For Abel, it would be for the last time.

Abel's college education helped him put things in a clearer perspective. Correctly, he reasoned that he would be better off than most Negroes. Twenty years ago, he probably wouldn't have been allowed on the bus in the first place. If he was cleaning it out, absolutely. But to actually buy a ticket and ride to another destination, Abel felt he was representing progress. *I'm better off than most,* he thought. *I'm educated, smart, can read and write, do figures. I have a skill to make myself a lot of money. I'm going to write books that help other Negroes become better people.*

In that short two-minute span, Abel laid out the manifesto to help all Negroes. *That's my purpose on earth,* he though. *That's why I am here.*

Sitting next to that bathroom reminded Abel of a story. Before the words eluded him, he quickly ripped pad and pencil out of his knapsack and began writing. He wrote about when he encountered his first toilet seat. Only affluent southerners had bathrooms with hot running water. Negroes cleaned plenty of them, just that they never owned or sat on them. Abel stopped. He thought. He wanted to get this right. That very first time. *Think back,* he told himself.

It was on a trip with his father to Montgomery. His father was going to look into a janitor job at the county courthouse building. The janitor job was his older brother Zeke's for the last five years. But Zeke died of a stroke, and Abel's father was hoping the manager would hire someone from the family to clean and mop the building. It would mean more money and a move to the big city. Everybody in the Johnson family was hoping for that.

When they reached Montgomery, they found out it was too late. The manager had given the job to a cousin of his. There was nothing left for Abel and his father to do but return to Tuskegee, return to sharecropping, return to a two-room shack and a life in the fields.

Before they got back into that old heap of a car Abel's father barely kept running for the trip back home, Abel needed to use the bathroom. He needed to use it in the worst way. A nine-year-old boy with a full bladder and load to release can't wait. So while Abel's father talked to the building manager about other work in Montgomery for Negroes, Abel did what he thought was the sensible thing at the time. He walked into a whites-only bathroom and ran to the first stall he saw available. His bowels were twisted in knots. He fumbled with his belt then the buttons. Finally he got his pants down and sat. To his dismay, Abel forgot one thing. He forgot to see if the toilet seat was down. His small and narrow butt plops right into the toilet bowl. His butt getting a bath of that cold water brought his father and the building manager running into the bathroom.

"Boy, you ain't supposed to be in here. Niggers ain't allowed in here."

"I gots stuck, sir."

The building manager didn't want to hear lame excuses from a Negro boy on how he stumbled into a whites-only bathroom. The thought was to get Abel and his father out of there as soon as possible before another white man came in there and reported the incident to the building owner. He would lose his job for sure. The building manager grabbed Abel by the arm and slapped him several times, feeling justified for doing it. Abel's father watched. He must watch. To retaliate would mean jail time for sure, maybe getting himself lynched. Abel's father reckoned better him than me. After all, they had no right being in there in the first place, he reasoned.

"Now y'all get."

Abel and his father ran out of the bathroom, never returning to Montgomery. For the entire trip back to Tuskegee, Abel's father cursed at him, told him he'd be nothing but a dumb nigger, a dumb nigger like himself. It hurt Abel that his own father thought he was stupid, let alone thought himself stupid. A burning sensation ran through Abel's blood, a sensation to prove to his father and the world that he wasn't stupid, that he will amount to something respectable and achieve great things. So Abel just sat and listened to his father's scornful oratory.

As Abel finished writing his entry, the realization of another hurtful memory of his past made the pages of his journal.

Abel thought, *This is why I must write. This is what a writer does. He uses words to influence people. I must use my words to influence other Negroes. People in America have to know that everything is not equal and fair as the Constitution states.*

If it wasn't for school, Abel wouldn't have known such a thing as a constitution existed, a document that actually says how people of all races, even Negroes, are supposed to be treated. Abel thought back to the days when he first started his diary. Somebody was always telling Abel to shut up. When they saw him coming, they'd run because if they didn't, they would be engrossed in a thirty-minute conversation with Abel on something he had just read. The other Negroes Abel's age in Macon County laughed at Abel. "Smarts ain't puttin' no money in your pockets, boy," was all Abel ever heard.

He had no girlfriend, not until Althea moved there. So Abel thought, *If no one will listen to me talk, then maybe they will read what I have to say.* From that day on, Abel wrote about his personal feelings. *I'll be a famous novelist,* he thought. *People of all kinds will read my books. I'll travel to Europe, Asia, South America. Speak at great universities like Yale, Harvard, Princeton.* Abel reasoned, if you dream, dream big.

2

Tall, handsome with steely blue eyes, Ian
McGregor looked more like an actor than a playwright
in Hollywood. He was the golden boy scenarist
for Universal Studios. Things were splendid for
this second-generation immigrant from Scotland.
The banter around Hollywood was that soon motion
pictures would have sound. Writers like Ian would
be in even greater demand. This industry that was
still in its infancy would mushroom into a million-
dollar business. People will move out west to live.
He had youth, money, looks, status, a beautiful wife
who was a famous actress, and steady employment.
Ian had everything.

As he stood on the Universal lot, Ian's fears
were coming to fruition. He could see studio chief
Carl Laemmle Jr. meeting in Laemmle senior's office.
Were they talking about him? His drunkenness and
obnoxious behavior? His bisexual affair with that
handsome actor from Von Stroheim's last picture? He
knew they were plotting to keep this as hush-hush
as possible. Not even Ian's wife, Katherine, knew.
Katherine wasn't going to ever know. Laemmle Sr.
arranged the marriage, a marriage of convenience.
One of the elder Laemmle's missions in life was to
keep the public thinking it was a blessed union. The
spirit doing the blessing wasn't God, but Laemmle

Sr. Ian and Katherine represented the all-American family, the wholesome couple next door. Mr. and Mrs. Goody Two-Shoes.

Universal's marketing strategy was simple: good meaningful, inexpensive silent films that end with a kiss and a happy ending, written by Ian, acted by Katherine—the all-American couple. Since 1923, it had made Universal millions of dollars. Laemmle Sr. would always tell Ian he didn't give a Frenchman's fuck what he did behind closed doors. Ian could have his male lovers, and Katherine could have Charlie Chaplin when the moment grabbed her as long as scandal and embarrassment to the studio stayed out of the newspapers.

Ian loved Katherine. Ian loved being married to a silent screen star even more. Katherine was always compared to the greats at that time: Bow, Swanson, Gaynor, Pickford. Katherine had everything: tall, leggy, busty, with long flaming red hair. She possessed the look of sex as well as the look of the farm girl from Indiana when the role called for it. Universal mad sure they capitalized on her developed vaudeville and Broadway acting talents. Acting in a mixture of films, she'd play the husband's mistress or the great heroine. She played the vamp. She played Mary, mother of Jesus. It didn't matter. The public loved her.

Was the meeting over? Ian asked himself. Were they about to forget he was a decorated war hero, an award-winning playwright from Broadway, and now a highly respected, well-paid motion picture scenarist? At that very moment, Ian knew he was watching the end of his job, back to Boston to spend freezing winters in soup lines. His ego would not allow him to sponge off Katherine. If he couldn't write, there would be nothing for him to do but drink himself to death. He'd rather divorce Katherine and move back east. He reasoned a writer without his quill is like a knight of King Arthur's Round Table going to battle without his sword.

Should I go to my office? he asked himself. *Now that's a stupid idea.* If he went to his office, he would have to walk by Laemmles'. He decided to delay his moment of shame.

He sat at his desk staring at his paper. Ian was angry, angry at Laemmle Jr. for putting him there. Junior ordered him to do a rewrite for Von Stroheim's next picture. As is the custom when Von Stroheim writes, it goes on and on and on. Ian knew he was just acting as an editor and not really creating any interesting story scenarios. Motion pictures were still silent—writers weren't required to supply actual dialogue. Von Stroheim was a pain in the ass. Only out of respect for Junior did Ian agree to make an insightful judgment regarding the script since Junior didn't have time to read it before meeting with Von Stroheim. Did Junior really care about this script? This film? Apparently not enough to read the script himself, Ian fumed. Von Stroheim is leaving for Metro after this next picture anyway. He'll be L. B. Mayer's and Thalberg's problem.

Halfway through the script, Ian knew it needed to be rewritten completely. He reached into his drawer looking for his friend, Beam . . . Jim Beam. When he felt fear of the dreaded writer's block, when it was time to generate creative energy, the call went out to Jimmy B. Ian was used to hiding behind whiskey. Once while in New York on Broadway, he went into hiding with Jimmy B. for months. A play he had written called *Remember Me* was playing. The play laid a great big egg, and he wanted to avoid the blame. That was only two years ago. Everyone thought Ian was finished. But look at him now. He held on.

He went back to the script. One more swig. The knock on the door was light, soft like a woman's. He jams his bottle back in the drawer just before

Katherine enters. Katherine was brought to Hollywood by Laemmle Sr. who saw her on Broadway in one of Ian's plays.

"It's me." Something was on her mind.

"You're in trouble, aren't you? Maybe I should call Douglas Kennedy."

Kennedy was their attorney.

"The old man is taking care of everything. No need to worry."

Ian waited while Katherine slowly paced the room, certain she was searching for the right words. There's no question their love for each other will overcome any and all obstacles. If Ian is banished from Hollywood because of his secret sins, Katherine will stand by him even if it means giving up her career in Hollywood.

"What did Junior say?"

He waited while Katherine lit a cigarette. "He said, eh, newspapers won't find out. Everything will be all right."

"What about my next picture, the talkie?" Katherine asked.

"It's going to be made. I'm doing the screenplay." Some kind of story about an actor's wife who cheats on him. How ironic.

"Maybe I should talk to Laemmle myself."

"No. I think we should wait."

"Wait? Wait for what, my dear?"

"He wants to tell the old man first. It's happening as we speak."

"Then I'll go home." Katherine moved toward Ian, kissed him to reassure him.

"Will you be home for dinner?"

"Yes."

"Good. I'll have Sloane prepare your favorite. Roast duck."

The door closed. Back to the bottle, back to Jimmy B., back to this wretched script, back to hating himself. Not for getting caught with that extra, but for having to grovel to Junior to keep his job.

Ian knew it was a mistake. His tryst with Sean Morgan began almost six weeks earlier. It was an early summer morning, and when Ian stepped out of stage 5, the streets of Universal Studios were empty. He didn't quite understand why, but the idea that Hollywood represented so much more than New York or Boston excited him. He felt alone in his excitement because there were no stampedes of swashbuckling pirates, Confederate soldiers, cowboys and Indians wandering around the lot. It was quiet, still. Many transplanted writers and newspaper journalists from New York hated these hangarlike buildings, but Ian was not depressed by this. It reminded him of Jimmy B., the merry feeling of getting drunk in the middle of the day. Hot late afternoons in Los Angeles were inebriating for him.

Why am I here? he asked himself. *I'm supposed to be here. I am a great writer. It's my right, my raison d'etre.*

Now Ian was mad at Sean, angry that Sean would be so stupid to even suggest he'd leave Katherine to live with him. Here came Sean toward Ian from across the street. Like two gunslingers in a B-picture western, they squared off to duel in the middle of the street.

"You said you'd call me back. We like each other. I told you my idea," Sean's voice got louder, loud enough for several studio employees to stick their heads out of windows to see what the commotion was all about.

"You said you'd get back to me. I told you I wanted to be with you. You said you wanted to have some time to think, and you'd get back to me."

Ian grabs Sean, shook him mightily.

"You stupid ass. Do you know who I am?" yelled Ian right back. Ian's hands around Sean's neck got tighter. A rage filled his body like gasoline in a tank. His mind sent signals: Kill him. Kill him. Kill him.

Is it his mind or someone else's? Who's controlling whom? Who really knows? Ian often thought about what drove a man to murder. One of his Broadway plays touched on that very subject. The play was called *My Two Minds*, and it brought Ian quite a bit of money and recognition. It was the play that initially attracted him to Universal. Universal won Ian's services over Metro-Goldwyn-Mayer, RKO, and Paramount because the Laemmles promised to make Ian a director in three years.

If a couple of janitors hadn't pulled him off, Sean he might have killed him. Now the talk has started around the studio. What did Sean mean when he told Ian he wanted him? Wanted him for what?

The whispers and innuendo might start. The talk might filter down to Metro, Fox, or Warner's. The Laemmles would get their own story out fast. Ian wanted Sean to do some writing work for him. Nothing more was the official word from Universal.

Junior's meeting with his father was over. Ian took one last drink. The end of his job was inevitable. There might be other work. Not if the truth got out. His popularity among the other studio heads would be lost forever. A new fear overcame him. He would end up selling something, toothbrushes or pots and pans door-to-door. If Laemmle fired him, it meant exile from Hollywood. All the names from the silent past rolled inside his head. Laroque, Normand, Arbuckle, Lester. He would be on that list. The list of Hollywood exiles, banished and not to be heard from again unless of course it was on a policeman's crime blotter. The sun was setting or had set, and he was next. He thought this won't happen immediately. He could get small writing jobs. Studios would hire Ian for small assignments, not understanding fully that alcoholism had robbed him of his wit and creativity. Eventually everyone would know he was a has-been. One day, he would be out of money. Everything he and Katherine had worked for would be gone. He'll be almost thirty-five. Ian tried picturing himself at that age selling pots and pans door-to-door. Why not suicide? The funeral would signal that the party would be over. He didn't ask himself how he would kill himself. Only that he would die as an alcoholic embarrassment. Quickly, those thoughts were banished.

He tried to envision himself a success, a real writer, maybe a director, a man to be respected. Nothing, not a damn thing. No such vision would emerge. The alcohol in his bloodstream was interfering, making things confusing.

The next morning, Ian had coffee at the commissary with Junior. They usually had coffee together at least once a week. Junior was so comfortable with Ian's drinking, he would allow him to spike his coffee with brandy right in front of him. But not today, he thought.

"How's Von Stroheim's script coming?" asked Junior.

"Okay."

"Good. Be through with it soon?"

"Another day or two."

"You know I saw him walking around the studio wearing Prussian boots and a helmet yesterday."

Ian smiled. "The other day I yelled at him, 'The war is over! The Germans lost!'"

"Quite." Junior continued, "In Von Stroheim's opinion, the man wins the girl from his brother but realizes it's a hollow victory, that his world is an empty world. Can you see that now?"

"The younger brother grows up in the story."

"I don't agree, Junior." Everyone calls Mr. Laemmle's son Junior.

"The audience will get angry, impatient. People hate ambiguity. They want everything reconciled before the third reel." Junior changed the subject, "I'm contemplating changes at the studio, lad."

"Am I in or out? Don't bloody bullshit me."

"I'm hiring another writer out of New York, a reporter from a newspaper. With talkies around the corner, we're going to need more writers."

"I'm not going to have some newspaper hack overlooking and editing my work. If that's the case, I quit."

"You can't quit. You have a year on your contract. I'll stand in your way, so forget about it. No use going to Metro, Fox, Warner Brothers, or Laskey at Paramount. I'll hold you to your contract and sue for breach unless you show up every day."

Ian felt the pressure mounting, impending doom hovering over him like an approaching thunderstorm. He imagined the executioner standing over his shoulder, sizing up the correct angle to attach his suntanned neck.

"Feel like a toad on a wet rock with a snake looking at the back of my neck," said Ian.

"Relax. Oliver is a very talented writer. He was available, and the studio can use him."

"Never heard of Robert Oliver," said Ian, irritated and acting sarcastic. Every writer in Hollywood had heard of Robert Oliver.

"You're joking of course," replied Laemmle. "He wrote that hit play *The Only Page*. Started his own newspaper back in Chicago."

"I know who he is," Ian said, still irritated. "So I'm not the golden boy anymore?"

"You haven't been for months. Your drinking has gotten the best of you. Your writing isn't as sharp. But you're still one of the best. Father and I want you here at Universal. If you don't want to write, you can produce or direct."

"Great—the chance I've been waiting for."

"Please, Ian, no more bitterness. Slow down on the drinking . . . and your male friends. Think of Katherine. Think of the studio. Do it for me, Ian."

As Ian pulled into his driveway off Sunset Boulevard, the smile he wore was as wide as the street itself. He hadn't been able to do that for a very long time. The studio was not going to fire him. Even better was that Junior had given Ian the green light to prepare a script for Katherine's first talkie. There would be good news at the dinner table for once. No dialogue centering around Ian being arrested for drunkenness. No angry fights about Katherine coming home and finding Ian entertaining male company. No confessions from Katherine about her one-night stand with Douglas Fairbanks. No, this was going to be a festive evening.

The servants had done a masterful job of setting the dining room table for dinner as Katherine had ordered. She was dressed in the sexiest full-length negligee she could find in hopes Ian would find her alluring. Her negligees always exposed most of her breasts, her "two biggest assets," she would tell the Laemmles at the studio. Katherine has never tried to figure out why Ian lusts for young men. She reasoned it's like the drunk who needs a drink, the thief that needs a score. Once they crave it, give it to them before they get violent. Katherine knew of other bisexual actors and actresses. Hollywood was still a small town in many respects. Everybody still knew everybody, and gossip spread quickly like Western Union.

Before Katherine married Ian, her affair with Charlie Chaplin was front-page news. Everyone was shocked by it merely for the reason that Katherine was the ripe old age of twenty-two and Chaplin usually found teenage girls more appealing.

When the gossip hit home, it made Katherine depressed. Not because of any pathos for Ian. She did not want any negative publicity jeopardizing and destroying her status as the no. 1 female box-office leader in Hollywood. She held on to that title like a heavyweight boxing champ holds on to his belt. All Katherine knew was that Ian loved her, that their love was honest and sincere. A marriage of convenience is what they both wanted, albeit for different reasons. Their home was a happy one as long as Katherine made money making films for Universal and Ian continued to write meaningful scripts and quench his occasional thirst for male companionship.

"The duck is delicious. I must compliment Sloane."

"He is a wonderful chef," replied Katherine. "I take it Saint Junior has forgiven you for your sins."

"And then some," said Ian. "Things are looking up."

"How soon before we shoot the talkie?" asks Katherine.

"He didn't say. I suppose when I finish the script," replied Ian.

"The whispers say DeMille will come over from Paramount to direct. I've always wanted to work for him."

Whenever Ian feels that Katherine is getting too submerged into Hollywood talk, he reaches for the decanter of wine and drinks it down like water. Ian loves the life that the motion picture business has brought him, but he doesn't want to be consumed in its blanket all day, every day like Katherine.

"I saw Marion Davies this afternoon," said Ian. "She and Hearst invited us up to San Simeon for the Labor Day weekend."

"We should go," replied Katherine.

"Why? So you can see Raoul Walsh?" asks Ian.

"I see you've been talking to that wretched nosey security policeman on the lot again," replies Katherine.

"I must admit he is a very good-looking young man, even with that eye patch," said Ian.

"There's no need to be jealous, my dear," says Katherine.

Ian replied, "It's not jealousy, my sweet. I realize you are a beautiful woman with big tits. Men are going to want you, especially sex-starved wannabe directors who wear an eye patch and have nothing better to do than try to fuck another man's wife."

"Must you be so crass?" asks Katherine.

"After five glasses of Chateau Lyons 1903, yes, of course," said Ian.

"I've something to show you upstairs," said Katherine.

"Goodie, I can hardly wait, my dear," replied Ian.

There was more of a spark than usual to Ian and Katherine's lovemaking. Ian's thrusts were much more pronounced. Their session lasted twice as long as Katherine reached orgasm much quicker. The explosion she felt inside mimicked that of a stick of dynamite being launched on the Fourth of July. They cuddled each other warmly. Both stared into space, not talking, merely caressing. The room remained silent. No one spoke. The moon's beam slit open the Venetian blinds in their bedroom. Katherine was thinking about her next picture and the possibility of working with the great director Cecil B. DeMille. Ian was thinking about a better way to conceal his attraction to that new assistant director Junior hired away from Howard Hughes at RKO. He was British, tall, with flaming red hair. All Ian knew about him was that his name was James.

"Thinking of me, I hope," said Katherine.

"I love you," replied Ian.

"I love you too, darling," said Katherine. "You haven't said that to me in quite a while."

Ian kissed Katherine passionately. They both were feeling that burning love they had for each other when they first started dating. Maybe it was the good news that the studio continued to want both of them. Maybe they were both horny. Soon they both fell asleep. A look of relief painted their faces. Tomorrow would be a continuation of the same euphoria that they experienced that night. Or would it?

It's just not the same, Ian thought. *Why do I continue living this charade? Do I love money and fame that much? Do I love Katherine that much, not to hurt her, destroy her career? What is true love? So many thoughts at such a late hour. Stop thinking and wishing for things that will never come about. Go to sleep.*

3

"New York City! Pullin' into New York City," the bus driver's yelling awoke Abel from his nap just in time to gaze out his window and see a concrete block row of tall buildings lining south Manhattan near Wall Street.

Abel felt the frenetic energy of a hustling and bustling metropolis within himself. What a feeling, what exuberance running from head to toe. Never had such energy been felt by Abel, certainly not in Tuskegee, he thought. In Tuskegee, the Saturday night dance in Thaddeus Howard's barn sufficed for entertainment for all Negroes within a twenty-mile radius. Abel would spend his time alternating between entries in his journal and dancing with Althea. Playing harmonicas and banjos, singing spirituals, and drinking cheap moonshine was not Abel's idea of entertainment, but it was the only social outing he and Althea would partake in. Most of Abel's writings centered on how Negroes worked and slaved on the cotton field they didn't all, all week, and how three hours of cheap entertainment on Saturday night was supposed to make all the pain and suffering everyone had endured the past 150 years go away, just in time for Monday's sunrise.

The people on Canal Street looked as if they were running to put out a fire. Quickly here, bustling

---

there. People scurried as if their very lives depended on being at their destination in the next minute.

Seizing the moment to make an entry into his diary, Abel rubbed the sleep out of his eyes, stretched, and quickly went to task. He wrote how the different shades of gray the buildings in Manhattan possess reminded him of a book he once read called *Build My Gallows High*. It told a story of a man hired to find a woman and return her to the husband. But when he locates her, they fall in love with each other and plot to kill the husband so that they may live together forever. Abel wrote of a similar parallel. A stranger, off to the big city to find one thing, in his case, writing employment. But he is afraid that once he finds it, if he finds it, instead of joy and happiness, pain and despair will reign over him like a dark cloud preparing to bust open with rain. A man can set out on one path but miss the many forks in the road to end up on another path. Abel reasoned that it's just the anxiety of the unknown. So he dismisses the anxiety as a bad dream. Instead, he writes about the electric charge New York City brings him.

My dream is coming alive, he wrote. Quickly, he composed a list of things he wanted to accomplish while in New York. First, a writing job. Next, to meet Paul Robeson. Third, to write his novel. Nothing on that list mentioned sending for Althea to come live with him.

A lot of Abel's writings were more hodgepodge than one clear, lucid story. But that was Abel's writing style—short bursts of words grouped together forming one thought. And now the faucet had been turned on. The words were flowing. Abel wanted to finish the page before the bus rolled into the Port Authority terminal. His excitement of finally reaching his destination was spewing over in his journal.

Already New York was everything his brother had said it would be. Abel wrote how a new place surely would mean meeting new people and experiencing new experiences. New experiences provide the kind of fuel a writer strives to have. It recharges the brain. It gets your writing hand moving places five minutes earlier you had no idea you would be going.

Keep writing, Abel tells himself. *Don't worry about the misspelled words. Keep writing,* Abel says.

At that moment, Abel looked out his window as the bus pulled up to a stop light. The white policeman that stared at Abel had a most ugly frown. When Abel saw him he stopped writing. That one look reminded Abel that even though he was north, he was not wanted.

Great—another nigger from the South, was the thought Abel had as if he was reading the white policeman's mind. Abel stopped writing and closed his journal.

Gripping his one suitcase, Abel stood before the Harlem YMCA. He checked the address on the piece of paper one last time, making sure it was the correct one his brother Isaiah gave him. Corner of Seventh Avenue and 126th Street. Yes, this was the place. Negroes from all walks of life whisked through him as if he was the invisible man. Pimps approached him, whispering in his ear. "Gots all kind of womenz, boy. You want a white one?"

Abel shook his head vehemently. Every man who didn't have a woman with him kept getting propositioned by the prostitutes working their beat. All he heard for the next few minutes was, "Baby, how bouts youz 'n' me havin' some fun."

Abel just stood swiveling his head in 360-degree intervals. It seemed like Harlem was one great carnival. All Abel could think of was the many great stories his writings would be able to produce from his new surroundings.

As Able walked through the lobby of the YMCA, he was hoping he would run into Isaiah on the spot. An hour had passed and night was beginning to fall outside before Abel conjured up enough courage to ask the desk clerk for Isaiah's room.

"203, stairs over yonder," the lady replies.

And with that small piece of information, Abel walked upstairs. As he approached Isaiah's room, he could hear the murmurs of other voices besides his brother's. Isaiah's voice could be heard talking above the others'. Abel's soft knock is barely heard.

Without warning, the door flies open, and there stands Isaiah, a revolver pointing at the figure on the other side of the door.

"Well, lookee here! If it ain't my baby brother, Abel." Isaiah grabbed Abel, and they hugged for minutes, not having seen each other for the better part of four years. "Let me look at youz, boy. Youz a grown man now, nigga.

"Hey, everybody, my little brotha is a college graduate," said Isaiah proudly. Isaiah walked Abel around the room, introducing him to the other members of his gang. "That there is Fat Moe. Just look at his fat ass, and you can see why. Next to him is Chauncey. Right there is Fetchit on account all he does is fetch thangs for us. Sittin' on the bed is Goldie. Show my little brotha why you called Goldie, nigga."

On cue, Goldie flashed the widest smile with his two front teeth exhibiting a gold cap on each. Abel didn't speak but nodded out of respect.

"Have a seat, little brotha. Wee'z talkin' bui'ness," said Isaiah.

Abel sat, casually listening to what's going on, casually gazing out at the window, marveling at the eclectic Harlem nightlife below. Abel was proud of

Isaiah. For whatever they were planning or talking about, it was obvious Isaiah was the man in charge.

In Isaiah's room, over ham and cheese sandwiches and coffee spiked with Irish whiskey, Isaiah gave everyone what they wanted to hear.

"I gots this tip directly from Bo Weinberg. He's Dutch Schultz's top cat. Says if we pull this off for the Dutchman there's fifty each for all of us. Listen up—these yids ain't payin' for protection, so the Dutchman wants to show 'em a lesson. This is a sketch of the block."

Isaiah unfolded a mock rendering of a map and spread it out on the table. Using his toothpick as a pointer, Isaiah continued, "Here's Forty-Second Street, here Fifth Avenue. The two stands are located right across the street from each other." Isaiah glanced at his wristwatch. "At exactly 4:00 a.m., the delivery boys drop off the bundle of papers right on the doorsteps of Guggenheim's and Schwartz's newsstands. Ain't nobody gonna get the stack 'till 'round four-thirty. At five after four, we show up. At four-ten, Fetchit keeps the car runnin' in this alley here. Me and Goldie walked down the street and torch both stands. Chauncey, you keep a lookout. Dutchman says we pull his off and there's more work, more dead presidents for us to count in the future. You niggas got it straight?"

Abel looked shocked, not believing that Negroes actually consorted with famous New York City gangsters such as Dutch Schultz. He also marveled at Isaiah, a real boss, truly in charge of a gang. Isaiah's gang kept munching on their sandwiches. Everyone nodded. Isaiah continued.

"I ain't 'xpectin' no gunplay, no trouble," said Isaiah. "On the other hand, if things get out of hand, coppers showz up, and somebody getting' shot can't be helped, well shit, that's the way it goes," Isaiah goes on. "This is the full-dress show. We wear gloves and the shoes that are too big for our feets. Can't leave any finger or footprints. Y'all know what they do to niggas who get caught torchin' shit. Our black asses ain't going to Sing Sing, they going six feet unda."

It was obvious to Abel that Isaiah was a perfectionist. He admired his older brother for that. Isaiah kept going over and over every detail, every eventuality. He went on and on. He left nothing to chance.

"I'll go over it once more," he said. "We show up at five after four. Fetchit keeps the motor runnin' in the alley here. Chauncey is on lookout here. Me and Goldie walk down the street, douse the papers, set 'em on fire."

Everyone nodded.

"Now don't y'all forget—once that shit goes up, we movin' fast like we stole watermelons off a goddamn farm back home in Alabama," said Isaiah.

Abel reasoned Isaiah said that so that everyone could relate to their childhood days down south, a recognizable reference point. Injecting a sense of nostalgia was just what the gang needed, make everyone feel comfortable. The gang all looked at each other and smiled as if they remembered an episode or two back home to match exactly what Isaiah was referring to.

All of Isaiah's repetitive briefings gave Abel the itch to write. He tried not to listen anymore. He tried to think of other things, so he pulled his notebook out.

Abel started to write. He thought back many years to the days when he, Isaiah, and Momma would sit huddled around the fire, eating chitterlings and collards, listening to Momma preach. After their father died, Isaiah assumed the man of the house leadership. He always acted like the boss and did all the figuring for Momma just as he was doing now.

Abel wrote how he and Isaiah were inseparable back then. He wished Momma could see how Isaiah had worked his way up into a Harlem big shot, how Isaiah had his fingers in operations controlled and instituted by the infamous Dutch Schultz.

Then Abel stopped writing. No, he didn't want Momma to know what her son Isaiah was doing. What if he's caught, sent to prison, or worse, executed for a crime? What if he's killed by a rival gang? This was inspiration better kept unsaid.

Isaiah's gang adjourned to their separate rooms down the hall. Abel and Isaiah both took catnaps. At 3:15 a.m., Isaiah tapped Abel gently and whispered, "Little brotha, time to get up."

Abel jumped up. He was glad Isaiah woke him when he did because he was having a mixed-up dream about the time his father was hung and castrated by the Klan.

"Glad you woke me. I was dreamin' 'bout Paw," says Abel.

"If that wasn't so funny, I'd laugh," replies Isaiah. "Ain't thought 'bout that dead nigga in years."

As Abel watched Isaiah get dressed and make coffee, he felt a peculiar combination of fear, respect, and pride in Isaiah's status as a gang leader, sort of a president of a club, albeit a club of a criminal nature. Isaiah was in charge of something, Abel reasoned, except this club played for keeps and didn't mind standing in the face of danger or death.

Abel wanted to ask Isaiah how he became such a big shot so soon. Abel even wondered if graduating from an agricultural college was worth it, seeing Isaiah with his own place, nice-looking pin-striped suits hanging in his closet, a roll of twenty-dollar bills on his dresser, plenty of food in the pantry.

Maybe a college education ain't needed to make it in this world, Abel thought.

Then Abel realized without the education he received at Tuskegee Institute, he wouldn't be the writer he is now. He wouldn't have the dreams, the aspirations to go on to bigger and better things. Abel was astute enough to realize that Isaiah's world was a world of violence, potential incarceration, maybe even death.

"Youz can stay here, little brotha. We've done this sort of thing before," said Isaiah.

Abel replied, "But I wanna go. I ain't afraid."

Isaiah gave Abel a wide big-brother grin of approval. "Who knows, you might want to mention me in one of your books one day?" Isaiah continued.

Abel got serious.

"Why do you do what you do?" asked Abel.

"Why do you what you do, nigga?" retorted Isaiah, suggesting that a real man controls his own destiny and that no one tells a man what to do and when to do it. "This ain't Alabama, boy," continued Isaiah. "Man gots to do what he can to make ends meet. In Harlem, that's the law of the land."

Abel watched Isaiah some more as he rummaged through his dresser drawer for a revolver. Isaiah handles the rod as if it was his firstborn. Slowly and with precision, Isaiah loads one bullet at a time. After loading the sixth bullet, he snuggly fits the gun into his holster then puts on his pin-striped suit coat. Now Abel understood why Isaiah wears suits one size too big. A loud hard knock occurred. It was the rest of Isaiah's gang.

"All set, boss man," said Goldie.

The car ride down Seventh Avenue was quiet. Were these gangsters or employees from a funeral home working a funeral? This was no funeral procession. No one wanted to be the poor soul to draw Isaiah's wrath for messing up the mission so everyone refocused on the task at hand. Abel wondered to himself whether the silence was some sort of pre-crime ritual gangsters undergo. He thought of nothing, but kept reminding himself of everything he would feel and see so that he could write about it when he returned to the YMCA.

The streets of New York were quiet and barren. They had a thin slick to them because of a predawn drizzle. With the windows down, Abel noticed the stark difference between the smell of the city and that of Tuskegee. An early-morning smell down south is fresh, clean. New York City suggested the opposite—something vile and dirty, something unfit, the perfect environment to commit a crime.

Abel and Isaiah sat in the back with Chauncey. Fetchit drove while Goldie snored in the front passenger seat. Isaiah placed his arm around Abel and smiled at him

"Proud of everythang you done did at that school. Ain't nobody from our family ever got no more than a fifth-grade education," said Isaiah.

Abel smiled back. Approval from a big brother is an honor a younger brother cherishes.

"How's Momma doing?" asked Isaiah.

Abel stopped smiling. "She's awfully disappointed I left," responded Abel. Then Abel began to justify his leaving to Isaiah. "I had to go. Ain't nothing in Alabama for me. Momma had to know once I got my degree I was leaving."

"Shit, wasn't nuthin' for me there eitha," said Isaiah. He turned his attention to Chauncey. "What's wrong with you? Chauncey, you looks like a little sleepy boy. This job has to be done fast and quietlike."

Abel cut him off. "Like we stole watermelons off a goddamn farm back in Alabama," he said.

Isaiah smiled and patted Abel on the back. He

called out to Goldie in the front seat. "Wake up, nigga. Gimme one of them stogies you got."

Goldie jumped up and without hesitation reached into his pocket for a cigar. Without turning, he handed it back to Isaiah. Isaiah lit the cigar as Chauncey looked at him for the next move. Quiet returned inside the car. Nothing to do but smell Isaiah's cigar smoke and think.

The brakes brought the car to a halt in an alley just off Fifth Avenue. "Showtime, goddamnit!" shouted Isaiah.

His gang emptied out of the car except Fetchit. When Abel began to exit, Isaiah pushed him back inside. "Keep you black ass here, little brotha. Do something useful. Write somethin' 'bout me."

"I wanna go," replied Abel. "Let me go with you, Isaiah."

Isaiah showcased his wide, bright smile, nodded, and he, Abel, Goldie and Chauncey began a predawn walk down a quiet, deserted Manhattan street.

Abel walked behind Isaiah, Goldie, and Chauncey to create distance between a law-abiding citizen like himself and the criminal element Isaiah and his gang seemed to wear like a soldier's Purple Heart medal. He could see an adrenaline rush in Isaiah's face. Each step closer to their intended target raised his exhilaration. Although he felt a brotherly closeness to Isaiah, he constantly reminded himself that they obviously were of two different worlds. He loved his brother, had tremendous respect for him because like himself, he managed to escape the simple ways of Tuskegee.

No running a farm for the Johnson men, Abel thought. *We're city slickers.* But Abel wanted no part of the dangerous, dark, and crime-ridden existence that Isaiah has managed to carve out for himself. Five years easily shape the philosophy of a man reared from Alabama, Abel reasoned. Life in New York City has had an effect on Isaiah. Capitalism took on different forms in New York. He no longer was the country bumpkin from Tuskegee, no longer walking around in torn denim, no shoes or socks, and a piece of straw sticking out of his mouth that acted as a toothpick. His big brother was now a slick-talking, gun-toting, sharply dressed city hustler.

Abel thought it strange everyone walked with both their hands in their pockets. *What are they concealing?* he asked himself. *Do they really have weapons to murder with? Or are their hands just cold?*

No one spoke to each other. He absorbed everything like a sponge to water. *This is going to be a great entry into my novel,* thought Abel. Now he was really thinking. A book about his brother and the gang, stories about Negroes who don't shine shoes, mop floors, constantly cater to the whims of white people in their homes, do jigaboo dances in the streets for money in front of white folks on Wall Street in lower Manhattan. Titles for his novel ran rampant through his mind. Soon he forgot that he needed a writing job to support himself, forgot about his wanting to meet Paul Robeson, forgot about seeking a job at the Negro newspaper. Rather, he entertained thoughts of devoting the next two years to writing his book.

As everyone reached the alley, Chauncey stopped walking. Isaiah and Goldie continued.

"Maybe you should stay back here, young blood," said Goldie.

Abel stopped, looked at Isaiah. They gazed into each other's dark brown eyes, and with that one look, a twinkle of assuredness became just the signal from Isaiah Abel was looking for. That

twinkle made it all right to accompany him. Soon
they stood before their intended target: a drug
store called Guggenheim's, another store across
the street called Schwartz's. Chauncey walked to
the curb and lit a cigarette. After gazing down
Seventh Avenue in both directions, he slowly nodded
to Isaiah that it was clear. Goldie walked across
the street to Schwartz's. Deftly, Isaiah pulled out
a small can of lighting fluid, dousing the bundle
of newspapers, rendering them soaking wet. Goldie
did the same thing at Schwartz's across the street.
Abel said nothing, only watched. Calmly, Isaiah
pulled a cigar out of his breast pocket, lit the
cigar, and before throwing the still-lighted match
on the bundle, gave Abel that wide gleaming smile
Abel had seen many times before over the years. In
an instant, the front façade of Guggenheim's and
Schwartz's were a raging inferno.

"Run, nigga! Run!"

That's all the coaxing Abel needed to hear. In
an instant, he was leading the sixty-yard dash
down Seventh Avenue back to the waiting automobile.
Once everyone reached the car and piled in, Fetchit
floored the accelerator. The car roared down the
street, zipping by Guggenheim's and Schwartz's one
last time. As everyone took a final look of approval
for a job well done, reality took its hold on Abel.
He was an accomplice to arson. *What if I'm caught?*
What if the police pull up this very minute and
engage us in a car chase? There will be shots fired
fir sure. What if I'm convicted and sent to prison?
How could I have been so stupid? What if one of the
gang is caught, made to talk? They could implicate
Isaiah. They could implicate me.

Rampant thoughts that run all at once seldom make
any sense. There was that smile from Isaiah again.

"How' bout some breakfast, little brotha?" asked
Isaiah. "Torchin' shit gives me a appetite."

4

The night sky over Hollywood Boulevard contained a soft white hue this particular evening. As Ian and Katherine's limousine approached that source of illumination, stacks of people were lining the streets as well. Now that source is evident: the bright lights and marquee of Grauman's Chinese Theatre were seen.

"For the love of Mary and Joseph, there's hundreds, maybe thousands!"

"No doubt we're early. Obviously Gloria Swanson has yet to arrive," says Katherine.

Their limousine accompanied a procession of autos along the street. Model Ts, Cadillacs, and Bentleys, all polished to a glistening glow, lined Hollywood Boulevard as if preparing for a long, loud, and bombastic parade. The excited murmur of fans, media, and spectators were heard as well as the squawks of radio personalities who have the task of announcing each arriving star.

A spring evening in 1928, a Hollywood Oscar night. It was Katherine's night, not Ian's. She had been nominated, along with Gloria Swanson, Marie Dressler, and Janet Gaynor, for the best actress. Compared to the other studios, Universal was noted for their frugal film budgets. Katherine's film *All My Love* was a box-office hit in 1927.

Her outstanding performance forced the critics to include her performance as one of the best. Ian supplied the written scenarios for the silent entry, but recognition on this particular night was not to be his.

The limousine moved forward toward the theater. The herd of fans and media slowly moved past throngs of men and women in their best evening garb, pressing against the barricades, gawking into each window.

Already drunk, Ian amusedly gazed back at everyone. "Look at those fools out there," he quipped. "What do these idiots hope to see?"

"Not me. I was an afterthought," Katherine retorted. "Just to make it an even field."

Ian began to brood. The writer's ego gets in the way. Always the ghost, always behind the scenes, always playing Mr. Incognito for the studio, Ian couldn't wait until the advent of sound so that words and scripts would be just as important as the casting and the choice of director.

One car up, a door opened, and a man and woman engaged themselves into an array of camera flashes.

"Well, will you look at this. They've paired Chaplin with that awful Anna Nilsson," Katherine declared.

"Are you jealous, my dear?" Ian asked. "I'm confident you'll have an opportunity to put your hat, or shall I say panties, in the ring before the evening is over."

"Nobody held a gun to your head to be here," Katherine snapped.

"I am not complaining, my sweet. I wouldn't miss this event for all the tea in bloody China."

"Then please give the sarcastic remarks a rest," said Katherine.

"Sarcastic? Was I being sarcastic?" Ian asked.

"You most certainly are," replied Katherine.

"Oh," Ian murmured between sips out of his flask. "Thought I was merely injecting a little humor into the evening."

Katherine was not amused. "I'm in no mood to hear you whine on in this drunken way. Anyone who didn't know you would think you were bitter."

"Don't be ridiculous. Bitter?" he said. "Of you?"

"We can't talk now," said Katherine.

There was one more car ahead of them. Ian stuffed his flask into his tuxedo coat breast pocket.

"Take that thing out and leave it in the car," Katherine scolded. "You look like a gangster with his heater bulging out."

Ian didn't want to be nasty to Katherine. Not tonight.

"Look at me," she said.

Ian faced her. Katherine softly straightened Ian's black bow tie then brushed his white dinner jacket. "There. Now you look absolutely handsome."

Ian and Katherine's car eased into the space behind the red carpet. The door \was opened. A beautiful usherette, attired in jacket and slacks and wearing a candy-box hat, smiled at them like a painted doll. Ian got out then helped Katherine to her feet.

"Time to play Mr. Katherine's husband," he muttered.

"And here comes Katherine Grant," announced the man at the microphone.

Ian always hated that Laemmle insisted on Katherine keeping her maiden name as her stage name after they married.

Ian and Katherine walked arm in arm up the red carpet, Katherine turning her head to allow her lavish long red hair to move a split second slower. She smiled brightly with the crazed fans along the ropes. Ian wore a faint smile of someone with a toothache.

"With her tonight is"—the announcer stumbled a bit, wanting to be certain who he was looking at—"yes, her husband, scenarist Ian McGregor who has come out to support his lovely wife."

Ian became incensed not to be identified as the scenarist of *All My Love*. Once again, the effort and the accomplishments of the writer were overlooked. Ian now felt that same burn of emptiness he experienced writing on Broadway. No recognition.

Does anyone ever consider that a play or even silent films need written structure? he asked. What of the seemingly endless nights of writer's block he has endured. It hurts Ian—maybe a small part of it is ego. But also human beings want to be recognized for their work. *It's that simple,* he thought. *His time will come. When sound is introduced, studios will be lining up for his talent, and he'll be recognized once and for all as a great writer.*

Ian and Katherine walked through the doors and right by the assemblage of studio executives: Mayer, Laskey, Warner, Fox, and Hughes, all licking their chops, sizing up Katherine's box-office potential for their studios. Those imaginary sounds were the explosion of cash registers going off like firecrackers on the Fourth of July. Obviously the word was out. Her contract with Universal was about to expire.

The ballroom was large, containing an elegance not seen before in Hollywood. Its décor was splendidly laced with hues of royal blue, purple, and cream. The tables were numbered, seating carefully planned so that altercations between studio adversaries do not occur. The orchestra played a European ballad as Ian and Katherine make their way to Universal's table. A small murmur of clapping for Katherine began. Perhaps more than anything, recognition from peers means more to an actor or actress than admiration from starstruck fans. This is why Katherine's smile was much brighter, Ian's face much sterner.

Ian and Katherine took their seats, greeted by both Laemmles and their wives. Katherine's *All My Love* co-star, the tall and handsome Martin Abbott, was there also.

"Martin and I have a publicity party to attend with Junior after the ceremony," said Katherine.

"I'll join you later," Ian offered.

"That won't be necessary. Go home," Katherine said curtly.

She was still angry, which made Ian angry. Watching Martin gleefully pick up on the tension made him angrier. He decided to nudge up to Katherine so as not to be overheard.

"Would you rather I went home now?" Ian said coldly.

Katherine looked into Ian's eyes. "You know I wanted you here. But I have no patience for that drunken sense of humor of yours."

"I'm sorry I lost my temper in the limousine," Ian said. Ian sensed Katherine wanted to make peace. "I am not bitter," he whispered. "Or envious or any such notion. I'm ecstatic for you and Universal. I happen to be in their employ as well. What's good for you is good for me."

"Can we discuss this later?" Katherine asked.

"You take this rubbish much too seriously," replied Ian.

"This might be the only time I ever get nominated for an Academy Award. How else am I to take it?"

"Your moment of fame darling?" asked Ian.

Katherine frowned. "I've supported you through everything. Your drinking, your trysts with those men. Just be happy for me this one time please. Is that so difficult?"

The crowd sat in a hushed tone. Adolphe Menjou stood at the podium poised to announce the winner for the Best Actress of 1928.

———

"And the winner is Janet Gaynor for *Sunrise*."

The crowd applauded loudly with approval. The actresses who lost applauded graciously but looked heartbroken. Ms. Gaynor kissed and hugged everyone in her path while moving toward the podium.

Ian softly grabbed Katherine's hand for support. "One day it shall be you, my sweet."

"Thank you, honey," replied Katherine.

For the entire time Ms. Gaynor made her acceptance speech, Ian and Katherine held hands and looked lovingly into each other's eyes. They said nothing, but it was obvious that no matter what instance beckoned upon their lives and marriage, they would see it through together. Katherine's career and Hollywood existence was more important to her than anything. Whatever support she needed from Ian, he would deliver. Despite Katherine's knowledge of Ian's bisexuality, that wedding night revelation of his seven years ago still haunted her, she truly believes in her Catholic morals and vowed to love Ian until the very end.

"You can make it home fine?" asked Katherine.

"Of course. I'll catch a taxi," replied Ian.

Katherine and Martin jumped into Junior's limousine and headed to a studio-sponsored post-Oscar reception. Ian detested such ass-kissing affairs, obnoxious producers, agents and press people with bad breath, those German directors who have migrated to Hollywood, possessing aspirations of becoming the next F. W. Murnau. They also would be there. Ian hated them the most. He was a corporal in World War I and felt that anyone with Prussian heritage had no right earning a living in America.

There was always a consortium of gay, lesbian, and bisexual industry people to entertain himself with, but Ian thought it not a good idea now that Katherine's star was obviously rising. Katherine would insist on attending these events. "Out of sight, out of mind," she would say.

Ian was bored with the Hollywood cocktail circuit. That's why he married Katherine. There was a time in the genesis years of their marriage that their focus was different. Even though he lived an immoral and sordid life and despite the fact he felt Laemmle's blessing was merely a cover-up to protect Katherine from scandal, Ian wanted children, a family, to come home after a hard day at the studio and have his children run up to him as he opened the door, to help his daughter with her multiplication, to help his son learn how to become the next Babe Ruth. Katherine settling down and having a baby was the furthest thing from her mind. The source of Katherine's fame and attention never worried her. It only became a concern when that fame and attention became suddenly turned off.

Ian was left standing in front of Grauman's, watching his wife scurry off to another night's session of hand kissing, back slapping, and the occasional producer trying to get a free feel of her butt.

"What a joyous evening, ladies and gentlemen!" yelled the radio announcer. "Joan Crawford and Billie Burke, part of the happy family of MGM."

The crowd went, "Oooooh."

The door to the ballroom opened. Janet Gaynor appeared alone, clutching her Best Actress Oscar. Ian thought Katherine would win. He felt she had as good a chance as the others. Ms. Gaynor stopped, stood perfectly still, then started toward the curb where her chauffeur-driven Bentley was parked. Along the purple velvet ropes, hundreds of arms belonging to fans reached out with their autograph books, desperately hoping to get a glimpse, an autograph, a touch, a feel. The crowd went wild; she was not visible to all.

"And here she is," screamed the announcer, "the 1928 winner for Best Actress, Ms. Janet Gaynor."

Yells and applause again. She stood and waved, thrusting her statuette into the air triumphantly. Everyone stared at her, even Ian. Ian moved closer, needing a tighter look.

"Ms. Gaynor? Congratulations," said Ian. Ian had seen her once before. During a holiday at Hearst's San Simeon castle, he watched her play tennis with Mary Pickford from his guest bedroom window. But even without the fine lens of the camera, she possessed the face of a wholesome and virtuous creature. Her only makeup was a small hint of rouge on her cheeks and the mascara on her long lashes. Her long coat concealed an elegant strapless silk gown. Suddenly Ms. Gaynor turned her attention to Ian.

"You are Katherine Grant's husband," she said. She smiled. "I saw your play *Me, Myself, and Her* on Broadway several years back. I absolutely love your work."

Ian was caught off guard by the recognition.

"Perhaps one day you could write something for me to star in." She laughed.

He laughed with her. "That would be interesting," said Ian.

Ms. Gaynor was helped into her car.

"Good night, Ms. Gaynor, and congratulations once more," Ian said proudly.

Ian told himself, *You are a goddamn hypocrite,* as he watched Ms. Gaynor's car pull off down the street. One minute he lamented how writers got no recognition. And yet, for that brief minute, the fact that Ms. Gaynor knew of his work on Broadway and complimented him on it, made Ian feel proud of his past accomplishments.

———

"What did she say, mate?"

Not immediately recognizing the voice, Ian hesitated before turning around. When he did, he stood before a young man of thirty with red hair, dressed in tails and top hat.

"I beg your pardon," responded Ian.

"Ms. Gaynor. That was Janet Gaynor, eh, gov'na?"

The young man's cockney accent gave him away as British. Ian immediately recognized him as the gentleman with Howard Hughes in the Universal commissary a few days back.

"We exchanged pleasantries. She was quite polite."

"I'm James."

They shook hands.

"Ian, Ian McGregor." Ian stared momentarily. At first glance, he found James handsome.

"I saw you with Howard Hughes at Universal, yes?"

James smiled. "Your memory is outstanding. I just got over here from England. Mr. Hughes has signed me to direct a picture."

"You'll find RKO an excellent studio to work for," offered Ian.

The Oscar crowd emptied out onto the street at a steadier pace than minutes before. On cue began a light drizzle. Springtime drizzles in Los Angeles could last for hours. Ian didn't want to go home. He knew Katherine wouldn't be getting there until late, maybe not until the very next morning. Ian began to fume. He thought of Katherine's co-star, Martin, who has always lusted over Katherine. He entertained thoughts of Katherine sleeping with Martin. Maybe they had already. Ian knew that Katherine, at times, would sleep with other men to get back at him for revealing his alter lifestyle after they got married. This was the price Ian was paying for his honesty.

The anger turned to resigning to fate. Marriages put together for reasons other than love and commitment sometimes brought excess baggage and a lot of painful nights.

"I said there's a friendly pub a short distance from here. Care to have a nightcap?" Even after the second time, Ian didn't hear James talking to him.

"I'm sorry, James. You were saying?" said Ian.

"I know of a friendly spot not far from here. How about a nightcap?" repeated James a third time.

"Splendid idea," said Ian.

The next cab became theirs.

5

Months passed. Abel had settled in comfortably as Isaiah's roommate. Isaiah had the bedroom. Abel made a corner of the living room his writing studio. There were always free and uninterrupted evenings to work on his notes for his future novel. He also had found a job as a print setter at the *Harlem Herald,* a Negro newspaper. On several occasions, Paul Robeson came into the office to submit articles to the paper he wanted published. Once, he walked right by Abel. That was as close as he got to him.

Isaiah and his gang used the days to collect the receipts from their policy numbers racket. The evening hours were reserved for their more-fiendish criminal work. Isaiah was adamant not to allow Abel to accompany them on their ventures. Just in case the cops showed up, he would say. Worse even, gunplay might be a part of the night's festivities. Isaiah respected Abel for what he was trying to accomplish. He wanted his brother to be a successful writer. He didn't want to see him killed or put in jail for the dastardly sins he was committing. Abel respected Isaiah, yet he was intelligent enough to know that his business was writing, not being a boss to a gang and running the numbers racket.

This particular evening, an all-night poker game

had begun. Abel didn't play poker. He just sat in a corner, writing.

Fetchit walked in and said, "Isaiah, Orpheus the bootblack is outside. Wants to see you. He's in some sort of trouble. Looks like he's had an awful whuppun'."

"Orpheus?" Isaiah asked doubtfully. Is he that bootblack by the polo grounds collectin' for us?"

"Yeh, that's the nigga," Goldie answered. He remembered him because they used to work at Lattner's Gym on Eighth Avenue and 126th.

Orpheus entered the room. His look resemble that of a pugilist loser fresh out of the ring. He had a bandage around his head. A black ring hung on his right eye. His lips were so swollen, he could hardly talk. Abel sat up only because he thought that this stranger's story might be worthy of an entry into his journal.

Goldie asked, "What's wrong with you, nigga? Wife kicked yo' ass again?"

Isaiah shoved a chair toward him and said, "Sit down, man. Have a drink and tell us yo' troubles."

He bowed gratefully with the drink in his hand. He said, "Ah," in appreciation after he drank up. Then he sat down with a groan and mumble through his swollen lips, "Wife trouble? Hell, naw," shaking his head to Isaiah.

Goldie asked laughingly, "So who decorated your eye, the mother-in-law?"

Orpheus turned and looked at Isaiah. He shook his head. "My wife and mother-in-law I can handle," he said. "It's bui'ness. I got into a fight." He rocked back and forth. "It's Bumpy Johnson," said Orpheus. "He sent one of his boys, Larry I think his name is, to give me the onceover. He took your cut of the action. After he kicked my ass, he said this was Bumpy's corner, that I was working for him now."

He looked helplessly at the gang as he continued

rocking back and forth in pain. "I axed you for protection," said Orpheus. "Can't go to the police. Gots a family too."

Orpheus looked at everyone's faces, hoping to read sympathy. Isaiah, angry, stood up and threw his glass against the wall, shattering it in a thousand and one pieces. Isaiah reassured him. "You did right by coming to us, Orpheus. Never go to the police. Weez a family. We take care of our own."

With that, Orpheus stood up, bowed his head and spoke softly, "Thanks, boss."

"Don't mention it," said Isaiah. "Far as I'm concerned, this conversation didn't happen. Go home. We'll handle it. Ain't nobody from Bumpy Johnson's gang gonna bother you no mo'."

Orpheus turned, walked out of the apartment.

Isaiah's anger continued. "That goddamn greedy-ass Bumpy Johnson. He don't take orders, it seems."

"Ain't none of 'em niggas any good," said Fetchit.

"Yes, this stinks," Isaiah agreed. "Dutch Schultz gives me a territory to work, and what does this nigga do? Tries to move in."

Goldie concurs with Isaiah. "Just last week you took that nigga to the Savoy. Bought his ass champagne and steak. You treated him handsome and look what the motherfucka does behind your back. Makes a move on your territory."

"Goldie's right," said Chauncey. "The Dutchman says we get Sugar Hill, the Jungle, and the Polo Grounds. It ain't right."

Isaiah slowly walked over to the window so that he may gaze out at the Harlem nightlife pulsating below on the sidewalks. The room took on a hushed tone. Everyone kept their thoughts to themselves as Isaiah decided what the plan for retaliation will be. There was the clue. When Isaiah pulled a cigar out of his pocket to smoke, he was thinking. Seconds, minutes went by. The apartment engulfed the cigar smoke. No one dared to interrupt his concentration. The gang had seen this moment before on many other occasions. They knew not to disturb Isaiah when his brain was set in motion like this. That was what made him so smart—because he was so pensive. He thought every move out to the nth degree. It was Isaiah's thinking abilities and street smarts that impressed Dutch Schultz the most. It was that reason Isaiah was put in charge of the Dutchman's numbers racket in Harlem. Dutch Schultz once told Isaiah he was the smartest nigger he ever knew.

Was he going to Dutch Schultz now and seek his blessing to take matters into his own hands? Or was this an incident of survival, and therefore, his call to make as the Dutchman's lieutenant? Isaiah had figured out long before that a well thought-out plan eliminated waste and, more importantly, mistakes. He shifted toward the sofa where Abel has been attentively listening to the dialogue.

"You need to blow for a few hours, little bro'," said Isaiah.

"Is it all right if I stay?" asked Abel.

"Naw, take a powder. Gots thangs to talk over with the boys. Betta off not known' what the fuck is going on," replies Isaiah. Isaiah walked to the bedroom door, knocking hard three times.

The door slowly opened. A young shapely woman with the legs of a ballet dancer emerged from the bedroom.

"Sweet cakes, here's two ticks to see Duke Ellington at the Savoy tonight. I want you to take my little brotha out and show him a good time," said Isaiah.

Florence was her name. But everyone called her Flo. She measured over six feet tall in her high heels. Her fair skin suggested she was part Caucasian. In all likelihood, a plantation slaveowner in a drunken stupor raped her great-grandmother many years earlier. Her large round breasts were perfectly shaped. She had dark brown hair and a round curvy butt so big, the men in Harlem said you could place a glass on it, and it wouldn't fall. The beige silk dress she wore clung to every curve she owned. She was every male Harlemite's wet dream and Isaiah's girlfriend.

"I thought we were going out tonight," a perturbed Flo said.

"It's bui'ness, get me?" replied Isaiah.

This was only the second occasion Abel had seen Flo. Last week, Isaiah first introduced her as his lady to Abel at the Apollo Theater. Abel couldn't take his eyes off her then and still couldn't now. Isaiah was careful not to have Flo spend the night on a regular basis, not out of respect for Abel or because he wanted to shield him from his own immoral behavior. Rather, it was because Flo bellowed and screamed like a wild animal when she and Isaiah had sex. Though he would never admit it, Isaiah became increasingly embarrassed about this event. It was also convenient that Flo lived in New Jersey. This allowed Isaiah ample opportunities to cheat on the side with his "Harlem Honies" as he put it.

Isaiah met Flo at a juke joint she was performing in across the Hudson River in Hoboken, New Jersey. Flo's dream was to become a professional singer, dancer, and actress like Josephine Baker. Isaiah had promised Flo he would help her launch a performing career in New York with his money and business connections. Abel had never seen such a beautiful woman like Flo. Country girls from Alabama simply aren't afforded the opportunity to devote time to rituals of vanity such as hair, nails, and clothing. There's too much time spent in the hot sun tilling fields, too much time brushing and combing the dust out of your hair, too much time rubbing the dryness off your sunbaked skin.

Abel quickly noticed that city women always had makeup, or their "faces," on, always wore lipstick, eye shadow, and rouge. New York City was about glamour and being glamorous. Glamorous fit Flo like a glove. He thought Isaiah was awful lucky to have Flo as his girlfriend.

"Betta get yo'self cleaned up. Gotta look sharp if you gonna take my girl out," said Isaiah.

Abel hurried to the bathroom to wash up, put on a clean shirt, and throw on Isaiah's black tails, which were one size too big, but he didn't have any formal wear of his own and, therefore, had no other choice. Abel wouldn't dare admit or let Isaiah see that he was quite infatuated with Flo. Any man with a pulse would be infatuated, but the object of his infatuation was his big brother's girlfriend. To pursue a romance would be a dead-end proposition.

Abel brushed the last bit of lint of his tails. He tried not to show too much excitement at the prospect of walking around the Savoy with a gorgeous well-built woman like Flo. Everybody in the joint would know that she was Isaiah Johnson's girl. But the whispers and murmurs would be about him.

"Who is he?"

"How come I ain't never seen him 'round here before?"

"Who is this nigga with Isaiah's lady?"

"Are Flo and Isaiah busto?"

The questions and innuendo this evening would be endless. Abel's plan was to relish it.

"Come on, baby, do me this one solid," Isaiah asked.

Flo smiled. "All right, baby, whatever you say. Just be careful."

"So what are you dinging up in Harlem, baby Johnson?"

They were the first words spoken since Abel and

Flo entered the cab almost fifteen minutes earlier. Abel, by no means, had any idea what a man about town is supposed to do with an obvious lady of class like Flo. Flo was being an accommodating escort only because as long as she thought Isaiah was her meal ticket to an established singing and acting career. Her credo was "whatever it takes."

The cab stopped right in front of the Savoy. The crowd making their way through the doors was as thick as a fog. Duke Ellington's band had a way of packing them in droves. The swing set was as hot as ever. Even Negroes at that time owned black tuxedos and tails and long shimmering gowns.

Abel, during the previous week, gawked at the neon signs blaring their messages: the Savoy, nightly jazz, twenty-five cent cover. A large poster board was mounted on the front façade promoting Duke Ellington's appearance. Abel, feeling like a big shot, reached into his pocket and paid the cabbie with the money Isaiah gave him to spend that evening.

"Not just yet," said Flo, sitting back in her seat waiting for something to happen.

Abel took his hand off the door handle and sat back in his seat.

"I thought we were going in," said Abel.

"Not just yet. Red, gimme one of them reefers," replied Flo.

On cue, the cab driver reached from behind his ear and handed Flo a reefer cigarette. There was no doubt as Abel watched, that Flo was proficient in the handling of marijuana. *Does Isaiah smoke reefers?* Abel thought. Isaiah had never smoked in front of Abel, nor had he detected any irrational behavior out of Isaiah other than too much drinking.

Flo dragged on the joint hard, holding, holding, holding. As she eased the smoke out of her mouth, she turned toward Abel.

"Don't smoke reefers," said Abel.

"Just more for me. Be a good baby Johnson and roll down the window," said Flo.

The maître d' immediately recognized Flo as Isaiah's woman. This was why he was so accommodating when it came to sitting Abel and Flo at one of the booths close to the band stand stage.

"Like being in classy joints, don't you?" asked Flo.

"Sure, who doesn't," replied Abel.

"Nothing like this in Alabama."

"You've been to Alabama?" asked Abel.

"Born and raised just outside Tuscaloosa. That's right. We do have something in common. 'Cept I got rid of my country-girl manner long time ago."

For the next hour, Abel's head was on a swivel, trying to recognize all the important people of the Harlem night scene. To his right sat Bojangles Robinson. To his left sat a young singer named Lena Horne with her date, Pittsburgh numbers kingpin Gus Greenlee. Abel's mind was on what he was going to write when he got home more than what the Duke was about to play during the next set. But what amazed Abel the most was that the crowd inside the Savoy was half white. The upper crust from Park Avenue and Wall Street had jumped into their Cadillacs and cabs and headed uptown to absorb Negro nightlife filled with greasy smells of fried chicken, swing, be-bop, and razzmatazz.

Just then Abel decided to devote a full chapter on this phenomenon. He thought, they hated, despised, looked upon as a lesser human being than themselves, and yet drive great distances to hear Negro music. One race was willing to embrace another race's culture and music but would not embrace that race as equal.

Isn't there something hypocritical about this? Abel asked himself. These rich white men and their women would get drunk, laugh uproariously whenever the Duke swang into a hot number while waving his conked hair wildly. Now Abel was upset he didn't bring his writing pad and would have to rely on his memory after several glasses of champagne.

He was right. Those in the crowd who knew Isaiah were whispering among themselves. "Who was this cat with Isaiah's woman?"

After more sips from his champagne glass, Abel didn't care who was looking or who was whispering. He felt like a real big shot—money in his pocket, escorting a beautiful woman to the Savoy for a Duke Ellington performance, absorbing the envy of the male crowd surrounding him.

New York City was becoming more and more his kind of town. That dream he had many years ago in Alabama about life in the big city was just as he had imagined—a city of life, a city of lights, a city with a million stories to write about. New York offered so many opportunities for a young and eager writer like Abel. *This is the best champagne I've ever had, the best time of my life,* he thought.

It had now become Abel and Flo's turn for a cab. When the cab approached the curb, Flo, quite gently, held her hand up against Abel's chest. "Tell Isaiah I went home to Hoboken," said Flo.

"Sure," replied Abel drunkenly.

Flo kissed Abel gently on the cheek. "I had a nice time, baby Johnson. Isaiah sure has a gentleman for a little brother."

As the cab pulled off, Abel thought of Althea, his old girlfriend back in Alabama. Abel has thought of Althea only once since he left Tuskegee. It was her birthday several weeks back, and when one specific date has been part of your existence for the past eight years, there becomes an attachment, an aura of nostalgia associated with that date. The day after Althea's birthday, he stopped thinking about her.

Any thoughts devoted to his past life in Tuskegee were forbidden. And so life moved on. But that kiss on the cheek Flo gave him had him reminiscing about the time he and Althea were teenagers.

Althea kissed Abel on the cheek on their first date also. Abel remembered the warmth inside, those initial buds of love blooming. He has those same feelings for Flo. But he can't have Flo. It's over before it ever began. He would never lust after his brother's girlfriend.

"I said, young man, are you waiting for the next cab?"

Abel turned. Paul Robeson, tall, stout, well-built, his writing idol stood less than one foot from him. He stared. No, he wasn't deciding whether or not to take the next cab. He was tongue tied, facing a legend.

"Why, no, sir," said Abel.

"Then I'll take this cab," said Robeson.

"You're Paul Robeson," Abel said proudly.

"Why, yes, would you like an autograph?" asked Robeson.

Autograph? Abel asked himself. The champagne was swirling in his head and stomach. The seconds seem like minutes as he fumbled with what words to say. "It would be an honor to write a play for you," Abel replied.

Robeson let out a loud, baritone laugh. "A collaboration?" asked Robeson. "You're a writer?"

"It would be an honor, sir," replied Abel.

The beautiful woman hanging on Robeson's arm was getting impatient. The look she delivered made it obviously clear to Abel that he was holding something up much more exciting.

"Well, young man, I'm always told never say never." Robeson smiled, got into the cab, and rode off into the Harlem night.

Abel's feet never touched the ground during his walk back to his room. There was a thought in the back of his mind Robeson was patronizing him. Mimicking Robeson's robust, baritone voice, Abel said, "Sure, young buck, you can write a play for me hahahahaha."

Abel was going to prove he was. Robeson was playing Shakespeare's Othello at Columbia University. Abel thought it would be a good idea to take in a performance or two in order to get a feel for Robeson's acting mannerisms and idiosyncrasies. Then Abel was going to write the best stage play Robeson ever read and starred in.

Even at two in the morning, Harlem nightlife was still abuzz, the city that never sleeps. At every second, every juncture, it seemed a different personality surrounded Abel on his walk: hookers, pimps, hustlers, out-of-towners, dope fiends. After several months, he had become used to this sort of urban environment. It didn't take long with Isaiah's guidance to develop urban or city instincts.

The temperature had dropped considerably, making the late evening chilly. Abel was oblivious to the cold air. His breaths were deep. He wanted Harlem to absorb him with all his might. For the first time, Abel truly believed his dreams were going to come true. For the first time, he showed confidence that his decision to leave Alabama was the right one. He had a job with a newspaper. He was writing. He met Paul Robeson.

Is it too good to be true? he asked. He reminded himself to write Momma a letter, only he had to send it to Althea so that she could read it to her. Now his thoughts were back on Flo. Abel wished she hadn't kissed his cheek. Her perfume was on his face and shirt. Her smell was poisoning his bloodstream. It was arousing him. He began to lust for her in his thoughts. He wanted to have sex with her. *You spend five hours drinking champagne, gazing at, dancing up close with a beautiful woman, and those things can happen,* he reasoned.

For every lustful thought about Flo, two thoughts of Isaiah beating him to a pulp would enter his mind. It was the one thing ruining a perfect evening. Abel's quick pace loosened the strings to one of his shoes. He took this time, this very moment, to turn the corner and perch his foot on the steps of a building.

"Abel!"

Abel recognized the voice immediately.

"This way!" Isaiah yelled from a car double-parked in the street.

Abel walked over to the passenger side and got in. Isaiah pulled off down the street, constantly checking his mirrors for unwanted followers or even the police.

"What's wrong?" Abel asked.

Isaiah motioned back and replied, "We gots company."

Abel turned toward the back seat—a Negro man bound and gagged, perspiration running down the front of his face, his eyes bulging out in fear, in fear of an impending death.

"Baby brotha, meet Larry Charleston. Why, he's Bumpy Johnson's number 1 collector. Yessir, he's a real top-flight Harlem nigga."

Abel turned back around to stare at Isaiah. As Isaiah kept his eyes on the road, Abel kept his eyes on him. He was trying to analyze Isaiah. Abel was beginning to realize that mayhem and murder was now a part of Isaiah's makeup. Now he wondered what was next. It was obvious to Abel that Isaiah already knew what he was going to do with this man.

"What happened to Flo?" asked Isaiah.

"She took a taxi home. Said she'd call you tomorrow," replied Abel.

The man's groans in the back seat grew louder. His pants were now soiled with urine.

"What'cha gonna do with him?" a frightened Abel asked. He knew that answer already. Isaiah always had a morbid-sounding laugh when he was about to do something diabolical. It reminded Abel of the time he and Isaiah were teenagers back in Alabama. That was the day Isaiah told Abel they were going to the store for Momma. Isaiah kept laughing morbidly for the entire walk. They ended up at Festus Whitaker's barn where Isaiah promptly swindled a group out of twenty dollars with a marked set of dice.

"What'cha think I'm gonna do with him?" replied Isaiah.

There was an eerie silence engulfing every inch of the car. An occasional mumble from Isaiah's prisoner in the back broke that eerie silence. Abel began to shiver. Isaiah turned into a dark alley by the Polo Grounds. Carefully parking the car against the brick wall of an abandoned building, Isaiah kept the motor running while opening the door.

"Need some help with this nigga," said Isaiah.

"I ain't killin' nobody," a defiant Abel replied.

"Just help me get him out o' the car!" yelled Isaiah.

The man weighed almost two hundred pounds, and it took both of them to get him out of the car and stack him up against the wall. Abel stepped back, disassociating himself from everything else that was about to happen. Isaiah ripped the tape off of the man's mouth. His screams and cries were that of a sobering man about to be shot at dawn after court martial or the murderer in Sing Sing right before he is strapped into the electric chair.

"Don't kill me, man. Beggin' you, don't kill me," the man pleaded.

Abel had never seen his older brother whom he loved and respected act like such a monster. Murder was seconds away, Abel was sure of it. He was going to kill him.

"Isaiah, stop!" pleaded Abel.

"Shut up!" Isaiah shot back.

Abel moved forward. Isaiah turned, giving Abel a look not to do one more thing. This was his business. A look from Isaiah to stay out of his business was all Abel needed to stop him dead in his tracks. Isaiah reached into his coat pocket for his switchblade knife. The quiet night was interrupted briefly by the click of Isaiah's blade opening. It took all but three seconds for Isaiah to cover the man's mouth and slash his throat from ear to ear. He was so deft at wielding his weapon of choice, the splattering of blood on the wall was kept to a minimum.

The man slowly slumped down the wall. His eyes absorbing life for the final time. His blood drenched his clothes like the driving rain of a summer thunderstorm. He stopped breathing. He stopped living. His eyes and mouth remained open. Abel ran back to the car. He couldn't keep his vomit from coming up and getting all over his clothes.

"Get a hold of yourself," said Isaiah.

"But . . . but you killed that man," replied Abel.

"Pull yourself together. Get in the car," Isaiah told Abel. Isaiah stepped on the gas, emerging out of the alley. Minutes later found him and Abel crossing the Hudson River on the George Washington Bridge.

"Where are we going now?" asked Abel.

"Jersey. You're going to stay at Flo's until the heat's off," said Isaiah.

"I can't. I won't," retorted Abel.

"You listen to me," said Isaiah. "You get wise. Bumpy Johnson is gonna come after us. He don't know shit about you. This is your chance to make a clean break."

"What about you?" asked Abel.

"Don't worry 'bout me. I got the Dutchman watchin' my back. Bumpy Johnson ain't no fool to start no war with Dutch Schultz," said Isaiah.

Abel couldn't control the tears streaming down his face. It was like water running down a mountain stream. How could one minute everything he was dreaming about appear to come to fruition and the next minute he's a witness to a murder his brother committed? For the first time ever, Abel thought about what would have happened if he had stayed in Alabama and taught at Tuskegee Institute. Maybe he and Althea would have gotten married. Maybe he would be an expectant father now.

"After things cool down, you need to move west," said Isaiah.

"West? Whadaya mean?" asked Abel.

"West, nigga, St. Louis, Chicago, KC, some goddamn place 'cept New York, get me?" Isaiah was trying to be as forceful as possible. He was preparing Abel for the worst.

"I'll have Fetchit bring you your clothes and books and shit in a couple of days," said Isaiah. He reached into his coat pocket and handed Abel five rolled-up twenty-dollar bills.

"Flo's a good woman. She loves my dirty stinkin' draw's. She'll do anything I say, so don't you worry 'bout her. It's going to be a long time 'fo' we see each other again, little bro'. Maybe never. Can't predict the future, so consider me already dead. Keep doin' what you do best, and that's writin' them books."

Abel never looked at Isaiah as he spoke. He merely clutched the money in his hand and kept crying while staring out the window into the dark, seemingly calm Hudson River.

6

"You're going to love Hollywood, James!" Ian said excitedly.

James smiled back in agreement.

"Sunny skies three hundred days of the year. The outrageous salaries these studios pay us for so-called work. And the women, all sizes and shapes and colors. I suppose a bachelor like yourself looks forward to tasting such wicked delicacies."

James replied, "If those are your wants and pleasures."

Ian didn't respond, only giving James a quizzical look. Now was not the time for elaboration. He quickly changed the subject. "How long do you plan on staying?" asked Ian.

"I'm here for two pictures," James replies. "After that, it's back to England and the theater."

"Give it some time," Ian said. "Once you have experienced California at its fullest, I guarantee you you'll never crave for cold, rain, and the boring European way of life again."

Approaching a small steel cart perched along the street curb, James became drawn to it like a pig to his slop box. He realized it was a cart that served food.

"And what do we have here?" asked James.

Ian replied, "This is a hot dog stand. This

gentleman serves what we Americans call hot dogs, a tasty treat if you are attracted to such primitive modes of cuisines."

"Sounds yummy. May I try one?" asked James.

Ian ordered, "Two with plenty of mustard."

The vendor moved quickly in preparing the small feast. James marveled how the vendor, with one hand, placed a hot dog in a bun, squirted mustard, and handed them to Ian and James in fifteen seconds flat. In an instant, James was munching hard through the soft bun and meat, enjoying every bite. Ian used his napkin to deftly wipe the mustard off of James's chin.

"Love that taste. What's it called again?" asked James.

"Mus-tard," Ian replied. "Quite good."

James kept making bigger bites until they become large chomps.

"Yes, very tasty," said James. He used his index finger to signal the vendor to serve him up one more.

As the movie played, Ian and James would often trade quizzical looks at each other. No words, just eye communication. Neither could read the other one's mind. That didn't deter them from trying. Every dashing move by Fairbanks on the screen seemed to flush Ian's and James's skin with excitement.

"Rather a good-looking chap," said James.

Ian was silent. "Yes," was his reply after several seconds as if he wanted to think about his answer. Was James making overtures for some sort of elaboration?

James asked, "The flickers have turned into quite the moneymaker, I see."

Ian never turned his head to acknowledge James's question. It was his way of telling him he didn't like to talk while the movie is playing. In the

movie, Fairbanks leaps off of a table to face an
awaiting swordsman. A fierce fencing battle ensues.
The fight ends as quickly as it began. Ian and
James both smiled at the actor's deft swashbuckling
antics. One more quick glance into each other's
eyes. It is at this very moment both decide to keep
all points of conversation concealed to themselves
until after the movie.

The look on James's face had Ian roaring with
laughter. James had never seen a restaurant shaped
the size of a large derby hat. James was so awestruck,
he nearly fell out of the taxi.

"This is actually a fun place." beamed Ian. The
loud red neon blaring the name *The Brown Derby* gave
James the impression that this was the venue in
Hollywood to see and be seen.

"I suppose a cavalcade of stars will be parading
through," said James. James had only been in
Hollywood one month and was still starstruck with
all the Hollywood regalia.

Ian quickly checked his watch. "Still early yet.
Just be yourself," replied Ian.

As they enter the bar area, a maitre d'
approached Ian.

"Good evening, Mr. McGregor. Table for two?"

James was unaware that this was the signal Ian
and the maitre d' used to secure a table in a
private room where Ian and his male friends could
be more cordial and inconspicuous.

Two hot dogs and sodas apiece made food an
afterthought.

"We've already eaten. We'll take seats at the
bar," replied Ian.

"Very good, Mr. McGregor." The maitre d' quickly
focused his attention to someone of more importance.
This night found the bar crowded more than most
evenings. Any time Douglas Fairbanks had a movie

premiere, the Brown Derby became transformed from a quaint restaurant to a boisterous party hall.

Before Ian and James could get comfortable on their bar stools, Ian was thrown into a vicelike bear hug by one of his drinking buddies, John, accompanied by his lovely and tall date.

"Ian, you twit! Where have you been?" John asked.

Ian replied, "Hiding from you, you bloody idiot. James, may I introduce Mr. John Gilbert and Ms. Greta Garbo."

James tried his best to camouflage his giddiness at the prospect of meeting John Gilbert and Greta Garbo. James was also impressed with Ian for being personal friends of the two stars. James nervously got out of his bar stool, grabbed Ms. Garbo's gloved hand, kissing it softly.

"The pleasure is all mine, Ms. Garbo," spoke James. As an afterthought, James shook John's hand.

"You and Katherine have stayed away too long," said John.

"You cheat at bridge too much for our taste and pocketbook," said Ian straightfaced. Everyone thought the joke was funny except James who didn't laugh until he was certain Ian was joking.

"Come by soon, ol' boy," said John.

"Of course you must come," said Ms. Garbo, chiming in.

"Soon as Katherine finishes her picture, we promise," said Ian.

Satisfied with Ian's response, John and Greta walked arm in arm into the Hollywood night. Ian's regular bartender, Sammy, appeared right on cue.

"Sammy, two scotches with water," ordered Ian.

It had been weeks since Ian went out alone without Katherine. His last scandal and warning from studio chief Laemmle Sr. was enough to ensure his best behavior while Katherine completed filming what would be her final silent movie. The studio had already decided what sound feature she would play the lead in. Ian was to begin working on the script next week.

"What does Hughes have you working on?" asked Ian.

"At the moment, nothing," replied James.

Ian threw his scotch down his throat like a Dublin Irishman on a binge. James coddled his drink, suggesting he'd prefer something British, like sherry. Two quick raps on the bar by Ian had the bartender bellying back up to pour him another shot.

"You got a girl here?" asked Ian.

Shot number 2 is finished.

"I haven't got a girl anywhere," said James. James sipped on his scotch and eyeballed Ian at the same time. It was a suggestive gesture usually reserved for a woman who is interested in a man, a signal of availability.

"Your wife is beautiful," said James.

"I know. I'm a lucky guy," replied Ian. He chose that moment to sound sarcastic, not letting James know he loved Katherine very much. Even though it was an arranged marriage through the studio for the benefit of Katherine's career, they had grown to love and respect each other. Ian cherished their relationship. But now he found James attractive. His stylish attire and flaming red hair gave him a lustful feeling. He had a feeling James was homosexual, but he was not quite sure. He decided to probe deeper before committing to another relationship, especially with the studio having him on a short leash.

"I know of a party," said Ian.

"A party, mate?" said James. "Sounds delightful."

Ian said, "Director friend of mine has a quaint home in Westwood. By the time we get there, things will be just starting. Finish your drink, and we'll leave."

"Actually, I prefer martinis," said James.
Ian replied, "Well then, shall we?"

The door to a large home off Sunset Boulevard opened. A Negro butler stood ready to greet the new guests.

"Evening, Mr. Ian."

"Good evening to you, Jenkins. Where's George?" asked Ian.

Ian and James entered the foyer.

"He in the wine cellar with some other guests," replied the butler.

"Splendid! We'll mingle around. I want to show James the house," said Ian.

"Very good, Mas'r Ian."

Ian and James entered a very large living room richly decorated with French provincial furniture. A pianist played Chopin. A large oriental carpet, plushly made, ran from wall to wall.

"Who is the owner?" asked James.

"George is an up-and-coming director," said Ian. "RKO just signed him to direct a picture starring Nora Wren. George also has exquisite taste as well."

A Negro servant offered champagne. Ian and James gleefully accepted. James went into a daydream. It would be so nice to own such extravagancies, entertain famous Hollywood and literary guests. In his mind, he just left England forever. This particular evening with Ian swayed him on never going back.

"I know what you're thinking," said Ian.

"Sorry?" replied James, hoping Ian wouldn't mind repeating himself.

"You have that same look I did twelve years after I left Scotland," said Ian.

"And what look might that be?" asked James.

"That you just fell in love with a time and place

in your life and that you hoped it would not end," replied Ian.

James smiled at Ian. He was becoming attracted to him. Was there a remote chance Ian would find him alluring, he asked himself. Eyes of lust seem to twinkle brightly after champagne. There attentiveness to each other was interrupted when a fat, balding white-dinner-jacket-wearing German director walked up to Ian.

"Ian, my lad, how's Katherine?" asked the director. The director shook Ian's hand forcefully.

James took the opportunity to pursue the waiter for another glass of champagne. He stood there watching, staring at the arrangement of couples mingling around the house—men with women, men with men, women with women. That's when it struck James that this was a party, a smorgasbord for whatever sexual tastes you desired. It was an orgy with a bit of class. James understood why Ian brought him here.

"Mr. Von Stroheim . . . I . . . I didn't expect to see you here," said Ian.

Von Stroheim was well aware of Ian's past bisexual sins since it was Von Stroheim's assistant director Ian had the fling with. On cue, he took the next fifteen seconds to yell out with a bombastic laugh, loud enough that the piano player stopped in the middle of his Chopin piece. Being from Germany and living in Berlin for many years, Von Stroheim was accustomed to actors, actresses, and artists possessing varying degrees of decadence when it came to matters of sexuality.

Von Stroheim said, "Of course you didn't think you would see me. Not at one of George's parties. So well-known for its lavish extracurricular activities."

Ian smirked.

"Thalberg and his lovely bride, Ms. Shearer, just left the party. Perhaps you've heard I'm leaving Universal for MGM," said Von Stroheim.

"It appears congratulations are in order. Impressive job directing *Husbands and Wives*," replied Ian.

"Yes, wasn't it?" said Von Stroheim.

The two were running out of complimentary things to say to each other. Von Stroheim had yet to state the real reason he walked over to Ian when he saw him.

"My first picture for MGM involves a very interesting part for a leading lady with your wife's talents. I want her to read for the part," said Von Stroheim.

"Why tell me? Tell Morry Adamson. He's her agent," replied Ian.

Von Stroheim took this opportunity to place his arm around Ian. He gave Ian a look that suggested he owed him a favor. "I'm hoping as a personal favor to me, you can convince Katherine to sign with MGM after she finishes this picture for Universal," said Von Stroheim.

"Do I owe you something?" asked Ian, taking Von Stroheim's arm from around his shoulders.

"Not me," said Von Stroheim.

"Who then?" asked Ian.

Von Stroheim reached into his pocket for his monocle and deftly placed it in his left eye socket. "If you don't know, then I suggest you ask somebody, Herr McGregor." Von Stroheim walked away.

Ian went looking for James.

There was no midnight moon to shine on the Olympic-sized outdoor pool. The pool neatly centered what was a large perfectly manicured lawn, containing what seemed an endless array of bushes of beautifully pruned roses. The only illumination to the yard was two small lights attached to both ends of the pool. Keeping the yard as dark as possible was the intended idea. All the swimmers enjoying the pool were naked. All the swimmers enjoying the pool were men.

Ian drunkenly stumbled around the grounds until he found himself by the pool. He took the first chair available. It was time to think. He was tired. James was nowhere to be found. At this moment, Ian's failures began mounting in his head: soon-to-be a has-been writer, sham of a husband, in-the-closet bisexual. Had he lost his meaning for life? Had he lost his vision of what he wanted? The champagne made it next to impossible for him to sort the cloudiness out. Failure was something Ian was not going to be able to handle. Should he pack up and go back to Boston? Should he kill himself?

Ian decided he was not going to be a burden on Katherine. No sympathy handouts. Not going to be in *Variety's* laughing stock column. Not going to be Walter Winchell's radio piece on how to be a bumbling idiot of a writer.

Ian quickly changed thought patterns. What possible motive could Von Stroheim have for thinking he would help him? Did Von Stroheim intervene with Laemmle on Ian's behalf? Ian also knew there were at least four other actresses better suited for an MGM picture than Katherine. Maybe Von Stroheim wanted Katherine for himself. It was hard for Ian to feel jealousy. Thoughts of another man wanting Katherine always entered his head. When you love men as well as your wife, there's always the risk your wife will seek another man's bed for sex. Ian knew of Katherine's affair with Chaplin. He harbored no ill feelings toward her. He never mentioned to Katherine that he knew about it. But he hated Chaplin. He went as far as to slash his car tires at a movie premiere several months back. That was the extent of his revenge.

A large splash drew Ian's attention to the pool. Two well-built men were caressing each other's pectoral muscles. This amused Ian. Their toned physiques illuminated odd-shaped shadows off the pool lights. And then it happened. A love story began brewing in Ian's head. Finally, something had happened to Ian that hadn't happened in a long time—an idea for an original scenario, actual inspiration.

Ian began smiling from ear to ear. *Get the story,* Ian kept telling himself. Two lovers flee the tight control of their religious parents, get married, and settle in a new town. Ian knew the protagonists in his story would have to be a man and a woman. The studio and the Hayes Code would never approve a storyline that included two male lovers. But so what? The writer's block had left momentarily. He wanted to leave so that he could go home and begin writing. The alcohol, combined with his sordid love life and serving as Katherine's husband for show only, had triggered long bouts of writer's block for months. Days, nights, would pass. Not one word written. Universal was about to put him under contract to write two screenplays for their first two movies with sound.

A hand gently squeezed his shoulder. Ian turned.

"Having a good time, mate?" asked James.

Ian looked up, saw a handsome face with red hair. He was galvanized. His pulse quickened. The pitch black background of the night sky produced a dark contrast to James's face.

Am I drunk, or is he beautiful? James asked himself. James cupped Ian's face tenderly. It was warm, affectionate, full of love.

Ian stopped.

"My flat is a short cab ride away," said James.

"I can't stay the night," replied Ian.

James said, "You don't have to."

Ian rose from his chair. A water polo game had begun in the pool. They briefly watched the nude men enjoy the hastily formed athletic contest. James softly touched Ian's hand so that no one saw him. That was his signal that it was time to leave. They walked back into the house to call a taxi.

It was after four in the morning when Ian walked into his bedroom at home. Katherine was asleep on her stomach, curled in a fetal position. She was dressed in a long silk gown that had been crumpled up to her buttocks. Ian undressed slowly, never taking his eyes off her. He took his underwear off and walked naked to the bed. He rubbed up on Katherine to warm her. She squirmed and turned, responding immediately. Katherine turned over to allow Ian to kiss her passionately.

"I wanted to wait up for you," said Katherine.

"Shhhhh," said Ian.

"Make love to me, darling," said Katherine.

This was what made Ian a unique person. His sexual meter could be turned off and on at a moment's notice. He could arouse himself regardless of gender. To him, lovemaking was the same. It was about providing pleasure to his mate at the time. Katherine loved his size, his movements, his ways of bringing her to orgasm like no other man could. Their wild and passionate sex life was enough to keep the marriage together. Their love for money and fame was enough to maintain their high-maintenance lifestyle that they had been accustomed to.

Katherine's groans had started to get louder. Ian's thrusts had begun. But he wasn't thinking about Katherine's impending orgasm. Von Stroheim's comments at the party had piqued his curiosity. Universal was going to pay top dollar to keep Katherine as their number 1 actress. At MGM, she would have to compete with Norma Shearer, Joan Crawford, Myrna Loy, and Miriam Hopkins. So why the pitch by Von Stroheim? Ian asked himself.

He also knew that Katherine ordered Laemmle to do so. A new contract would be tendered to Ian as well. From a business point of view, going over to MGM made no sense. Ian decided not to mention Von Stroheim to Katherine.

As a faint hint of dawn appeared through Ian and Katherine's bedroom window, Katherine sighed loudly after her orgasm. Satisfied, she could now go back to sleep. It was Sunday morning. The McGregors were going to sleep in.

7

This evening was quiet, uneventful, the sort of an evening every writer loves. Abel's work on his novel moved briskly. Still, his creation bore no title. His carefully planned words filled his writing pad like a thirsty Roman emperor's chalice. Outside his window, the streets of Hoboken in the early hours of the morning bore no resemblance to Harlem. There were no prostitutes, no drunks, no lepers of the night to disturb the peace.

Months had passed since Abel had seen his brother Isaiah. Flo's weekly messages were his only way of communicating with him. The distance from Harlem to Hoboken was eight miles, separated only by the Hudson River. To Abel, Isaiah might as well have lived in China.

Flo's apartment had become the kind of reclusive abode he needed to concentrate on his book. Flo spent her evenings singing and performing in Harlem. She was never there to be in Abel's way. Nighttime was when he did his best work. Writers know their peak creative period—Nights, days, just before sun up. For Abel, it was after midnight when the streets became barren, when the slickness can be heard. Abel loved to mix his thoughts and the world outside. It's why he kept his windows wide open, even on the chilliest of evenings. The words flowed with regularity. The protagonist's character began to take shape. His character was similar to Abel himself—confident and filled with reassurance in some areas, doubt and fear in others.

He stopped writing. His character reminds him of an episode with Althea. It was a warm intimate episode between the two. It quickly became another reason why he couldn't respond. At least he thinks he knew. But Althea is never to know. It caused great friction, anger, and frustration for both of them.

Abel decided to focus on another aspect of his story. He had now rid himself of a memory he was not ready to face.

There's that sound again. The slow deliberate creep up the stairs outside his door, a light tap of a stiletto heel. It was Flo, her evening performance complete. The last round of applause ceased to be heard. The door slowly opened, that familiar creek before completely opening. Flo stood in her performance dress. Black, tight, revealing in all its clarity, an hourglass figure. At times, Abel didn't want to look at Flo. She aroused him, and he was embarrassed. He dared not tell Flo because he was too scared she might tell Isaiah. So he always kept his head in his notes whenever she walked around the apartment.

"Hey, baby, decided to stay up 'n wait for me?" asked Flo.

Abel slowly looked up out of his notes. Flo stood before him, looking lovely as always. Abel stuttered and stumbled for his reply. "Huh, naw, just felt like writin' somethin'."

"When you gonna finish that book?" Flo asked.

"Still a ways away," replied Abel.

Flo gave Abel that sexy smile she always gives

him and walked over to the kitchen. She knew Abel was watching her. She had a sixth sense when a man was checking her strut out.

"Want some tea?" asked Flo.

Abel shook his head no and returned to his writing. Every now and then, he managed to look up and sneak a peek at Flo. What a beautiful woman, he thought. He thought how lucky his brother was for having a girlfriend as attractive as Flo.

"You see Isaiah tonight?" asked Abel.

Flo ignored the question, continuing with filling her kettle and starting the gas on her stove. She stopped to stare at the wall. Did she see a cockroach running up the pipe, or was she deep in thought searching for an answer to a yes or no question?

"Said did you see—" Flo interrupted Abel before he finished.

"Heard you the first time," replied Flo. She was angry, obviously angry at Isaiah. Now Abel wanted to pry as to make sure Isaiah was all right. Abel took the opportunity to get up from his table and walk over to Flo. He got within inches of her back. He can see how smooth and silky her skin was.

"Everything all right?" asked Abel.

"Sure everythin' all right for Isaiah. He gots more women friends than I can ever keep up with."

Abel was smart enough not to pry any further. He wanted no elaboration. He could sense Flo was upset, upset at Isaiah. He surmised that another woman involved with Isaiah was the source of Flo's anger. Before Flo could begin to speak, the tea kettle whistled. Flo turned the gas off, but she didn't prepare her tea. She bolted for her bedroom and slammed the door.

Abel walked back to his desk and resumed his writing. He returned to the part in his story where the protagonist questions his girlfriend about their sexual inadequacies. Abel was an expert in sexual inadequacy. He learned early on in his writing career that personal experiences in life make for the most compelling stories. The words come from the heart. The stories are more believable. First, he had to answer the question, what is sexual inadequacy? Abel was no an expert on women. He and Althea were lovers only on a few occasions, his barn serving as their love nest. But they were young, and lovemaking is supposed to be awkward, so he thought and wrote.

As Abel lay on his cot, a bluish-gray hue peeked through the apartment window. The dawn had arrived. His eyes slowly opened. He hated the advent of a new day. All his thoughts seemed to jam his brain at once. Momma back home, Althea, Isaiah, his future, his novel, who he really was as a man. His attention was drawn to Flo's bedroom door. It cracked. It opened. Flo stood in her doorway, the sleekest and most revealing negligee she owned draped her curvy figure as if she was poured into it. Abel turned his head toward the window. He heard the sounds of the heels on her slippers moving toward him. *What could she want*? he asks himself when the scent of her French perfume was more than he can bear. He turned toward her. Flo stood above him saying nothing.

"Good morning," said Flo.

Abel didn't know what to say. It was so unusual for Flo to be up at the crack of dawn the morning after her performance. She usually slept through mornings. Abel had a morning routine. A thirty-minute walk, coffee, back to his novel. He sensed his morning routine was about to be altered.

"Mornin'," replied Abel. "Can I get you something" he asked.

Flo smiled, moved closer to Abel. Without warning and with the sleekness of a cheetah pouncing on her prey, she mounted Abel. "Funny you should ask," replied Flo.

Her kisses from those rich full lips she possessed engulfed Abel's lips passionately. Abel broke away. Guilt that he's kissing his brother's girlfriend overcame him.

"You Isaiah's girl," said Abel.

"I ain't nobody's girl. Not no more," replied Flo.

The kissing resumed. Abel wanted to stop but can't. With her breasts clamping his chest, his arousal was now complete. There was but a slight moment left to stop before Flo saw how inadequate of a lover he was. Certainly he couldn't match the prowess of Isaiah, he thought. Too late. The point of no return had been reached. Flo's touch and feel was no match to the country girl awkwardness of Althea. Now he was loving a real woman who knew what she was doing. No more fumblings in the farmer's hay loft. A move to the city has transformed Abel in the past months. Isaiah showed him how to be a big-city man. Now Flo was showing him how to be a big-city lover. It felt good. Her pounce was orchestrated as if it was part of a concerto at the Metropolitan. Abel wondered how long he could control himself.

"Not yet, not yet," groaned Flo. "I'll show you how to control yo'self," she groaned.

Abel couldn't control himself. He tried, he tried hard. But Flo's movements and sensual deftness were too much for him to overcome. The eruption within himself had begun. Flo jumped off before Abel's seed was planted. Their moans became synchronized.

"Can't be havin' no babies," sighed Flo.

Sleep for both had begun.

The sun was shining brightly into Flo's apartment. Flo had nestled herself snuggly on Abel's chest. They held each other closely as if they had been lovers for years. Abel remained silent, satisfied, feeling like a real man for the first time. *So this is how a man feels after making love to a woman,* he thought. Sure, he and Althea had done it. Then he didn't have an inkling that he was doing it right or effectively to please Althea. A pile of hay in Alabama didn't exactly make a nice place for lovers to express themselves lovingly. Abel wondered after each awkward session whether he was capable of loving a woman. Maybe he wasn't supposed to love women at all. Now he lay with his brother's woman. Confusion seeped in. *What am I?* he asked.

Flo awakened. "Mmmmm, hello, you," said Flo.

"Hello back," replied Abel.

"Did you like it?" asked Flo.

Abel hesitated. He didn't want to say something stupid and upset Flo. "Yes," he replied.

"That's all you gots to say to me?" asked Flo.

"Not sure what I'm supposed to say," replied Abel.

"I'm gonna show you a few thangs 'bout how a woman's body operates," said Flo.

A disappointed look now turned to a bubbly feeling of anticipation. Flo's kisses on his neck had begun. He closed his eyes because her wet lips feel so good to him. Her nude body has fused into his. They were one. His small cot used for sleeping didn't seem so small for lovemaking. Flo had a way with men. She knew how to send a man to the heights of ecstasy.

She's mine, all mine, Abel thinks to himself. The guilt of making love to his brother's girlfriend haunted him no longer.

The sunrise ferry across the Hudson River included Abel as a passenger. The "Negro Only" section was especially full. Mondays, the first day after a typical boisterous Manhattan weekend, always was a busy day for housekeepers, maids, and janitors.

Abel's new job as a busboy at the Cotton Club would bring him enough money to live on. It also enabled him to continue his writing aspirations. His book shall be completed no matter what, he often told himself. *It must be written. My voice must be heard.*

Inner compulsion often drove Abel. His novel was the prime example. Flo was more than happy to have Abel living with her rent free. They had become not only lovers but friends as well. Months had passed, and neither one of them had heard a peep from Isaiah. Rumors abounded in the streets that Isaiah had moved on to Pittsburgh. Some said Boston. No one knew for sure. No one cared.

The early a.m. shift at the Cotton Club was always the quietest. The club was closed. The clean-up crew from the night before was the only ones present this early. Abel was part of this crew. From six-thirty to two in the afternoon, his job was to clean tables, wipe the floors, then set up place napkins and silverware for the stage and performance area. His last hour was spent shining the owner's shoes.

Owney Madden was a bootlegging Irishman who made the Cotton Club a "whites only" front for his illegal businesses. Owney Madden took an immediate liking to Abel. His intelligence and articulate manner were characteristics Madden found appealing. He often wondered how Abel became such an intellectual though he never asked him. Madden looked at Abel as some sort of circus freak of nature.

Abel would shine shoes, engage in lighthearted conversations with Madden. Sometimes Abel was privy to business conversations between Madden and his business associates, henchmen, or gun molls. For some unknown reason to Abel, Madden trusted him.

Abel was having a particularly hard time removing a spot from Madden's brown shoe.

"Spot seems to be givin' you a bit of trouble, lad," said Madden.

"Yessa, can't seem to work it right," replied Abel.

"Blood on leather . . . twist a pig's ear."

"Sir?" replied Abel.

"Let it drift. Finish up. I'm in a hurry," said Madden.

Madden bolted up from his chair, his patience with Abel's insistence on getting the spot out of his shoe coming to an end.

"But I ain't got that spot out yet," said Abel.

"Never mind that. I got a meeting with me business partner," replied Madden.

The doors of Madden's office bolted open. Arthur Flaggenheimer, known to everyone in New York and New Jersey as Dutch Schultz, the Dutchman, slowly entered, his diminutive stature a characteristic no one notices because of who he is. He would always tell anyone who'd listen that "It's not how big you are. It's how big you kill." And everyone believed him.

Abel's eyes caught Dutch Schultz's as he walked by. That brief moment made Abel want to watch and listen to him as much as possible. As quickly has he could focus on him, a briefcase was being presented to his boss, Mr. Madden. A hug, a brief whisper in each other's ears, and the meeting was over.

Dutch Schultz turned toward Abel, staring momentarily before speaking.

"You, boy, get me a cup of java."

Abel replied, "Yessa," and walked over to Madden's desk where the pot of coffee stood. Quickly but without hesitancy, Abel returned to Schultz with the cup.

"Haven't seen you around here before," said Schultz.

"No, suh, just started workin' 'round here a few weeks back," replied Abel.

"Off you go, Abel. Do what I told you to do," interjected Madden.

Abel turned and exited the office. As he left the office, while walking down the hall, a realization hit him. Dutch Schultz was the first real important person he had ever met, a real celebrity, someone who garnished instant respect. When a man walked into a room, he wanted his presence felt. That's what Abel wanted for himself.

The Harlem Café was the place where Abel could write. He went there every day after work, at least three hours. His usual corner of the café was available when he walked in. He took his seat, pulled out his notepad, and began writing. His thoughts were lucid, quick, sharp. He liked what he had written. He read his words over and over again. He beamed with pride. All writers do when they produce words that please. He would have kept writing had an interruption not stopped him.

Casting a large shadow over his prose was Isaiah. No one had seen him for months, but there he stood, heavily bearded but appearing healthy. He took a chair next to his younger brother.

"I thought you were dead, or in Philly," said Abel.

"As you can see, I ain't neither," replied Isaiah.

Abel gave Isaiah a faint smile, glad to see him, glad to see him alive. Isaiah kept his hat down over his eyes. He wasn't sure who might be watching. He was still wanted by the New York Police for suspicion of murdering an officer.

"You takin' care of Flo?" asked Isaiah.

"She takes care of herself," replied Abel.

That response brought a chuckle to Isaiah. He

already knew Flo took care of herself and quite well.

"She layin' that good lovin' on you yet?"

Abel pondered Isaiah's question before answering. Why does he want to know the answer to that, he wondered. He stared, continued to think to himself. *Do I lie, do I tell the truth?* Abel kept thinking, never looking Isaiah in the eyes.

"Come on, nigga, ain't gotta think 'bout that one, do ya?" asked Isaiah.

"Naw . . . naw, I ain't. I just write," replied Abel.

"Sure you do. That good-lookin', fine piece of woman walkin' round there, and you ain't touched her?" asked Isaiah.

Abel became really nervous. He wasn't sure if his face painted a look of guilt. Then it hit him. He would lie and deny. He would lie and deny for the rest of his life. "Hey, look, man, I just live, eat, got to work, write. That's all," said Abel.

Isaiah smiled broadly and sipped out of Abel's coffee.

"Sure, sure you do," said Isaiah.

"So where you been hidin'?" asked Abel.

"Anywhere and everywhere," replied Isaiah. "Been watchin' you come into here fer the last week."

A thought pertinent to Abel's novel hit him at that precise moment. He quickly reverted to his novel just to get it down. Isaiah watched him for seconds, watching Abel's pencil glide through the paper. Isaiah was proud of Abel. Isaiah could barely read and write, let alone formulate words to produce a book.

"How's that writin' goin'?" asked Isaiah.

"Okay, I guess," replied Abel.

"Want'u write a book 'bout me," said Isaiah.

"'Bout you?" asked Abel.

"Sure, you knows how a nigga becomes a big shot in the big city," replied Isaiah.

Abel chuckled. Finally something Isaiah said made him laugh. It took an edge off the seriousness of the moment. It was not lost on Abel that Isaiah was still a wanted man.

"Want'u to do me a favor. I need some dough," said Isaiah.

Abel began going into his pockets. He could muster up only three dollars. "That's all I got," said Abel.

"Where the fuck you think I can go on three dollars?" asked Isaiah.

"It's all I got," replied Abel.

There was that wild boisterous laugh of Isaiah's again. Not as loud as usual, he didn't want to draw too much attention to himself just in case there was a snitch in the café.

"I want you to go home, tell Flo to go into my box in the floorboards 'n' get my dough," said Isaiah. "Meet me in Hoboken at Jefferson Park tonight, seven o'clock. Can you remember that?"

"Sure. Jefferson Park, seven o'clock," replied Abel.

One last bright smile, then Isaiah stood out of his chair. "Knew I could count on you," replied Isaiah. "And you ain't seen me either." As quickly as he sat down, Isaiah was gone.

The evening wore on. The unproductive minutes that mounted made the writing session unbearable for Abel. Hours had passed. The sky outside had been transformed from sky blue to black. He had been staring at his paper for hours and had written seven measly words. The beginning of his next chapter was one of his most important. His lead character refuses to sleep with his girlfriend not because of another woman, but because of his confusion, his awkwardness of who he is. Rather, what he is. Perhaps he struggled because the subject matter paralleled his own personal experiences with Althea back home in Alabama. Abel never intended to draw his own turmoil into his novel. It just happened. Now he wanted to forget thinking about Althea, about Momma, about Isaiah, about anyone or anything that reminded him of Alabama. He wanted to write but couldn't.

I'm stuck. I'm stuck, he said to himself. There was no solution to his problem, but he tried intensely to figure out a solution for his character. Writer's block is a disease all writers eventually catch. It is up to the individual writer to come up with their own cure. A writer has two choices: allow the block to kill you or find a cure and go on writing. Now it was Abel's turn. He had a system when he struggled to find his next words—a cup of hot coffee and intense meditation.

Neither the coffee nor the meditation was working this evening. As a last resort, he resorted to lying on his cot, staring at the ceiling. He continued to ask himself what he was trying to say. What did he really want to put on that paper of his? Althea kept popping back into his head. That's the problem. Thinking about their problems. Thinking about problems that mean nothing. Abel was in New Jersey. Althea was back in Alabama. Her situation was nothing like his. It all led up to Abel's refusal to do a self-examination.

Maybe I should go to sleep and try again in the morning, he thought.

The silence became broken by that familiar sound. The wheel brakes of a cab being heard outside. The door closed. The sounds of high heels were next. The vestibule door opened. Those heels moved upward. It was Flo. Abel knew she'd want to talk about her meeting with Isaiah. Abel was certain there would be no writing this night. Most men on earth know of that one woman in their lives that whenever she walked into a room you were in, you lost the rhythm in your breathing. That was what Flo did to Abel. And when the door opened and Abel saw Flo enter, this time he smiled. He smiled brightly.

"Youz look happy to see me," said Flo.

"I am," replied Abel.

Flo sauntered over to Abel's cot and planted a very wet kiss on his lips. Abel's smile reappeared.

"Fixin' to get out of these clothes," said Flo. She moved seductively across the room to her bedroom and softly closed the door.

Abel watched the light go on as well as his thought process. He knew by now that Flo liked to clean up, get sexy, then leave the door slightly ajar. That was Abel's signal to enter. This evening, Abel felt different. His confusion began to set in. There were evenings he found Flo alluring, sexy. He wanted to make love to her. Tonight was not that night. Tonight confusions reigned. No rational explanation would enter Abel's mind why he shouldn't do what he'd been doing for the past several months. The lust wasn't there. The lust was elsewhere.

On cue, Flo's bedroom light was seen going off. The bedroom door was slightly opened. Abel knew what he was supposed to do next. This time, hesitancy existed. Abel allowed his instincts to take over. He slowly got up off the cot and moved toward Flo's bedroom. As he entered, he saw that Flo had taken her usual place on the bed. This evening, the color was vanilla, a vanilla silk negligee that contrasted well off her caramel brown skin. Abel knew what to do next. He took his clothes off and joined Flo in bed. The cuddling and kissing began. As quickly as it had started, it ended.

"Somthin' wrong?" asked Flo.

Abel remained silent. Flo wasn't interested in a verbal response. Her massaging continued. As did her soft kisses.

"Somethin' is wrong," said Flo. "Youz ain't respondin' like you usually do."

"I'm not sure," replied Abel. "It's like my desire leaves my body, and I don't know when it's coming." What Abel was trying to say was that he was confused, confused about his manhood.

"You ain't worried 'bout your brother, is you?" asked Flo.

"What'u mean worried 'bout Isaiah?" asked Abel. "You ain't told him 'bout us, have you?"

"Sure did, when I saw him tonight and gives him his money," replied Flo. "He gone. He leavin'. Headin' back south he told me."

Abel relaxed. His guilt for sleeping with his brother's girlfriend subsided. His trepidation about his manhood increased.

"I want to tell you something," said Abel.

"You can tell me anything," replied Flo.

So there Abel was, naked in bed with a beautiful woman and struggling to find the words to tell her that she was unable to arouse him. It was starting all over again, the bad memories, the fights with Althea as Abel struggled to express his feelings. He would try once more.

"At times, at times, I can't do it," said Abel. "I have trouble getting myself ready."

"That's my job," replied Flo.

"No, I mean I don't wanna do it with a woman," said Abel.

"You don't wanna do it with a woman, or you don't wanna do it with me?" asked Flo.

"I just don't know," replied Abel.

"Well, I know one thing," said Flo. "I love you."

Abel had heard those words from a woman before.

Although hearing them flattered him, not being able to reciprocate saddened him.

"You ain't gotta say nuthin," said Flo. "You stay here as long as you want. I'll help you figure thangs out."

These words comforted Abel. He felt compelled to kiss Flo, and he did. The hug was warm. The warmth moved down from his lips to his stomach, reaching his inner thighs. For at least this evening, he wanted her.

8

Universal Studios' stage 24 was Katherine's favorite to shoot her scenes. A large number of Hollywood actors and actresses had a superstition that they lean on. They can't act, can't perform without the knowledge that their idiosyncrasies have been satisfied. For Katherine, familiarity was hers—the same faulty light in her dressing room, that creaky floorboard just off stage left, the water cooler in the corner that never worked, the stench of mildew when the humidity reached the right level.

Ian nestled comfortably in an unused director's chair, a mere number of steps from Katherine as she and her leading man, Rod Laroque, shot a love scene. Ian had been ordered by studio head Carl Laemmle to observe how sound in motion pictures affected what a writer puts on paper. The studio had been pressuring Ian to produce a feature-length shooting script for Katherine's next movie. The past two months, his nights were spent increasing his drinking levels until completely passing out on his office sofa. Nothing clicked. No story. No dialogue. No passionate love scenes. No action sequences.

Sound brought huge financial possibilities to the studio head's bottom line. But for a writer such as Ian, the writer's block becoming a heavier albatross around his neck, it was a time of sheer panic. Last night's headaches had been the worst so far, so excruciating it brought him out of his chair and onto his knees. *Where are the words? Where are the words?* he kept asking himself while cradling his split-opened skull.

"Cut—print it!" yelled the director.

Katherine took this time to turn and smile at Ian. Ian waved back and mouthed the words "love you" under his breath. Back to his daydream, that daydream about James. His flaming red hair parted to the side was sexy to Ian. His British manner was as alluring to Ian as a woman's perfume is to a man. They had a rendezvous scheduled for later that evening. Ian couldn't wait to see James again. He hoped terribly that James felt the same way. He had not expressed any sort of affection for Ian, but Ian felt it in his head, his heart, his loins. He liked kissing James. His lips were soft and moist like a woman's.

Before the next take, Katherine took a second to smile at Ian once more.

He hated Katherine. He hated that he had to stay married to her to keep his bisexuality under wraps. Ian always thought that marriage was like a dull meal with the dessert served at the beginning. Laemmle knew. Ian's lovers all over Hollywood knew. Katherine knew. If Ian was to keep his standard of living as high as the Hollywood Hills, his sinful, secret life must remain a secret. He hated giving in to create a script for Katherine's next film to star in, making Universal millions. And for what? he asked. His screenplay by-line? His next plum writing assignment?

But the reality was as plain as the nose on his face. Ian knew it would be since Katherine was Universal's golden calf. MGM had Crawford and

Shearer. Paramount had Dietrich. Columbia had Colbert. Everybody had somebody. Ian had Katherine.

There was that excruciating pain again. That pain that accompanied Ian whenever it was time to write. Dusk was appearing outside his studio lot office window. There were no clanging of keys from his typewriter. Instead, the typewriter was being used as a pillow to rest his throbbing head. His left hand ably poured him another drink. The next scene to be written was simple. In the story, Katherine is to burst into her husband's office and confront him about the affair he is having with his secretary. Simple enough, Ian thought. But he didn't know or couldn't put onto paper the words. What would a wife who knows she has been betrayed say?

Ian's inability to create dialogue was a threat to his job, his self-worth, his life. *The hell with it,* Ian thought. The last shot had gone down. He began hacking away at the keys. He didn't care if it was good, bad, or downright awful. He was going to put something on paper, something he could show Laemmle. If he threw it in the garbage two seconds after reading it, c'est la vie.

The more he thought about his impending failure, the more the keys banged. Sometimes when you know your words aren't up to par, you write with a nothing-to-lose mentality. That's how Ian felt. Nothing to lose. As long as he was married to Katherine, he was all right. He was employed. The headache kept getting worse. Now he was afraid that these ills weren't stress related. *Maybe I should see a doctor,* he thought.

Ian kept on with his typing. *A bad story is better than no story at all,* he thought. His mind shifted between the tripe he was writing and the meeting with Laemmle tomorrow morning. He kept typing even though his phone rang incessantly. Annoyed, he answered.

"Yes, hello," Ian snapped.

He did no talking, only listening.

"Tell Mr. Laemmle I'll be there," replied Ian.

He went back to his typing. It was Laemmle's secretary. She was calling to confirm tomorrow's meeting. Ian was supposed to show Laemmle the rough draft of the script. In his office, first thing after breakfast. Ian knew he was going to be working all night. He wanted to keep his tryst with James also. Ian was confused. When confused, he reaches for Jimmy Beam. One more swig. *Just finish the bloomin' thing,* he kept telling himself.

But he couldn't. There's that roadblock in the middle of the scene. *Finish the conversation,* he kept telling himself. Another swig of Jimmy. The minutes mount. His desperation grows larger, his headache more pronounced. Writer's block doesn't happen to writers such as Ian. He kept telling himself that over and over again. He was telling himself that more times than the keys hit the paper with fresh dialogue. The block was happening at too frequent a clip the last few months. The studio yelled at him for the script. Katherine yelled at him for the script. *Daily Variety* wrote about the script. Never had a scenarist received so much attention for something that had not yet been written. Frustration had reached its zenith. Ian knew no more would be written. His urge returned that urge, that urge that made him happy.

"Penny for your thought," whispered James into Ian's ear. Ian was thoroughly drunk and lying in James's bed satisfied. They held each other close as a soft rain started pelting the windows. The only apparent illumination was the street lights peering between the spaces in the Venetian blinds.

Ian wanted to confide in James. He wanted to tell him how much of a failure as a writer he was feeling. As soon as Hollywood was about to go boom with talking pictures, Ian was about to go bust.

"You can talk to me, mate," said James.

"I want to confide in you very much," replied Ian.

James thought a soft tender kiss on Ian's cheek would loosen the feathers, help Ian get over his shyness. Now Ian and James's embrace became warmer. More pillow talk was to follow.

"I can't finish Katherine's script," said Ian. "Old man Laemmle wants to see it tomorrow morning. I've got sixty of the most awful pages of rubbish ever known to man."

"What do you mean you can't? You must finish it," said James.

"Can't, meaning unable," replied Ian. "I can't find the bloomin' words. I don't know how to set a scene. Silent pictures meant no words. My job was a bloody lot easier."

"If you don't, the studio will find someone else," replied James. "The next step for you will be the unemployment line."

Ian took this moment to break from the embrace and get out of bed. Now was not the time to be curt with James. He liked James. They were just getting to know each other. James liked Ian. They were both from the United Kingdom, and James had made very few friends since crossing over last year. Ian paced the room. James had angered him by reminding Ian he was not far from not even working at all. Ian paced. Ian thought. He wished he could go back to last year, two, three years ago. *Why do people have to have sound when watching a movie?* he asked. *Why do I refuse to move with the times?*

The future was talkies. The future had arrived, and Ian wanted to stay in the past. His silence was broken by James's voice.

"This is the last time," said James.

Those words froze Ian in his tracks. He returned to the bed to stand over James. He hovered over James like an angry father about to scold his firstborn son.

"This it, the last time?" spoke James.

"I don't understand," replied Ian. "I thought we had been having a smashing time of it."

"We have. I'm leaving Universal. I'm to be an assistant director to Howard Hughes at RKO."

"You're going to work for that Texas grease monkey?" asked Ian.

"He's make *Hell's Angels* a talking picture. A lot of aerial fight scenes. Very action packed."

On cue like a baby searching for the elusive pacifier, Ian paced toward the dresser for the bottle of scotch. It was James's turn to be a smoother. Quickly, his embrace on Ian is felt from behind. He wanted to comfort Ian. James's hand felt good to Ian. But he didn't want to turn around and face him. Ian was going to miss James. He loved the sex from men but hated the goodbye endings. It depressed him. He believed James was going to be a soul mate, a friend, and confidant, a friend in the motion picture business to bounce ideas off of. No man had ever been Ian's lover for more than a year. He liked it that way. This time, someone was walking out on him. Ian felt James's lips on the back of his shoulder.

"Hughes has a private detective following me," said James.

Ian knew what that meant. James was getting scared he might be found out, a career snuffed out before it ever began.

"I think I understand," said Ian. "Don't want your name associated with such a deviant scoundrel like myself."

"No, it's not it at all," replied James.

Ian broke from James's caresses. He was angry. The anger triggered his headaches. Another shot of scotch would help that. It was bad enough Ian's lover no longer wanted him. But to lie about his true feelings made Ian angry.

"Just say the truth, ol' boy," said Ian. "You are in fear, my friend. In fear that all of your precious Hollywood dreams will go up in bloody smoke if Mr. Hughes found out about our trysts."

James began to tremble. He wanted his cake and eat it too. He wanted Ian. But he wanted fame and stardom. That is why he left Bristol, England, in the first place.

"I love Hollywood," said James, "I love being here in America. I damn well don't want to go back to that life of stale toast and drippings."

Ian wanted to hear no more. *Let's not stall the inevitable,* he said to himself. One more shot of scotch awaited him. After wiping the remnants, he bolted for the door.

"Not a problem, mate," said Ian. "Plenty of buggers like you floating 'round Hollywood."

Ian never saw James again.

The rain had stopped. Ian could drive home with the top down of his convertible. The cool, chilly air placed a scratchy feel to his throat. His coat lapels went up immediately. Ian stopped thinking about James. *Jolly good while it lasted,* he thought. His intersection appeared. Sunset and Santa Monica Boulevard. Ten more minutes and home. *Home to what?* he asked. *A typewriter with no dialogue. A wife you're not in love with.*

The right turn for home suddenly became a left turn toward Hollywood.

The Leopard Club on Melrose was quiet for a Thursday evening. Provided the bartender kept the scotch flowing, Ian was not about to budge. She was pretty. Long red hair like Katherine's. Ian and she were on a first-name basis. That's what happens when you frequent the same place for years.

"Keep 'em comin, love," Ian said.

Anna was her name. But Ian always called her love. She liked it. Most women in Hollywood went head over heels with Ian and his smooth-as-silk British accent. Anna was like most women. Ian was very aware that their casual flirtations over the years were going to lead to something naughty. Anna had what Ian liked in women. When those opportunities arose for loving women, Anna had what Ian liked—red hair and a large bosom.

Anna, like all beautiful young women in Hollywood, hoped one day that serving drinks and doing sexual favors to the male Hollywood elite would be her ticket out of the Leopard Club.

"Your eyes are very alluring," said Ian. "Can't make up my mind what shade of blue they are."

Anna blushed. Men had been telling her how beautiful she was for years. But every time a compliment came her way, she still blushed. Anna liked Ian enough to bed him. He was well endowed. But Ian was just a writer, a hack scribe. Anna was smart enough to know Ian couldn't get her a screen test at Universal. But Katherine could. Anna thought back to the other times she slept with Ian, wishing it was Katherine instead so that she could get a part in a picture.

"Thanks," replied Anna.

"No, thank you." A fifty-dollar bill appeared on the bar.

"You spoil me, Mr. McGregor."

Ian smiled, turned his head away to peek toward the corner of the bar, the focus being the storage closet. One instant later, it was a wink, a smile, a shot of scotch, and a trip to the storage closet.

———

The space was tight, cramped. For its purpose, more than enough room. The smell of dirt, floor wax, and sawdust camouflaged the heat and eroticism Ian and Anna generated. With Anna on top, Ian was able to look into her eyes. He masked his true dislike for Anna, his dislike for women. Ian puffed his chest, not because of his sexual prowess, but because he knew Anna had no idea. In Ian's mind, this was his sense of duty. Sex for him was whoever wanted his libido. Men, women, it was the same for him. Self-satisfaction by any means necessary. Ian never looked at himself as mentally unstable or depraved. He saw himself as a liberal lover, full of artistic expression. An artist just doesn't paint for women. He paints for men too. That's how Ian felt. His libido was for all who thirst for it.

This night was no different than the hundreds of others. That long winding drive down Sunset Boulevard at 2:00 a.m. Having loved a man and a woman on the same night had become passé with Ian. It was who he was about. James and Anna quickly left his mind. Laemmle's script was due in six hours. He had enough time to fake out the third act and bullshit Laemmle on a rewrite. It will give him more time. More time to conquer his fear of failure, his writer's block.

There was Al Jolson's billboard promoting *The Jazz Singer*, a cruel reminder that talking pictures were here to stay. If he didn't master dialogue creation soon, his writing career would be dashed. Katherine will leave him for sure. *Maybe it's best,* Ian thought. The one thing about Katherine he could not hate was that she accepted him for who and what he was. He loved her for that.

The grandfather clock in the foyer struck 4:00 a.m. Ian's home office had become a smoke-filled abode, his cigarette butts strewn every which way on his desk, the balls of rolled-up typing paper overflowed the wastepaper basket. His headache was excruciating. The last sip out of his fifteen-year aged scotch had become a one-hour memory.

A moment of genius struck Ian. He remembered a funny story Katherine told him about the time she slipped and fell, the back hem of her evening dress splitting all the way up to her butt. It would become a funny scene in Ian's screenplay. *That's the ingredient that is missing,* Ian thought. *Slapstick.*

Even though the main storyline was to be a somber one all the way to the end, Ian always felt the first two acts dragged on way too much. It needed a bit of slapstick. The scene with Katherine falling and splitting her dress all the way up her backside would be a welcome comic relief, he thought. *Just write,* he said. *Let the director and editor finish the rest.*

Finally. . . inspiration. It was working well. The typewriter bristled. The keys banged in a symphonic rhythm. Ian felt good. Out of twenty scenes written with lousy dialogue, he finally had one that sang. Now Ian thought maybe his flair was comedy, not drama. He always seemed to find a laugh or comedic tone to almost everything in life. That was until six months ago when the rush to talkies began, the confrontation of his writer's block, the various medical maladies, the alcoholism and depression. Fear of losing your career will do that. For those few precious minutes, he liked what he was creating. A writer's chest swelled from the inside when those poetic moments of creativity engulfed the air. This was one of those moments.

It was unknown to Ian. Ha had no idea why he did it. Why did he pick this moment to take a break from his typewriter? As his head peered up, a gaze through a crack in the draperies proved interesting and revealing. It revealed something he did not want to see—Katherine exiting a man's car. Her kiss was not of friendship but of passion. Ian remembered the binding agreement he and Katherine had: Don't ask. Don't tell.

These were the steadfast rules for a marriage of convenience. It is what Ian and Katherine wanted, and it was exactly what they had. Ian returned to his typewriter, a moment to pause. *Get it back,* he said. It was becoming increasingly difficult to do that. He hated the man that was kissing Katherine. Adolph Menjou was a notorious womanizer.

Katherine loved the attention men gave her. She felt it kept the publicity where it should be, on her. If Katherine liked a man enough, she would sleep with him. Katherine saw Ian was home, so she didn't invite Menjou in for a nightcap.

Ian returned to his typewriter. The door opened. He heard Katherine's high heels making their way to his office.

"It's late," said Katherine.

"Junior wants this script at ten o'clock."

"I'd like to read it before you give it to him."

Ian replied, "Prefer that you didn't, love. Good night, what's left of it."

Katherine knew Ian had seen her kissing Menjou. Saying nothing, she left the office and headed upstairs to bed. Ian was relieved. Sometimes after an evening out, Katherine would want Ian to make love to her. But not tonight. Thirty more minutes of work, a four-hour nap on his office couch. Katherine would sleep alone.

Ian was not fooled one bit. The look on Laemmle's face spoke volumes. Ian's screenplay was terrible. He had reached only page fifty. Laemmle's look said he wished it was the end so that the rest wouldn't upset the digestion of his breakfast.

"Just a rough draft, mate," said Ian. "All the guts aren't quiet in it just yet."

Laemmle did not buy it. "Ian, I'm afraid this won't do," said Laemmle. "We might have to go in another direction with the script."

Ian knew his career was about to be placed in jeopardy. There was no way he was going to allow himself to be Mr. Katherine Edmonds.

"Look, Junior, I can do this," said Ian.

"I just don't see it," replied Laemmle.

"Give me another chance."

"We're running out of time."

"I can do this," pleaded Ian.

Laemmle wanted to give Ian another opportunity. But Universal's bankers in New York were getting nervous. Every studio was going to sound. They needed a film to star Katherine in. The silence in Laemmle's office was deafening. Ian bravely walked up to Laemmle's desk.

"Well, what's it going to be, mate?" asked Ian.

"All right, Ian. One more draft. Back in my office two weeks from today."

That was all Ian needed to hear. Nothing needed to be said. He flashed his brilliant white smile, winked, and zoomed out of Laemmle's office before he changed his mind.

9

It happens at times. At times, it happens in days, weeks, months. Sometimes it never happens. Sometimes it is called inspiration. Abel now had everything in balance, word for word, description for description, emotion for emotion. Inspiration surged through his body. Flo would not be home for hours. The middle chapters played out right before him. All that was needed was what he had plenty of—time, time to write.

And so he thought and wrote and wrote again. The protagonist in his story was a self-image, a Negro occupying a minute piece of the world that does not want him. *Don't stop writing,* he told himself. He didn't. He wanted to finish. A writer doesn't care if it makes sense or not. Literal coherence becomes moot. Just write. It is what Abel did best. To think. To feel. To imagine. To learn. To reflect. And after all of that, he did what was in him. He wrote.

It couldn't have been helped. He knew he was headed in that direction. It was why he didn't object, didn't try to fight it. Althea, his Althea back home in Alabama, she was everything to him. He didn't love Althea. She was a lot of things a man likes about a woman—cute enough, warm, funny, a good cook, a good mender. She showed Abel what he

was really like to be her man, her lover. It never
felt right to Abel. It never felt like love. Every
time Althea told Abel she loved him, he wondered
to himself why he couldn't say those words back.
It bothered him. It bothered him immensely. It got
to a point that he resented hearing those words.
Lovemaking was awkward, uncomfortable. Nothing
sensual or erotic. Certainly nothing loving about
it. He went on for many months giving Althea the
impression that he cared for her, that he loved her.
But there was no place for her in his heart. Not
the kind of love Althea wanted from him.

It was what confused Abel. The internal struggle,
turmoil, angst, ambiguity, the sense of feeling like
a man, the feeling of a man who had prowess as a
lover of women. As Abel wrote, he asked the same
question of himself that his protagonist in his
story asked. A simple question, a simple question
he struggled to find an answer to: was he a man
himself?

Wasn't that the determining factor for a man?
His physical presence in the bedroom, his ability
to send a woman to unreachable orgasmic heights?
A woman's moans and groans signal to a man he is
hitting the right spots. Abel wasn't hitting any of
those notes with Althea. Neither was the character
in his book.

He remembered that first time he called on
Althea, the first time he gave her flowers, the
first time he sung to her. He remembered that first
time he made love to Althea. Two virgins in a hay
loft on a hot summer day can spin numerous and
humorous events and takes. The fumbling, crying,
hurting, sweating Abel and Althea did to each other
that evening made for so many memories for the two
of them. It also made for some awkward memories
for Abel. Those nights holding Althea close to him,
those nights of caressing, those nights he could not

reciprocate the depth of caring Althea showed for him, those nights he wondered if it was different loving a man instead.

Why were the sounds of woman's heels on those outside steps appearing at this moment? Abel wondered. Flo was not due home until 2:00 a.m. The clock on the wall read twelve-fifteen. Abel had completed exactly two pages. He was becoming increasingly perturbed with each approaching step on that porch. He wanted to work more, and he knew Flo would not let him. Flo loved to drink. She loved to drink a lot. She loved to talk a lot too. If she did just that, Abel would be happy. But Abel knew better. He knew when Flo started to drink, it meant he would have to make love to her whether he wanted to or not. Screwing Flo only confused Abel more. His sexual orientation issues became magnified. But for those moments, the two of them became intertwined in Flo's bed.

The door opened, that familiar creak. Those familiar high heels stood in the doorway.

"Well now, nice to see you waitin' up for me."

"Not exactly waitin' up for you. I was doing some writin'," replied Abel.

Flo smiled as she sauntered across the room. She made sure Abel got a glance at the hourglass full figure she possessed. She walked to the kitchen and opened up the cabinet, the cabinet with the whiskey in it. It was a nightly habit for Flo. A long night of singing, playing to the crowd, flirting with the men who gawk at her captivating beauty. She was thirsty and ready for refreshment. She threw the shot down like it was a tall cool glass of lemonade.

"Want some?" she asked.

"Sure," Abel replied.

One shot for Abel, one additional shot for Flo. That's how it always ended up. Abel knew what would be next. But for some reason, Flo didn't immediately change into her long black negligee. Abel didn't notice right away. His mind was still on trying to finish that chapter, that chapter, that chapter on love, men and love, men and love together. The words he wanted to write ran through his head like a herd of deer scurrying through the woods. Abel knew how he was. If he didn't get everything down on paper immediately, he would lose the flow, the pace.

"How's that book comin' along?" Flo asked.

"Slow. Very slow," replied Abel.

"Must be somethin' I can do about it."

"No, no, there isn't. I need to work on the book myself," said Abel.

"I ain't talkin' 'bout yo' book, you crazy fool." So Flo walked away, not without grabbing the bottle and walking to the bedroom. The bedroom door closed slowly. Her singing began. It was a sultry, sexy tune emanating from her lips.

"One day I will have to leave," replied Abel.

"And why you wanna do that?" asked Flo.

She didn't wait to hear Abel's answer. It was her clue to start rubbing Abel around his groin. Her hand and the friction of the bedsheet aroused him. He wanted more. She wanted more, more from Abel, more of his loving. Over several months, they had become quite passionate in their sexual escapades. Despite Abel's misgivings about who he was as a man, what his orientation was, when he was in bed with Flo, the turmoil and feeling of ambiguity dissipated.

Once more this time, Flo was on top riding Abel like a cow poke on a Texas ranch, reminiscent of a rodeo, a bronco rider trying to set a record. With all the windows open, it was a miracle everyone in New Jersey did not hear Flo's moans of ecstasy. Abel liked to hear Flo moan. He was feeling big of himself. Flo told him what a better lover he was than his older brother. For once, he was the big man in more ways than one.

"I meant what I said," said Abel.

"What was it that you said?" asked Flo.

"I ain't getting' much done with my book."

"That ain't my fault, is it?" asked Flo.

Abel wanted to get out of Flo's bed. He did. He wanted to dress and go back to his writing.

"Don't leave," said Flo. "Wanna ask you something."

Abel continued putting on his boxers. His pants were next. The silence between the two was broken when Abel walked out of the room. She was quick, very quick putting on her nightgown and following Abel into the living room.

She found him at his typewriter and stood behind his shoulder. Something triggered Abel's inspiration. The typewriter keys clickety-clacked with regularity. Abel's character was in bed with his lover. He wanted to tell his girlfriend he was going to leave her, leave her for a man. Abel's character was not feeling like a man. That was the whole point. His unyielding desire to feel a man inside him was all consuming. It is why he knew he had to leave her. The dialogue Abel wrote for his characters was frank, honest. It enlightened both of them. Abel felt good. For weeks, he had been struggling to find how his character would reveal who he was to his girlfriend. He would never tell Flo that having sex with her would unclog his writer's block. Maybe because it was the most passionate sex he had ever had. Maybe it was because Flo told him he was a better lover than his brother. Maybe because it clouded his own trepidations about who he was as a man. Abel did not want to address the true reasons he left Althea back in Alabama. He did not want to ask himself who he was—a man, a man who liked men, a man who liked men and women. No, those thoughts and feelings stayed locked up in his closet. His mind had become quite a large closet.

There, that sound again. *Clickety-clack. Clickety-clack.* Total immersion. Why does he feel the way he does? Abel asked himself. Why does he want men? At it again, finding himself the contradictions of his own life and his characters.

"Been standin' 'hind you for almost five minutes," said Flo.

Abel kept typing. He was on. He was hot, on fire. The keys to his typewriter carried a glow. The words flowed with the regularity of water through a faucet. He was not going to be mean to Flo and tell her to leave. He was going to remain silent, focused, writing. He liked Flo. As a girlfriend? No. As a woman who gave him bountiful and passionate sex? Absolutely. He continued to ignore her.

Flo allowed her breasts to nestle on the back of Abel's head. She tried to read what he had been feverishly typing. She couldn't make sense of it.

"Ain't neva' told me what yo' book's 'bout," said Flo.

"It's about people and relationships," replied Abel.

"There a chapter 'bout me?" asked Flo.

Abel smirked, chuckled to himself as he kept typing. And then, he stopped. A moment had arrived, a moment to confide in Flo.

"I want to ask you something," said Abel.

"Ask Flo whatever you want, suga' pie."

He took this moment to get up from his typewriter. It was time to circle the room, time to let Flo watch him and wonder exactly what was going on in his mind. Flo sat on the couch and waited for Abel to lap the living room one last time before sitting down next to her.

"I don't know how to say what I am feeling. But I

will try my best. I think I like men in a way that I like women, in a way that I like you."

Flo handed Abel a look of disbelief. Total shock. She did not want her head to believe what her ears had just said to her. Most certainly, it was something a man had never told her before. It was why a look of shock painted her face, why her mouth dropped.

"Ain't sure what I am s'pos' to say," said Flo.

"Don't want you to say anything. Just listen."

"You some kind of one of them suga' boys?" Flo asked.

Now it was Abel's turn to be speechless, to struggle for words. The opportunity to unleash the torment he had kept bottled up since Alabama was before him. But he was helpless. He felt helpless, acted helpless.

"I've had these feelings, these feelings for a long, long time," said Abel. "When I was with Althea back home, I used to lay up with her and wish I wasn't. There was this guy back at school. Leroy Marberry. We were alike in many ways."

"Alike how?" asked Flo.

"We both like to write," replied Abel. "He was really good at poetry. He was good at making me laugh. He was good at showing me what real true feelings about someone was all about."

Flo smiled, not to mock Abel, but she was hearing words that she was not accustomed to. It was a look more of astonishment than derision toward Abel. "But youz still likes women, don't youz?" asked Flo.

It was Abel's turn to smirk. What else could he do? "I still like women," replied Abel. "That's what makes this all so hard, so doggone hard for me to handle."

His mind swirled like a Kansas tornado, too much to process at such a late hour. He wanted to confide in Flo. He wanted her to be more than just a lover.

He wanted a friend. Abel couldn't find the words. He was having a writer's block of the spoken word.

"Back home, me and Leroy used to go by Deer Creek Lake. Sometimes the full moon would light that lake up like fifty street lights," said Abel. He sighed. He was feeling comfortable. "First time he touched me, my heart sped so fast, I thought it was gonna jump right out of my chest. I felt like I was really wanted. With Althea, I felt she was sizin' me up as a husband. It was different when I was with Althea. After being with Leroy, I wanted to be a real lover to somebody. That's what I wanted, and the more I was with Althea, the more I felt that way."

Hearing Abel talk about his inner feelings excited Flo. She was turned on. She wanted Abel to make love to her once more. When she was sure he had stopped talking, she laid Abel back on the couch. She placed her exposed breasts right in his face.

Not this time, he thought. He wanted out. It was the moment he picked to jump up.

"Not now, Flo," said Abel.

"You mean you don't want me?"

"I mean not now," replied Abel.

"'Cause I ain't no man, right?"

It was a comment not worth responding to. Abel took that opportunity to rise from the couch, finish dressing, and walk out of the apartment. Flo did not run after him. The phone rang.

At 3:00 a.m., Hoboken, New Jersey, in the colored section of town was desolate. That was how Abel felt as he walked. Alone, alone with his thoughts, with his feelings, with his fears, with his desires. He tried his best to think about his book and not about the unhappiness he was feeling about himself, his manhood, his lack of manhood. He could not confide in his brother Isaiah. He could not tell him the turmoil that ravaged his insides. Isaiah had a certain image of his baby brother Abel, and Abel was going to make sure that image, that illusion would not be tarnished. Isaiah was interested only in Isaiah. How much money he could make. How much power he can absorb. He wanted to be the leader, the leader of a gang. He wanted to be Dutch Schultz's main nigger. Abel did not try to understand the man Isaiah had become. He did not want to understand the psychosis of a criminal. He wanted to keep the happy thoughts of Isaiah in the front part of his mind, those years they were young kids on their farm in Alabama.

He didn't keep track of the seconds or the minutes he walked. It was a warm summer night that was turning into a warm summer early morning. His thoughts bounced every which way. He thought about Momma. She was getting along. His cousins working the farm helped a lot, but Abel vowed never to go back to Alabama. There was nothing left for him there. He would never become the writer he aspired to be if he stayed. He knew that. He knew in all likelihood he would never see Momma alive again.

He thought about Flo, what to do about her. He was feeling an increasing emotional connection with Flo. He thought about her but not like he used to. It would never be like it was in those early moments of their relationship. Hurting her now would be better than crushing her later, he thought.

He thought about Leroy. He really missed him, their connection, their physical chemistry.

And then he remembered something. Abel remembered Mike's All-Night Café would be open. He remembered he was hungry. He could get some bacon and eggs and a cup of coffee while he made notes.

"Lookin' for a good time, big boy?" The prostitute came out of nowhere. Abel didn't see her. But there she stood. She stood there sizing Abel up. Her dress revealed the two large assets. Her dress was torn, probably as a result of her last encounter. Her assessment of Abel ended quickly, how much money he had for whatever services she was going to provide.

"Sorry, can't help you," said Abel. Startled, he didn't break his stride as he brushed right by her.

The café was less than three blocks away, and satisfying his hunger was all that was on Abel's mind at the moment. He walked. He thought. Was that a chance meeting? he asked himself, a coincidence, or was there a hidden meaning? On second thought, she did resemble Flo. She had the body, the allure. But her face was not one of fresh appeal. It was weathered, aged older than her obvious twentysomething figure. It had a look of a woman who had been kissed many times over, numerous years. Abel couldn't put his finger on it. There was something about her that made him think of Flo.

He loved the café. Even more during the wee hours of the morning. Only Mike, the owner, and a couple of drunks trying to sleep it off were ever present. He sat in the corner, sopping up the last drop of the homemade gravy and biscuits with his left hand, writing notes for his novel with the right. He was on to something. His character had an identity, a man of torment and confusion, a man filled with ambition—to be a Negro doctor, to be a great man who contributes to the betterment of mankind, a flawed man because he wanted to experience unnatural acts, acts that his friends and family would never condone. But there was one man who would condone them—his lover.

He stopped writing. A premonition befell him. He stopped thinking about his character in the story and started thinking about Flo. Nothing mattered now. His coffee tasted bitter. Mike's coffee never tasted great in the first place. But the last few swallows went down with an awful taste. Abel reached into his pocket, paid the check, and left the café.

Abel opened the door to Flo's apartment. Those inner fears, his trepidation that something was amiss had presented itself before his very eyes. There on the floor was Flo, beaten, bloody, a black eye, ribs hurting. He rushed to her side as if she was the lady of his heart. Acting like a caring man, he lay next to her caressing her head on his stomach.

"Flo! Flo, what happened?"

She was too hurt to speak. She tried. She wanted to. There was something she needed to tell Abel. The pain was excruciating even in attempting to pucker her lips to form words.

"You gotta go. You gotta get out of here now. Tonight," said Flo.

"Why?" asked Abel. "What's happened?"

"It's your brotha, Isaiah. He found out 'bout us. He's comin' back to whup on you. You needz to pack."

Abel stood. He didn't know what to make of all of this. It was happening fast, too fast. *Where do I go?* he asked himself. *What do I do?* he continued to ask himself.

Flo was badly hurt. She needed a doctor. His brother was on his way back to do the same to him. He bent down and helped Flo onto the couch. He ran to the bathroom for a cold face cloth and tried his best to clean her face up. The following minutes became a total turbulence in Flo's apartment as Abel ran from room to room, gathering up his belongings, his book, his typewriter. He had made up his mind he was not going to wait for Isaiah and attempt to talk him out of whatever he had in mind for him. He wasn't going to wait for Isaiah to storm in and beat on him like he used to do when they were kids.

No, not tonight. For the last time, he knelt before Flo and kissed her gently.

"Can't thank you enough for all you did for me," said Abel.

Flo smiled as best she could. She cupped Abel's face into her hands and kissed him softly on the lips. She reached into her bra and handed Abel one hundred dollars in cash.

"Take care of yourself," said Flo.

And so Abel walked out into the wee hours of a new day. That walk to the Hoboken train station signaled more than just a stroll. Reality was settling in. A clear realization washed his mind with clarity. He would never see Flo or his brother again.

10

Ramon knew something was amiss. Ian's attention span continued to waver as the evening evolved into an early-morning light. His stroking of Ian's chest hairs could not arouse him. Ian wanted to sleep. Too much champagne. Too much revelry. Too much Ramon. Insecurity took hold of Ramon. He was Ian's new plaything. He wasn't sure if Ian wanted him for him or if he was going to use him for influence with Mayer at MGM. He knew of Ian's long list of male lovers, but he had no worry about becoming his next. They had hit it off very quickly. That chance meeting at the Brown Derby remained fresh in Ramon's mind.

"Wake up, my sleepy head of a man," said Ramon.

"What time is it?" asked Ian.

"Six-thirty, still early. You make love to me again, yes?" replied Ramon.

Now Ian wanted to taste Ramon's lips. Soft. Moist. Ian quickly broke from their embrace. His mind was elsewhere.

"Something wrong?" asked Ramon.

"No, nothing wrong. I have worries," replied Ian.

"Worries?"

Enough time to pause, enough time for Ian to reach on the nightstand for his cigarettes. Quiet draped the room. Two people together, side by side yet traveling different roads. Minutes of silence can be measured in many years traveled in one's mind. Ian did not want to confide. Ramon was not his friend. No man like James. He was deeply attracted to James.

"Can't talk about it. Not now," said Ian.

Ramon's hopes evaporated quickly. He longed for Ian to confide in him. And as Ramon lay in bed expressing his desires to Ian for a serious relationship, Ian stood there not listening to a word of what was being said. He looked at Ramon as he talked. He looked him square in the eye. But he didn't hear him. None of it. He was thinking about how much of a failure he had become. He wondered about what one did after a studio like Universal dumped you. Laemmle cared for Ian more than most studio execs do for their staff writers. At one time, Ian was the number 1 talent. Katherine had become the household cash cow not him. Ian had become a man of no principles, no morals, married to a woman merely for her fame, her status, her wealth.

He was on the verge of losing it all. His writing skills were diminishing. His affair with scotch and soda water became his entire existence. Writer's block pounded him repeatedly. Ramon kept talking. Ian listened but didn't hear. No, it was time to leave. Ian walked over to Ramon and kissed him softly without saying goodbye. No promises of ever seeing him soon. Next week. Next month. Ever again.

"I will talk to Mayer for you," said Ramon. "I can get you writing assignments. Do not go."

Ian didn't hear him.

A writer's office on a studio lot is usually small, cramped, poorly ventilated. More times than not, you share that office with another recognition-starved aspiring scribe as yourself. Most of the writers in Hollywood were from the city newspapers, acquainted with cramped spaces. But Ian was from Broadway, once hailed as the next Eugene O'Neil. He also had a penchant for letting anyone within earshot knowing about his so-called claim to fame, how his path to Hollywood was far more noteworthy than the others.

That combination of a rare humid Southern California day and Ian's rampant cigarette smoke only made his office murkier, dank. He sat in his familiar place. Ian had a new cigarette lit seconds after the last one had been extinguished. He only wished the words were as rapid. The keys moved slowly without any real cadence. *How awful this reads,* he thought.

It didn't stop him from writing, writing slop, garbage. *It beats not writing at all,* he thought. *It beats turning in blank sheets of paper to Laemmle in a couple of days,* he reasoned. He found it so difficult to write for Katherine. The studio had never asked him to be a scenarist for one of her pictures. But what was the big deal? Ian reasoned. She is no different than Mabel Normand, Janet Gaynor, Juliet Dee. Not true. Katherine was his wife.

He stopped typing. Strange how little a man knows about his wife after ten years of marriage. That thought made him snicker. His snicker became a howling laugh. They loved each other, but it was a love only the two of them would ever understand. Because of that special love, Ian always hoped that Katherine would be more condoning, more understanding of his sexual appetites for men. They would never leave each other. He was sure of that. The number of men and women the two of them loved in secrecy was not going to break them up. But he couldn't do it. He could not come up with a workable love scene for Katherine in her new picture.

It should have been easy. She was beautiful. She

was gorgeous. A tragedy color film had yet to be created to expose her bright red hair to the rest of the world. What was there to write? he thought. The camera would do all the work. She could say anything she wanted with those eyes of hers.

The commotion outside Ian's office provided just enough of a distraction for him. He was annoyed. At least he was writing unworthy trash, and it thrilled him not having to stare at a blank piece of paper. He read what he had written. It was comical instead of romantic. Perhaps good material for Harold Lloyd, he thought. He didn't hear his office partner Jimmy bust in.

"Did you hear?" asked Jimmy.

"'Fraid I haven't, ol' boy. Too busy creating Laemmle's next masterpiece," said Ian.

"They did it!"

"Did what?" asked Ian.

"Warner Brothers. Al Jolson. They finally did it. They did a talkie. All the studios are changing to sound PDQ."

So the rumors have now become fact. Yes, it would mean more writing assignments for writers. But only the good ones were going to survive. Only the exceptional writing talent will be getting those jobs. Ian knew he was not one of the good ones. His eroding talent will be scrutinized more, more transparent for the studio to see. From the Toast of Broadway to Hollywood Washout. Not even the fact that he was married to Katherine was going to be enough for him to stay. Those very thoughts sent Ian through a very tumultuous internal rollercoaster ride. His seizure had returned.

Jimmy, used to seeing this before, knew what to do and got Ian a glass of water. Ian's head felt like the size of a medicine ball in his hands. His groans grew louder. With a steadfast hand, he reached into his pocket and struggled mightily to get one of those tablets into his mouth.

"Thanks, mate," said Ian.

"Don't mention it," replied Jimmy. "Just came by to tell you the news. I got a meeting with Bob Florey. Catch up with you later."

There he was again, alone in his office and back in front of that typewriter. Ian forgot one thing. The medicine prescribed for the headaches by his doctor always went down with a couple of swigs of scotch. His desk drawer opened and a slight gleam in his eyes appeared. It wasn't a big swig but rather intervals of large gulps. But it worked. Something clicked in Ian's mind. He had an idea—the idea, the idea for Katherine's love scene. He was off. *Clickety-clack, clickety-clack.* A wonderful sound, Ian thought.

Yes, he thought. *Katherine will reject the advances of her lover at first. The camera moves in closer. But her eyes do not say no. They say, "I still love you."*

More scotch. His headache, although still there, was quickly becoming a faint memory. He was sure Laemmle would like what he had written. What he wasn't sure about was whether the star, his wife, Katherine would like it. Actors and actresses were very particular about storyline scenarios that involved them. Ian kept typing. He didn't let potential rejection interfere with his explosion of genius at work. It felt good. No writer's block, just free flow movement of the typing keys. The scotch tasted good. The nicotine seething through the cigarette and into his mouth tasted good. Ian felt good. He was in desperation mode. He was trying to save his job.

The Formosa Restaurant was Ian's favorite place to relax, to drink to drink some more, to drink until he was drunk before he went home. Katherine was on location shooting and would not be home until late. He sat at the bar, and a feeling of disaster began to sweep over him. It was those new scenes he had written. Suddenly they didn't feel as wonderful and awe inspiring as they did two hours ago in his office. Those scenes went from being moving, from potentially producing not a dry eye in the movie theater to a series of words that read as mindless dribble.

How could that be? Ian asked himself. *What happened? Why does everything seem so uninspired?* He grabbed a pencil out of his pocket, began an impromptu editing job right there at the bar.

"Charlie, another scotch and water?" yelled Ian.

Ian could not tell if he was blowing everything out of proportion or if all of his efforts were going to be the result of crumpled-up paper in someone's waste basket. He crossed out. He rewrote. He read. His scotch and water could not have come any quicker.

"Thanks, mate," said Ian.

It gulped down quite easily. He signaled Charlie for another. A panic was settling in. Ian was afraid another one of his headache seizures would follow. *Remain calm,* he told himself. *One word at a time. It's not really as awful as you make it,* he said to himself.

The seconds passed. He became frightened, scared, mortified, fearful of the one thing writers fear—that their creation, their birthing has become refuse right before their very eyes. He was sure everything he had written stunk to the highest order. It should be burned, not discarded in a trash can. Even the garbage can would be too good for it. At the moment where his mind reached a plateau of panic, he felt a man's hand softly caress his shoulder.

"I have been thinking about you, *mes amis*."

Ian wanted to bellow out with a hearty, drunken laugh. He felt hearing a man with a Spanish accent speak words of French was amusing. He knew it was Ramon. The seat next to Ian happened to be available.

"Fancy seeing you here," said Ian. "Pull up a chair. The wake has just begun."

"Funny custom here in California. Not returning phone calls," replied Ramon.

The bartender had adapted to Ian's clever signal for another shot of scotch. This time he needed it to break up the intensity Ramon was bringing to their relationship. He could not think clearly. His livelihood, the core of his total existence was at stake. A washed-out hack he had become in five very short years. *What's next?* he thought. He panicked. *What shall it be?* he asked. *Editor of a newspaper in Ames, Iowa?*

And here was Ramon sitting next to him, his soft light brown eyes expressing an admiration for Ian. Craving and expecting things that Ian was not prepared nor cared to deliver upon him. Ian nodded once more. The bartender obliged him once more.

"Ramon, you are nice, but my life is about to go up in bloody smoke," said Ian. "Stop with the pressure, mate. I'm not leaving Katherine."

He turned his head from Ramon. He didn't want to become perturbed. The relationship had gotten out of hand, Ian thought. It was supposed to be fun, light, carefree, no strings attached, and certainly no dialogue about committed relationships and leaving his wife.

"I said we could be friends," said Ian. "You want more than I could give to any person at this time in my life."

"My feelings for you are stronger than you know," replied Ramon.

Ramon was becoming more emotional than Ian cared to deal with at the moment. These things seem to run their course after a month or two, he thought. Poor Ramon, he was on his way out of Ian's life as quick as he entered. That was Hollywood—sin for all, all kinds of sin, a pool of decadence to swim, wade in if you chose to do so. As long as you kept your trysts out of the newspapers, it was whatever your heart desired. Ian was an avid swimmer in this pool. Men bored him as quickly as they excited him.

Just chalked up another boyfriend—that's all he would often say to himself. He was okay with who he was. It is why he loved Katherine so much—because she understood him and accepted Ian for who he was.

While he sat at the bar listening to Ramon once more, trying to remember where he had parked his car, he felt happy and relieved. It would be the last time for Ramon.

Home was home, a beautiful and comfortable home Ian and Katherine had made for themselves over the years. Hollywood, in its genesis stage, had been very prosperous for the both of them. Many fond and lively memories in their home, those were Ian's thoughts while making that drunken trudge up the stairs to the bedroom. Those circular, winding stairs from the foyer to the second level forced Ian to hug the wall, for it made him dizzy. Ian held on to the banister tightly. He could see that their bedroom light was still on. It was the sole source of illumination throughout the entire house, shining brightly, serving as a beacon, a lighthouse to steer Ian in to safety. The landing felt firm.

Who was Katherine talking to on the phone at this hour, Ian thought. He remembered that toothy, silly laugh she gets at those times when she is feeling particularly giddy. Whoever was on that phone was entertaining Katherine royally. He opened the door.

No, it wasn't. It was not a late-night phone call with Mary Pickford.

"I would appreciate it very much if you would stop tickling my wife's fancy with your bloody tongue, Mr. Laroque."

Together, as if choreographed, Katherine and Mr. Rod Laroque's head rose from their respective resting places. Nothing was said. There was nothing to be said from any one of them. The only thing moving in the bedroom were those sonic speed, breakneck moving thoughts each individual had. Ian didn't want his apparent drunken manner to get the best of him, to make him look weaker than the situation already suggested.

It was not the first time Ian had caught Katherine with another man. It was the second time in their home. It made Ian angry. He felt Katherine was disrespecting their pact, their pact of "Ask me no questions, and I shall tell you no lies." Ian felt Katherine violated this pact by bringing her lovers to their home. He prided himself in keeping his friends away from their house. He wondered why she had become so careless, so ambiguous toward their inner sanctum.

Ian stopped exuding anger. He wanted to feel and show he was still the so-called man of the house. "Now if you don't mind, I would like very much if you gather your belongings and leave my home," said Ian.

Mr. Laroque began to oblige.

"Ian, please," said Katherine.

Ian held his index finger to his lips, telling Katherine to be quiet. "I'm sure that Hungarian tart of yours, Ms. Banky, would be none too thrilled to hear that her fiancé places his nose in things where they ought not to be," said Ian.

"Ian, please," said Katherine.

Patience escaped Ian quickly. Too much time at

the scene of the crime. He lunged at Mr. Laroque, connected solidly to his jaw with a right cross. Katherine could do nothing but crawl on the bed and shield her eyes as Ian picked Mr. Laroque off the floor and escorted his half-naked body out of the bedroom, down those long winding stairs, and out of the house.

Now, back upstairs. There she was in bed. As Ian stood over Katherine, his rage filled him up as if he was a tank receiving gasoline.

"I'm sorry you had to see him," said Katherine.

"Are you?" replied Ian.

"We need to stop hurting each other, Ian."

"My dear, you have no idea what pain is."

He became a raged-filled cobra just prior to a preemptive strike. Ian pounced on Katherine. In seconds, her silk nightgown became tattered shreds. Her beautiful body became a silhouette as the light of the evening moon shone through the bedroom window.

"Stop it," said Katherine. "Leave me alone. Don't touch me."

He wanted nothing between him and her, nothing between what he thought was rightfully his that no man should ever have. She fought him with all her might. A powerful struggle between a couple as if they never had met. Ian enjoyed the scratches Katherine applied to him. He tasted hi own blood as it trickled down his face. His force became too much for her. He struggled to fight her and unzip his slacks simultaneously. The struggle ended.

It was rape, penetration without consent. He tried his very best to hurt her with each thrust. He wanted to hurt her. He was hurting himself. For the life he had, the life he was living, for the life he gave Katherine as a weak and shallow husband. Katherine's tears soaked her face then the bedsheets. No one was going to hear her screams, her moans of pain and ecstasy at the same time.

She and Ian hadn't made love to each other for weeks. As he pinned her arms down to the bed, neither remembered how long it had been.

"You will never feel another man after tonight," said Ian.

"You're hurting me," replied Katherine.

"I want to," Ian continued.

Katherine's face contained many hues and expressions. Shock . . . pain . . . orgasmic revelation . . . desire . . . disappointment . . . contriteness. Ian was not going to stop, not until he released himself. Katherine knew. Years of being each other's lover told her so. She knew he was close. She grabbed him, clutched him with everything she had. And then she felt him, felt Ian's release, felt each other's wetness trickle down her leg, felt Ian's hard and panting breath on her neck. There was nothing left but for the two of them to hold each other. They both got what they wanted.

11

"Los Angeles in forty-five minutes. Los Angeles in forty-five!" the porter yelled loudly as he made his way through the first-class compartment cars. The Santa Fe-San Francisco–Los Angeles line was running on schedule this particular Sunday. Cars were full, Canadians from Vancouver, businessmen from Seattle and Portland, a number of Hollywood stars fresh from a visit at Randolph Hearst's in San Simeon. That's where Ian and Katherine had been.

Ian and Katherine sat across from each other in club car 502. It was the usual four days of revelry and sin at San Simeon. This trip, Ian and Katherine used the weekend to mend fences, to establish that caring and understanding they had for each other, to agree that there will be no more lovers between them. Both were not stupid. Both knew that they needed each other in a business sense. Both knew there would be more lovers. Sexual compatibility with more than one soul was one of the few things they had in common. Katherine needed Ian as long as Ian could write. Ian was still in charge of writing the script for Katherine's new film. Laemmle was going to want to see something tomorrow morning, first thing. Ian frantically scribbled notes.

"How's it going, darling?" asked Katherine.

"It's going," replied Ian. "It's going bloody awful."

Katherine knew Ian was serious. The mood went from airy and light to dark. Katherine knew that Ian's existence in Hollywood was on the line. Their marriage was a contrived scam. Still, she loved Ian, didn't want to see him down on his luck.

"If you don't complete the script, you'll be through at Universal," said Katherine. "Nobody else will want you either."

"My darling, you state the obvious so eloquently," said Ian.

All of those happy moments at San Simeon had quickly eroded, that seemingly endless night of romance and lovemaking, the hours of telling each other how sorry they were. It was back to business for Ian and Katherine, back to that common ground, their careers.

"Coffee, sandwiches, candy, cigarettes!" It was Abel, Abel the train porter, many miles and months away from New Jersey, a working man but also a writing man, a man still pursuing his one passion, his work. His passion. He was serving the public, but his mind was elsewhere. He was anticipating getting home tonight and finishing his next chapter. But for the moment, he made his way down the aisle.

"Get your coffee, sandwiches, cigarettes, chewin' gum!"

Nobody was paying any attention to Abel.

"Over here, boy!"

That was music to Abel's ears. A sudden about-face and he was facing his customer. Ian was his customer. "Yessah."

"I say what sort of sandwiches have we today?" asked Ian.

"Ham and cheese, sir. Ham and cheese only."

Ian took this moment to look at Abel, a very long gaze, up and down, back up again. He saw a handsome well-built Negro man with a cleft in his chin, a chocolate brown complexion. Everything Ian saw of Abel he liked. *Is this an attraction?* he asked himself.

"Sir?"

"Ian, the boy wants to know what you want," said Katherine.

Ian and Abel looked at each other for different reasons. Yet this glance at each other would be their first communication.

"Ian, stop staring at the man," said Katherine.

"Yes, quite sorry. A ham sandwich."

"Yessuh," replied Abel.

Abel dipped into his basket. He wanted to find the freshest ham and cheese sandwich he had in order to give to Ian.

"Here you go, freshly made, yessuh."

"Excellent. I have seen you before?"

"No, sir, 'less you been on this train in the last year," replied Abel.

Ian smiled. He found Abel appealing. It was something Ian was very good at—sizing up men in a carnal fashion. All of this did not get past Katherine. She has seen that glint in Ian's eye before.

"That'll be fifty cents, sir."

Still smiling, Ian reached into his pocket and handed Abel a one-dollar bill. "Keep it."

"Thanks youz, sir," replied Abel.

As he ate his ham sandwich, Ian watched Abel intently. Abel moved slowly through the car, serving the other passengers, not knowing his every move was being inspected. Suddenly and without warning, the ham sandwich became a tasteless morsel in Ian's mouth. In an instant, Ian's appetite changed from food to desire. He was contemplating, scheming how to get him in his employ, into his confidence.

"I see you insist on embarrassing me," said

Katherine. "And now with this. This new obsession with Negroes? Nothing stops you, does it, Ian?"

Ian saw opportunity, the opportunity to ignore Katherine. His balled-up scribbles impersonating remnants of a screenplay filled his hands. He licked the lead off his pencil, a twirl, a lick once more. In thought, ignoring Katherine. The *San Francisco Chronicle* became Katherine's entertainment. All was normal once more. The McGregors were ignoring each other.

Ian tried to conceal the writer's block. It plagued him once more. Even though Katherine buried her face in that newspaper, occasionally her curiosity would rear up, and she would want to see what Ian had written. There was no way he would let Katherine in on his dilemma. So he wrote. He wrote more. He wrote more. Dialogue filled the sheets rapidly. But it was tripe, useless dribble. Laemmle would ball it up and toss it in the garbage. Ian knew that.

That corner behind the bar was Abel's favorite space during his break. He leaned back in his chair. He could tell how close the train was to Los Angeles by listening to the speed of the wheels. They were close, he thought, thirty minutes. He wanted to finish two more sentences. What would his character feel when he met his friend for the first time? he thought. It was a key moment in Abel's story. An initial meeting of a unique friendship had to be expressed in words in just the right way. It was starting to happen. Abel had been having writer's blocks. He never experienced it before. For the past six weeks, every time he wanted to write, every time he wanted to get it down on paper, he froze. He froze with emptiness, a writer's nightmare, ready to say with nothing to say, pen or pencil in hand. Your grip gets tighter and tighter with each second that you come up with nothing, nothing to say, nothing to write. These feelings made Abel feel awful, sick to his stomach. He never had to face failure at anything, especially his writing. It was his one release, his one vehicle he was going to use to tell his story, his own story, a story of conflict and pain and loss love.

A giant shadow was cast over Abel's paper. It appeared suddenly. His concentration on his work was so keen, he didn't realize its appearance. It was sudden. Another reason to stop writing. One more reason his creativity would be halted. He looked up. Ian stood in the doorway. His ever-present look of a man dying of thirst was so obviously apparent, dying of thirst for scotch, not water.

"Club car closed, sir, we almost in the station," said Abel.

"I say would you be a gent and provide a thirsty Scotsman a shot of something?" replied Ian.

Ian moved closer to the bar. He wanted a better look of Abel. Each second he had him in his eyesight, he liked what he saw. Abel was used to drunkards like Ian who always wanted to keep the bar open past closing. Abel remembered him from earlier when he served him. He thought Ian was a nice man.

Abel spoke up again, "Sir, club car closed."

Ian's broad and beaming smile appeared. It was a captivating smile. Abel noticed. No man ever smiled at him the Ian did. He wasn't sure what to make of it. He thought it polite to smile back. He watched Ian's hand reach into his pants pocket for a twenty-dollar bill. Abel liked the way Ian smacked in on the bar.

"Well now, mate, shall we make it worth your while?" asked Ian.

"Yessah!" replied Abel.

And Abel poured Ian a double. And in appreciative fashion, Ian drank. And Abel poured another. And

Abel drank. Ian's soft tap on the bar was his signal for more.

"Tell me, how long have you worked for the railroad?" asked Ian.

"'Bout a year," said Abel.

"Like it?"

"It's work. Man's gotta toil at somethin'."

In the brief time of their acquaintance, Ian seemed to find something about Abel he considered attractive. Every so often, Abel's intelligent manner would peer through. Ian liked that, was attracted by that. While he sipped his scotch, he gave Abel a curious look. Abel stared back. He could not figure out Ian's stare, so he gave him a faint smirk back. He nervously grabbed a towel and began wiping the bar.

"Toil? I see. Where does a colored boy learn to acquire such an expanded vocabulary?" asked Ian.

"Went to college. Back home in Alabama," replied Abel.

"I was supposed to go to college, Yale. But Father died and left us penniless. I had to work selling pots and pans in Boston to support me mum and younger sisters."

Abel listened. He listened carefully as Ian opened his heart about a missed opportunity in his life. For a brief moment, Abel felt superior to Ian, superior to a white man. He had attended college. Here he was face to face with a white man who hadn't. *But look at the difference,* he thought. *The college graduate serves sandwiches, cigarettes, and coffee. The high school dropout is a successful businessman living in Los Angeles.*

Abel felt he should say something to let Ian know he was paying attention. "Circumstances ain't suh'pose to change your ambitions," said Abel.

Ian's eyes twinkled once more. The wheels in his

head turned. He wanted to see Abel again after the train arrived in Los Angeles.

"What is your name," asks Ian.

"Abel Johnson."

"I like your manner. Suppose you come work for me in Los Angeles."

"Work for you, sir?" asks Abel.

"I'm in desperate need of a valet and chauffeur. How much do you make working the train line?"

"Seven dollars a week, plus tips," replied Abel.

"I'll make it twelve, plus your meals. Your own room in the coach house garage."

It was happening so very fast for Abel. He was never enamored of being a porter on a train line for the past nine months. And now, here was this man, a stranger to him no more than an hour ago, offering him the chance to vacate the Santa Fe existence, offering him his own room, offering him more money, offering him a life besides six days a week trips between Los Angeles and Portland, Oregon. He wanted to make a decision, make a quick decision. *This is an opportunity to do something completely different,* he thought.

The *L.A. Herald* would not be offering him a job as a beat writer. Neither would the *L.A. Examiner.* Neither would any newspaper. He liked Southern California. His two-day layovers were always a welcome relief. Abel spent quite a bit of time writing on secluded beaches near Los Angeles. Negroes weren't allowed on public beaches in Los Angeles, so it was always a challenge to find secluded areas where he would not be forced to move or even arrested for trespassing.

"How much did you say a week?" asked Abel.

"Twelve a week plus your meals," replied Ian.

"Like to think it over Mr. . . . Mr. . . . Mr. . . ."

"McGregor, boy. Mr. McGregor."

Ian didn't want to seem pushy and anxious. But he wanted Abel in his employ. He pulled a piece of paper out of his suit coat and wrote down his address and phone number.

"I'll keep the position open until I hear from you," said Ian.

Abel took the piece of paper and placed it in his shirt pocket. He smiled and nodded back at Ian to let him know his answer would be imminently soon. Ian acknowledged Abel's smile by tapping twice on the bar for one more shot. Abel obliged. Ian gulped.

"It would not be a good idea to keep me waiting too long," said Ian.

Abel received that infectious smile from Ian one last time before he turned and left the club car. He placed his hand over his breast pocket, the one containing Ian's phone number and address. He wanted to return to his writing, but he stared at the spot on the floor where Ian was standing. He thought Ian went out of his way to be nice to him. He wasn't sure why. He felt most white people were patronizing him when they exhibited kindness, especially while he was working the trains. Maybe they were afraid Abel would spit in the ham and cheese sandwiches. That thought made Abel laugh out loud.

Now he was ready to write again. This time Ian's interruption was good for Abel. The words flowed with a symphonic regularity on his writing pad. His thoughts made complete sense. He expressed his character's thoughts and desires precisely the way he wanted. It is difficult writing about a character's feelings that carry an ambiguous tone. Abel tried, tried very hard. For the first time, Abel realized that his main character was resembling him in personality. He was writing about himself.

He thought about Althea back home perhaps because the day before was her birthday. He didn't call her.

He didn't write her. Abel didn't want Althea to read anything into a phone call or a letter, so he thought it best not to communicate at all.

Mr. O'Brien, his boss, interrupted his thoughts about Althea. "Johnson! Goddamnit, boy, you best not be sleepin'."

Abel was startled. He did not hear Mr. O'Brien enter the club car. Quickly he shut his thought process down and slowly closed his notebook before O'Brien saw it.

"Yessa," said Abel.

"Get to them dishes and be quick about it," said Mr. O'Brien.

"Ain't finished my break just yet, Mr. O'Brien."

"Your break, 'tis it?"

"Yessa, the union says—"

Mr. O'Brien, a big rotund Irishman who weighed over 250 pounds, got right into Abel's face, as close as he could. Abel smelled the cheap gin on his breath. It wasn't the first time, but he dared not say anything to management. He was afraid Mr. O'Brien would find out and make his life a living hell then have him fired. As much as Abel hated working as a porter, it was the only job he had. Some of Mr. O'Brien's tobacco chaw hit Abel in the face. He pretended he didn't notice.

"Look here, boy, that niggra union you belong to don't carry any weight in me club car, get me?"

Abel continued to listen. He continued to smell bad gin and get pelted with tobacco juice. He wanted to tell Mr. O'Brien where he could take this job. He wasn't sure what was holding him back.

"And another thing that lazy shiftless SOB Lucious is out sick, so you have to take his Sacramento run tomorrow. Be back here at 4:00 a.m."

Abel replied, "But, Mr. O'Brien, tomorrow is my day off."

"Now you see here, Sambo, it's a depression out

there. Either do as I say or hit the streets. Stupid niggras like yourself are a dime a dozen for washing dishes." Mr. O'Brien took the liberty to blow his liquored breath in Abel's face once more. "What's it going to be, boy?" asked Mr. O'Brien.

"Yessa."

By the time Abel had reached his rooming house, night had fallen. The stairs leading up to his room seemed steeper today than usual. Mrs. Gibson, his landlady, stuck Abel on in the fourth floor attic. The room there was the cheapest, and it allowed Abel more privacy for his writing. He had made up his mind on a very important decision. The incident in the club car with Mr. O'Brien was the straw that broke the camel's back. He had enough of Mr. O'Brien. As he stood in the hallway, his frustration mounted. What he wanted to do badly he could not. No newspaper in Los Angeles would ever hire Abel as a writer. When a man can't do what he is called out to do in his life, he feels lonely. He feels as though he has been outcast into an abyss of failure. His sense of worth is thrown into a cauldron of despair.

He reached into his pocket for that nickel, his next to last nickel. He hesitated before placing it into the phone an dialing. It had to be done.

"Hello? Yes, ma'am, may I speak to Mr. McGregor?
"Yes, ma'am, I'll hold."

It was his last chance to change his mind. He thought about other things he could do—bootblack on Western Avenue, bust dishes at Auntie Ann's Kitchen on La Brea. It was too late.

"Yessa, Mr. McGregor, it's Abel Johnson the train porter. If that job is still open, I'd like to take it."

12

Abel could not believe his eyes. His coach house apartment was much larger, more warmly furnished than Ms. Ophelia's one-room rooming house bedroom overlooking a wheat field across the street. Abel now had a picturesque view of the Hollywood Hills. The view that day was clear, not a cloud in the sky.

Abel smirked. *This is going to be just fine,* he thought. His pace around the room slowed. He imagined his work table in the corner next to his bed. A gleeful thought about how nice writing was going to be here paraded through his mind. His confidence rose with each second. His novel would be finished soon. He felt he made the right decision coming to work for the McGregors.

"Not the Beverly Hills Shores of course. Still, a step up from that rooming house," said Ian.

"Yessa," replied Abel.

Ian watched Abel circle the room. Whenever Abel had his back to him, Ian smiled. His lips moistened. He studied his walk. He studied the emotions painted on his face. He could see Abel was pleased. He could see happiness and satisfaction at his decision to work for him. It appeared. It appeared suddenly. That twinkle in Ian's eyes emerged. A yearning inside his body guzzled. Ian was starting to like Abel.

"Mrs. McGregor has a number of items to discuss with you in the house. I'm off to the studio. Breakfast is promptly at eight unless otherwise stated. The cars are to be washed every other day. We leave for the studio promptly at eight forty-five," said Ian.

"Yessa."

It was Abel's turn to watch Ian as he paced the room. To see what was not working or broken, he thought. He continued to wonder why Ian had taken such a liking to him. Why he was going out of his way to make him feel so special as though he was better than the other Negro servants.

Ian quickly turned around and glanced at Abel. He wanted to catch him looking at him. It startled Abel but tickled Ian's offhanded sense of humor. He wanted Abel to see the serious tone of his face.

"One last thing. We have a colored woman in our employ. Her name is Mabel. Fornication with the staff is expressly forbidden," said Ian.

Ian took the moment to walk up closer to Abel. He wanted to see his eyes in a different light. He was looking for something in his eyes. There was apprehension in his steps. Abel felt Ian's hand softly caressed his shoulder. "I will assume a smart, good-looking boy knows what fornication means."

Abel nodded yes. He thought to himself, *What a strange man.* But as Ian turned walked out of the coach house, he reminded himself how glad he was to be there.

Ian sat in his car, frozen, terrified. He did not want to move. He sat there watching the studio population hustle and bustle around him. His whiskey flask pounded through his suit jacket. It was singing Ian's tune. He answered the call with a huge swig and swallow. He wanted to garner as much courage as possible before his meeting with Junior. Now it was time, time to get out of his car and make the 150-foot walk to Junior's office. He lightly closed the door to his car and proceeded, stopping only to blow his breath into his hand. It didn't make any difference because Junior would already assume he had been drinking. Ian always drank before meeting with Junior. One more meeting in that richly decorated, plush office of Junior. Ian hated going there to talk studio business. It meant he had to stare at the large photograph of his wife, Katherine, on Junior's wall.

"Have a seat, Ian," said Junior.

Ian sat. He tried to get a read on what Junior was about to say to him. Junior never raised his head out of the script on his desk.

Junior spoke. "I've read the script and—"

Ian wanted to have his say before Junior finished. That was the strategy, the motive, head him off at the pass, admit right off the bat that the script wasn't very good, but the best was yet to come. Ian wanted to keep Junior convinced he was still the writer for the job.

"Have no fear—it's only a first draft. The next one will be decidedly better," said Ian.

"I'm afraid there won't be a next time."

Those words shook up Ian. He wasn't expecting it. He thought Junior would encourage him, urge him on. Ian wanted a drink, a drink in the worst way. His head began to throb. *Not those blasted headaches at this time,* he thought. He didn't want to let on that his flask was in his pocket.

"I don't understand," said Ian.

"Lewis Milestone has been assigned to direct *All Quiet on the Western Front*. He wants Maxwell Anderson to write the script."

Ian's surprised manner quickly turned into anger. He was being replaced, a sure sign to a writer working in Hollywood that his services soon would no longer be needed. He knew Maxwell Anderson personally. He was an inferior writer to him. Certainly Ian had more writing accolades to boast of, especially during his tenure at Universal.

Ian spoke, "Junior, you told me this was my big shot, not Maxwell Anderson's. You're snatching it from me as if you were removing candy from a naughty child."

"You're overstating," replied Junior.

"I can write for sound. Just going through a bit of writer's block. Blimey, give a bloke a proper chance."

He was seconds from just standing up and bolting for the door. He wasn't going to allow Junior to belittle him, not after eight successful years, not after all he has accomplished for Universal. The films he wrote that Katherine acted in had grossed over two million dollars.

"It's just not working out, Ian. It's your writing. We have a production schedule to adhere to. You've had three months to crack it. I'm sorry."

Ian had had enough. He stood and turned toward the door. From there, it would be a beeline to his office to clear out his desk. He was quitting Universal. Today. He would talk to his friend James later and ask him to speak to Howard Hughes about a writer's position with RKO. *What would Katherine say?* he thought.

Junior's voice halted him as he placed his hand on the door knob. "One second, Ian," said Junior.

Ian slowly walked back to Junior's desk.

"My father says give you one more chance. He likes you a ton, Ian. You've been a valuable employee for Universal despite your sinful male escapades. We're going to assign you to write the script for Katherine's first talkie."

It was music to Ian's ears, a concerto that spoke

volumes. He did not want to leave Universal. The Laemmles had been very good to him. He was living a luxurious lifestyle during the Depression, and Ian knew where his bread was buttered on. Junior had Ian's attention. He reached into his desk drawer and pulled out a treatment for Ian to read. The title appeared before Ian's eyes. It read *Another Man's Poison*. Ian picked up the treatment and tucked it under his arm.

The walk back to his car didn't feel like a walk to Ian. He was exhilarated. He had been given a new lease on life. He was floating on a cloud. As he walked back to his car, he read the treatment. In the story, Katherine's character was a nineteenth-century countess who was married and in love with another man. *Here we go again,* thought Ian, *doomed love.*

The sunny afternoon skies turned into a cloudy and overcast late afternoon for Ian and James. A light drizzle had begun on this November day. The rain drops that pelted the window contained a linguistic rhythm to them. Ian found James's buttocks a very warm and comfortable pillow to rest his head after their lovemaking session.

"I struggle with creating dialogue," said Ian.

"Rubbish. You are a very talented writer," replied James.

"If I don't write a smashing script for Katherine's first talkie, I'm through."

James didn't hear Ian. He was preoccupied with his own thoughts. There was something he had to tell Ian. It had to be done that day. It would upset him terribly. Still, he knew it had to be done. That moment he felt Ian's head nestling up on him, he moved slightly to sit up on the bed.

"Something the matter?" asked Ian.

"I imagine it is a good-news-bad-news scenario," replied James.

"Let's have the good news now, shall we?"

James squirmed ever so slightly. His uneasiness intensified. He thought it better if he held Ian's hand. Slowly James spoke, "I'm leaving RKO for Universal. Three-picture deal. I'm to direct a horror picture. Shelley's *Frankenstein.* We start production right after Lugosi finishes *Dracula.*"

Ian was elated, very happy for his friend from England. "James, that's wonderful," said Ian. "Simply marvelous. It means we'll see a lot more of each other. Pray tell what could possibly the bad news be?"

James broke away from the embrace. It was his way of telling Ian what he was about to say would be bad news. It would be hurtful for him and toward Ian.

Once more, he spoke slowly. "We can't see each other again. Ever. The Laemmles instructed me never to see you again. They know about us. Don't ask me how, but they know. I gave them my word. They'll tear up my contract if I go against their wishes."

It was unfamiliar territory for Ian—a man telling him he was no longer needed. Usually it was Ian giving his lover the heave-ho. Not this time. James hadn't been in America long, but he was astute enough to realize and understand he was not going to allow Ian to ruin his vision for fame, for wealth, for recognition in the film industry. Ian could do nothing but stare back at James. He felt hurt, rejected. He liked James very much. They were wonderful lovers together. They had also become very good friends. He felt James was letting him down at his lowest point. A lonely feeling painted Ian's heart. He didn't want James to know how hurt he was, how disappointed he felt. James touched Ian on his shoulder as he spoke.

"I say we have had loads of fun. Yes, we are

sexually compatible. But I am not the answer to your sexual needs. Nor you mine. As your friend, I'm saying to you to go find a boyfriend, someone who is more of a total package than myself."

As he finished dressing, Ian decided to put on his proud face.

"I hope you understand and won't be cross. Let's be just friends, shall we?" said James.

Ian didn't hear a word James said as he headed for the door.

"All the luck in the world, mate."

The drive down Sunset was a solemn one for Ian. He was hurting. He felt rejected. The pain inside his heart increased with every half mile. He was beginning to realize how much he cared for James, how much he liked him, perhaps how much he was in love with him. And now the thought rummaged through his mind. What could he do to salvage the relationship he and James had initiated? He did not want it to end. He wanted to continue seeing him even though James informed him the studio would be watching. They already had knowledge of their trysts. The Laemmles had decided that one known queer was enough.

And at that moment, it hit Ian like a ton of bricks. He somberly realized that he and James approached their friendship from two different altitudes, two different perspectives. James liked Ian for his sexual prowess, for their bedroom chemistry, for the way he made him feel, for their unique level of friendship. Ian wanted James, wanted him as his everlasting friend, wanted him as a relationship partner. He wanted to write wonderful screenplays and allow James to direct, a collaboration both professional and emotional. That is what Ian wanted more than anything else. The reality was becoming prominent. For he knew as long as they felt differently, there would be no forging as one. And so as the rain slowly and intermittently struck his windshield, Ian was saddened, saddened with the grave possibility he would never see James again. He thought of a line he wrote in one of his Broadway plays:

"If you love someone, set them free. If they come back, it is a relationship that will last forever. If they do not return, they were never yours to begin with."

Ian used one hand to drive. The other hand gripped his flask. It was full, full of scotch, enough to last him the remaining drive home. He was hoping Katherine would not be home when he arrived. He did not want to see her, did not want her to see him with his eyes welled up from crying, from crying over a man, a man he cared for, a man he wanted unconditionally, a man he loved. For the first time ever, Ian wished Katherine was not home. He wished she was with another man in another man's bed, feeling another man's member inside her. He could not face her. Katherine would see that something was amiss. Ian had no desire to confide in her. Not tonight.

The winding roads on Sunset proposed an ever-increasing challenge to Ian's driving skills. He managed. The speed of his car increased. His drinking intensified. With each sip of his flask, his heart cracked a little more. He wondered if James was sitting in his room thinking about him. He wondered if James was sitting in his room longing for him. *Watch that bloomin' curve,* he said to himself.

The thought only prompted the desire for another swig out of his flask. It was at that moment his memory kicked in, reminded him of things James had told him, told him how he really felt about Ian. He once told Ian, "Let's not make this into anything more than what it is."

But Ian never asked him specifically what *it* was, what the true definition of their relationship would be. There was his memory again. Another recollection. The evening James told him, "I don't want to be responsible for your happiness or your unhappiness."

Abel was stuck, perplexed. He struggled trying to find the words to his novel. This had never happened to him—only briefly when he was in New Jersey staying with Isaiah's girlfriend Flo. He stopped writing. He thought about Flo, those times they made love. Even though this woman appeared at a confusing point in his life, Abel remembered their intimacies fondly. She excited him, made him feel like a man, not the way Althea did back home in Alabama. With Flo, he desired a woman. With Althea, it was different. She was only a fraction of the woman Flo was, he thought, never a whole woman. With Althea, he never felt like a whole man. She would give her body but was incapable of emotionally giving herself up to Abel.

His mind played tricks on him, made him wonder if he was destined to be intimate with a man. Being intimate with a woman wasn't feeling natural to Abel, especially those early years with Althea. These thoughts, whether unnatural or unholy, filled Abel's mind with confusion. The character in his book was filled with confusion as well. His character's name was Robert. Robert was a musician. Robert loved women. But one day, a woman cut him with her knife after they made love. He sought comfort, both physically and psychologically from his best friend, Charles. Soon, Charles and Robert were lovers. Robert was confused.

And now, Abel was confused, confused about himself, confused about Althea, about Flo, about what he wanted, about who he wanted. He felt it best to start writing again. He liked his new home. His coach house apartment was very comfortable. He was eating well. Ian was a very good boss to him.

Abel wanted to finish the chapter he was working on before Ian returned home. He would want his usual late-night snack, a ham and cheese sandwich and coffee. He wrote. He was in a hurry. He wasn't concerned whether it was good, whether he would keep it. He just wanted the satisfaction of saying tonight he had finished another chapter.

His pen moved quickly. A thought had occurred. It would connect everything he had written before in his earlier chapters with what he wanted to say later. He felt good. Abel always felt good when his work was uninterrupted. He wanted Robert to appear to have as much ambivalence about men and women and relationships as he did. He wanted Robert to act as troubled as he was. He was living his life through Robert, a character in his book.

All creativity stopped upon hearing Ian's car pull up into the driveway. Abel stopped writing. Instinctively, he reached for his white servant's jacket. Working as Ian's valet and chauffeur had become acceptable.

The door slowly opened. Ian saw what he had hoped. As he looked up the stairs into his bedroom, he saw the light off. It meant Katherine was not home. Katherine always kept the bedroom light on until Ian arrived home. A drunken stumble through the foyer to his office was next. He slumped into his chair. He stared at his typewriter, the typewriter that hadn't written anything good for over three weeks. A piece of paper remained sitting still in the typewriter. There was nothing on it, white as snow, nothing for Ian to jump up and finish an idea he had. It was as blank as the expression painted on his face. His headache, those headaches that have been getting worse for the past few months, appeared once more. It was Ian's green light to take a swig out of his flask.

Another memory of James haunted him—that night James told him, "I am destined to hurt you." Those words upset Ian terribly. Later that week, he asked James not to say such hurtful things. But James refused, said he was only being honest. A soft knock at the door interrupted his pain.

"Yes, who is it?"

The door opened. Abel appeared.

"Yes, what is it?" asked Ian.

"Thought you might want somethin' to eat, sir."

"Is my wife here?"

Abel replied, "No, sir, said she was gonna go out with friends 'bout three hours ago."

"I see. Fix me a ham sandwich, scotch, and water."

"Look like you could use some coffee, sir," said Abel.

"Damn it, man, do as I say."

"Yes, sir," said Abel.

"Bring it to my bedroom."

"Yes, sir."

Ian had what he wanted—silence, a moment, a moment to think about James, a moment to cry, a moment to allow his pain to escape, to allow his cheeks to moisten with his tears.

13

"Darling, you haven't heard a word I've been saying."

Ian hadn't. His mind, his thoughts, his whims, his heart were with James. A sunny morning breakfast with Katherine was painful to him, heartbreaking. He was hiding internally his anguish. Another one of James's hurtful remarks pierced his mind. "I don't want to be withholding, but I don't want to be misleading either."

James had a unique way of being hurtful at the wrong moment. Yet it was Ian who blamed himself. He blamed himself for not heeding the warnings, the warnings that James was not, could not, would never love him the way he loved James. He was remembering the times, the instances James picked to be particularly hurtful and insensitive, when he told Ian his calls during the day had become oppressive. He never thought of himself as oppressive. No man had ever thought of him as oppressive.

"Did you hear what I said?" asked Katherine.

"Huh? Sorry, my pet, I did not."

For a change, Ian welcomed a conversation with Katherine. It got his mind off James. Ian and Katherine did share many components and characteristics: their voracious sexual appetites, their love for money and fame, their love and desire to maintain their opulent Hollywood lifestyles.

"I asked you, do you know this Tod Browning?"

Ian replied, "Only that MGM loves him and Junior wants to get in a bidding war with Thalberg."

"Doesn't tell me much, Ian."

"I don't think he is a good enough director for drama. The horror genre is where he belongs, where he should stay. My advice to you is to tell Junior to find another goddamn bloody director for your picture."

As breakfast elapsed, Ian's internal pain intensified. He was hiding it well from Katherine. Pain, remorse, feeling he had been used and taken advantage of, the money, the gifts, the trinkets, the weekend getaways to Catalina Island. And now he blamed himself for not heeding the warning signs that read, "he is not the one."

Abel had Ian and Katherine's breakfast ready at precisely 8:00 a.m. It was Tuesday. Tuesday morning meant eggs benedict, toast, and coffee.

"We'll take the Packard today, Abel."

"Yessah," replied Abel.

Katherine chimed in. "I have a script for you to deliver to my agent on Wilshire. You are to drop it off after you take us to the studio."

"Yes, ma'am."

It was Abel's cue to return to the kitchen. Ian's voice stopped him. "Abel."

"Yessuh."

Ian asked, "Are you finding things to your liking so far?

"Yessah."

"Splendid. It's important staff feels wanted. That's all."

"Yessah."

Abel had a few free minutes before he was to

bring the car around front. He sat in the corner of the kitchen. His small notebook pad was full of notes for his story. Now that his character, Robert, was beginning to shape up, his mind became clearer on his storyline. Mabel, the maid and cook, was finishing the dishes. She ignored Abel. Abel ignored her. His attention was drawn to the occurrences outside in the yard.

Ian and Katherine stood holding hands and talking. Abel sensed whatever they were talking about was not adversarial. Katherine took that moment to kiss Ian gently on the lips. Abel saw a look on Ian's face, a look he had been attempting to capture and depict for his character, Robert. An inspirational moment to write had struck. Abel's character, over time, had become like Abel—ambivalent to sexual encounters with women. He wasn't confusing, perplexing, unnerving. Like Abel, Robert had an inner compulsion to be someone, to be a success, to make an impact on people's lives, to leave a legacy behind. For Abel, it was his writing. For his character, Robert, he wanted to be a musician, a pianist, a great pianist.

"What'cha thinkin' 'bout over there, college boy?"

Mabel's voice startled Abel. Mabel never called Abel by his name, always college boy. She would say it in such a tone, it sounded as if she mocked him. Abel never acted condescending to the other Negro servants. But for reasons unbeknownst to him, Mabel's ways disturbed him.

"Nuthin'," replied Abel.

"What'u writin'?"

"Some notes for my book."

"Yo book!" exclaimed Mabel.

Mabel could not help herself. Her loud, bombastic laugh engulfed the entire kitchen. As quickly as it started, her laugh ended. She did not want the other servants hearing her mock Abel.

Abel saw something in Mabel that reminded him of his momma. Perhaps it was the way she wore her hair: a cinched bun pinned up in the back. Momma did not have the brash mouth that Mabel possessed. There was nothing demure about Mabel. Mabel's mother was a domestic as was her grandmother. As Mabel put it to anyone who would listen, her great-grandmother was a slave and lover to James Madison, bore him two children. "I've heard that story before," said Abel.

Abel had stopped Mabel cold in her thoughts. He really wanted some quiet time to work on his notes before having to drive the McGregors to the studio.

"Let me say somethin', college boy. Ain't nuthin' changed 'round here. What? Just 'cause it's nearin' 1929 and you ain't in Mas'er's field pickin' his cotton that thanz is betta?"

Abel placed his hand further into his notes. He had heard Mabel's rants before that Negroes were not better off. Every chance she got Mabel would put down Abel's academic achievement from Tuskegee Agricultural, that Abel's intelligence and articulate manner were nothing to be proud of.

"Look at youz," said Mabel. "Still Mas'er's boy. Ain't it time for you to be drivin' anyway?"

Abel raised his head up and peered outside into the backyard. Ian and Katherine were still strolling. Abel knew it would be time to leave soon. Mabel was preventing him from writing, so he stood up from his chair to leave.

"Let me tellz youz somethin' else," said Mabel.

Abel stared at Mabel. He wanted to speak his mind. He wanted to tell Mabel that ignorant, narrow-minded thinking by colored people like Mabel were the main reasons Negroes had not advanced further. It was the exact feelings Abel longed to convey in his writings, expose to the world that a Negro can attain and achieve what any man can. But he didn't. Mabel would never understand. So once more, he allowed himself to be snickered at by Mabel while walking out of the kitchen.

The spring morning provided Sunset Boulevard with a sunny, glowing picturesque drive for the McGregors. An early-morning weekday drive was usually filled with long traffic lines and motorists who cannot drive. Sunset had become the main thoroughfare into Hollywood and Los Angeles. But the traffic was light, smooth running, uneventful. The inside of the McGregors' Packard was quiet.

Ian and Katherine rarely spoke to each other while riding together to the studio. The exception was if it was a continuation of an argument the night before. But not this morning. Katherine usually spent the time reading and preparing her lines for the day's shooting. Ian spent the time determining how many martinis he would put down before two o'clock.

Abel had been working for the McGregors for almost three months. He immediately noticed one thing about Ian and Katherine, that they were creatures of habit—same time for breakfast, same time to leave for the studio, same time to be picked up from the studio, same time for dinner, same time on Saturday night to get drunk and start arguing with each other.

Abel was feeling good about his new surroundings. He had a feeling that the McGregors liked him and wanted him around. They considered Abel a valuable addition to their domestic staff. And with each passing day, Abel felt more at home. His comfort level rose. He had his own room above the garage. He was making more money than being a porter on the trains. He was able to spend a large amount of time working on his book. With each passing day, he was feeling he had made the right decision.

Ian said nothing. His thoughts were elsewhere. His thoughts were with James. James had become an omnipresent fixture in his mind. He was a mark on his blackboard that could not be erased. His love for James continued to engulf his soul. He softly touched the breast pocket of his suit coat, the pocket that carried the letter James wrote him, the letter that told Ian how sorry James was for breaking his heart, how James told him there was nothing he could do but cease communication and with him well. James's words pounded his head like a hammer on an anvil. "I cannot be both the source of pain and the source of comfort to you. I hope you find peace, and I truly wish you great happiness."

James was right, Ian thought. To think of James brought Ian moments of pain, heartbreak, despair, a sense of loss. He wanted James in his life more than any other man. He had told one person, one person his entire life that he was in love with that person. That was Katherine. He told James he loved him. But it was over. They were moving on and going their separate ways. His heart ached, and yet he continued to hide his pain from Katherine quite well.

He grabbed Katherine's hand and squeezed it gently. He was attempting to channel energy. No man had ever touched Ian so like James had. He missed James terribly. He was gone out of his life as if he had died, had passed on. Trying to embrace a mind-set of death toward James, to grieve, and then to move on with his life. He knew he would have to stop being in love with James. But he was also sure of one thing. He would always love him.

Katherine remained worried. Frightened. There were younger upstarts vying for the studio and the public's attention. Vilma Banky at Universal. Joan Crawford, Greta Garbo, and Norma Shearer at MGM. Irene Dunne at RKO. Kay Francis at Warner Brothers. Sound in pictures would be a certainty in months. Katherine's career for the next five, the next ten years was in Ian's hands. He had to write a fabulous screenplay. But was it in him? She turned her head slightly to glance at Ian. For a brief moment, they shared eye contact with one another. Katherine thought a glance of reassurance would relax Ian. He might have a productive day writing.

She turned her head slightly to glance at Ian. For a brief moment, they shared a look of love. Or was it? For Katherine, it was a glance to help Ian relax, to make him feel reassured. She slowly placed his hand beneath her skirt. The gesture brought a smile to both. Katherine took that moment to softly kiss Ian on the lips. It was an unexplainable passion Ian and Katherine possessed. They could engage in a battle royale in front of many one minute and the next, with the right touch at the right place, a heated very sensual exchange would develop between them.

"Busy day planned?" asked Katherine.

"Working on the screenplay for the better part of the day."

Katherine replied, "Can we meet at Cirro's for lunch?"

"Noon, better make it one o'clock," said Ian.

Abel stole a glance at Ian and Katherine from his rearview mirror. He made sure neither Ian nor Katherine caught him. A Negro servant was to always pretend he never saw anything or heard anything. Playing the role of hear no evil, see no evil, speak no evil was as important as the clean white shirt and bow tie Abel put on every day.

His dialogue with Mabel earlier that morning triggered thoughts about Momma. And when he stopped thinking about Momma, he thought about Althea. He could not forget. He would never forget how terrible and unsatisfying a lover he was to her. All the support, love, and compassion Althea had bestowed on Abel never resulted in Abel exhibiting any degree of manhood, any degree of sexual prowess. And that is when it started. One failed lovemaking attempt after another, one failed attempt after another to achieve an erection, one premature ejaculation experience after another, reliving the too many to count one-minute-and-done moments he and Althea shared. And that's when it started—the questioning in Abel's mind, the questions whether he should or could love a woman altogether. Or was it just Althea? he asked himself. She certainly was no sensual vixen compared to Flo. It had to be. It had to be Althea's fault. Flo made Abel feel like a man, like a man is supposed to act when bedding a woman. And yet the questions of his sexuality clouded his mind, gave him doubts.

The evening moved slowly as Abel stared out of his coach house window. He was able to count the numerous seemingly patterned stars that laced the clear midnight-hued sky. Minutes passed. The writer's block was overtaking him. The blank pages consumed him. A new chapter meant new thoughts, new ideas, new frustrations. In two hours, he managed to write less than ten words. It has happened to Abel before. More times than he cared to remember. He was trying not to be so hard on himself. It was his first novel. The moments where no creation was being depicted on his paper sent Abel into a myriad of moods: depression, anger, loneliness, despair. A writer who is unable to perform, to create, loses his self-worth. The pages remain blank. His life mirrors emptiness. Even a warm Southern California evening filled with peacefulness and solitude could not trigger inspiration. That is the lifeblood for a writer: inspiration.

Frustrated with his non-productivity, Abel thought a walk in the backyard would clear his mind and give him what he was lacking.

The still of the night was just as it had been while upstairs in his room. A faint distinct cool breeze had started. Abel felt chilled with just his shirt and slacks on. He looked up to the sky as if the words he lacked would fall down on him in an instant. He liked walking in the backyard at night. It was always quiet. The McGregors had trees, landscaping, and an eight-foot solid wood fence surrounding their property. Privacy was never an issue. Abel always felt secure and at peace back there. The solitude allowed him to think and hash out his story lines, the right dialogue for his characters, the perfect emotions he was trying to depict. But not this evening.

There was a particular spot on the coach house that Abel liked to lean on, right next to the entrance door. His solitude abruptly ended. Something or someone was around the corner. The coach house wall resonated with periodic thuds. It startled Abel. His heart began to race. He wanted to gulp but was afraid he might be heard. He reasoned it could not be a raccoon or a deer. Living in the backwoods of Alabama taught him that. His pace was slow. He needed to find out what the noise was. He turned the corner. The glow from the moonlight beamed on the silhouette of Ian. Standing, his head turned up toward the heavens. He was in his own moment. Abel's eyes began to cast downward. A man was on his knees before Ian. Ian's moment was sexual pleasure. The man served up fellatio to Ian as if he performed such an act many times before. Abel leaned on the garage just hard enough to startle Ian and his friend.

"Yessah, heard a noise back here," said Abel.

Ian found Abel's interruption more amusing than embarrassing. On cue, Ian's friend stood up and quickly fixed his shirt and slacks as he brushed by Abel and off the property.

"Good night, Mr. McGregor."

Ian replied, "No, stay."

Abel was not sure what Ian meant by that. What was his motive, he thought. As Ian moved toward him while lighting his after-fellatio cigarette, Abel became more nervous.

"Just wanted to chat a bit," said Ian.

"Fine by me, sir."

There was that smirk again, that smirk that painted Ian's face when he faced Abel alone. He'd never found a Negro man physically attractive before, never saw the striking, artistic, and geometric facial features of a man like Abel.

"You spend a lot of time here in the yard at night?" asked Ian.

"Quite a bit. Good for thinkin'."

Ian continued smirking at Abel between puffs.

"You don't say. Thinking about what?" asked Ian.

Abel paused, pondered Ian's question. It excited Ian watching Abel be so intellectual before him.

"Whatever's on my mind," replied Abel.

"Well, there's an in-depth answer."

They looked at each other as the seconds went by. Ian was amused. Abel, not sure what to say next.

"I did not intend for you to see me in the act as it were," said Ian.

"Didn't see much," replied Abel.

"No, Steven is not very large to begin with."

Ian thought his joke was funny. He got a kick out of it. It was way over Abel's head so he just stood there, not laughing, wearing a blank expression on his face.

"We've never spent much time talking to each other, have we?" asked Ian.

"No, sir."

"Have somewhere to go?" Ian's blue eyes perked up.

"No, sir."

Abel's last response brought a smile to Ian's

face. He wanted to get to know Abel better. He never had the chance—until this evening. A one-on-one conversation with the hired help was rare.

He found Abel very intelligent. Certainly more intelligent than the other servants. He stared intently at Abel. Those seconds felt like hours to Abel. Ian's intensity made him feel uncomfortable. Both men had the same thoughts in their heads. What was next?

The urge to speak to Abel in a blunt manner struck Ian. Abel had that sort of an effect on him. It was always so subtle. Ian never knew when that magical, mystical moment would strike. He thought better not to act on his impulse this evening.

"It's getting late. Good night, Abel."

"Good night, Mr. McGregor."

Abel returned to his coach house apartment with the ocean view. Ian returned to the house to tackle what was perplexing him the entire evening.

Catching Ian in his awkward and embarrassing moment inspired Abel to sit with his notebook. Finally, he found a name for his heroine in his novel. She would be called Cassandra. And now, his chapter had meaning, substance. His hero and heroine met for the first time at a dance for the Negro slaves in Master William's hay barn. From the first time they met, their eyes glistened with reciprocating care and love for each other. Abel smiled as he wrote. He stopped momentarily to allow the tug boat to yell its horn many miles from El Segundo Harbor. The still of the night returned. That flash in which his pencil moved across the paper was illuminating. The glee of accomplishment that painted Abel's face was evident. He had that feeling back inside of him. When a writer writes, when a writer's words are complete and free from error or contradiction, when his thirst for creativity has been quenched, there is no more grand a satisfaction.

Abel had it, the end of his chapter. Robert sat off in a corner of the barn. The dancers before him do-see-doed in a merry fashion. It was the moment Robert's focus centered on the group dancing before him. As he stared, she appeared before him. Her dance moves captivated him, kept his attention for minutes. He felt his breath being sucked away. He could not take his eyes off her, tall, willowy, a smile that outshone the moonlight above. The music ended. Robert stood up. He hoped Cassandra would notice as she moved toward him.

He knew it would be futile. He knew he should, for all practical reasons, just go to bed. Just sleep off the drunken stupor. Ian was hoping that late-night inspiration would beckon. That somehow, someway, his typewriter would be transformed into an active machine, and he could contribute some meaningful dialogue to his incomplete screenplay. All day long, he wrestled with an idea for the second act. The studio had implored him to implement a comedic element to offset the accidental murder that Katherine's character commits. Until now, Universal always portrayed Katherine as the heroine, dutiful wife, or damsel in distress, never as a murderess caught in a scandalous affair. With talking pictures now a reality, Universal Studios felt it was time to broaden Katherine's range to the audience. All of this resulted in intense pressure on Ian. Katherine's picture was Universal's talkie debut. It had to be a smash, a financial bonanza. He was responsible for their first original screenplay, a responsibility he did not want.

To quiet his fears, to soothe his anxiety, to bolster his lost confidence as a writer, he needed Katherine. She had not arrived home. Ian didn't care if it was another boring Hollywood cocktail party or a late-night romp with John Barrymore. He wanted her in bed with him at the moment. Rarely were they ever there for each other. When it was time for passionate sex, always there. Their physical and sensual chemistry knew no bounds. Ian tried to sleep. Midnight had long passed. He was used to Katherine nestled up on him. The soft summer breeze was soothing, a humid air that Ian liked.

His thoughts remain centered on just one point: Not which bed Katherine was in at two o'clock in the morning, not what Von Stroheim said about his screenplay, he thought about James. He missed him. His heart ached with excruciating pain. James had cut off all communication now. He refused to return Ian's phone calls or reply to his letters. It was over. He was gone as if James had passed away. Grieving James's loss consumed Ian. The sadness, the heartbreak painted his face, moistened his eyes. He loved James more than he would ever know.

It was his day. His off day. Abel had already made his plans. After serving the McGregors' breakfast, a bus ride from Brentwood to Jefferson Park, the Negro section of Los Angeles. Lou's Barber Shop was the place where he relaxed, the place he did his writing on his day off. His only duty on his off day was to wash and wipe Ian's Packard before he left for the studio. A cloudless morning gave Abel the hope that the bright sunshine would serve as a catalyst to a productive day to work on his novel.

The sunny Southern California weather always brought the cheerful disposition out of Abel. Today was no different. He was so much in a trance thinking about all that was going well for him, he almost missed his stop and did not exit the bus in time. The bus stopped right in front of Lou's Barber Shop. As he approached the storefront entrance, he was able to peer inside and see that the place was bustling. All was good. The small table and chair where he sat while writing was open and available. Every barber chair was filled, every spare chair taken. Count Basie's Radio City performance was emitting from the radio.

The crowd at Lou's Barber Shop served Abel well. The home-spun stories that flowed freely between 9:00 a.m. and 6:00 p.m. could fill Abel's diary twice over. Time to work. Time to be creative. Abel became nice and snug in his chair. He relieved the notepad from the inside of his coat pocket. Abel had one superstitious quirk. Before he began to write, he would twirl his pencil while licking the lead point. First a thought. The thought ended with a loud roar made by the patrons as Ruby Thompson walked past the barbershop window. The ooohs and aaahs amused Abel.

"What'ya think of that East Coast?" asked Lou.

Abel snickered. His lead needed an additional lick. Seconds seemed like hours while he stared at his empty page. He was working on a new scene. There is a moment where his characters, Cassandra and John, share a touching while walking down a country road. They have known each other for a couple of months. Cassandra has let John know in her own feminine way that she likes him. John is not as reciprocating as fast as Cassandra would like. Not out of arrogance. Not out of conceit. He is shy. Unsure of himself as a man. Abel was pouring himself into John's character. He thought back to the so many awkward moments he and Althea had back home. As much as he wanted to write, he was having trouble. Writer's block had shown up. Not today. Not on his off day. The one day he had to himself. The one day he did not have to cater to the McGregors, or listen to Mabel's rants about what he could not become because of the color of his skin. Whenever it was time to inject a more personal feel for John with respect to his personal self, Abel had trouble finding those exact words. He was looking for the exact words in his mind. Words for his fear. Words for his doubts. Words that questioned his sexuality.

"No, cut!"
Bruce Humberstone, the director of Katherine's film, was not pleased with the scene.

"Let's do it again, shall we?"

When he heard Humberstone repeat those words a fourth time, Ian's eyes were drawn to Katherine. She was standing off in a corner alone, attempting to compose herself. Humberstone was a task master. Katherine was used to the soft touch by a director such as Cukor or Van Dyke. Not the abrasive sort like Humberstone. Leammle liked Humberstone. Their families emigrated from the same village in Germany. Humberstone also understood budget and time. He was very adept at getting a picture completed. Completed and on time within the prescribed budget. The Leammles loved him for that. Ian could see by the way Katherine puffed on her cigarette that she was unnerved. Sound stage number 9 was Katherine's favorite. It was where she made all of her greatest successes. If it was not for Lon Chaney and Katherine, Universal Studios would have been bankrupt years earlier. Ian had Katherine's rewrites in his pocket. He wanted to show them to her before his meeting with Junior later that afternoon. He decided to walk over and say hello. It only took him a few steps to halt in his tracks. Humberstone was now in the corner, giving Katherine a stern talking to. His voice became raised.

"Are you an actress or not, Miss Edmonds?"

The entire crew heard him yelling at Katherine. Ian didn't like it, but he knew it was part of the business. A director will try any and all tricks in his bag to inspire an actor to a better performance. Ian did not know Humberstone personally. He sat in on a couple of poker games at Mack Sennett's home when Humberstone was present. He saw Humberstone place his hand on Katherine's shoulder. His voice had become murmured, subdued. Perhaps he was being encouraging, Ian thought. He did not like Humberstone sliding his hand down the small of Katherine's back and placing it on her butt. It was a quick gesture. Long enough for Ian to steam up. He stopped himself, refusing to allow a jealous impulse to enter his body. It was part of the pact Katherine and Ian had forged together. No jealous tantrums over or about any of their extramarital excursions. He was sure that Humberstone was not one of Katherine's lovers. He was aware of Chaplin and Barrymore. He knew about the long weekend to Catalina Island she took with Valentino. About that night at Hearst's estate in San Simeon when she left their bedroom to be with a young, unknown, big-eared actor named Gable.

With their conference over, Ian walked over to Katherine. He wanted to encourage her. Be a friend. He wasn't sure what he would say to her. He grabbed the rewrites out of his pocket and rolled them up in his hand. He took his time so that Katherine had a few extra moments for herself.

"I say Humberstone can be a bloody twit," said Ian.

Ian's remark brought a slight smile to Katherine's face. For a moment she relaxed.

"How long have you been here?" asked Katherine.

"Maybe forty-five minutes. Enough to see your last eight takes."

Katherine loved and respected Ian's bluntness about her acting.

"That bad, huh?"
Ian replied, "I wouldn't say that. Relax, you can play this role in your sleep."

Ian kissed Katherine gently. It made her feel better. They held hands and took a minute to exchange a look of love.

"I have something for you, my sweet," said Ian.
"Is it better than a bread box?"
Ian replied, "No, but perhaps just as enjoyable."

Ian placed his rewrites in Katherine's hand. She unraveled the notes and began to read his work. Ian tried to read Katherine's reaction, hoping for the most minute clue that she liked what he had written. Sitting in a studio exec's office waiting for a response to your work can twist a writer's insides into numerable knots. That same anxiety was attempting to overpower Ian. He needed someone—anyone—to love his work. He needed the rejection to end. He needed to feel that with the advent of talkies, the introduction of the written screenplay, he could survive and be a success as a writer in Hollywood.

"Well, I am waiting with bated breath," said Ian.

Katherine looked up from Ian's notes. She was perplexed, unsure what to tell Ian.

"Have you shown these to Junior?" asked Katherine.

"No, we have a meeting this afternoon," said Ian.

Katherine re-rolled Ian's notes and softly placed them back in his hands.

"I have to get back to work. I'll see you at home tonight."

Katherine walked away as Ian stood dumbfounded. The cameras for the next shot rolled into place. The stage lights were turned on. The actors blocked their movements on the set for the next scene. Humberstone talked to his crew one last time before ordering the cameras to roll. It was as if Ian was not there. He was hurt. Hurt that Katherine didn't even offer an opinion of his rewrites. He now was afraid. Afraid that Katherine would not support his work in front of Leammle. Afraid that Katherine might go so far and demand a new writer. First a feeling of rejection. Next a feeling of betrayal. The quiet was interrupted by the voice of the assistant director yelling, "Quiet on the set." Ian slithered toward the door. No one noticed his exit. It was another example of his anonymity among his peers, his colleagues, even his wife.

Abel had not written much. Almost the whole day had been spent doodling, twirling the lead of his pencil in his mouth, and transcribing obscure notes that made very little sense. Cassandra and John were nowhere near having a relationship than this morning when Abel sat down. It frustrated him. He has tried desperately to tie John's sexual inadequacies with his own. Parallel the frustrations of Cassandra with Althea. It did not work. The shadows from the sun had changed. It was now late afternoon. The summer sun continued to illuminate the barbershop. Plenty of natural light to help Abel with his writer's block. The view out the window didn't help him with his motivation. A mother walked by with her young son. A teenage girl chasing her younger brother down the block. Two cars stopped in the middle of the street for no apparent reason. And then quickly his view outside became quiet. A man's voice towering over him interrupted his concentration.

"Excuse me."

Abel looked up. He didn't recognize him. But the man looked at Abel as though he had seen him before.

"Sorry, my man, can't place the face," said Abel. "You don't remember me, douz you?"

Abel shook his head no. He became a bit nervous. He didn't know the gentleman standing before him. He left his eyes on his hands.

"May I set fer a spell?" asked the man.

Abel nodded yes. The man sat. Still nervous, he sensed something unpleasant was going to happen.

"You Isaiah Johnson's brotha, ain't 'u?"
"Yes. How did you know me?" asked Abel.
"I'm Orpheus. Your brotha helped me a while back."

It was coming back to Abel. He recognized the face this time. He didn't have a black eye. His lips were healed, not the size of a balloon when he saw him back in Harlem.

"What brings you to Los Angeles, Mr. . . . Mr. . . . ?"
"Orpheus Banks," replied the man.

Abel wanted to ask him how Isaiah was getting along. Almost a year had passed. Almost a year had passed since he skipped out of Flo's house in the middle of the night to run away from Isaiah. Abel knew Isaiah would never forgive him for sleeping with Flo. He knew all too well he was also prone to periods of violence. He listened intently as Orpheus spoke in glowing terms about Isaiah. The words entered his ears, but his mind was back in Harlem. Abel was waiting for the right moment.

"Hear from Isaiah lately?" asked Abel.
"Since when?" replied Orpheus.

Abel appeared startled. A bad feeling engulfed him. Something wrong had happened, he thought.

"You ain't heard, have you?" asked Orpheus.
Abel asked, "Heard what?"
Orpheus replied, "Isaiah doing a thirty-year stretch in Sing Sing."

Abel's heart sunk to his stomach. He shook his head for seconds. His remaining brother was now in prison.

"What happened?" asked Abel.
"Killed his girlfriend Flo. Strangled her one night."

The news visibly shook Abel throughout his entire body. It was the wrong time to express a great outpour of grief, and yet he did hide the fact how hurt he was.

"Why?" asked Abel.
Orpheus replied, "Don't nobody know for sure. He

went over there one night. They started to fightin'
and arguin'. He killed her. That's all I know."

Abel knew why. It was because of him. It was
because he was sleeping with Flo. It wasn't for love.
It wasn't for sex. Flo was trying to make Abel feel
like a man. Make him believe that his doubts about
his orientation were unfounded. The sex with Flo
just confused him further. Abel's guilt over Flo's
murder was too much to comprehend at the time.
Instantly his pencil, pad, and belongings were in
his hand as he bolted out the barbershop.

There was nothing for Ian to do but wait. To just
sit there and wait. Fifteen minutes. Thirty minutes.
Forty-five minutes. Ian felt Leammle was being
unreasonably cruel, making him sit in his office,
waiting for him. Cigarette number 3 was just about
finished. He contemplated lighting up a fourth. He
wouldn't have to. Leammle walked into his office.

"Sorry for being late. The dailies from Browning's
picture were awful."

Ian said nothing. He wasn't interested in
Browning's picture. Todd Browning's future with
Universal was secure. Ian's concern was focused on
his future. Leammle took his seat behind his big,
oval mahogany desk.

"Cigar?" asked Leammle.

Ian shook his head no. He wanted to get right
down to business.

"Understand you let Katherine see my rewrites,"
said Ian.
"I did," replied Leammle.

"Any particular reason why?"

Junior replied, "It's her picture. She has first refusal for the script."

Leammle's response did not sit well with Ian. He felt Leammle should have given his feedback first to him. It was evident to Ian that Leammle and Universal Studios' loyalties were with Katherine. Ian was seething inside. The silence in the office added to his contempt.

"I saw Katherine on the sound stage. Humberstone is giving her a tough go," said Ian.

Junior replied, "Humberstone is a tough SOB."

They seemed to nod in agreement. For the past several months, Ian and Leammle have not been in agreement on many things. Especially the direction Katherine's script was developing under Ian's hand. Ian was not there to talk about Humberstone's treatment of Katherine.

"Katherine wants to see some major changes. I am inclined to agree with her," said Leammle.

"As for instance?" asked Ian.

Leammle replied, "She wants more humor. Especially that scene in the second act."

Ian's blood simmered. He felt the scenes involving Katherine in the ice cream shop were hilarious. Some of his best work. And now Leammle was siding with Katherine that a rewrite was in order. Another rewrite. It will be the fourth one.

"I just don't know what you expect from me," said Ian.

Leammle replied, "I expect you to write a screenplay that is excellent. Top drawer. Your best work. A screenplay that will make Universal's first talkie a big success. That is what I expect."

Those seconds Ian and Leammle stared at each other seemed like minutes. Leammle issued the ultimate challenge. Give him exactly what he wanted. Even if Ian was full of fear and doubt in his ability to deliver what Leammle demanded, he was never going to let him see it in his face.

"So we understand each other," said Leammle.

So Ian did what he always did. He smirked back, rose from his chair preparing to exit.

"No worries, mate."

He gave Leammle a wink of confidence and walked out of his office.

14

The setting of the sun began many hours earlier. It was peacefully quiet. The McGregors were tucked in their bed. Abel's writing session ended a long time earlier. He was alone in his room. Alone with his thoughts. He allowed his mind to take him wherever it wanted to. On this night, at 2:00 a.m., his mind and thoughts found Althea. He was thinking of her and that night before he left for New York. The last night he and Althea spent together. Those hours, one after another, he failed to achieve an erection. He kept telling Althea he was tired. But he knew otherwise. He wasn't feeling attracted to her. Not just Althea, but any woman. For the first time Abel wondered whether he was supposed to be attracted to a woman, or was he supposed to be attracted to men. That last night left him confused. Those evenings with Flo only left him more confused. Flo took it upon herself, trying to rescue Abel from himself. To help him before he made the fatal mistake of declaring himself a homosexual. He wanted to cry. He did cry. Before he knew it, his pillow had soaked itself with his own tears. He wanted to erase the flashback.

Unable to make love to Althea, he bolted from the bed and dressed hurriedly. Not even Althea's uncontrollable sobbing was enough of a deterrent to stop him. He wanted to leave. He was embarrassed, tired, frustrated, angry at himself. He was confused, wasn't even sure he even belonged there. Standing there facing a beautiful, naked woman sprawled across clean white sheets, he begged Althea to find another man.

"I ain't capable of lovin' no woman back."

Althea didn't believe him. Althea thought Abel's erection issues were brought on by his nervousness and anxiety about his trip to New York. She would never been able to fathom that Abel was not capable of sexually making love to a woman. Not in the current frame he was in. As he made his way out of the bedroom, through Althea's house and out the door, all he could here was Althea yelling at him, cursing him.

"Abel Johnson, you ain't no real man. A man who can't get himself ready to love a woman ain't no real man."

As he moved across the field, Althea stood on her front porch yelling at Abel. "You ain't no real man." Her words took residence in his head long after he reached his own home. He didn't want Momma to see how visibly shaken he was. He sat, wanting to be alone, not wanting to share his inner turmoil. Not wanting to explore his inadequacy.

It was if he woke up from a dream. But it wasn't a dream. It was for real. The feelings were real for Abel. The feeling of confusion. The feeling of helplessness. His watch now read 3:00 a.m. Tomorrow's wake-up was set for 6. Close your eyes, he said to himself.

He was close. The screenplay was almost finished. Like the thoroughbred that sprints around the far turn heading into the home stretch, after months, Ian sniffed the finish line. He had locked himself in his den all day, and he liked what he had written. He didn't care who else did. Ten pages to go, he proclaimed to himself. A sense of pride beckoned. A sense of accomplishment filled his spirit of nostalgia. Those moments right after he finished one of his plays on Broadway. When he was the toast of New York, swimming in the same circles as Eugene O'Neil and Edna Ferber.

The sound emanating from Ian's den had not been there in weeks. Perhaps it was the intense pressure he felt trying to complete Katherine's script. Trying to make something great out of something mediocre. Perhaps it was the looks Katherine cast upon him during breakfast that was making him feel inadequate. Not as a man, a lover, a husband. But as a writer. That hurt him most. The knock on his door interrupted his writer's creativity. It was Abel with the afternoon mail.

"Your mail, sir," said Abel.
"Toss it over there."

Abel didn't toss it but softly placed it next to Ian's typewriter. As quietly as he entered, he exited. Ian took a moment to glance at the envelope on top. He noticed the name on the return addressee portion. It was from James. For a moment, he thought, he hoped James was writing to tell him what a fool he had been. That he wanted another try at their relationship. Ian hoped James was writing for forgiveness for his nastiness, his cold-heartedness, his betrayal. At one fell swoop, Ian ripped the envelope open and yanked out James's letter. His heart raced over a hundred miles per hour. The beads of sweat on his brow and the moistness in his hands made him feel like a wet sponge. He wanted to take his time and read slowly.

Ian,

You have failed to either pay attention to my words (stop) or my unresponsiveness. I will be brief and blunt. Do not call me. Do not suddenly pop over to my flat for anymore visits. Do not write me anymore letters. Do not send me anymore packages to the studio. Leave me be. If you want to prove you can be friends to a man, it will have to be someone else. You and I can never be friends. This is the absolute last time you will hear from me. I will not respond. Period. I have moved on in my life. You must do the same.

James

Ian softly folded James's letter up and placed it in his pocket. He knew then he would never hear from James again. It would have to be as though he has died. As if he had passed away. Sadness engulfed Ian. He had lost a person he loved very much. Perhaps more than he loved Katherine. He could not help it. Overcome with grief, he cried uncontrollably. His sobs reigned throughout the house, almost assuredly alarming the servants. He didn't care if the servants heard him. His pain, his anguish was too severe. He stopped long enough to ask himself how he could feel "loss" when it was apparent he never had James's heart or his love. In order to feel loss, you have to lose something or someone that was at one time in your possession. James's heart, his love was never in Ian's possession. James was never going to see Ian as anything more than fun, frolic, a good time, a holiday. And when the fun and frolic was over for James, he was over Ian. It became painfully obvious to Ian that it was just too, too many never(s) for him to overcome. And he cried once more. He stopped. He wanted to respond. He wanted to put down his feelings while they were fresh in his mind and heart. He used the back of James's letter to write.

My Dearest James,

It would have been much too easy to walk away and say nothing. For me to ignore what you have written. What you have expressed to me. In essence, your true feelings and how you have always felt about me. I could not say goodbye to someone I loved deeply with all of my heart, all of my soul, all of my inner being, by simply walking away. Walking away without letting you know how I truly felt about you. You will never know just how much I loved you so. In James-esque fashion, you did your very best to hurt me, belittle me, make me feel as worthless, useless, and insignificant as one can. Bravo, my friend, bravo. I loved you very much. All that I did, all that I endured, all that I bestowed onto you I did because I loved you very much. Alas, dear James, I could not make you love me back, could I? You said leave you be. I shall. You said stop calling. I will. You said stop coming to your flat unannounced. As you wish. You said stop sending you packages. I understand. You said stop loving you. No, James, that I cannot do. I shall always love you. If it was so damn easy to stop loving someone, then it was never really love in the first place. Shakespeare's Hamlet once said, "Even our loves should with our fortunes change. As our lives change, so must our love." All the best, my Cockney bedfellow.

Ian

He was done. He folded up the letter, now filled with sentiment on both sides. The letter went back into his shirt pocket. Ian sat at his desk, staring out the window. He remembered a line he once wrote in one of his Broadway plays, "To be in love means to give someone permission to break your heart, but trusting them that they won't." From that moment on, he knew he would have to proceed through life without James. For ten months everyday communication. Phone calls, meetings, telegrams, scented letters, intimate rendezvous on Catalina Island. And without warning, he is betrayed. His lover walks away and ceases all communication with him. Strange, he thought, how you can spend ten months with a man and not know the first thing about him.

That next scene for the screenplay needed to be written. He was ready to write. He was willing. But the words stopped. The *clackety-clack* ended. He became angry at himself. Should have never opened that bloomin' letter, he thought. The headache reappeared. Ian stood up and began pacing the den. With each lap, he grabbed the whiskey bottle. With each lap, the swigs off the malt scotch became bigger. With each lap, his headache became more excruciating. Too excruciating for him to endure. The pain dropped him to his knees. He murmured a long and drawn-out moan. In an instant, Ian found himself passed out on the floor.

Mabel was just finishing the dinner dishes when Abel entered the kitchen, fresh from wiping down the McGregors' cars. It was customary for Mabel to prepare a small snack for Abel. The usual, half a ham sandwich and coffee.

"'Bout time you finished washin' them cars," said Mabel.

"You gettin' paid for opinions or to clean?"

Mabel hated when Abel smart-mouthed her. Her tone suggested she was in no mood for back talk.

"Make yo'self useful, college boy, and fetch them dishes out the library. Mr. McGregor been in there since this afternoon. I wanna finish this here kitchen 'fore my eight o'clock radio program come on."

Abel stood and stared back at Mabel. He was contemplating to reciprocate with a flippant remark.

"I ain't gots all night, boy, now get."

Abel voted not to say anything and left. He had his own plans. He wanted to get back to the coach house and work on his novel. He had finally come up with a way to bring John and Cassandra closer together. He would have Cassandra become stricken with a virus. An infection that renders her bedridden. John takes care of her. Nurses her back to health. At that point John realizes he is in love with Cassandra. Easy when you know how, Abel thought.

Abel entered the library. He did not immediately see Ian. What he did see was a chaotic mess. A cigarette was lying in an ashtray. It had burned itself from one end to the other, filling the room with a haze of cloudy smoke. The whiskey bottle was tilted over its side and had been slowly dripping itself onto the oak desktop and the expensive imported rug from China. The lunch tray hardly touched. Two bites out of the sandwich; the soup was now cold. He didn't even touch Mabel's delicious-tasting chocolate fudge that he loved.

As he stepped farther into the den, there he found Ian, passed out on the floor. A tattered mess. His loud, drunken snore only assured Abel that he wasn't dead. Several more steps found him at Ian's desk. It was his task to commence cleaning up. He did so promptly. The area around Ian's typewriter needed picking up as well. Countless number of balled- up paper surrounded the entire area. It was at that moment Abel noticed Ian's screenplay. He noticed the title, *"Another Man's Poison."* The temptation to read his boss' creation overcame him. Page 1. Page 20. Page 67, and so on. Ian's snoring became distinctively louder. And now Abel thought the unthinkable. How he could improve upon what Ian had already written. The ideas that filled his head were numerous. He was tempted. Abel felt it was a way he could help Ian. He took that moment to glance down at him. For the first time, he saw Ian as someone more than just his employer. He saw him as a man that he admired. He cared for him. Felt pathos for him.

He saw a man curled up like a baby on the floor, sleeping off a drunken stupor. He saw him as attractive, as good-looking. A metamorphosis began inside of Abel. A degree of affection saturated his soul. His affection became his motive to want to sit down and retype Ian's screenplay. Punch up the weak dialogue. Realign the scene sequences. And so he sat. Reading. Retyping. *Clickety-clack. Clickety-clack.* Reading. *Clickety-clack, clickety-clack.* Ian was so filled with booze, sleep deprivation, and aspirin for his headache, he didn't move one muscle. Abel liked what he had written. He amazed himself at how he was so easily able to adapt, edit, and create from what Ian had produced. The screenplay became better. The story sprung a life on its own.

Abel had never written a screenplay. *Not ever. I can be good at this*, he thought. More *clickety-clack. Clickety-clack*. An occasional peek at Ian confirmed he had not budged an inch. He stared at Ian once more. Was that his heart going *ping*? he wondered. It never went *ping* for Althea. It never went *ping* for any woman. He chose not to explore his newfound feelings for his boss. His creative juices flowed like it never had before, not even when he worked on his own material. Without his being conscious of it, the evening had spun into the wee hours of the morning. As he read the final pages, two things overcame him: a feeling of accomplishment and a feeling of hope. That Ian never notices what he had done to his screenplay.

Whenever you do something for someone you care for, there is an inner working of happiness. Not only for yourself, but for the person you steer your good work toward. You want to be acknowledged. Perhaps one day reciprocation will be bestowed back onto you. And so, *Another Man's Poison* by Ian McGregor was complete. There would be no "by" line for Abel. Not ever. He would have to carry his secret for eternity. The secret. His secret. He helped a man he suddenly and inexplicably had grown fond of, attracted to, subconsciously desired in an intimate way. Ian's clock in the den softly struck 3:00 a.m. He grabbed Ian's pages that he substituted his own for and tucked them under his arm. As he tiptoed out, he turned to look at Ian. He gave Ian his first warm and faint smile. The door softly closed behind him.

The morning sun shone brightly through the Venetian blinds of Ian's den. This time he did hear the clock strike. It struck 7:00 a.m. Ian rolled over onto his back and allowed the dribble of saliva to roll down the side of his mouth. He lay there for a moment to get his bearings. To remind himself what day it was. It was not the first time he had passed out on the floor of his den. He knew the routine well. Lie there and stare at the ceiling while he worked the cobwebs out of his head. He managed to rise to his knees and move forward toward his desk. A cigarette beckoned, inviting him to smoke it. Ian obliged, and as he held the cigarette in one hand and rubbed his head with the other, he glanced over to his screenplay. It was stacked neatly next to his typewriter. It looked complete. Finished. Ian couldn't recall exactly what time he finished writing. He managed to get himself on his two feet. His pace toward the window was a slow, stumbled one. As he gazed out the window, he saw Abel helping Katherine bring groceries in the house. He smiled as he admired how broad and strong Abel's shoulders looked in his white servant's jacket. His smile quickly turned into a pained expression. He remembered James's letter was still in his shirt pocket. He took a moment to place his hand where the letter snuggled his breast pocket. He dare not read it again. Instead, he replayed the words in his mind. As if they were lyrics to a song playing off a record from his phonograph. It was enough to moisten his eyes. He could still see Abel unloading the car. His cigarette was now finished. He extinguished it using the windowsill and walked back to his desk. Ian smiled. Seeing the words "screenplay by Ian McGregor" made him feel very proud. He picked up his script, began flipping through the pages. One pause, to study a particular scene. A quizzical look painted his face. Yes, that's what I meant to write, he thought. He smiled. Smiled broadly. He liked it all. He couldn't wait to throw his work into Katherine and Leammle's face. The two people who doubted him the most. The two people who never thought he could manage to not only finish it, but produce an excellent body of work at the same time. Laemmle, at Katherine's behest, had already lined up a couple of writers in case Ian fell flat on his face.

As he exited the den to head toward the breakfast nook, he decided in his mind not to gloat. To wait until Katherine had read it. He entered the breakfast nook and found Katherine having her morning coffee and toast.

"Good morning, my darling."

Ian kissed Katherine on her rosy cheek. The Cheshire grin on his face could not be hidden.

"Something the matter?" asked Katherine.
"I am full of vim and sparkle."

He placed his screenplay on the table before Katherine.

"Have you finished?" asked Katherine.
"Yes, it's done."

Just a moment to glance at each other. A moment for Ian to look proud. A moment for Katherine to look skeptical.

"Off for a shower."

Ian left. Katherine grabbed her reading glasses and began reading. The subsequent glow on her face suggested she was enjoying whatever she was reading. She even found a scene to smile and snicker at. Finally, something funny and clever, she thought. She continued reading. Continued flipping through the pages. Continued to be engrossed.

"More coffee, ma'am?"

Katherine, so mesmerized with Ian's screenplay, did not hear Abel enter the breakfast nook.

"I'm sorry, no, thank you."

"Will Mr. McGregor be having breakfast?" asked Abel.

Katherine replied, "I am not sure. Give him two three-minute eggs, bacon, and toast."

"Very good, Mrs. McGregor."

Katherine did not look up out of the screenplay. She was riveted. Abel checked the hot plates to see if more bacon for Ian would be needed. Every few seconds, he would glance over his shoulder, trying to get a reaction from Katherine. As if on cue, she bellowed out with a loud laugh. Abel was proud of what he had done. If his writing could please Katherine, if she had harbored no doubt in her mind that the work was Ian's, then he accomplished what he set out to do. Another chuckle erupted out of Katherine. She closed the screenplay and cradled it against her bosom. "It appears we have a hit," said Katherine, not realizing Abel was still in the room. Abel watched Katherine rise from her seat and leave the breakfast nook. Ian's screenplay remained nestled against her chest. Mabel stuck her head in.

"Is Mr. McGregor eatin' breakfast this mornin'?"

Abel replied, "Two three-minute eggs, bacon, toast, coffee."

That was all Mabel needed to hear. A little extra pep in his step while cleaning the breakfast nook. He believed in his heart he had done a noble thing in helping Ian. It was his hope that his endeavor would relieve some of the pressure Katherine had placed on Ian. He was very happy working for the McGregors. He was very happy not to be working on the trains. He was happy that his novel was moving along well. And then, suddenly, he stopped being happy. He stopped feeling excited about the way his life was moving. He thought about his brother, Isaiah. His older brother who was doing thirty years in Sing Sing Prison. Thirty years for murdering Flo. Because of what he had done. Slept with his brother's woman. It was the ultimate betrayal, he thought. No one was present to see his eyes water with sadness, with grief for his self-perceived sins.

Ian leapt out of the shower. He knew in his heart it was going to be one of the best days he will experience in a long time. He stood before the mirror, drying off, combing his golden hair. Not even the sight of a gray hair nestled along his temple would discourage him today. He merrily hummed an old Scottish song his father Angus once taught him. Without him noticing, Katherine was behind him in the reflection, clutching his screenplay as it was her own. Ian turned and faced her.

"Hello again."
"I wanted to tell you I think your screenplay is wonderful," said Katherine.

Ian smiled. He had not heard Katherine compliment his writing in many months. There was a time he would share all that he wrote with her. But not anymore. She became too critical. His drinking did not help, but Ian always dismissed his boozing as a legitimate reason why his worked had slipped. It was evident that Katherine's opinion mattered to him very much.

"It's a hit. I am sure of it," said Katherine.

"I am afraid our two opinions won't matter. Junior and Universal have to love it as well."

Katherine replied, "Junior is going to fall madly in love with it. You have your zeal back, my darling. It's New York, it's Broadway all over again."

"Fancy that," said Ian.
"You're going to make your loving wife a big star in talkies."

Katherine moved closer to Ian. She opened her robe, exposing all that was Katherine. With each kiss, their bodies felt each other's warmth. Happiness was back in their lives once more.

15

Picture-perfect. Another picture-perfect, cloudless bright and sunny afternoon was smothering Southern California. Abel had exactly three hours before his customary late-afternoon drive down Sunset Boulevard to pick up the McGregors at the studio. Today was a writing day. Abel stretched across his bed. His shoes off, his servant's jacket unbuttoned to the waist. A comfortable pose and moment. He loved his coach house room. It provided him the quiet and privacy he desired. Cornelia and the other servants had to leave for their own homes at the end of their workday. Not Abel. The other servants were envious and jealous of Abel. He had the least seniority, but there he was. Occupying the coach house apartment. All to himself. He had quickly become Ian's favorite, Katherine's do-it-all servant. Invaluable to both.

Abel liked what he had written. He wanted to take his story in a different direction. Thoughts of Isaiah in Sing Sing was the fuel for his inspiration. His next chapter involves John and Cassandra in bed together. John picks that moment to tell Cassandra about his fifteen months on a chain-gang in Georgia. Before moving to Alabama, John was a young man living with his grandmother just north of Valdosta, Georgia. There was nothing to eat that day. He was starving. His younger brother Enis was starving. His older sister Hazel was starving. A potato and one three-week-old carrot was all they had. To that day John could not rationally explain to Cassandra why he picked that day that time to attempt to steal a chicken from Chester Taylor's henhouse. There was no mistake. John knew his motive. Starvation. Intense hunger. Starvation for his family. He had to have that chicken at all cost. He knew Chester Taylor would be in the south field all afternoon. One chicken missing from thirty or forty was not going to be missed, he reckoned. What he didn't know was that Sheriff Timmons would be visiting Chester that afternoon to return his hunting rifle. As he emerged from the henhouse, there standing in his uniform and dark-rimmed glasses was Sheriff Timmons. The wrong time, plus the wrong place, equaled months of donning cufflinks and ankle shackles made of steel.

"Clark, we can't meet like this anymore."

Katherine was ending it. Her affair with Clark had run its course. He was a married man. She was married to Ian. Despite the total understanding she and Ian had about their extramarital affairs, guilt always plagued Katherine. Sex with another man was always in retaliation to one of Ian's trysts with his playmates. Clark was also ten years younger. Clark was a neophyte at MGM. There was something ruggedly handsome about him she found attractive. He had a husky voice, big ears, and was not well endowed, but she liked him and found Clark amusing.

"Missy, don't you like the fun we havin'?" asked Clark. He always called Katherine Missy.

Katherine replied, "Yes, grand fun. But the fun is now over. You are under contract with MGM. You are just getting started. Mr. Mayer and Thalberg love to keep close tabs on their actors. The operative word here is investment."

"I'm in the chips, Missy. Start shooting my first picture in two days. A Western called *The Painted Desert*," said Clark.

"How nice. Do I know the director?" asked Katherine.

"William Boyd."

Katherine replied, "Not one of L.B.'s top directors, but he will do a serviceable job."

Clark firmly grabbed Katherine by the shoulders. A wrestling match ensued. He wanted more. Letting Katherine go was not Clark's intention at the moment. He wanted more. Katherine had a 4:00 p.m. call at the studio to shoot night exterior scenes. Career first, she said to herself. It helped her quicken her pace to dress and leave.

Ian sat before Laemmle, feeling very proud and full of himself. The head of Universal Studios was patting him on the back for a job well done. Ian's screenplay was now in pre-production phase. His mind roamed. He contemplated his next move. He was feeling he had acquired the necessary leverage.

"The big bosses in New York are happy with the script, my boy."

Ian replied sarcastically, "I'm so happy they're happy."

Laemmle had not smiled at Ian in months. It was a long time coming between credible writing work submitted by his top writer. Laemmle felt it was the right time to reach into his desk and pull out a treatment for Ian to read.

"What have we here?" asked Ian.

"Swashbuckler," replied Laemmle. Ian liked the title *Captain's Cove*. "Lon has agreed to star. We want you to write the script."

Ian knew immediately the implications to all that Laemmle was saying to him. It meant that the studio star, Lon Chaney, had specifically requested Ian to write the script. What it meant was that he had arrived. Ian flipped through several pages of the treatment.

"Yes, I see the possibilities."

"We start shooting in sixty days," said Laemmle.

"Blimey, sixty days?" asked Ian.

"Yes, can you do it?"

"Not so fast, Junior," said Ian. "I thought we might have a chat first."

"What about?"

"About me directing *Another Man's Poison*."

Laemmle tempted himself not to bellow out with a loud laugh. A ridiculous notion, he thought. He just chuckled in Ian's face. Ian was not laughing back. He was serious. He saw it all as an opportunity to do more than be just a writer. Laemmle's smirk was lifted off his face when Ian didn't budge.

"My God, you're serious, aren't you?"

"As a bloody heart attack," replied Ian. Immediately thereafter, tension had announced itself present in the office.

"No, can't be done. DeCava is all set to direct. Besides, your wife picked DeCava."

Ian stood taller in his chair. "Then break the contract. I'll have a chat with me wife. I am ready to direct a bloody picture. It's my turn."

Laemmle rose from behind his large oakwood desk and circled it until he found himself facing Ian.

"My boy, this is our first talkie. Every nickel Universal can beg, borrow, steal goes into this picture."

Ian sat stone-faced, his right leg crossed over the left. He switched. Left leg over right. "Have you a cigarette?"

Laemmle obliged him, reaching into his pocket and softly tossing the pack to Ian.

"Katherine will have to approve you as director. It's her picture."

Ian lit up his cigarette. Drag. Puff. Drag. Puff.

"Well, why wouldn't she want me to direct her picture? After all, I'm her husband."

Laemmle replied, "This isn't one of your productions on Broadway, and I am not Ziegfield. The way a scene is blocked. The way we shoot it. The way a scene is edited. We need someone with experience within our silent division. DeCava has experience. You do not."

Ian's voice became terse.

"Look here, you don't want Variety getting wind that your top scenarist was leaving for RKO or MGM over a tizzy."

"No director deal, Ian. I'm sorry," said Laemmle.

"Have you forgotten Katherine's contact is up in six months? No, of course, you haven't. We will walk out the doors together. She will go wherever I go."

"Care to wager on that?" asked Laemmle.

Ian replied, "Do you? Think of it in these terms. The husband-wife duo of Ian McGregor and Katherine Edmonds brings happiness to an audience of millions while filling the silk-lined coffers of Universal Studios."

It was Laemmle's turn to puff hard on his cigarette.

"You think you've got it all figured out, don't you?" asked Laemmle.

Ian replied, "We serve others best when at the same time we serve ourselves."

It was a seemingly easy scene to shoot. According to the script, all Katherine had to do was walk down the dimly lit street on stage 9. A brisk pace for several feet. Then, she hears a noise she does not recognize. She becomes startled. Simple for an actress of Katherine's caliber. Today it would not be so easy. Katherine stumbled, fell, and skinned her knee on the sidewalk.

"Cut!" yelled the director.

The assistant director ran to Katherine's aid. He

helped her up. Just a scratch and a small trickle of blood. The director stood in front of the cast and crew, yelling out the next direction.

"Let's break for lunch. Let Katherine get cleaned up. I want everyone back on the set in one hour. We will pick it up with scene 16."

The cast and crew dispersed. The stage lighting was turned off. Max the caterer rolled in with his sandwiches and coffee. Katherine, with the aid of the assistant director, hobbled to her dressing room.

Katherine's dressing room was larger than most. Her status as the reigning queen of the silent era rated such opulence. Long, plush suede couch and lounge chair. A dressing mirror twice its normal size. Dressing room closet large enough it could easily fill three weeks' worth of wardrobe. Ian stood lurking in the shadows, smoking a cigarette while waiting for Katherine. His eyes panned across Katherine's dressing room. Gazing at every artifact, at every piece of memorabilia that represented her illustrious film career. That reminded him how big a star she was, and how insignificant his writing career had become. He began to smoke his second cigarette when Katherine entered with the help of the assistant director.

"Just take me to my dressing table, Harold," said Katherine.

"Is there anything else I can get you, Miss Edwards?"

Katherine replied, "Be a good soul and bring me a cup of tea, please."

The assistant director nodded his head yes and walked out of the dressing room. Katherine sat before her mirror. Her first thoughts were directed toward the swelling in her injured ankle. Those thoughts quickly vanished as her sense of smell kicked in. Someone was smoking in her dressing room.

"Hello, my darling."

"Ian, you startled me. What are you doing here?" replied Katherine.

Ian walked over to Katherine and kissed her softly on her lips.

"Have you another cigarette, darling?" asked Katherine.

Ian placed his cigarette into Katherine's mouth.

"So, what brings you here?" asked Katherine.

"To gloat. I wanted to share some wonderful news," replied Ian.

The Cheshire grin that painted Ian's face was as loud and glaring as a neon sign in Times Square. Ian stood before Katherine, not saying anything. He wanted Katherine to guess.

"I gather we are playing some sort of guessing game," said Katherine.

Ian softly grabbed the cigarette out of Katherine's mouth for a few puffs.

"Junior gave me the green light to direct your picture," said Ian.

"You must be joking."

Ian took a drag off the cigarette and blew out the smoke as he shook his head no.

"I'm your man."

Katherine said, "This can't be. DeCava is supposed to direct. Why, why you have no experience directing a picture. This is my *first* talkie."

Ian replied, "Apparently Junior is not concerned with my inexperience. The director's chair and my screenplay is a package deal."

Katherine struggled to lift herself out of her chair. She wanted to stand and face Ian eye-to-eye. With her heels on, she and Ian stood six feet tall. Not at this moment. The pain in Katherine's ankle left her shoeless.

"Darling, we are talking about my career," said Katherine.

"It's my career too," said Ian.

Katherine believed in Ian. She believed in what she thought was Ian's screenplay. What she believed was Ian's own words, his own creation. She was astute to know that by having Ian as her director, the picture would continue to have her stamp all over it. Everything would still be under her control, including Ian. Ian felt Katherine's arms around his neck.

"Darling, you know that I love you very much."

Ian replied, "Prove it to me. Give me your stamp of approval. Show that you believe in me."

"I'll do better than that."

The stamp of approval turned into a kiss of approval. The stamp of approval turned into an interlude. Right there on Katherine's dressing room table. The scripts, the makeup and hair, the accessories flew in every direction. All that rested on the table was Katherine's exposed buttocks. Ian knew where he was going. He had been there many times before. Ian could have been completely blind and know how to reach under Katherine's dress to remove her stockings and panties. He did not need a roadmap to find her spot. And as he entered her, as they made love, with every deep thrust Ian could bestow, as Ian listened to every groan and moan of pleasure Katherine whispered into his ear. Their agreement became consummated. Universal Studios had their creative team in place.

The very expensive automobiles of Hollywood's very rich lined the circular driveway at Pickfair. A driveway that belonged to the lavish and gorgeous home of Douglas Fairbanks and Mary Pickford. This night was a gala celebration for those blue-blooded HollywoodLand actors, actresses, and studio executives who were fortunate enough, and had the foresight to sell off their stocks and bonds before the October Stock Market Crash of 1929 eight months earlier. So while the vast majority of the country wallowed in despair, poverty, financial ruin, and omnipresent hopelessness, this group of Americans living in a small desert town bordering the Pacific Ocean basked in the reality that their vast fortunes and property holdings remained safe and secure.

The massive and opulent ballroom filled itself up quickly with the elite of the HollywoodLand motion picture business. A ten-piece orchestra played an Argentine tango. The male guests dressed in their black tie and tails held their gorgeously dressed escorts tightly around the dance floor. Ian and Katherine stood in a corner together. They held each other closely. Happiness and bliss painted their faces. The excitement of working together on Universal's first talkie galvanized their relationship and marriage. Ian did not convey to Katherine his proclivity for men until after their wedding. It was too late. Katherine loved Ian deeply. Loved Ian unconditionally. There was so much history between them. All the way back to when they first met after World War I at a fraternity dance on the campus of Princeton University. During those years Katherine was on Broadway and Ian was writing scenarios for Ziegfield. Nothing like cooing in a cozy corner at Pickfair. Ian and Katherine enjoyed the spotlight as one acting colleague after another approached them to offer their congratulations. Von Stroheim, dressed in his black tuxedo and knee-high Prussian army boots, could not just walk by without speaking. It was his custom to click his heels and kiss a lady's hand before speaking.

"I'd rather thought you kiss my hand first, Von Stroheim," said Ian.

Von Stroheim replied, "Only women. No more lovely than your beautiful wife."

"Always the gallant gentleman, Erich," said Katherine.

"Congratulations are in order for the two of you. And you, Heir McGregor, your first picture as a director. You both must feel proud and excited," said Von Stroheim.

Ian was becoming tired of Von Stroheim's Prussian boorishness. He softly squeezed Katherine's hand, precisely on cue as the orchestra began a waltz. Katherine nodded yes and provided a faint smile. The dance floor awaited them.

Ian and Katherine gracefully painted the dance floor for nearly ten minutes. It was a wonderful mixture of grace and elegance. They held each other tightly. Ian allowed his hand to slide down the small of Katherine's back. He found the curvature of her hips. He alternated his touch between her hips and her back. Katherine wore an open back dress. She loved the touch of Ian's fingers on her skin. There was that glint again. That glint Ian and Katherine have shared between each other ever since college. No matter what had happened between them, each knew that they loved each other very much.

"Love me?" asked Katherine.

"*Oui, ma amour*," said Ian.

"*Une peu*?" asked Katherine.

"*Beaucoup*."

The still of the night provided Abel an abundance of restlessness. Writer's block. A myriad of thoughts, anxieties, and fears. He found himself in bed, on his back wearing only his T-shirt and boxers. A June evening in Southern California is usually cool, but a weeklong heat wave has rendered the weather to a closer resemblance to Texas. Warm and muggy and reminding Abel of Alabama instead. He thought about asking Ian for two weeks off so he could take a train back to New York and visit Isaiah at Sing Sing. As he thought deeper, he realized the logistics of such a cross-country trip on the train just would not work out. Two weeks without pay just wasn't an option. Abel worked the dialogue in his head. The things he wanted to say to Isaiah. Perhaps more important than anything, to say how sorry he was for betraying him. How his betrayal has now cost him the next twenty years of his life.

A sound outside his coach house broke Abel's trance. Someone was walking up the outside stairs to his door. It felt like an eternity of seconds before a soft knock sounded. Abel slowly got up from his bed and moved to the door.

"Who is it?"

The voice on the other side of the door replied, "It's Mr. McGregor. May I come in for a moment?"

Abel hesitated before responding. "Just a second." He ran back to his bed to put his pants and servant's jacket back on. Before he opened the door to let Ian in, he took one deep breath.

"Yessa, Mr. McGregor. Somethin' I can help you with?"

"May I enter?" asked Ian.

"Yessa."

Ian slowly entered Abel's coach house apartment. His white dinner jacket was still on, but his dress shirt was out, and his black bow tie was untied and dangling from his neck.

"Somethin' I can help you with, sir?"

Ian smirked and while pulling a half pint of whiskey out of his pocket, he began to walk around Abel's room. A very long swig ensued.

"Mrs. McGregor and I just had a lovely evening at Pickfair and I was feeling a bit daffy. Thought I would come up here for an aperitif."

Abel replied, "Apera-what, sir?"

Ian chuckled and chose that moment to take another long swig. There was no doubt to Abel that his boss was drunk beyond recognition. It wasn't the first time he had seen Ian drunk. Not by a long shot.

"So tell me, dear Abel, have you a girlfriend in these parts?" asked Ian.

"Ain't got no girlfriend, suh."

"Where are you from?" asked Ian.

Abel replied, "Tuskegee, Alabama."

Ian was becoming increasingly intrigued, interested in how Abel found himself living in California.

"Have you family there now?" asked Ian.

"Yessa. Just my momma. Got a brotha livin' in New York City."

"I'm from Boston," said Ian. "They say all native Californians are from someplace else. Ever been to Beantown?"

"No, suh," replied Abel.

Ian replied, "Spent quite a number of years in New York. I was writing and directing Broadway plays back then. Quite good ones, I may add. Big hits—made me a star and a lot of money. Motion pictures provided myself and Mrs. McGregor a new challenge for our creative spirit. It is why we moved out here."

Abel began to wonder why Ian picked two o'clock in the morning to come over and start a conversation about his life and family. An awkward silence permeated the coach house. As each second mounted, two different looks developed. Abel had a look of bewilderment. A look of fatigue after a very long day at work and interrupted sleep. For Ian, an interesting combination of interest and lust. Like a fox eyeing his prey of a prairie rabbit, his mouth watered.

"You have the most, the most expressive face," said Ian.

"X'cuse me, suh?" a shocked Abel replied.

Ian asked, "How do you manage to stay so fit?"

On cue, a very slow, up-and-down glare of admiration of Abel's physique followed. Abel felt very uncomfortable with Ian's frankness. Especially at two o'clock in the morning. He said nothing. Thought nothing. Ian decided one large swig off his bottle was warranted.

"This may be a wonderful moment to say good night," said Ian.

Ian placed the bottle in his pocket. Abel walked toward the door, except Ian would not move out of his way. Four inches separated their two noses in the middle of the night.

Ian said, "My gorgeous man, you are about to be kissed good night."

He gave Abel no time to react, quickly cupping his hands over Abel's cheeks, and quickly, yet softly kissing him on the lips. Abel stood frozen in a complete and total shock. Too shocked to say or do anything except watch Ian turn and walk out of the coach house.

The day had finally arrived for Universal Studios. The day of arrival for Ian. For Katherine. It was day 1 for shooting *Another Man's Poison.* Universal Studios' first talkie would be conceived this day. Its birth, its premiere, would be unveiled to the rest of the world in less than four months. Ian stood alone in the corner of stage 4. He was nervous. Very nervous as his hand holding his cigarette shook slightly. *I wish this blasted headache would go away*, he thought. He gulped his morning coffee down just as the assistant director approached him.

"Ian, the cast is assembled."

Ian replied, "Thank you, Miles."

Ian handed Miles his cup of coffee then watched him walk away. He dropped his cigarette to the floor, extinguishing it using the tip of his shoe. He took a moment to go through a pre-production ritual he started when he was writing and directing his plays on Broadway. He closed his eyes, bowed his head.

"One minute at a time. One hour at a time. One second at a time. And you shall do great things."

As he made his way to the center of the set, all eyes of the cast and crew became riveted on Ian. Including Katherine's. *Another Man's Poison* tells the story of illicit love. Katherine plays the wife of a barrister in Victorian London. She meets and falls in love with the son of a bootmaker living in the London section of Notting Hill. When the man realizes he will never have Katherine for himself, he murders her, then kills himself by jumping into the Thames River. It was time to address the cast and crew. Ian had conducted this ritual many times before. There was no need to prepare anything. He asked the assistant director to hand him the shooting script.

"Ladies and gentleman, I am holding here a piece of history. We are here to make history. What do I ask of you? The same things I ask of myself. Be on time, be prepared. Give this picture your all. Your very best. If we work hard together, have a bit of fun with this, I am sure we will be quite proud of our finished project. Remember this, everyone . . . remember, this is our passion. This is what we love. Bring that passion, that love to *Another Man's Poison.* Shall we begin?"

16

A number of weeks passed since that night. Since that night Abel felt the soft touch of Ian's lips on his. While Abel finished washing and waxing down Ian's Packard, the afternoon sun felt refreshing on his skin. Abel, to that day, had not fully processed the meaning of it all. The true meaning of Ian's kiss. He was ambivalent. It was not a particularly good or sensual feeling. He was not aroused. And yet, he was not repulsed by it either. His thoughts turned to Ian. The bright sun took this moment to play peek-a-boo. Now an overcast shadow hung over him. The shadows perturbed Abel. He wanted the sun to coat Ian's Packard with a beautiful gloss for his wax job. Coming from New York, Abel was enjoying how the sunny California days made him feel. Free. Exhilarated. Inspired to write. Abel made a decision. His feelings about Ian, his points of view, his inner turbulence with respect to his sexual orientation would all go to the back burner for the moment. It was not important. Not relevant. What was important, what was relevant was that he worked as hard as he possibly could on his book, and on being the best valet and chauffeur he could be for the McGregors. Period. The sun reappeared. An excellent time to write, Abel thought. He had a couple of hours before he picked up Ian and Katherine from the studio.

He sat by the car and pulled out his notebook and pencil. Not much had been written since that night of the kiss between two men. Abel tried, but so much had been thrust upon him. He continued to work through the guilt of betraying Isaiah. Deep down in his heart, he knew he would never be able to make things right with his brother. So there he sat. Thinking. The palms of his hands, moist from the hard work of washing and waxing. The aroma of Simonize car wax permeated his sense of smell. So he sat. And he thought. He grabbed his pencil, twirling it in his hand as he licked the point. I've got it, Abel said to himself. And so he feverishly wrote. Cassandra picks an awkward moment to convey to John the deep pain she feels for her older brother Cassius. The Ku Klux Klan arrived at Cassandra's house in the middle of the night and rousted Cassius out of his bed. Cassandra's father grabbed his rifle. But before he could fire, a Klansman shot Cassandra's father in the leg. Although he survived the shooting, his leg was amputated from the knee. Cassandra's brother was not found until months later when his decomposed body surfaced in the Tallahatchie River. The police and coroner's office ruled it a suicide. Everyone in the Negro section of town knew different. It was the first time Cassandra shared her inner pain and loss with someone outside the immediate family. John at first remained silent. He had no idea how to show any compassion for Cassandra at that moment. Cassandra was not the first Negro to lose a family member at the hands of the Ku Klux Klan. What John was not capable of seeing was the huge amount of trust Cassandra was placing into him and their relationship. Abel stopped writing. There was a word he was trying to comprehend. Trust. What is trust, he asked. He saw trust as an inner belief, a sense of faith, a degree of self-knowing that whatever or whomever you are placing your trust in is true. That trust is built on a solidly poured foundation. Always strong and never cracking through the test of time. How Abel's character Cassandra trusted John. How a newly founded trust between himself and Ian had been hatched. But he can't know what I have done to his screenplay, Abel said to himself. No, that must always remain secret.

"Cut!"

It was the fourth time in ten minutes Ian had yelled "Cut." Scene 37 was not moving as planned. Ian wanted more passion from Katherine, the wife of a barrister, and her co-star Simon, the son of a Notting Hill bootmaker. They have found a moment to sneak away from their spouses for an adulterous interlude between each other. This is the scene Katherine's character breaks the affair off. Ian and Katherine do not see eye-to-eye with the way the scene is to be played. Ian calls his two stars over for an artistic discussion of the material.

Ian said, "Simon, my boy, this woman that you love desperately has just told you that the affair is over. She never wants to see you again. And what do you do? You tiptoe behind her like a bloody coward, and you speak your lines with her back to you. No! No! I want you to move quickly and forcibly grab her shoulder and turn her around. Make her face you. Make her look into your eyes."

Katherine saw fit to interject her opinion. "Ian, perhaps now is the time Simon shows how tentative he is with his feelings."

Ian replied, "No, absolutely not! I want the character to be forceful."

"It may be too soon. There is still the scene at the railway station in the third act," said Katherine.

The "I am perturbed" look had presented itself on Ian's face. A very pale, reddish hue. No actor, not even Katherine, was going to tell him how to direct his picture. The picture he also wrote the screenplay for. He didn't want to embarrass Katherine in front of her co-star.

"Darling, a moment, if you please," said Ian.

Simon took Ian's words as his cue to move on to another part of the set.

Ian said, "I want to have a word with you. And I want you to listen carefully to what I have to say."

Katherine replied, "All right, my darling."

Ian reached into his pocket for his pack of cigarettes. He guessed Katherine wanted one as well, so he offered. Katherine accepted and lit hers first.

Ian said, "For your entire career, going back to Broadway, you've had hack directors more interested in looking at your big tits, holding their cocks at night, and wishing they were fucking you instead of helping you to become a better actress."

"I've done quite well in this business, thank you very much," said Katherine.

Ian said, "Quite well? You've done quite well? Is that all you want? Let me share a bit of reality with you, my lovely. In ten years you will be too old to play young heroines and newlywed brides. No one will want you. Not even that blowhard Harry Cohn at Columbia. But everyone will want you if you are a great actress. You can be great. Academy Award great. And I am going to make you a great actress. Look at me. A great actress."

Katherine asked, "Just how do you propose to do that?"

Ian replied, "You may begin by doing whatever the hell I say on this bloody picture."

Ian threw his cigarette to the floor, providing Katherine with a glance of a director's defiance as he walked away. She stood in shock while listening to Ian address the cast several feet away.

"Let's get started!" yelled Ian.

Abel was writing feverishly. He had only five or ten minutes before Ian and Katherine appeared from the set for their ride home. Pencil lead was flying all over the paper in order to get one more train of thought down. Cassandra and John plan to pack up and leave Alabama for Tennessee. John's uncle has opened up a small general store for the town Negroes, and John has agreed to work there. It will be a wonderful beginning for them. Abel stops writing. A very delicate moment for Cassandra stands before her. How does she tell the man she loves dearly that the same night her brother Cassius was abducted and ultimately murdered, was the same night she was brutally raped by a Ku Klux Klansman.

How does she tell the man she loves dearly that because of her refusal to give birth to a Klansman's child, a backroom, late-night botched abortion has left her unable to bear children for John. Abel has to stop writing. Ian and Katherine could be seen approaching the car from his rearview mirror. Quickly his notebook goes into his breast pocket. He stands by the door, opening it, allowing Ian and Katherine to enter the back seat. The twenty-five-minute drive down Sunset Boulevard to Brentwood had begun. Most days Ian and Katherine would chatter the entire trip home. Sharing sips of brandy via Ian's flask. Gossiping one minute, arguing the virtues of theater versus motion pictures the next. Sometimes exchanging barbs on which wine should go with which fish.

Abel sensed that there was something wrong, something amiss. It was quiet in that back seat. Abel glanced in the rearview mirror. Katherine was upset about something. Her face remained turned, staring out the window. As Abel's eyes moved toward Ian, Ian was looking right back at him. A smirk, suggesting a most devilish and carnal desire.

"I thought the first day shooting went quite well," said Ian.

Katherine replied, "If that is what you think."

"Yes, that is exactly what I think."

Nothing else was said. Abel watched as Ian slowly ran his hand up Katherine's skirt. Ian looked at Abel. There's that wicked smile again.

The evening was quiet. Abel lay in his bed wondering why the McGregors were giving each other the cold shoulder on the ride home that afternoon. In the back of his mind, he knew it was none of his business. But since that day he revised and rewrote Ian's screenplay, since that evening Ian kissed him, Abel had developed a fondness and attraction for Ian. He respected him. Their relationship was evolving into more than a worker/boss relationship. He felt he could confide in Ian. He wouldn't go so far as to do so, but he did not fear him either. His coach house phone was ringing. The clock on his dresser said nine o'clock. It was still Abel's job to respond quickly to his employer's demands no matter what the time.

"Yes, Mr. McGregor. Sorry, yes, yes, Mrs. McGregor . . . right away, Mrs. McGregor."

Abel got up from his bed and dressed quickly. Katherine called for the car and wanted Abel to take her out for the evening. A servant, a valet, gets trained quickly to respond to their employer's needs and demands in an expedient and efficient manner. Abel was no different with respect to Ian and Katherine's demands and orders. If you wanted to remain employed, you had to learn your employer's idiosyncrasies in a hurry. A policeman gets a call at the precinct station; the alarm goes off at a firehouse. It was the same for a Negro servant.

Phone rings, you answer, you respond in a timely and efficient manner.

Abel sat in the car waiting for Katherine to come out of the house. He wasn't sure how late of a night it was going to be so he lay his head back and closed his eyes for a short cat nap. Then he wondered. If he was going to be driving Katherine around all evening, what was Ian doing. Why did he care so much how Ian spent his evenings without Katherine. What was Momma doing back home in Alabama, he thought. Who did she get to help her with the sharecroppin' this season. What was Althea up to. He had not spoken to her since that last night they were together. That last night when she challenged his manhood. He kept his eyes closed. He kept on thinking. What was Isaiah doing in that prison cell in Sing Sing. He's sittin' there hatin' me for all it's worth, Abel thought. Too many thoughts swimming through his head with his eyes closed. So he opened them. He saw Katherine making her way to the car. For just a quick moment he saw Ian peering through the living room curtains. It appeared like they locked eyes on each other for a brief moment. And then the curtains closed. Ian was gone. Quickly Abel had to exit the car and open the door for Katherine.

"Chaplin Studios. San Vincente and Melrose."

"Yes, ma'am," replied Abel.

"You are not to tell Mr. McGregor where you took me this evening. Is that understood?" asked Katherine.

"Yes, ma'am," replied Abel.

Of course Abel knew better not to say anything to Ian. He loved his job and was not about to betray a trust between himself and his employer. He was hoping the ride would be quiet. He was not in the mood for small talk.

"How are things working out for you so far?" asked Katherine.

Abel was shocked, taken aback a bit. Katherine had never initiated a personal conversation with him before. Be polite, he said to himself.

"Yes, ma'am. Real good. Workin' fer youz and Mr. McGregor has been mighty nice," said Abel.

"I'm glad to hear it. Mr. McGregor seems to be happy with your work as well," replied Katherine.

"Yes, ma'am."

"You don't socialize with the other servants. Why is that?" asked Katherine.

Abel smirked. He thought Katherine's question was funny. Cornelia was the only one he talked to at length. He was helping her to read. He used his novel about Cassandra and John as a study tool.

"Not sure. Guess everybody has their own bui'ness. I pretty much keep to myself," said Abel.

"Just as well," replied Katherine.

The car ride became very quiet. Just the way Abel wanted it. He liked driving at night. Not so much traffic. Los Angeles became serene once the sun went down. It resembled more of a sleepy desert community instead of an up-and-coming bustling metropolis. The motion picture industry resulted in an enormous migration boom westward. A shot in the arm for the economy, but for a small-town country farm boy from Alabama, the less hustle and bustle the better. Katherine remained quiet, just staring out the window as Abel drove. What is she thinking about, Abel wondered.

What is she thinking? The same question Ian asked as he sat in his den. It wasn't the first time Katherine would leave for the evening without Ian. A marriage with a "don't ask, don't tell" mantra often leads to the playing of merry-go-round mind games. Ian thought a writing session would be beneficial. The studio asked him to begin the screenplay for

Lon Chaney's new film, *Captain's Cove*. It was not going particularly well. It didn't stop Ian from drowning himself with large quantities of scotch. Didn't stop his massive headache from reappearing either. Ian did not handle his writing block spells very well. He was weak, losing confidence in his abilities. A panic set in, just as it did when he was writing *Another Man's Poison*. Then he remembered. He remembered how he found the inspiration to write a magnificent screenplay. Or so he thought. Those thoughts, remembering what he accomplished, was enough for him to grab his pen and give it another try.

Katherine was enjoying the feel of the silk sheets caressing her naked body. She closed her eyes and nestled softly in the comfort of an expensive king-size bed.

"You Brits and your tea," said Katherine

"How do you take yours, Mrs. McGregor?"

Katherine replied, "Two sugars and cream please, Mr. Chaplin."

Two accomplished, famous and well-known actors in the motion picture business enjoy their tea after a late evening of passionate sex. It was not the first time they had enjoyed each other's company. Their meetings were not intended to go over lines for their next film together. Until now, they had never done a film together. They did have one thing in common. Sex. Even better, sex without strings attached. A HollywoodLand perk for many.

"I always wondered something, Mr. Chaplin," asked Katherine.

"Pray tell, and what might that be?"

Katherine replied, "Why me for your little fun? I am almost twenty years too old for you. You usually troll the local high schools near Sunset Boulevard for your conquests."

"My dear, you excite me so much more than those virgin, wet-behind-the-ear debutantes. Besides, we sometimes make exceptions to our little rules. Now suppose we finish our tea and continue what you and I do best. Then you may return home to that devoted, free-thinking husband of yours."

Abel found himself with a free three hours. There was only one place to go. To the Negro section of Los Angeles. There would be only one place open late. A smoky back room dive called Lulu's. Abel entered and found an open table by the stage. He was glad it was blues night. He liked blues, and as his luck would have it, the band was in the midst of a hot set.

"Hey, Abel, cha doing here on a Tuesday night?"

Abel replied, "Killin' some time, Ruthie. How 'bout a beer?"

The waitress said, "Busta made some of his sweet potato pie."

Abel replied, "Bring me a slice of dat too."

Abel had what he wanted. A relaxing moment and free night out. Most evenings when he waited for Katherine he spent sitting in his car near Echo Park. Some days he would write; other days he would watch individuals slowly paddle their canoes in the pond. He was enjoying the night, his beer, his sweet potato pie, the music. A figure slowly approached him. It was the figure of a woman. The night club was too dark to make out the face. Abel sat up, braced himself, and then he saw who it was. It was Cornelia. Happy to see Abel. Moving in a wobbly way, a way that suggests she had been drinking.

"Hey, college boy. What'cha doing here?"

A group of Cornelia's friends walked up from behind and took a place at Abel's table. It was apparent all had been drinking. Abel's solitude moment suddenly became a raucous party for six at his table.

"Hey, Cornelia. Looks like youz been havin' a good time."

"It's my birthday, college boy," said Cornelia.

"I didn't know. Happy birthday!" replied Abel.

"Come on, college boy, have another drink with us."

Abel didn't want to act like a party pooper. Over the months Cornelia was the only servant he grew to feel comfortable around, even to like. Once a week he would sit down and help Cornelia improve her reading. One hour a week helped the two of them build a rapport between each other. Abel felt obliged.

"Come on, college boy. We drinkin' shots of rum Ruthie's momma brought from Jamaica," said Cornelia.

Abel replied, "Order the drinks. Let's have a good time."

A full moon was now casting a bright glow against the hue of a midnight sky. It is all Ian could do while he smoked his cigarette on the veranda. Gaze at a beautiful and clear, starry, moon-filled evening. He gave up working on his screenplay over an hour ago. It was going nowhere. The booze and the headaches left him unable to write anything coherent. His attention turned to Katherine on that veranda. With each thought on where Katherine might be, he gripped the next day's shooting schedule tighter in his hand. He puffed harder on his cigarette. He hated the feelings he was going through. His lust for men and his amoral behavior have turned his wife against him. She was seeking the sexual prowess of other men not because Ian could not satisfy her. It was Katherine's way of exacting revenge against Ian. Her way of getting back at Ian for his betrayal, for his dishonesty in not telling Katherine about who he really was before they married, for the huge cavern it created in their marriage. Their marriage had nothing to do with the deep love they had for each other. You can't have it both ways, Katherine would always say to Ian. Was it the anger for not being able to write five decent lines in two hours, or was the anger toward himself for turning his wife into a promiscuous whore.

Ian had started playing a drum rhythm with the shooting script against the post of the veranda. What else was there to do? Writing or sleeping was not an option. The car pulled up into the driveway. Katherine exited the car, and Abel continued down the driveway to the garage.

"Good evening. Out late considering we have to be on the set at 8:00 a.m.," said Ian.

"Mary called me. She needed to talk about her and Douglas. They're having issues. We went out for drinks."

Ian replied, "I see. Everything okay?"

"Yes, I talked her off the ledge," said Katherine.

Ian and Katherine shared a look. A look they had shared before. Once again they were playing that game called "don't ask, don't tell."

"Going to bed. You coming?" asked Katherine.

"Be up in a minute."

Katherine stroked Ian's faced and kissed him before going inside the house. Ian turned to look at her. He was battling the anger. The last time his anger overcame him he raped Katherine. She brought that actor into their home to fuck him. He reached into his back pocket for his flask for another one of those huge swigs. The full moon looked so peaceful.

With each step Abel stumbled a little more. That short trek up to his coach house, usually a quick endeavor, was becoming an Olympic athletic adventure. Abel's alcoholic consumption was always one beer on a Saturday night. Cornelia's birthday celebration and the three shots of Jamaican rum left him in a state he had never been before—completely and totally intoxicated. He was elated

Katherine didn't notice he was drunk and that he did
not run the car into a light pole. He made it. He
entered his coach house and thought of nothing else
but taking off his clothes and falling into bed. He
collapsed on his bed, completely exhausted. He had
a 7:00 a.m. wake-up in four hours. He rolled over
on his back, hoping his head would stop spinning in
circles. The tighter he closed his eyes, the bigger
the circles became. Spinning. Spinning. Spinning.
Spinning. His head kept spinning.

Then, he felt something. His bed was moving. Not
from his drunkenness. Someone was in his bed. It
was Ian. Next to Abel. Looking at him. Admiring his
chocolate brown, well-toned body.

"Mr. McGregor, what'chu doing here?" asked Abel.

"Just laying here next to you. Admiring your
strong body," replied Ian.

"You shouldn't be here. This ain't right."

Abel was too drunk to do anything but lie there.
If he moved one inch, it would make his head spin
fifteen times faster. He felt Ian caressing his
neck, working his hand downward toward his chiseled
chest. Ian couldn't resist. He planted a warm kiss
on Abel's cheek.

"You've been out drinking. I thought you were
driving Mrs. McGregor this evening," said Ian.

Abel remained silent. His response was to moan
louder.

"You shouldn't be here," said Abel.

"Shhhhhhhh," replied Ian.

"This ain't right, Mr. McGregor. You gots to go."

Ian ignored Abel's words. Abel felt Ian's hand
slowly move down his torso. He reached into Abel's
boxers.

"My God, you are massive," said Ian.

Abel couldn't fight. He wouldn't fight. His
drunken stupor combined with the erotic sensation

Ian was providing left him totally paralyzed. All he could do was moan.

"I've never seen nor felt such a big cock as yours," said Ian.

Ian grabbed tightly. Slowly massaging Abel. Tighter. Gripping tighter. Pulling, jerking Abel. A vice grip with Abel's manhood in his hand. Ian was enjoying it. Enjoying the moment to its fullest.

"Won't be long now, will it, Abel?" asked Ian.

Abel couldn't hold himself. The next sound was Abel exploding into Ian's hand.

"That's a good lad. My goodness, so much oozing thru me fingers," said Ian.

Ian licked his fingers clean. He enjoyed Abel's release as though it was a twelve-ounce T-bone being served at La Boheme. Now he was finished. Now he felt control over Abel. As he got up and made his way to the door, he turned and looked at Abel, fast asleep and snoring.

"Sleep well, my chocolate prince."

17

There was no bright sun this morning. No bluish hue. An overcast sky existed instead. Morning rush hour on Sunset Boulevard was a congested mess. A milk truck had rammed into the back of a farmer's fruit and vegetable wagon. Cars sat motionless, completely still, lined up one behind the other on a one-lane road while a middle-aged man struggled to gather his produce. Horns blared repeatedly, to no avail. Unfortunately for Abel, he had to arise by 7:00 a.m. and take Ian and Katherine to the studio. As his head throbbed, he vowed to never allow himself to become that drunk again. There was that dream still swimming in his head. A dream about Ian. How he climbed into bed with him. It felt so real, so intense that he ejaculated himself into a wetness he never experienced before. He took that moment to gaze into the rearview mirror. Katherine was reviewing her lines for the morning shoot, but Ian looked at Abel with the most satisfying smile.

"My God, how long with this traffic? We are already late for the studio," said Ian.

"Clearin' up a bit yonder down the road," replied Abel.

There was that sinister smirk of Ian's again. This time Abel realized the truth. It was not a dream. Something did happen between him and Ian.

Abel looked back at Ian and provided him with as blank an expression as possible.

Ian asked, "My dear, why don't we have Mary and Douglas over for dinner soon? Douglas and I are going golfing on Sunday. Shall I set it up then?"

Katherine looked up. "No, no, that won't be necessary, darling. I shall speak to Mary this afternoon and invite them myself."

Ian was enjoying the mind game he was playing with Katherine. He knew she was lying about the previous night. When Katherine told a lie, the brow on her forehead would raise upward. Perhaps she never knew that was her giveaway, her blink. But Ian knew.

"As you wish, my love."

The traffic cleared, the cars began their procession. Abel did his best to nurse his hangover as he drove. Katherine went back to her script. Ian pulled out the *Daily Variety*. Suddenly Ian found an article of keen interest. He could not believe his eyes. He read on. The article said that Universal had signed his friend James to a three-year contract. He was to direct the picture *Frankenstein* the following year. Universal Studios had found its niche. It was to become the studio for the horror picture. Lugosi's *Dracula* was in pre-production, and now they were going to cash in and shoot Mary Shelley's novel *Frankenstein*, followed soon thereafter by *The Mummy*. What's becoming of this place, Ian wondered. Writing photoplays that will star ghouls and monsters in the lead role? So this is the studio's way of battling for the Depression dollars.

"Have you seen this?" asked Ian.

"Seen what?" replied Katherine.

"This bloody article in the *Daily Variety*. It wasn't enough that Junior decided to make Bela Lugosi a ghastly vampire, but now more pictures with monsters. What's next, a picture about a shipwrecked crew of niggers playing zombies?"

Ian did not notice what he had said. More importantly, he was oblivious to the notion that he was in the company of Abel when he said it. Katherine and Abel shared a quick glance at each other through the rearview mirror. Katherine slapped Ian on the thigh and motioned to the front of the car. Abel kept driving. He ignored the slur. It wasn't the first time a white man made a racial slur in front of his face. It was 1930; certainly it would not be the last. He had been called nigger in Alabama on so many occasions he lost count. If I had a dollar for every time, Abel used to say to himself. He would joke how rich he would be. The thought of that joke brought a smirk to Abel's face.

Ian realized his error, but he would never acknowledge his mistake to Abel. To apologize to a Negro suggests they are equals as men. Instead Ian thought about James. How he would have to see him on the studio lot. Run into him in the commissary. Attend the same studio events and parties. It was breaking his heart. He crumbled the newspaper up and angrily threw it down to the floor. Katherine watched but said nothing. She felt learning her lines were more important at the time than reading her husband's mind, or expressing concern about his anger.

A light, very faint drizzle had begun. The rain did not stop a number of canoes from gliding along the pond in Echo Park. Abel had found a quiet and serene place to park the car so that he may immerse himself in some very deep, contemplative soul-searching. Despite the fact that he swallowed six Bayer aspirin tablets, his head continued to pound him mercilessly. What was bothering him at this very moment was what Ian had done to him the night before. He felt his touch. He felt the kiss on his cheek. He felt his strong grip on his loins. He felt his explosion into Ian's hand. And now, what was the meaning of it all? What was to be next? His emotions wavered up and down like a ship navigating choppy seas. A feeling of a euphoric erotica he had never felt before, versus a deep sense of guilt and remorsefulness

He thought about Althea back home. Wondered how she was doing. He wondered why her touch, her taste, her sensuality felt so different to what he had just experienced with Ian. Up next for Abel was to garner enough courage to confront Ian about what happened between them. It made him feel very afraid. Can I trust a white man with my feelings? Abel asked himself. Was confronting Ian, his boss, worth the risk of possibly being fired? Was it all worth the risk of having to pack up and move back to Harlem? These questions were weighing on Abel. Abel reached into his pocket for his notes. He thought writing would get his mind off things. Perhaps focusing on John and Cassandra and his book would bring him a bit of peace before picking up Ian and Katherine from the studio. Nothing was clicking. His writer's block had entered through stage left. There was nothing to put down on paper. Just a blank stare. A writer faces this fork in the road on many occasions. He must be brave, face the beast called creative abyss, and forge ahead as best he can. Hold the pencil tightly. Focus. Grit your teeth if you have to. Anything that turns the lightbulb in your head on. Anything that gets your hand moving and making lead marks on your paper.

"Quiet on the set. Roll camera. Speed . . . and . . . Action!"

With Ian's direction, Katherine is seen entering the study of her husband, John McLaidlaw.

"I have some bad news for you, Olivia," said John.

(Olivia) Katherine replied, "Yes, John."

At this moment John reaches for a match inside his smoking jacket. He looks at Katherine and lights his pipe simultaneously.

"I'm afraid that son of a cobbler you have been amusing yourself with for the past year has met a tragic end."

(Olivia) Katherine walks up close to John. She had no idea her husband knew of her tryst. Katherine had to provide on camera the look of shock that she had been found out, while at the same time exhibit no level of grief to her husband that her lover was dead.

"Cut!"

The actors looked startled. They both glared at Ian, wondering why he stopped them. The flow was perfect, the energy just right. The tension was building at the precise tambour. There was nothing wrong with the scene and Ian knew it. Katherine's screen character Olivia was striking an inner chord with Ian. He was personally struggling with

her off-camera infidelities. Chaplin . . . Barrymore . . . Beery. He knew all the men who were bedding his wife. At least he thought he knew all of them. It was the price he was paying for his own sins. What really tormented him was the thought of knowing he was apt to run into James from time to time on the studio lot. That thought was creating inner discord in his heart, exacerbating his headaches that seemed to make its appearance every four or five days with regularity.

"Let me see the script again," said Ian.

The assistant director brought Ian the script as Katherine and her co-star stood awaiting Ian's direction. Ian said nothing. Just reading. He rolled up the script and approached Katherine. Deliberately, he spoke just loud enough for the cast and crew to hear him.

"My dear Katherine, what I saw was the look of

a woman who just allowed her puppy to shit in the house on mommy's little carpet. What I want . . . What I want you to give me is a woman showing fear to her husband because she has been found out to be a lying adulteress. Can you display that look for the camera after I say Action?

"Yes. Yes. Let's have another go at it, shall we?" said Ian.

The view from the coach house, although not necessarily breathtaking, often could tell a story as you gazed through a clear glass-and-frame jalousie window. Today's story as Abel watched was a spirited argument that Ian and Katherine were having on the back terrace. Both of them took turns waving their shooting scripts in each other's face. And as he looked at Ian, he realized how complex this man was. A tranquil gentleman one moment, and suddenly and without notice acting like a drunken, mad, raving lunatic. Months had passed since that night he rewrote Ian's screenplay. His hope was that it would in some way make Ian's life easier. Instead, he saw a more intense man. A more driven man. Abel's motive back then was not clear; today, that motive could not have been more clearer. He was feeling an attraction toward Ian. He no longer regarded Ian's intimate advance toward him repulsive. He was not repulsed. It is all he has thought about for the past several weeks. He was coming to grips with the realization that a man's touch on his body tingled him and made him feel alive and wanted sexually. And now he had two secrets to hide from Ian. His edit and rewrite of Ian's screenplay, and that he was falling in love with him.

He got it. Right at that moment, at 11:00 p.m. at night the inspiration beckoned. Abel ran to his writing desk and began to scribble earnestly into his notebook. John and Cassandra have made a new home in Tennessee. One evening as they cuddled closely in their bed, Cassandra confided in John and told him she could never have children. It took her weeks to build up the courage. The fear that John would run out on her was too much to bear at times. She needed to trust John. To not only trust John with her horrors and secrets, but to trust herself. Having the belief and the faith that the man in her life loves her unconditionally. That no matter what happened, moving forward Cassandra could trust John. There was that word again. Trust. This word that makes Abel freeze dead in his tracks. His entire life he has trusted no one but his Momma. Not his father, not his brothers, not Althea. Not one childhood friend either. And so he stood, trying to inject a level of trust in himself, so that he may trust Ian with his inner feelings. Ian's and Katherine's bickering outside broke up Abel's train of thought. He focused deeper to get the right dialogue between Cassandra and John. His effort was not going to work this evening. Abel's curiosity got the best of him. He stopped writing and walked to the window to listen.

"Why do you insist on embarrassing me in front of the cast and crew?" asked Katherine.

Ian replied, "There is no reason to shout at the top of your lungs, my dear."

Katherine took a moment to cool down, a quick sip of her wine. She reached into her bra for a cigarette. She sat down next to Ian.

"I have something to tell you," said Ian.

"Speak," replied Katherine.

"Every day for the past six weeks I have looked at the dailies of our picture. I have seen your performance," said Ian.

"So?" asked Katherine.

"So, you have been magnificent. Your beauty exudes thru the camera lens, but most important, your acting has been the best I have seen. The best."

"Thank you for that, Ian," replied Katherine.

Ian said, "You are going to be nominated for an Academy Award. I know it."

Abel continued watching from his window. The yelling and screaming between Ian and Katherine ceased. They acted civil. Laughter was heard. As Abel watched, Katherine kissed Ian and grabbed his hand, and they walked into the house. The war between the McGregors resulted in a ceasefire. Too late to write now, said Abel. Not too late to lie in bed and think about Ian.

Ian stood on the fairway of the ninth hole. He took a long gaze at the pin that stood a little over 150 yards away.

"What do you think, 8 or 9 iron?" asked Ian.

"9 iron, sir. A little length needed here. Yes, sir."

Every second Sunday of the month Ian went golfing. Eighteen holes. Four hours of fresh air and California sunshine. His Sunday matinee routine has not always gone the way of the past. This was the first Sunday since *Another Man's Poison* started production he was able to get out to the course. The premiere was set for Grauman's Chinese Theatre in six weeks. The end of shooting was near. One more exterior scene to be shot. Ian and Katherine would find out just how far their careers were going to go.

"Abel, it seems I have turned you into a damn good caddie," said Ian.

Abel smiled. "Yes, sir. I do my best."

It was the first time Abel and Ian had a moment alone. Ian approached the ball and lined up his next shot. His shot went straight, a very small bend to it that landed on the green twenty feet from the hole.

"Nice shot, Mr. McGregor," said Abel.

Ian smiled, and for the first the first time ever he looked at Abel as something other than his butler and chauffeur. While Abel carried his bags, the normal procession would be for him to walk behind Ian. But Ian walked toward the pin side by side of Abel.

"Blast it all, Douglas has already finished putting. He runs thru a golf course like a bloomin' wild tractor. I wanted to ask you something, Abel," said Ian.

Abel replied, "Yessuh?"

Ian slowed the walk to a pace resembling a crawl.

"You may find this a bit awkward. What do you really think of me? No, seriously. I would like to know your true opinion."

So much in such a short time for Abel to not only digest but to answer. Right in the middle of the Beverly Hills Country Club.

"Not sure what you mean, sir. I can't really talk 'bout somethin' like that out here," said Abel.

"Well, when can you?" replied Ian. "I say, it's rather important to me."

Just too much for Abel to handle. Too much for him to comprehend. If Ian was attempting to place Abel out of his comfort zone, he succeeded. A Negro knows his place, always knows his place. A Negro is told to never interject his opinion. Abel's only response back to Ian would be the first words that popped into his head at the moment.

"Sir, if you don't mind, I mean . . . if it's all right with you, Mr. McGregor, I kinda like to just focus on caddying a round of golf for you this here afternoon," replied Abel.

"Very well. Shall we catch up with Douglas at the 7th hole?" said Ian.

One last exterior shot left on the schedule. It would be a perfect day to shoot an exterior scene.

No sun, plenty of cloud cover, and no wind. Ian conferred with his art director to make sure the exterior shots had continuity with the interior boards painted to show a Victorian England background consisting of shots of the Thames River. He had a moment to himself. A moment to look back at his accomplishment. Directing his first motion picture. A moment to take a second to pat himself on the back. To stick his chest out with conviction. To feel proud. Everyone, every studio executive at Universal, including Katherine, doubted he could not only write a superb screenplay, but direct it as well. Hollywood was about to be his town, his oyster. Just as New York City and Broadway was for him right after World War I. He thought back to that night when he picked himself up off the floor of his den, and handed Katherine his script that morning. The script he is convinced that he wrote. How Katherine was in love with his writing again. The day Laemmle told him his writing was topnotch once again and gave him the assignment to write and direct Lon Chaney's next picture. He believed he is back. Like the phoenix, he has risen from the ashes of literary doom and destruction. His life has been turned around on that script. In his mind, his script. Sole ownership. Ian thought of his future where people will recognize him and not Katherine when they are out in public. The press will run to him for quotes, opinions, and points of view. Not Katherine. The studio bosses will seek his opinion on matters regarding his pictures. Not Katherine's.

"Ian, we're ready."

"Thank you, Roger."

He stood in the middle of a cobblestone street set, conducting one more once through with the cast. The dolly of the camera follows the young man walking down the street. He stops in front of his favorite store, a chocolate shop called Ipswich Chocolatiers.

One last look as the camera close-up captures a tear welling in his eye. He resumes continuing his walk toward London Bridge. He commits suicide by jumping into the Thames. Unable to have the woman he loves, he chooses not to live. One long shot, one or two close-ups. *Another Man's Poison,* Universal Studios first talkie, has completed shooting.

"Cut, that's a wrap!"

Katherine had three days off in the past four months. She went from finishing her picture *Joan of Arc* straight into production of *Another Man's Poison.* Today would make number 4. The view from her den window provided her a tranquil scene of her terrace and landscaped garden. The roses need pruning, she said to herself. Her mind wasn't on her roses. She needed to respond to the knock on the door first.

"Yes?"

Abel entered the den with Katherine's tray of tea, cookies, and the afternoon mail.

"Your tea, Mrs. McGregor," said Abel.

Katherine stayed focused on her rose garden.

"Place it on the table, please, thank you."

Abel did as instructed and exited the den. Katherine began to fix her tea, one lump of sugar and a spot of cream. She liked her tea warm but not too hot. As her custom, Cornelia had prepared Katherine's tea perfectly. Back to her garden. Back to her thoughts. Her future, her film career was the current agenda topic. She trusted Ian throughout the entire shoot of their picture. She trusted Ian with every direction he gave her. She trusted that Ian's screenplay would bring her the recognition she thirsted for. The movie-going public had been watching Katherine on the screen for the past ten years. They had never heard her voice. And in two months they will. *What would be their reaction to me?* Katherine asked herself. Will she remain famous and well-known now that talkies have arrived in HollywoodLand. In HollywoodLand to stay. Fear. Fear had arrived. It always shows up in a woman actor's life as she begins to knock on the door of forty. Katherine is three years from forty. A blank stare had taken hostage of her face. She began rubbing her face as though she was magically removing every wrinkle. Frantically she searched the den for a hand mirror. She remembered she always kept one in the desk drawer. Katherine stood, tilting the mirror in every direction. Examining her profile, her smile, her hairline, the faint appearance of crow's feet at her eyes. There was a photo album near. Photos that spanned the past ten years she had been at Universal Studios. Katherine was one of Laemmle's first stars. Quickly she grabbed the photo album, going through each picture, reminiscing about each picture, each scene she was allowed to cast her beauty. Each accolade bestowed on her. The conclusion she drew was that she was not the aging, has-been actress her rivals gladly portrayed to the studio moguls. A smile appeared. A smile that reassured her she remained the gorgeous, sexy, best actress of her time.

"Come on now, Cornelia."

Abel was helping Cornelia with her reading. Today's word that required a tutoring session was consternation.

"Come on now, Cornelia. Let's try this again," said Abel.

Cornelia replied, "Cuss tern nation."

"Watch my lips," said Abel. "Watch my lips. Con-ster-na-shun."

The phone interrupted the session. Cornelia rose from her seat to answer.

"Good afternoon, McGregors' residence. Yes, ma'am, he right here."

Cornelia stood holding the phone, covering the

mouthpiece. Abel looked up Cornelia. Cornelia looked up at Abel.

"Abel, it's a Mrs. Parker callin' all the way from Alabama. She sez she's yo auntie," said Cornelia.

Abel jumped up and grabbed the phone from Cornelia. Auntie Mae, his momma's younger sister, would only be calling if it was bad news from home.

"Hello? Hey, Auntie Mae, how are you? How's Momma?"

Abel listened for a moment. Cornelia saw the sadness on his face. Whatever news was on the other end, it was not good.

"No, no, not Momma. Not Momma."

Abel took a moment and clutched the phone to his heart. He felt his momma's last breath sear right through him.

"I'll catch the bus home first thing in the mornin'."

Abel slowly hung the phone up. He turned, planted his face against the wall, and began to cry uncontrollably. Cornelia rushed to his side.

"Abel, what's wrong? What happened?" asked Cornelia.

Abel replied, "Momma's gone. Momma's gone. She passed away yesterday."

Abel sat on the edge of his bed, the weight of his world pinned against the brass bed frame where his shoulder rested. Everyone from his family was gone in one way or another. His father, dead. His brother James, dead. His brother Isaiah, in prison. And now Momma. Gone. If he could stop crying just long enough to pack, he could manage a few hours of sleep before his forty-hour bus ride home to Alabama. Katherine told Abel he needed to be back at work in six days to work a cocktail party for Ian and Katherine. Two days to Alabama, two days for the funeral and burial, two days to return.

The soft knock at his door got Abel to spring

up off the bed and begin packing. There would be another knock.

"Come in."

Ian entered and stood at the doorway.

"May I come in for a moment?" asked Ian.

"Yessuh."

Ian moved closer to Abel. Abel stopped packing and turned to face Ian.

"Mrs. McGregor just informed me of the terrible news. I am sorry about your dear mother's passing," said Ian.

"Thank you, suh. She went pretty quick," replied Abel.

"I understand you will be leaving tomorrow and be gone for six days," said Ian.

"Yessuh, be back Friday night."

Ian asked, "Have you any other family in Alabama?"

Abel replied, "Just some aunts and cousins now. My daddy and my brotha John they dead."

Before he could mention Isaiah and what happened to him, Abel paused and thought about the exact words he wanted to say to Ian.

"My brotha Isaiah he in jail. Now momma's dead."

Ian became intrigued with the notion that Abel's brother had been incarcerated.

"What did your brother do . . . kill somebody?" asked Ian.

Ian began to chuckle. He thought Abel was going to say Isaiah was in jail for making moonshine or running numbers.

"He killed his girlfriend," replied Abel.

Ian raised his eyebrows. Shock painted his face.

"Well, well now. A murderer in the family. How mundane," said Ian.

Ian walked closer toward Abel and softly grabbed his hand while squeezing.

"I am very sorry," said Ian.

"Thank you, suh."

One more squeeze of Abel's hand by Ian.

"Travel safe. See you Friday," said Ian.

Ian turned and headed for the door.

"Shall we have that chat we talked about upon your return?" asked Ian.

Abel paused for seconds. He took a moment to gaze into Ian's eyes from across the room.

"Yessuh."

He watched Ian respond with a sly smile, then turned and exited. Back to packing. The packing wasn't going as planned. The ever-present visual of Momma sitting in an ice-filled casket awaiting his arrival was becoming a bit too much to bear. There were also thoughts of moving on without his family. For a brief moment he contemplated leaving the McGregors' employ and move back to Alabama. As quickly as that idea appeared, it vanished. He was happy living and working in Los Angeles. He was happy to work for Ian and Katherine. He was happy his novel was moving well. And what was becoming most important to him was the change in the way Ian treated him. He understood the boundary lines clearly. In public, at any moment, any day, any time, he was a Negro servant. It was those brief moments in his coach house where he and Ian shared a different respect for each other. Share the ability to confide in one another. Perhaps a friendship was budding before his eyes.

18

The Johnson living room had always been a scene of happiness. A scene of celebration and joy. A scene of laughter and revelry. A scene of family togetherness. This morning resembled anything but joy, happiness, or revelry. The living room he had known as home for the past twenty-two years became Momma's resting place. A resting place of a handcrafted oak casket filled with dry ice to preserve his momma as much as possible. Only one additional day would be needed. She will be buried tomorrow. Right next to her father and mother. Anger and hurt engulfed Abel on the inside. He sat stoic, strong, not willing to allow his family and friends to glance at any grief. Hurt because he was not present during Momma's last days. Anger because that is what life in Alabama reminded him of. A life of loss. A life of pain. A life of unforgiving moments. A life of watching family and loved ones be murdered for unjust reasons. Simply because they were Negro.

She is at peace now. Reverend Tompkins, a large man with a deep baritone voice, stood before a few in that tiny living room and reminded everyone that a better life was ahead for Momma. He pleaded and encouraged all that although this wonderful woman

has been called home at the young age of forty-
seven, her spiritual connection with everyone would
live forever, especially Abel, her youngest child—
perhaps her most loved child. Certainly the child
she placed the most faith and hope in for a better,
more prosperous life. In the end, as those minutes
transpired with Reverend Tompkins urging every
ounce of inspiration he could, did not deter the
flow of tears to cascade downward Abel's cheek. He
would be back on that bus to Los Angeles tomorrow.
I reckon I needz to move on, he said to himself. One
thing remained for Abel to do before his journey.

The next morning a brazen and intense desire
befell Abel. He refused to leave Tuskegee without
visiting Althea's house one last time. The familiar
path down Route 15 was upon him. The landscape
and the scenery had changed drastically in almost
three years. Fewer children running and playing
around. Fewer farm animals grazing in the grass
and fields. During his walk he saw a familiar
face. Rufus Calley, known for the biggest, widest,
happiest toothless grin in Tuskegee County. He
waved. Rufus waved back. He knew he was heading in
the right direction. Abel's aunt, Hazel, had told
him Althea had moved away. His curiosity piqued,
for he wondered who was now residing there. Several
yards away Abel recognized the wood picket fence
with the painted rooster mounted on top. Thaddeus
Lincoln's floppy-eared bloodhound always took his
afternoon nap at the foot of the fence entryway.
That was all he recognized.

"Hey you!"

Abel had not walked within thirty feet of Althea's
house when he heard an unfamiliar voice yelling at
him in a most angry way. Abel stopped and looked

left and right. From behind stood a thirty-ish, tall and big man. He was Caucasian and dressed in bib overalls, with a bare chest and a big round belly and a straw cowboy hat. His scowl could only suggest he was not happy being face to face with Abel.

"The hell you doing on my property, boy?" asked the man.

Abel nervously stared at an imposingly large figure of a man. He was angry. Perturbed. Ready to impose violence if need be. A Negro in Alabama develops a sixth sense to white human beings bent on being racist.

"Sir, so sorry, sir. I was passin' by cuz I used to know the family that lived here," said Abel.

Abel's response was met with a most vicious and thunderous slap across his face. So hard a slap that it knocked him off his feet and down to the ground.

"Nigga, git off my property. I mean now!"

Hearing the distinct click of the man's revolver helped Abel snap out of his cobwebs in a quick fashion. Abel picked himself up off the hard ground and ran. Kept running. He was not going to stop until he had his bags packed and was on that bus for Los Angeles.

If the afternoon could get any sunnier, if the blue skies could get any bluer, neither Ian nor Katherine would have noticed. It was the morning after. The morning after of Ian and Katherine's talkie premiere, *Another Man's Poison*. The movie reviews were nestled in the morning papers. Ian and Katherine's rear yard bluestone outdoor terrace faced east, which made for abundant sunshine on those cool Southern California mornings. This day it made for a very bright morning to spend in their robes enjoying their coffee, juice, and toast.

"I sure beeze glad when that Abel gets back," said Mabel.

Mabel was not pleased the past few days with handling her usual cooking and cleaning chores, and doing Abel's job serving and doting on the McGregors. It meant more hours, more work. And no extra pay.

"There, there Mabel. Abel returns in three more days," said
Katherine.

"Isn't that so, dear?"

Ian paused for what seemed like minutes. "My God, has a week gone by that quickly," he asked himself.

"Yes, my darling, this Friday," replied Ian.

"Lord have mercy, that is good news," said Mabel.

It was Mabel's subtle way to let Ian and Katherine know as she walked away that the longer days were becoming tiresome. The no-extra pay more irritating with each day.

Ian found a moment to refrain from the reviews and placed his newspaper on his lap. To close his eyes and reflect. To quickly relive the past disappointments with his writing, and to bask the morning sun feeling good about his well-received screenplay by the motion picture critics and writers. There was that one scene. That one scene as he watched the premiere that Ian did not quite remember writing. All the bloody scotch you threw down, how would you remember anything, he said to himself.

He did not allow a blank moment to deter him from his basking. It wasn't to improve his bronze tan. He was basking in his success. His screenplay turned into an overwhelming success and made Katherine Universal's star to rival MGM's Garbo and Shearer. There would be more plum writing assignments, he thought. More jobs directing. More acclaim and recognition. There was a bit of irony thrown in as well for Ian.

He wanted desperately to outshine Katherine. He wanted to put her back in her place. It had become a competition between them. And yet, his success made Katherine an even bigger star.

There are those thoughts about Abel again. Wondering how he was doing. Wishing he could have gone to Alabama with Abel to attend Momma's funeral. Ian could not stop thinking about Abel. He missed him. Their brief but passionate interlude only ignited a deeper passion inside of Ian. He planned to rid of all his male friends and sexual playmates and devote his time to Abel. He wanted Abel even more. A new and fresh relationship would help him forget James. And now, he felt he had truly moved on from that pain and rejection.

"Darling, listen to this," said Katherine.

Ian opened his eyes, but the bright sun forced him to squint. "Drat it all. Abel would have made bloody sure my sunglasses were in my robe pocket," said Ian.

Katherine replied, "Listen to what Hedda wrote. If Universal Studios are the 1932 New York Yankees, then Ian and Katherine McGregor are Babe Ruth and Lou Gherig. An all-powerful couple in today's Hollywood day and age."

"Bless Hedda's little heart," replied Ian.

How a few words could be such a comfort, emit such a warm and loving smile between a married couple. It appeared the sun shone its brightest as Ian held Katherine's soft petite hand in his.

The duel-to-the-death swashbuckling scene had finally begun to take shape. The action sequences were pleasing to the director's eye. Ian as director wanted his cameraman to focus on the tight close-up shots of the hand, wrist, and swords clashing between his two actors.

"Cut!" yelled Ian. "How did it look, Rollie?"

Rollie Montgomery had a particular way of letting Ian know if he got the shot the way Ian wanted it. A simultaneous nod and wink.

"On the money, boss," said Rollie.

"Good, then shall we do it again?" asked Ian.

Rollie replied, "I think we got it that last time, boss."

"This time we will set the camera back two feet and tilt the lens so high, say this much. I want to give Raoul something to work with in the editing room," said Ian.

Exhausted as they were, the actors took their positions.

"Now, Gordon, this time a tad more grit in the teeth," said Ian. Ian's star of *Captain's Cove*, Gordon Simon, nodded in understanding what his director was asking of him.

"If you please, Scott," said Ian. Ian's assistant director, Scott, took his cue to scream at the top of his voice, "Places, quiet on the set!" It was now Ian's cue to yell even louder.

"Roll speed! Lights! Camera . . . Action!"

The swords clashed with might. A fencing synchronization presented itself in magnificent glory. Ian witnessed just what he had hoped. His desire was to keep the audience captivated and wondering if the hero will be up to the challenge of defeating and killing his archnemesis. Despite the wound to his shoulder, the hero wields his sabre with deft and grace. In the corner of His Majesty's castle stood the heroine, frightened beyond her imagination, at times, unable to watch her hero fight for his life. Suddenly, one deft move, one jab, and the drama ceases. Our hero is victorious.

"Cut!" yelled Ian.

Ian looked at Rollie and received the customary nod and wink. The scene had been captured.

"Let's call it a day, shall we, everyone?" asked Ian.

Cast and crew began dispersing. The air quickly filled with cigarette smoke. Ian failed to see his boss Leammle walking up behind him. A smile of satisfaction swashed Ian's face like the surf embracing a beach cove. Ian basked in his success, and he loved every minute. First as an Academy Award winner for his writing, and now as a director of this new, exciting, and revolutionary medium called motion pictures with sound.

"Well done, my boy," said Leammle.

Ian's Cheshire grin reached from one end of stage 12 to the other.

"Coming from you, Junior, I take that as the ultimate compliment. Which everyone on the lot knows you throw out compliments like bloody concrete blocks."

Both men enjoyed Ian's joke—or Ian's barb, depending on who you asked.

"How about a round of golf at my club? Say, Sunday noon?" asked Leammle.

It was the first time in over a year Junior had invited Ian for a round of golf. When Ian's writing was at the very bottom of the pits in hell, when Ian was on the brink of being released from his contract with Universal, he was transformed into a pariah among the other writers. No other writers on the set wanted to socialize, even be seen with him. And now, Ian's perch on top of all of his colleagues gave him a feeling of euphoria, a reaffirmation that he truly belonged. He relished his moment looking down and sneering at the other writers. The plum assignments were going his way. And because he was also able to market his directorial talents as well, it would not be long before the A-list studios like MGM and Warner Brothers would be beating down his door.

"What time is our tee time?" asked Ian.

Katherine stood visibly upset. For the third time this week Ian's shooting schedule ran overtime. For the third time this week she stood outside stage 12 waiting for Ian. If there was one thing that irked her more, it was Ian's penchant for tardiness. Between her bouts of fuming and daydreaming about her next picture playing Queen Elizabeth, she obliged an occasional fan with an autograph. An Academy Award Oscar win has a distinct way of getting one noticed, and noticed quickly. Like any adoration-seeking actress of her time, Katherine basked in the sunshine of such recognition as often as she could. The screeching tires that beckoned at her feet could only mean Ian had finally arrived.

"My apologies, my love. Junior showed up to the set unannounced and uninvited," said Ian.

"Isn't it always something with you, Ian?" asked Katherine. "I had to do this and I had to do that. My, my, my, haven't we become Mr. Bigshot Director in such a short time."

Katherine knew that sometimes in Hollywood all it takes is one hit of a picture to catapult you to the top of the heap, but a flop of a picture, coupled with nasty critic reviews, sends you back down the mountain as quickly as you got there. Such a beaming glow devoured Ian. While he drove, he found enough manual dexterity to reach into his breast pocket for his whiskey flask.

"Aaaaaah!" said Ian. "Care for a nip, darling?"

Katherine shook her head no. There were other things on her mind she wanted to discuss.

"I am rather irked at Junior at the moment," said Katherine. "He informed me at lunch today he has given you total writing and direction control over my next picture."

"Oh that," replied Ian.

"Yes, THAT!" said Katherine tersely.

Ian took another swig and looked skyward, basking with pride and allowing the late-afternoon sun to beam down on his tanned face. He was soaking up the rays of the golden sun and at the same time soaking up the glee and enjoyment having power over Katherine's career brought him. That power being a gift from Carl Leammle. A power Ian had no intention of ever relinquishing.

"We start shooting *Elizabeth, Queen of England* in three months," said Ian.

"How can this be?" asked Katherine. "You haven't even finished writing the script yet."

Ian replied, "My love, such a formality is just that, a formality. I will be putting pencil to paper to typewriter in a matter of days. Of course, the first draft is always the more coarse, but the finished product will be my masterpiece."

"Just take me home, Rembrandt. I have the most dreadful headache," said Katherine.

"As madame wishes," said Ian.

Quite a number of weeks had passed since Abel found a moment to write. The preparation for Ian and Katherine's Oscar night party, the sudden passing of Momma and the bus trip home to Alabama for the service, the writing block episodes—when he did find the time to take pencil to paper—had not added up to very much production. From the very last row of a crowded Greyhound bus, the desert soil and sand of New Mexico as his backdrop, Abel was close to the end of his chapter. How does a man say goodbye to the woman he loves, asked Abel. Of course, he thought of Althea. He thought about her. Only able to wager a guess where she might have moved to. Nobody in Tuskegee seemed to know. Nobody seemed to care either. What saddened more than anything was that none of his close friends, even Momma, bothered to contact him in Los Angeles and let him know Althea had left home. He wanted a chance to say to Althea how sorry he was for everything that went wrong between them.

"Why, I didn't know they let niggers ride on this here bus line."

The couple sitting in front of Abel uttered those words just loud enough for Abel to break his concentration. His focus reverted back to his immediate surroundings. That of a lonely Negro passenger on a crowded, foul-smelling bus. A bus filled with an odor of weekly body mustiness, cheap booze, and spoiled food. There Abel sat. Sunken into his seat. Not wanting to be seen, definitely not wanting to be heard.

He nervously dropped his pad. He watched his pencil roll toward the very couple who voiced their racist remarks within earshot. It seemed that pencil laid still for hours. There was no possible way Abel was ever going to ask them to return his pencil. Slowly, Abel got up. Left his seat, walked over to the couple.

"Excuse me, sir, ma'am," said Abel. There was no response. As if Abel was not there.

"Excuse me, just gettin' my pencil," said Abel.

Quickly and deftly Abel bent down, holding his breath, hoping not to disturb the couple and ignite more racist hurts to be hurled at him. Quietly Abel sat back down in his seat, "Back at it," he said to himself.

He really wanted to write now. Channel the negative energy that permeated him. That odor of rejection because of his skin color.

Over the months since his move to California, Abel had become more oblivious to the racism around him. The opposite approach to what his defiant brother and father exhibited. He had come to realize in his heart it was why they were both murdered at the hands of Alabama white supremacists.

Eyes to the ground, head bowed. "Where was I?" Abel asked himself. He thought about his heroine, Cassandra. She lay in bed alone in her room. Her face buried deeply into her pillow. The faint sighs provided the only clue that she was crying. Now Abel's pencil glided quickly. One pause . . . "Yes," he said to himself.

This is where Abel is at his best, when he immerses himself in his writing. He focuses on his heroine Cassandra. She loves, but she feels betrayed by the man she loves desperately. She wants him back. She is willing to do anything to get her man back. Murder, if it will quench her passion and desire.

There was no need for Abel to look up. No need to feel the scowls, the looks of hate, the words of racism from those who surrounded him on that crowded bus, on that hot day in New Mexico. For Abel, communicating in words was his escape. The words flow quickly now. Soon it will be too dark to write. He will be back in Los Angeles. Back home. Back to work. Back to Ian.

19

———

"Fore!"

Ian's errant drive off the seventeenth tee managed to find its final resting place on the adjoining fairway. The near decapitation of an unsuspecting golfer missed its mark by several feet.

"Goodness sakes, Ian, it may be better time spent working on your golf game instead of writing these disappointing screenplays for me to read," said Leammle.

Ian became taken aback. He was puzzled. He could not be certain if Leammle said those words in jest, or was sending a message back to him. Before that day he had no clue Leammle had become dissatisfied with his work on the Queen Elizabeth screenplay. Queen Elizabeth was to be Universal's second talkie. Katherine would star in the picture, Ian slated to write the screenplay and direct. This union, affectionately known as "Team McGregor" in all the Hollywood newspapers, already had two Academy Awards for their efforts, and Ian believed his first few pages were progressing well. It was because of his confidence he showed the pages to Leammle the previous week.

"I'm not quite sure what we're talking about," said Ian

Leammle acted as though he didn't hear Ian. As

if he hadn't said a word. Instead, he walked over to his golf bag, re-lit his cigar, and signaled to his caddie to hand him his 9-iron. Ian felt obliged to lend Leammle a moment of gentleman's sportsmanship and took a step back to allow Leammle a chance to place his next shot on the green.

"Drat, another damn sand trap," said Leammle.

The stroll down the fairway felt like hours to Ian. He wasn't thinking about golf. He was curious. He wanted to know what Leammle was thinking. Ian was set to direct Queen Elizabeth in addition to writing the screenplay. But he also knew if the studio doesn't approve his script, another writer and director will be attached to the picture.

"I have gathered you weren't impressed with those first forty pages," said Ian

Leammle replied, "To be honest, Ian, I was quite disappointed. There is something missing. Your script for *Another Man's Poison* was on the mark. Sharp. Witty. Intense when it needed to be. It showed in the picture. You made Katherine a talkie star."

"Bloody right I did. And I will continue to do so, Junior," said Ian.

Leammle paused a moment to think about what he would say next. He loved Ian like his own son. Universal was a low-tier studio competing with the MGM, Paramount, and Warner Brothers of the world. Every picture had to end up in the black.

"Our banks in New York are nervous after the crash. We are talking about individual investors who were smart enough to keep their money in their mattresses and not on Wall Street. I guaranteed them *Queen Elizabeth* will end up in the black. I made that guarantee because I believe you and Katherine can pull it off. As far as you are concerned, I still do. Now I don't know what has happened to your writing. But I need you back on the ball here. I've had my say. Shall we finish the round?"

Ian sat in the projector room, staring at the dailies from *Captain's Cove*. The movie screen flickered his latest work. His body was present, but his mind was still on that golf course. Leammle was dissatisfied with Ian's screenplay. And if he was not happy, then Katherine was not happy as well. How is this possible? he asked himself. It wasn't making any sense. *Another Man's Poison* won him an Academy Award for Best Original Screenplay. It garnered him praise from not only Leammle, but the other studios inquired about his contract status with Universal. He smiled when he thought about how Louis B. Mayer from MGM approached him in the men's room to compliment his work while holding his penis over the urinal. He recaptured the artistic respect from Katherine. She won an Academy Award for best actress because of Ian's screenplay. To the bottom of his heart, Ian felt that every word written was his.

"Mr. McGregor. Mr. McGregor?"

Ian's secretary voice shook him out of his daydream.

"Your wife is on the phone. She says it's urgent."

Abel entered his room, quickly seeking a spot on the floor to drop his bag. He was emotionally spent and physically exhausted from the long trip. It was good to be back in California. Good to be in the McGregors' employ once again. Good to be back inside that room above the garage. His sojourn home to Tuskegee, attending Momma's funeral, to learn that Althea had moved away, shook him up and upset him visibly. Those few short days of events back home disrupted his sense of stability. Completely gift-wrapping Abel with an unsettling feeling to his life. Just the opposite being employed by the McGregors had brought him. The three-day bus ride back to Los Angeles while working on his novel gave him some peace and solace. He was ready to move on.

How wonderful it felt to lie in his own bed. Having his window always open so he may smell the ocean breeze off the Pacific, instead of Alabama's stifling and oppressive heat and humidity. He had missed all that had evolved as his Southern California existence. The blue skies. The sunshine. His work as a valet and chauffeur. The lavish parties he had the pleasure of being a servant for. Writing in his bed as his feet dangled over the side. Selling sandwiches and cigarettes on the train had finally become a distant blur. He felt he was even missing Ian. Or did he? What do I really miss? he asked himself. Not the physical energy they shared for the first time. Not that he has become Ian's ghostwriter. It was the way Ian would talk to him. The same level as a human being. An equal. Not as the ignorant, illiterate, shiftless, and lazy Negro servant that the rest of the world had embraced and cultivated. Even hated and loathed in the South. This here is 1932. There ain't no such thing as a Negro being equal to a white man, Abel said to himself. His last thought brought a wry smile and chuckle to his face. Who am I kidding, Abel thought to himself. His mind saw Ian as a friend and confidant. But his heart said something different. That because of the way the world was, he was a Negro. Always the lowest on the social and race scale. Second class. Third class. Fourth class in every way. He couldn't even vote. How dare he think he could be the equal of a Caucasian. Starting in the morning, it would be business as usual. Up at 4:30 a.m. Wipe down the cars. Prepare Ian's suit and wardrobe. Help with breakfast preparation. Drive Ian and Katherine to the studio. Pick them up from the studio. Help with dinner preparation. Shine Ian's shoes. And whatever else was needed to do. And now, what else was needed was Abel's attention. His affection. His heart raced haphazardly; each second moving forward saw his forehead moisten with perspiration. Stop it! Abel said to himself. Abel shut himself down. Just like the many times he shut down before Althea. He felt he would never be able to emotionally connect to anyone. If you ain't felt love in your heart, it ain't never gonna be broken, he said to himself. Abel's eyelids began to weigh heavily on his pillow. He was home.

"Don't you dare patronize me!"

And now, it was Katherine's turn to feel the wrath and frustration of Ian. Leammle's conversation on the golf course led Ian to believe Katherine was behind the studio's bluster and nervousness about the Queen Elizabeth screenplay and picture. She had backstabbed him before during the production of *Another Man's Poison.* The heavy drinking began at the country club at one. The heavier drinking made its presence known at five. By dinner, Ian was in full roar.

"I demand you tell me what you said to Junior!"

"Don't you dare talk to me in that fashion," replied Katherine.

Abel entered the dining room, keeping his head down as he hurriedly cleared the dinner dishes.

"We'll have coffee now, Abel," said Katherine.

"Yes, ma'am," replied Abel.

"Blast it all. Fetch me that bottle of scotch from my bloody office," said Ian.

"Yes, Mr. McGregor."

Katherine waited for Abel to exit the dining room. She needed to take a second. A brief moment. To think about what she wanted to say to Ian. Her blue eyes stared looking across the table at a very drunk Ian. She had been down this path before. A road well traveled. Katherine worried. Worried that

Ian has lost his writing and creative touch again. Worried that if Ian failed, her luster will vanish, and the younger actresses trying to break through during the talkie boom would take over. She was dreadfully worried she would become a soon-to-be-forgotten has-been. An over-the-hill has-been at thirty-five. She thought back to those earlier days when she and Chaplin had just started with Mack Sennett. That was fourteen years ago when she was a fresh-faced, starlet two years removed from a highly successful Broadway run starring in *Romeo and Juliet*.

"Suppose you tell me what Junior said that has you all riled up," said Katherine.

Abel quietly entered the dining room with Ian's bottle of scotch. Ian wasted no time snatching the bottle off the tray and pouring three full shots into his glass.

"Will that be all, sir?" asked Abel.

Ian simply waved his hand to signal Abel to leave and enjoyed his first gulp.

"You bloody well know what Junior said to me because you told him what to say. I'm not an idiot," said Ian.

"Ian, you know it, I know it, and yes, Junior knows it. We all loved *Another Man's Poison*. But that was almost three years ago. We have made two flops since, and everyone is getting nervous. Including me."

Ian didn't even bother pouring the scotch into his glass.

Long swigs became the course of action.

"That's it. There you go. Find a way to steer your career failures on me. I can't write young heroine scripts for a woman closer to forty than twenty-five."

"Asshole!" yelled Katherine.

Katherine angrily threw her wineglass at Ian, narrowly missing his head. Minute bits of glass smash up against the wall behind him.

Ian asked, "Well, who's angry now?"

Abel could hear Ian and Katherine arguing a distance away from the garage outside. He kept his head down and focused on washing and buffing up the McGregors' automobiles. It was his usual evening chore. Things appeared to be back to normal. And like every normal evening, there would be a moment where Ian and Katherine would start yelling and screaming at each other. Two actors, effusing each other with melodrama, as though they were rehearsing lines for the next day's shoot. Once again, this evening, the McGregors were right on cue. The loud and excessive screaming at the top of their lungs was heard throughout the property by all. It did not deter Abel from his job. Head down and focused on his work. His soapy sponge moved a mile a minute across Ian's canary yellow Packard. And when every drop had been removed, Abel buffed the car finish to a moonbeam glow. He looked up in time to realize the shouting had stopped. He wasn't even certain how long the argument had been over. Ian's office window light turned on. I reckon he's a writin' 'bout now, Abel said to himself.

Just as over a year ago, Ian found himself in familiar territory. The familiar scene was playing itself out. The excessive drinking beyond being drunk. The headaches that pounded his head like the tympani drum from a symphony orchestra. The back-and-forth pacing in his office. His Corona typewriter sat squarely on his office desk, begging for attention. A white sheet of paper staring blank into space.

There was nothing left to do but sit down at his desk. To sit there as best he could to create something of use. A crafty script cloaked in sense and screenplay dialogue form. Something. Anything. Words on the paper making absolutely no sense was far better than that blank piece of paper laughing loudly at him from the typewriter. The intense pressure he felt, the overwhelming fear of failure and ultimate rejection. The headaches had become worse over the past few months. Universal Studios had transferred itself into a horror film factory during the Depression. There would be no competing against the MGM's and Warner Brothers of the world. Everything was riding on Ian. Without a well-written script, the entire production fails. No actor or actress can wring an outstanding performance from a badly written script. Since 1914, Ian and Katherine had been with Universal for eighteen years. Longer than any other studio employee. They rode the train westward from New York with the Leammles. So much talk. So much promise. So much expectation. Things quickly swirled in Ian's head. The pacing picked up. The panic made its entrance. Ian's cigarette just draped from his mouth. He gave no interest to the trails of ashes that dropped from to the carpet. There would be no going back to New York. No going back to Broadway to be a playwright. Since the success of *Another Man's Poison,* Ian had written and directed two box-office flops. The talk around Hollywood was that he was a flash in the pan, one-hit marvel. He needed a hit in a desperate way.

The quiet evenings in Hollywood reminded Abel of Tuskegee. He could lie still in his bed and absorb a blend of peace, calm, and happiness. He could hear the faint sounds of the ship's bell from Santa Monica Harbor. It was late: 1:00 a.m. A temptation to sit up, flick on the light, and finish his latest chapter became. All of those tranquil thoughts and desires to write dissipated at the sound of a faint knock at his door. He knew who it was. He just didn't know why he was knocking. Why he was at his door at

1:00 a.m. What he wanted. Abel knew there was only one way for him to get his answers.

"Sir?" asked Abel.

"Hello, Abel," replied Ian. "I say, it is a bit awkward just standing outside here in the chilly air. May I come in?"

Abel stood frozen for seconds that seemed like minutes. He was replaying in his mind the last time Ian came to see him. Thinking back to that moment Ian pressed his lips on his. Replaying in his mind Ian's hand pressing firmly against the small of his back. How they spent hours cuddled up on his floor. His heart pitter-pattered, fluttered in the hopes it would happen again.

"Let me in, Abel," said Ian.

Abel slowly opened the door and watched Ian slowly enter his room. He didn't want to look Ian in the eye. Not out of shyness, but in respect.

"Try closing the door."

Abel slowly closed the door. Two men, for different reasons, stood before each other.

"Welcome home, Abel," said Ian.

Abel replied, "Thank you, sir, it's good to be back."

Ian moved closer to Abel. Abel, over six feet tall, forced a shorter Ian to gaze skyward up to him. Ian loved playing worshipper to his chocolate brown Adonis. He was different. Like no other man he had ever met, or had ever bedded. Ian could feel his blood surge with passion as he inched closer. On his second visit, Ian's kiss meant more to both. Closer. Closer. Ian softly caressed, slowly cupped his hands around Abel's face. Closer. Closer. He wanted to kiss Abel. Abel stood very still, not moving one inch. As their lips pressed against each other, Abel stood there kissing back, but his eyes remained open, looking at Ian the entire moment.

He felt it was the right moment to break away and ensure some space was between them.

"You do not want to kiss me?" asked Ian.

Abel did not answer, only a blank stare present. He did not want to answer. Feeling something, but not sure. And now, the longer he felt Ian's embrace, the more confused he became.

"I ain't sure what's I want," said Abel.

"That's easy. I can help with that," replied Ian.

And an intense kiss took center stage. Their intertwining embrace became a synchronized waltz. One step back. Pause. One step back. Each moment, each embrace tighter. Their waltz has ceased. Abel's bed stood before them. It took Ian's kisses on his neck for him to finally close his eyes. Ian's slow and deliberate massaging of Abel's groin provided him with the clue he hoped for. Ian became clumsy. Awkward. Abel's belt on his trousers gave him trouble. Much longer than he wanted. Abel was ready to be pleased.

"Allow me," said Ian. "I have waited many a sunset to enjoy your wonderful thickness."

"Penny for your thoughts," said Ian.

Ian lay curled up inside the strength and prowess of Abel's arms and bare chest. The darkness engulfing Abel's room became interrupted with the brightness of a full moon cascading through the bedroom window. Abel did not sleep, just choosing to keep his eyes closed. Not wanting to look at Ian. Not wanting to answer his question after all that had transpired for the past forty-five minutes.

"Maybe it might be a good time to leave 'fo'e Ms. McGregor come lookin' for you," said Abel.

Those were not the words Ian had hoped to hear from Abel. Ian desired words of warmth. Words of desire. Words of comfort. Something romantic. Words to let him know he enjoyed their intimate moment.

"Do you want me to leave your bed?" asked Ian.

All remained quiet. Still as the evening that surrounded them outside. Abel shared no thoughts, no feelings, no affection or love. Guilt was painting Abel as though it was a freshly coated wall.

"Mr. McGregor."

"Please, Abel, during our special moments, you may call me Ian."

Abel replied, "This . . . this . . . this has been nice 'n all. I mean, what I am trying to say is . . . well, I ain't sure what to say."

Ian snuggled up even closer into Abel's chest. A massage of his groin gave Ian something to do with his hands as well. Abel turned his head to face the open window. He was fighting. Fighting to not become aroused again. He felt the blood surging toward his loins. Dear God, don't let that happen, he said to himself.

"I thought we had become friends. Good friends since the discovery of our feelings for each other," said Ian.

A wry `smile mixed with confusion painted Abel's face. Abel kept his gaze toward the window, as though he desired a message from God to strike him in the worse way. Feelings of ambivalence swirled through him with a monsoon-esque fervor. Abel teetered between shame and adoration for a man he respected, liked, and admired.

"Of course, we must continue to be discreet," said Ian.

"Dizzcreet?" asked Abel.

"Careful," replied Ian. "Subtle, quiet in a way to not bring attention to oneself. To us and what we are doing, and what we have. You see, Abel, it is not just about me and you. There is Katherine. A scandal involving her writer husband that involves the sexual exploits with his Negro servant can be embarrassing for all. Worse, a career ender for me and my beautiful wife. And that, my handsome Abel, is forbidden. Have I made myself crystal clear?"

So now Abel knew what Ian wanted. He wanted Abel's affection. Abel's trust. Abel's respect and honor. He wanted Abel's erection when the moment presented itself. In a quiet and discreet way. Abel didn't have an answer or response. He wanted Ian to get up and leave. He wanted to just sleep. He just wanted to see the sun come up so that the advent of a new day would signal in a new beginning.

"Friends?" asked Ian.

20

"I just noticed somethin'."

"And what might that be, my chocolate friend?"

Abel enjoyed running his long nimble fingers through Ian's hair. He found what he was looking for. A long, thin strand of gray hair protruding from Ian's scalp.

"Ouch! Bloody hell, what are you doing up there?" asked Ian.

Abel held the strand of Ian's gray hair between his thumb and index finger. Smirking like a Cheshire cat while displaying the hair before Ian's eyes.

"Have I aged that much in five years?" asked Ian. "Can it be 1935 already? You've been here what?"

Abel replied, "Pert'n'ear four years."

"Where has the time gone by?" asked Ian.

It was a moment to embrace each other warmly. The sheets of Abel's bed suffocated his and Abel's skin tightly.

"I've enjoyed workin' for you 'n Ms. McGregor," said Abel.

"Let's not get too weepy and start painting the moment with sentiment, shall we?" replied Ian. "We've enjoyed having you in our employ. I hope you stay with us for a very long time."

Ian softly clasped Abel's hand. Out of gentleness. Out of affection and admiration. One smile evoked one kiss between the two. Ian felt an undeniable urge to kiss, grab, and massage Abel's loins at the same time.

"I must go. Have to be at the studio early in the morning," said Ian. "Have the car out front by 7:30."

"Yessuh," replied Abel.

Abel had a moment to himself. He heard his apartment door close softly. Ian was gone. The break of day began to slowly emerge through his Venetian blinds. A wry, satisfied and happy smile painted Abel's face. The hummingbirds chirping outside his window reminded him of a Josephine Baker song that Althea used to sing to him after they made love. Wonder where she has gone off to, Abel said to himself. He wanted to see Althea in the worse way while he was home for Momma's funeral. He was all but certain there would be a moment for her and Althea to catch up. A chance for Abel to say he was sorry for the way things ended between the two of them before he left for New York. Abel was never one who could express his inner and intimate feelings with any level of ease. The hummingbirds changed their tune outside Abel's window. A quicker-paced chirp aided Abel in rotating his thoughts to Ian. This man named Ian. This man from Glasgow, Scotland, who met, rescued, and hired Abel from menial porter work on the trains. A man who, in his own way had shown Abel respect, kindness, affection, and friendship. A man who gave him his own room and freedom to come and go as he pleases. How can I pay him back for all he has done, Abel asked himself. Abel felt certain there will be a moment in the future that he will be able to reciprocate all that Ian had bestowed upon him.

Ian entered the foyer. Slow paced, a very slow pace. It was his way to help him get through the alcohol hangover. He was on the proverbial heavenly cloud after a most pleasurable evening sharing

Abel's bed. Ian embraced the early-morning quiet. Only Mabel singing out gospel songs in the kitchen could be heard. He had a notion to peek into the kitchen to make a special request for breakfast. His stomach growled softly but consistently. French toast with peaches on top. Mabel made the best french toast in Hollywood. Her other Southern dishes tempted Ian and Katherine to open a chain of restaurants as an investment. Mabel was never interested. "No, sir, I ain't interested in cookin' up for a bunch of folks," Mabel would always say. He glanced toward the breakfast nook. He did not see Katherine having her morning coffee and reading while reading the trade newspapers. Strange he thought. Katherine was much more a routine person about her mornings than Ian. The end result of the last two minutes meant Ian was to take the long walk up the stairs to the bedroom.

"And just where were you all night?" asked Katherine. "Or shall I bother to inquire? I have had a dreadful night, and this morning is shaping up to be even worse."

This role Katherine was playing before Ian was a rerun many times over. Ian had seen the bedroom scene time after time again. The over-the-top melodrama. The panic Katherine would bathe in when the public or the press wouldn't praise her celluloid self. Katherine didn't see Ian rolling his eyes around his head. A half-hearted yawn. So apparent that Katherine was more interested in her current plight than where he had been all evening. Katherine stopped years ago being inquisitive about Ian's nocturnal escapades.

"Did you hear me?" asked Katherine.

"I'm sorry, is there something amiss in the papers, my love?" replied Ian.

"You obviously have not read the morning edition of *Variety*. Look at what they are saying about me."

Katherine softly tossed the newspaper at Ian, who caught it on the fly.

"Hedda's column, page 3," said Katherine.

Over the years, Ian had become adept at reading Katherine's newspaper clips without giving her the old here-we-go-again look. This time the scribe's words weren't kind, supportive, or full of adulation of one of Katherine's performances. To this writer, her portrayal of Queen Elizabeth was tepid at best.

"Oh dear, I say this is rather nasty," said Ian.

"That is so you," replied Katherine. "Make light of the demise of my career. Thank you so very much, my husband."

Ian watched Katherine slowly stroke her coffee cup as though she was rubbing Aladdin's lamp. Hoping, wishing for three wishes, one of which would grant her the fame, recognition, and studio prominence she once enjoyed in the twenties. The tears slowly cascaded down Katherine's cheek. Eight years ago she was more famous than Garbo, Crawford, and Bow combined. And now, a writer was stating for all the Hollywood world to see that she was now a has-been. Hollywood had given Katherine a new name: Box-Office Poison. Katherine was now closer to forty than thirty. Fame can be as fleeting as a Kansas tornado in September.

"I am a total has-been," said Katherine. "Maybe I can be dress extra or car hop at Burger Bill's."

"I understand Cirros needs a hat check girl," said Ian.

Katherine replied, "I don't find that comment the least bit funny."

Ian could sense Katherine was about to embark on a spiraling trek to a depressive day. One of his husbandly duties that he detested with intense passion was being Katherine's ego inflator whenever seepage from this air balloon commenced. She needed to be at her best today. The studio was holding a press conference to announce Katherine's next picture, *Remembering Tomorrow*. Leammle decided to move forward and start production in spite of the box-office failure of *Queen Elizabeth*. Leammle always looked at everyone who worked for Universal as family. Family equates to loyalty in his book.

"Darling, aren't you being a bit melodramatic?" asked Ian. "For goodness' sakes, it is not the first time Hedda has written something about you that bordered on nasty."

Not the words Katherine wanted to hear. The conversation was about to head south. For Katherine, her career, her livelihood, her fame was in the balance. The thought of being anything other than an adored actress always in the spotlight instilled an omnipresent panic. Those fears opened up the valve to more crying. It was Ian's moment to show compassion. Katherine felt Ian's hand on her shoulder.

"Darling, you are a wonderful actress," said Ian. "Your public adores you. Laemmle is going to announce to the press the news of your next picture. Now, get out of bed, put that lovely pink and white dress on, paint your gorgeous face, and let's get to the studio."

Ian softly grabbed Katherine's hand and placed a kiss of reassurance on her lips. It was what Katherine needed. Attention and affection from Ian.

"Still my number 1 fan?" asked Katherine.

"Always, my darling."

The moment echoed for a deeper passionate kiss. Panic and depression in Katherine's life had become the fuse to her libido the past few years. The feeling that her career of fame, fortune, and adulation was dissipating turned her on sexually. Sex and intimacy became a thirst that needed to be quenched.

"I need you, Ian," said Katherine. "Take me, darling."

Ian didn't have a moment to respond. Katherine had grabbed him to the bed and pulled him closer. Their hands grabbed, yanked, and tugged at whatever dress shirt, belt buckle or panties that were in the way.

"You know what I want. You always know when I need you inside me," said Katherine.

There were not many moments over the years where Ian could make Katherine happy. He had become invisible as nothing. A non-facto husband. Unfaithful, conniving, self-serving, and narcissistic. Through it all there was always a mutual respect and a close and deep friendship between Ian and Katherine. Ever since they met in New York, Ian was at Columbia and Katherine was performing with her family troupe. Almost twenty years. They were friends and sex partners, but a total disaster as a married couple. The arrangement suited them fine. They knew what they had in each other. There would never be children. Those years were over for Katherine. Her choice. It would always be about her career. Her center was being on that screen in front of an audience. And there was also their hot and passionate sex life. The deeper the depression Katherine allowed herself to get into, the more passionate Ian's and Katherine's sex life became. Ian obliged her, of course. He always loved sex. She always loved sex. The bedroom was the only place they found bliss together. Katherine did not care who Ian slept with. He was the only man she had any intimate history with. Ian satisfied her in every way.

"Be good to me," said Katherine.

Ian held Katherine tightly so they were able to fuse as one.

"Be good to me."

"Nails in my back, my Kate," replied Ian.

"Be good to me."

"Always good to you, my Kate."

The studio commissary was unusually quiet this morning. There were no individual conferences between actors and actresses. No hustle and bustle from extras in between jobs. No producers and directors negotiating. No lovers and combatants bickering. Waitresses walked around desperately looking for people to serve, their daily tips hanging in the balance. Ian sat alone in the corner reading the latest draft of his script. His pencil spent more time being twirled in his mouth than creating snappy dialogue on his screenplay. In between twirls evolved a forlorn and disgusted look on his face, he was not embracing what was on paper. He hated what he had written. He was two seconds from balling up every piece of paper and tossing every page on the floor. Nothing was working. Everything being put down on paper came back into his face as tripe. It has been six years since *ANOTHER MAN's POISON*. Ian couldn't figure out what had happened. How he lost the touch writers covet. How can I win an Academy Award for my writing one year and be the worse bloody writer on earth the next, he asked himself. He refused to believe that perhaps his talent was fleeting. He wanted to believe that he was still a great writer. That his Academy Award was not a fluke. He thought it may be the headaches. The drinking. Ian, just as Katherine, battled depression demons himself. For Katherine, it was her fading beauty and good looks.

For Ian, the power of his pen was fleeting. Neither one could fathom what the future was going to bring them. Ian became so absorbed with his perceived future doom and career being blown to smithereens he didn't hear the voices saying hello to him.

"Ian. I say, Ian."

Ian raised his head up out of his script. James stood before him. He wasn't alone. His two friends were also acquaintances of Ian.

"I say, Ian, fancy you being here so early," said James.

Ian gave James a very long and cold stare. It startled James. He always thought as the years have gone by that him and Ian would remain friends. It was always a rare occasion when a jilted lover had a desire to remain friends during the aftermath of a painful breakup.

"You remember Elsa and Boris," said James.

Ian replied, "Of course. Please, won't you join me?"

The surprise in seeing James sped Ian's heart from still to a flutter, *pitty-patter* rhythm. He had decided to be nice and cordial to everyone.

"Why the happy faces?" asked Ian. "Is Louis B. Mayer coming to Universal?"

James could not resist hiding his glee. His feelings were more of relief and satisfaction. It was a celebration. *Bride of Frankenstein* was completed and in the can. Universal was relying heavily that his picture would reap in large box-office receipts. James's films over the years, *Frankenstein, Show Boat, The Invisible Man* kept the studio in the black during the Depression. Ian had been jealous of James's success for years. His career skyrocketed, while Ian's had floundered into becoming the future has-been. A one-hit writer.

"We just wrapped up *Bride of Frankenstein*," said James.

"Well, now, it appears congratulations are in order," replied Ian. "Milk shakes for everyone!"

Ian signaled to the waitress to bring over three vanilla milk shakes. His amusing comment brought a boisterous laugh from everyone at the table. James saw it as a discreet opportunity to softly massage

Ian's leg under the table. Ian continued to laugh and chuckle so that the others weren't informed on what was happening under the table.

"I can imagine, Boris, you are quite happy not to no longer wear Jack Pierce's makeup caked all over your face for twelve hours a day," said Ian.

Boris replied, "You have no bloody idea."

"Absolutely stifling," said Elsa. "Every time I looked at those dailies it reminded me how ghastly I looked."

"Well, my dear, it is a horror picture," said Ian.

Boris replied, "You shouldn't complain, Elsa. You know what that troll Hedda wrote about me in *The Reporter*? She said Frankenstein is a stark improvement to my own bloody face."

Boris's remark was funny to all. James felt inclined to chime in on the conversation while rubbing Ian's leg. He was enjoying listening to the banter between Ian, Boris, and Elsa.

"Well, if you don't mind, I best get a move on. Enjoy your milk shakes," said Ian.

James was hoping Ian would look up at him while he left the table. He didn't look up. Ian made a straight line to the door and exited quickly. He was running late for Katherine's press conference to announce her next picture. He didn't care if he was late or not. He was happy to take twenty minutes for a five-minute walk through the studio grounds. Ian was still upset Leammle assigned someone else to direct Katherine's picture. He's losing confidence in my writing, he said to himself. Now it was Ian's turn to feel paranoid about his job. The sense of losing everything he has worked for over the past twenty years. Now he was even more incensed. James had dumped him unceremoniously, found another lover named David. They even moved in together. Bought a home in Pacific Palisades. Ten-minute drive from Ian and Katherine. He hadn't seen James for months.

Mostly on the studio lot, and every time he did see James, he would go out of his way to avoid seeing and talking to him. What happened in the commissary made Ian feel like a cheap throw-away whore from Boyle Heights. He thought about returning to the commissary to give James a big round black eye. All the bloody nerve for James to take the liberty by rubbing me leg under the table, he raged to himself. Ian fumed with each step he made toward stage 17. He stopped. He needed to light up a cigarette. It was time to compose himself. Time to remember what was crucial at the time. What needed to be addressed. What had become imminent. The survival of his career at Universal. Between puffs he gazed around at what was before him. The studio buildings. The offices that housed the writers. The constant hustle and chaotic bustle of staff, colleagues, and actors. The directors who recognized him and nodded in acknowledgment. It helped Ian to remind him what was important to him. There will be more bloody buggers to bed, he said to himself. Ian took great joy in extinguishing his cigarette with his shoe while pretending he was stepping all over James's penis.

"Ladies and gentleman, thank you for attending our press conference to announce the new Katherine Edmonds picture *Remembering Tomorrow*," said Leammle. "We at Universal Studios feel we have put together a fine cast and crew. Production will begin next month. Now without further ado, I am going to ask Katherine to step up here and answer a few questions."

The newspaper reporters and cameramen stepped up a few feet closer to live on every word that Katherine was about to evoke. She was already used to the lightbulbs bursting and exploding in her face. Her flaming red hair served as a demure background to the navy blue business suit she decided to wear for the occasion.

"Thank you all for attending," said Katherine. "It is always so much fun to share the excitement of announcing my new picture with so many friends. Yes, all of you are my friends. Even the ones who haven't been so kind."

Katherine's last statement brought a chuckle from the press. The reporters knew who the nasty ones had been accentuating Katherine's downslide over the past few pictures. Ian stood several feet in the background, unseen and unheard from. He was supposed to attend, after all; he was the one chosen to write the screenplay. But he was not asked to join Katherine and Leammle at the press conference table. Shunned again. Asked to sit in the corner as though he was in grade school being punished for throwing a pencil on the floor in order to bend down for a peek at young Molly's panties. It was beginning to become a habit. Ian stood listening to all the accolades being hurled at Katherine. The hope that this picture would resurrect her staid career. Ian needed a hit. He was desperate for one. It is one thing to have the cure back to writer's heaven. It was another to stand there without a clue on how to go about it. Ian was the latter.

21

Ian's typewriter *clickety-clacked* with a rhythm reminiscent of a Bach overture. A rousing and boisterous pace. Orderly. Filled with passion. His long love affair for writing and creating words of meaning were excreting through his fingers. He was on fire behind his huge oak desk. A writer has that creative flow; a breakthrough from writer's block has been broken. It must not stop. Not even for a bathroom break, a fresh cup of coffee. Your twenty-fifth cigarette of the day. The cries from a child in another room. At a quick glance, it appeared the keys were emitting smoke like a steamboat engine.

"No! No! No!" screamed Katherine. "Surely you cannot mean this."

Ian ignored Katherine's loud outburst and kept typing. His subconscious conveyed negativity in the form of Katherine criticizing his work. Her screams grew louder in his head. Reverberating at will. A headache ensued. He began to misspell words. All in a matter of a few quick seconds.

"Damn it, Kate!" yelled Ian. "What the hell is wrong now?"

Katherine balled the script in her hand while circling the sofa to face Ian. Ian kept typing. He didn't want to stop. He was wishing Katherine was not there. She stood before him, her hands planted firmly on her curvy hips.

"Ian, we need to talk about this scene," said Katherine.

Ian kept typing.

"Ian!"

Ian kept typing.

"For God's sakes, Ian!"

Having Katherine yelling at the top of her lungs was enough to get Ian to stop typing. It was also a very good reason to continue the binge drinking he had started at sunrise.

"What can I do for you, Kate?"

"This love scene in the second act. It is simply not going to work. You just have to rewrite it," said Katherine.

Ian replied, "Blast, Kate, I have rewritten that scene six times."

"And you have failed to get it right six times."

Ian rose up from his chair and slapped Katherine violently across the face.

"You ungrateful bitch. I have written some of your greatest lines since New York and Broadway. And I suppose you now feel that gives you the right to degrade me. I know all about the times you asked Junior to replace me on our last three pictures. You didn't even have the guts to tell me in my face you think I stink. Why, you are nothing but an over-the-hill has-been. If it wasn't for me these past five years, you would be passed out on some bar stool. It was my screenplay, my screenplay, that I wrote that got you that Academy Award. You ungrateful bitch."

Ian's violent, unpremeditated outburst triggered another one of his excruciating headaches. It forced him to stop yelling, direct his attention to the unbearable throb in his head. He leaned on his desk to maintain his balance. Katherine saw Ian's collapse as an opportunity to regain her balance and run out of the office.

"Get out!" yelled Ian. "I said get out!"

Katherine was able to close the door seconds before the glass hurled by Ian made its mark. The past few minutes didn't deter Ian from pouring another shot of scotch. And another. One more, simply because it was available. For reasons only known to him, he thought a round of boozing with forty-year malt scotch serving as ringmaster would alleviate his throbbing headache. He did the right thing. At least he thought he was doing the right thing—return back to his typewriter. This time, there was no *clickety-clack*. No pulsating beat. The mood, the unwavering flow of words were long gone. Damn that Kate, Ian muttered to himself.

He wanted to blame someone. Anyone. There always appeared to be a convenient reason for Ian to blame another person for his writer's block. For his unavoidable, increasing tumble toward certain literary failure. The majority of the time, the blame was placed on Katherine. Their self-serving, vicious competition to show up the other was beginning to take its toll on him and their marriage. For those other moments of travel through the depths of pain and depravity, it was his swilling of alcohol. And suddenly, without warning, his writer's block appeared. The painful, inner reliving of James's rejection of him for a much younger man. The mounting pressure and stress heaved upon him to create screenplays for Universal that could be made into something for the viewing public. Always a reason. Always a ready-made excuse to make it easy for him to accept the writer's block spells. Always the two-headed monster named failure standing before him. Ridiculing him. A derisive, mocking laugh swam inside his head. The pain drove him to loud screams. Cries of agony. Psychotic madness. The voices inside his head cursed his every word that had missed its mark in all of his scripts. It was not the first time he had slapped Katherine. It was the first time he slapped her after she had denigrated his writing. Stood there in his face, looked him in the eye, and proclaimed his failure. His shaking head reached for the bottle and poured. Not even enough for a shot. Ian reached into his desk drawer for another bottle. He had given up for the night. The writer's block would not be lifted this evening. He wanted to celebrate. To do what he did best. Drink scotch until he passed out so he may see the next morning.

"Abel."

Abel stopped emptying the ashtrays in the living room to turn around to see Katherine standing fully dressed with packed suitcases.

"Yes, ma'am," replied Abel.

"You may finish that later. Bring the car around. I will be taking a suite at the Biltmore for a few days."

"Yes, ma'am."

Abel quickly gathered his cleaning rags and exited the living room. All the while as he moved through the hallway, he could not help but ask himself why Katherine was leaving. Why now. It wasn't the first time she packed her bags and left for a few days. What piqued Abel's curiosity was the look on her face when she told him to bring the car round front. It was obvious she had applied extra makeup under her right eye. Wearing sunglasses at night. He did not want to keep Katherine waiting, zooming through the kitchen and past Mabel like the white hue of a fast-moving comet.

Katherine always required Abel to wear a chauffeur jacket and hat. He dressed quickly, started the Packard, and slowly pulled the car out of the garage. He stopped the car long enough on the driveway to notice that Ian's office light was still on. It was against his better judgment. The temptation had become overwhelming. He knew Katherine was waiting. Abel wanted to take a peek inside the window to look at Ian. Just for a moment. He pressed his face against the windowpane. There Ian sat. His battle with the scotch bottle was over. Passed out and sprawled unconscious on top of his desk. His face buried into his script. The same script Katherine said was awful. The same script Katherine got slapped in the face for. The same script that remained unfinished. Abel pressed his face harder against the window. He thought about the special moments he and Ian had shared over the years. How their special relationship, unbeknownst to all, meant so much to him. Abel possessed a fierce loyalty comparable to a well-trained dog toward his master. He gave Ian a faint smile, returned to the car, and drove around to the front of the house.

It was never Abel's place to speak while driving Ian or Katherine. It was a cool evening for a July summer. Katherine looked outward toward a quiet Sunset Boulevard. On occasion, she would use her handkerchief to douse the tears off her cheek. Abel kept driving. Quiet. To himself, an every-now-and-then peek at his rearview mirror to see what Katherine was doing.

"Kinda cool evenin' for this time of year," said Abel.

Katherine continued to stare out the window. She didn't hear Abel, or she did and decided to pay no mind to him. Silence continued.

"Kinda cool evenin'," said Abel.

Katherine removed her sunglasses. It provided her a moment to light up her cigarette.

"I would like to ask you a question," said Katherine.

Abel wasn't certain that Katherine was speaking to him. He was the only one in the car, but Abel could not remember the last time Katherine wanted his opinion or point of view.

"Ma'am?" replied Abel.

"May I ask you a question?" asked Katherine. "It's a simple question."

"Yes, ma'am."

Katherine took a moment to stare at the back of Abel's head. She could see Abel looking at her in his rearview mirror. The moment needed one more puff off her cigarette.

"Have you ever been in love, Abel?" asked Katherine.

Abel paused. He was never one to voice his thoughts at a moment's notice. It was an easy question. Abel only had one girlfriend in his entire life—Althea.

"Not sure, ma'am," replied Abel.

"Well, have you ever had a girl?"

Abel replied, "Yes, ma'am. Back home in Tuskegee."

"Does she have a name?" asked Katherine.

"Althea."

"How cute," said Katherine. "It must be hard for you being away from her."

Abel drifted away from Katherine's voice for a moment. What was hard was not having the chance to achieve a bit of closure with Althea. There was no way for Katherine to know that he and Althea were no longer together.

"Me 'n Althea ain't together no' mo', Ms. Katherine," said Abel. "Been like that fer a while now."

"I'm sorry to hear that," said Katherine. "Love can be very fleeting. One day, you cherish and keep it close to your heart endlessly. Then something happens. One thing. A small thing. And what you thought was solid and true and wholesome, what you thought in your heart was unyielding bliss, is actually ice cubes on a sizzling hot sidewalk in summer. It dissipates ever so quickly."

Katherine decided that she was through talking. She didn't want Abel to see her tears streaming down her face. Just as well. Abel had no idea what she was talking about. She slowly slumped into her seat and closed her eyes, wishing inside, and desperate to run away from all her problems. Abel didn't want to talk about Althea anyway. Not enough good memories to fawn over and too many bad ones that remain lodged in his heart. *Why, I ain't sure what love is,* he said to himself. It was easy to conjure up inner feelings for Althea. She was Abel's best friend for many years. A relationship hatched when they were kids in knickers and socks. Abel was born when Althea first kissed him. She died when he left Alabama, and he lived for many weeks when she said she loved him.

It became well after sundown when Abel returned to the McGregor home. The muted *chong* of the hallway grandfather clock began to strike twelve. Abel needed to finish cleaning up Ian's office. Tomorrow was his day off. He was required to have all his duties completed. Ian and Katherine were always fair to Abel, but they demanded tidiness and order in their home at all times. Their marriage was a classic horror film in every aspect, but their lavish home had to remain pristine. Whisking Katherine away to the Biltmore Hotel placed him hours behind his schedule of duties. Ian's office was basked in a dark black hue seconds before Abel flicked the light on. As he stepped inside, he witnessed what he always saw, which is nothing new or out of the ordinary—Ian's office in a tattered mess. The sofa cushions were on the floor. In every direction, whiskey and scotch bottles were strewn all over. Balled-up papers representing one failed attempt after another were found crumpled up on his desk. Centered within Ian's self-imposed destruction was his typewriter alongside his neatly stacked screenplay, one page on top of the other. The title of Ian's creation stared right back at Abel. *Remembering Tomorrow*. Abel knew exactly what needed to be done. He had seen this motion picture before. Sprawled and passed out in the corner of his office lay Ian out cold for hours. With each drink, with each failed attempt to write something of meaning, Ian felt the failure noose being tightened around his neck. And now, hours later, his final resting place for the duration of the night had been found.

The temptation placed on Abel's shoulders began to mount as he stared at Ian's screenplay. Four years earlier, his heroic effort to save Ian from catastrophic failure yielded an Academy Award for Best Screenplay for him. But his efforts this time had a broader consequence, a deeper meaning. Abel's and Ian's relationship had taken a life of its own. A bonding had formed. A friendship was consummated. An intimacy unbridled like never before. His heart tugged ferociously. So Abel sat down, ready, willing, and prepared to take Ian's screenplay to another level. Hopefully, his efforts will provide Ian the ladder to a new and unachieved level of fame and notoriety. There's that sound. *Clickety-clack. Clickety-clack. Clickety-clack.* Suddenly, without warning, Abel stopped typing. Suddenly, he became fearful that the noise emitting from the typewriter would wake Ian. He stopped long enough to leave his perch from the desk and walk to the corner of the office. He looked down at Ian with a concerned look. *What a troubled man,* Abel thought to himself. Ian's snore and the cascade of dribble oozing from his mouth were distinct signals to Abel that Ian would not be waking up anytime soon. He returned to the typewriter. He read what Ian had written. His eyebrows furred. He winced. Nothing written flowed. Nothing written contained any elements of drama. Nothing written was remotely funny. That was all about to change, thanks to Abel. *Clickety-clack. Clickety-clack. Clickety-clack. Clickety-clack.*

Katherine had visited the Biltmore Hotel on many occasions—wedding receptions, studio functions, and family gatherings. Sitting in a hotel bar, sipping on martinis, and waiting for a secret lover made her edgy and pensive. It was late enough for the press to be nowhere in sight to take sneaky and unwanted pictures in order to supply their newspapers with unfounded innuendo. It made Katherine feel a bit more comfortable to signal the bartender for another martini.

"Well, hello, Katherine."

Katherine raised her head out of her martini glass while hearing her name. She faintly recognized the voice but couldn't quite place it.

"I say Katherine."

Now there was no doubt. Katherine recognized who it was. She stood a few feet behind her.

"Norma. How are you, dear?" asked Katherine.

"Oh my goodness, never better," replied Norma. "Irving and I were just leaving, celebrating LB's birthday. Face time with the boss is a necessity, I'm afraid. What brings you here?"

Katherine didn't really want to say the real reason. *Loose lips sink ships,* she thought to herself. Small talk was the avenue to be taken.

"Oh, I like being in the city at times," said Katherine. "You know Ian has become so accustomed to Hollywood Hills. I guess I miss New York and Broadway more than I ever would have thought."

Katherine's wistfulness toward New York City presented a perfect moment for Norma and her husband to graciously say goodnight and walk away. It was also the perfect moment for Katherine to look over her shoulder and focus on what she had been waiting for the better part of an hour—a twentysomething, tall, handsome, blond man standing by the elevator. It would be so unladylike to chug down her martini. A Hollywood star never forgets that all eyes are always on them, especially if you are Katherine Edmonds. The list began running in Katherine's head as she walked toward the hotel elevator—why he should sleep with this young Warner Brothers hopeful and why she shouldn't. What were her real motives for this evening tryst? Certainly not to make Ian jealous after fourteen years of marriage. *Give him everything you got, missy,* Katherine said to herself.

"Good evening, Mr. Flynn," said Katherine.

The afternoon shooting schedule afforded Ian an opportunity to watch the cast act out his latest rewrites. For Ian, as he stood in the corner of the soundstage, his whole rewrite episode the past few days had become a complete blur. It started as hoped, a chance to improve his final body of work. All he could remember from last night was grabbing his head in pain and passing out by his office window until the next morning. How he wished the cup of coffee that he cradled in his hand was really a glass of scotch. His head stared down into his cup. He saw a deep abyss, his very life swirling in the balance. Six ounces of black coffee was able to convey so much.

"Oh, Ian, nice job on the rewrites. I think they will work."

By the time Ian realized that it was the director of the picture paying him a compliment, he had briskly walked past him and was now talking to Katherine on the set. The director's words brought a faint smile to Ian's face. More of an act of relief on his part, for he was certain that if the director approved of what he had written, the studio boss, Leammle, must have as well.

"Quiet on the set!" yelled the director.

"Lights!

"Speed!

"Camera!

"Action!"

As Ian listened to the scene being played out before him, his pride and sense of accomplishment turned to amazement and bewilderment. He had become perplexed. The actors were acting out the scenes he had written, but Ian could not remember the words. He had no recollection of ever putting the dialogue down in writing. He reached inside his raincoat and pulled the script out. It was all there, the exact dialogue with his name on the front of the script. His head slowly looked up to the stage toward Katherine. How poetic and romantic the words he had written enhanced Katherine's beauty. *By God, she still has it because of me,* Ian thought. But it wasn't clicking. He could not remember writing those very words. He didn't remember. Convincing himself that he did write it all was an easier task to accomplish.

22

Abel sat in his usual seat—that beat-up old desk and old, wooden, unvarnished chair placed right against the windowpane at Ken's barbershop. It was his same routine every other Saturday on his off day—writing down precious words on his crumpled-up notepaper in hopes that his special self-creative flow remained for the rest of the afternoon. The twirling of his pencil in his mouth once more signaled that he had run into a brick wall. No cohesiveness in the storyline and no snappy dialogue between his hero and lover. A moment of an innovative idea presented itself. Abel decided to change course. His novel would now become a three-act play. *Of course, why didn't I think of that before,* he said to himself. The story would play to Abel's writing strength—creating dialogue. He sought satisfaction in taking a moment to gaze out at the people strolling back and forth on Washington Street. It had not rained for thirty-eight straight days, and the look of perpetual thirst painted the faces of everyone who walked by. It was not the most productive of writing days for Abel. Having spent a late night immersing himself in Ian's screenplay in a clandestine fashion left him feeling tired and sluggish. Concentration was lacking.

"*Ho! Ha ha ha ho ho!*"

The loud boisterous laugh emitting from the barber chairs pulled Abel away from his people-watching exercise through the barbershop window. The neighborhood pimp, Big Charley Whitlow, had finished his haircut and was now entertaining the group with one of his famous street stories.

"*Ho! Ha ha ha ho ho!*"

This time, the entire barbershop joined in unison with Big Charley's bellowing as he made his way out the door. Abel managed a wry smile and small chuckle himself, keeping his smile while watching Big Charley converse with a man in front of the barbershop. The conversation seemed to last for minutes. Abel watched Big Charley slowly grab the woman's hand while giving her a reassuring smile. For such a large imposing man, his gentle nature pleased Abel. Suddenly, a split second occurred that Abel could not believe his own eyes. He began rubbing them ferociously. He dropped his jaw. *Naw, it couldn't have been,* he said to himself. He leapt out of his seat and bolted out of the barbershop. There was nothing left to do but to stare down both sides of Washington Street. He chose to look right and run in that direction. Abel quickly became adept at engineering a full-speed sprint while not bowling anyone over on a crowded sidewalk. He arrived at his corner destination, panting feverishly. Looking frantically in every direction, Abel did not see who he was looking for.

The doctor's stethoscope felt very cold running down Ian's back. It reminded him of those moments Katherine would slowly pour cold water on his back to wake him up in the morning. It was one of a few rare funny moments the two of them shared over the past number of years.

"Breathe deeper, please, Ian," said Dr. Owens.

Ian obliged as best he could. His eyes began to roll around the room. The task the doctor was performing was starting to become monotonous to him. He wanted this over in a hurry. The meeting with Leammle later that afternoon was in the forefront of his mind. Even though he was not directing *Remembering Tomorrow,* the production was going well. Shooting was on schedule. Katherine looked radiant and convincing during her performance on set. The director was happy. The producers were happy. The banks in New York were happy. Ian should be happy as well, if it weren't for the splitting headaches he has had to endure. Those ear-splitting headaches seemed to be getting gradually worse with each passing week, with each passing month, and with each passing year.

"I'm going to give you something for the headaches," said Dr. Owens. "It would help if you cut down the boozing, stress, and make a serious effort to get a decent night's sleep on a regular basis."

Ian replied, "Now that, mate, will never happen."

"Try, Ian. Try harder for your sake," said Dr. Owens.

"I suppose I should say thanks for the prescription and advice."

Ian looked tall and proud as he walked out of Dr. Owens's office. There was a wry smile on his face as though he knew something the rest of the world didn't. No matter what the doctor said, no matter what medical advice was disposed onto him, he would not heed his words of warning. To prove his defiance against good health, he lit up a cigarette the moment he stepped outside as he walked to his car. By the time he entered his car and drove away down Sunset Boulevard, he already had a second cigarette going. Meetings with Leammle always unnerved Ian. Leammle never let on what he wanted to talk to Ian about. It was an opportune time for Ian to reach into his glove compartment for his flask. One sip.

One puff. One sip. One puff. Whatever the subject matter, Ian's nerves would be calm.

"Mr. Flynn, you are quite the bull between the sheets."

Another escape romp for Katherine. Another moment to sink her self-esteem to new lows. Whenever she felt stress from the studio or the strain from being married to Ian, she would seek and find solace in the arms of another man. It was so easy for her. She used a man's libido to punish herself for marrying a man like Ian. For not seeing the signs as he was different before the wedding. For thinking about her selfish motives to enhance her career, instead of what kind of husband Ian could be to her. She would always be grateful and beholding to Ian for one thing. Because of his greatness as a writer, she became a star. First on stage on Broadway and now before the cameras in Hollywood. Ian and Katherine's twelve-year-old marriage brought them many highs. And with the many highs, usually many lows followed. Both were narcissists. It was always their personal needs and gratifications that came first. This day, a twentysomething, tall, handsome man from Tasmania just signed to a Warner Brothers contract was her lover, her amnesia tablet for past mistakes.

"Mmmmmm, I always feel like a purring cat after an orgasm," said Katherine.

"I always feel like more scotch and sex," said Errol.

Katherine replied, "Well, now it is usually the man that needs to rest up. You mind if we just cuddle? No time for another round, I am afraid. Have to leave for a meeting at the studio in a few."

Errol gently grabbed Katherine's hand and placed it on his groin. Katherine enjoyed massaging all his muscles in the area.

"How long have you been at Warner Brothers?" asked Katherine.

Errol tried to relax and enjoy being pleasured while answering Katherine's question at the same time.

"Five months. You really should stop if there is no time."

Katherine replied, "Who said there wasn't time?"

Leammle's office was quiet. His cavernous space was void of phone calls, secretary interruptions, or the endless stream of staff meetings. This was an occurrence that was rare during shooting season. Their biggest film for that year was *Show Boat*. It became a box-office and commercial success. Leammle practiced his putting stroke in the corner, while Ian sat in a chair before Leammle's large oak desk, puffing on a cigarette while staring upward as though the Sistine Chapel lay before him. As each second elapsed, the more perturbed he became. Ian, always a man without patience, detested waiting for someone more than anything. Cigarette number 3 beckoned.

"I wonder why Katherine is so late. Have you talked to her?" asked Leammle.

Ian pretended that he didn't hear Leammle. His attention stayed right where it was—blowing circles of smoke with his cigarette.

"Ian, did you hear me?" asked Leammle.

Ian replied, "I haven't the faintest idea."

And now the truth was out. Ian was doing his very best at not showing how irked he was at Katherine for being over an hour late. He and Leammle had not said more than twenty words to each other in that time frame. He had no idea why Leammle wanted to talk to the both of them at the same time. With his anger was also a look of remorse. He slapped Katherine very hard across the face the night before. And with that realization, Ian knew why Katherine left. She was going to be in the bed of another man, lying there and feeling the touch, thrusts, and embraces of a stranger onto her body. How many lovers of the years had she taken in retaliation to the pain Ian had injected on her. It was her way of getting back at Ian, to punish him as though he was a young lad who just hit a baseball through a neighbor's window and then ran away out of fear of the repercussions that followed.

"So sorry, I'm late," said Katherine. "Traffic from downtown was horrific."

Ian replied, "Now there's an hour I won't get back."

Leammle returned to his desk, while Ian, always the gentleman, let Katherine have his chair before grabbing another.

"Shall we?" asked Leammle. "Good then. I have some good news. The early box-office receipts from *Show Boat* are excellent. We should clear over a quarter of a million dollars. It will keep the studio in the black until we get Deanna Durbin's pictures shot and released. *Variety* will run a nice piece on how the picture saved Universal. Oh, by the way, the Mrs. and I are having a dinner reception in honor of the picture's success. I expect to see the two of you there. Together."

It was a moment for Ian and Katherine to take a glance at one another. Not a glance of love. For Katherine, a glance of defiance. A glance that said, "I got you back, you bastard." For Ian, it was a glance of anger. A glance that said, "You have never appreciated one thing I have ever done for you."

"Of course we will be there," said Katherine.

"Will *Variety* be writing anything else?" asked Ian.

"Oh Ian, this is not one of your Broadway melodramas," said Katherine.

"He asked us here for a reason, my sweet."

Leammle took a very deep breath. His face filled up with sadness and loss, a look that suggests that he was about to announce a death in the family to his loved ones.

"The banks in New York have taken over. They called in their note yesterday. They own the studio. I'm out."

It was the lone time Ian and Katherine shared the same feelings that day—the feeling of shock and disbelief. They sat before a man that had been the head of the studio for over twenty-five years. A Jewish immigrant from New York who packed up his family's vaudeville business and moved west to California in the hope that something new and exciting was on the horizon. One of a small number of pioneers forming a new and booming industry. And next week, he would be walking out the door and walking out on everything that he had built.

"Blimey, how could this happen?" asked Ian. "You just said *Show Boat* saved the day."

Leammle replied, "The picture will keep the doors open and the lights on."

"What dreadful news," said Katherine.

Leammle replied, "The studio took on a ton of debt after the Depression. We recovered a bit with our horror film unit, but it's simply a case of too little, too late."

"So what now?" asked Ian.

Leammle rose from his desk and walked over to the bookshelf containing all the classics he had collected over the years. His back remained facing Ian and Katherine. He found a copy of Melville's *Moby-Dick* and began to flip through the pages.

"I was hoping to shoot this one day," said Leammle. "Lon and I talked it over for years. Even started writing a script. He was going to play

Captain Ahab. Pity, one more dream that will not see the light of day."

Leammle placed the book back on the shelf and walked toward Ian and Katherine.

"New York told me they will not offer contracts to either one of you after your current deal expires in a few months. You will finish the *New Orleans Belle* picture. And, and, you will be free to sign with another studio. I'm sorry, you two."

Ian extinguished his cigarette, stood up out of his chair, and made his way to the office door.

"Where are you going?" asked Katherine.

"Getting fired makes me thirsty."

Ian's abrupt exit managed to unnerve Katherine more than Leammle's nerves for having to tell her that she had been fired. She lost track that her cigarette was dropping ashes all over Leammle's carpet. Quickly realizing her bad manners, she placed the cigarette in the ashtray.

"Have no fear, Kate. You will find a studio," said Leammle.

Katherine replied, "The consummate optimist. Warners, Fox, MGM, and Paramount all standing in line to hire a thirtysomething, almost fortysomething actress who has just started coloring her recently emerging gray strands of hair."

Katherine's cigarette burned slowly in the ashtray, but it didn't stop her from lighting up another one.

"You already have one going, my dear," said Leammle.

Katherine addressed the embarrassing moment by burying her hands in her face and sobbing uncontrollably. Leammle rose from his chair and in his customary fatherly fashion consoled Katherine as best he could.

"There, there now, Kate," said Leammle. "None of that. You are and still a talented and marvelous actress. Me personally and Universal Studios have been so proud at what we have accomplished with this business these last sixteen years. You and Ian were with me at the very beginning when we left New York together in '17. Greatness doesn't ever wane; it only flourishes. Don't ever forget that."

It was this particular cocktail party that Ian and Katherine loathed together and did not want to attend. Twenty years of black ties, evening gowns, champagne, smiles, laughs, and debates bringing the Hollywood elite together for one studio function after another. The remainder of the day was spent locked up in their home trying to make sense of the devastating news delivered earlier by Leammle. Katherine, lying in bed, crying her eyes out. Ian, consoling himself the best way he knew—taking laps in his bottle of scotch. Both wondered what the future as individuals and as a couple lay before them. Leammle's soiree was to be a celebration of the great financial success *Show Boat* had brought to the studio. And it was for everyone involved. Everyone but Ian and Katherine.

"Look!" said Katherine. "Everyone is glaring their eyes at us, whispering under their breaths. The word is out that we are looking for jobs."

Ian listened with one ear and kept his focus on the Negro female servant walking by with the tray filled with glasses of champagne.

"Thank you," said Ian to the waitress. As was his custom, Ian did more gulping than sipping. He also took notice of the room inhabitants staring at him and Katherine.

"The vultures are circling the prey, my love," said Ian.

Katherine replied, "Look at that damn Joan Crawford. Without question, I hate that self-serving bitch with a passion."

"You're in good company, darling. Everybody except MGM hates that self-serving bitch as much as you."

Abel stood outside, leaning on the car and waiting for the party to end inside. He was right at home. It's what all the other chauffeurs were doing. He knew the other Negro chauffeurs personally by name and who they worked for, but he was not friends with any of them. Abel was the only one of the group to finish high school and attend college, and the less fortunate ridiculed him for it every chance they had. He was hoping beyond hope that Ian and Katherine would want to go straight home and not make their usual after-party nightcap at Ciros, followed by a sunrise breakfast at a greasy spoon on Sunset. Abel would never tell the McGregors that their all-night revelry always meant that he had to be exhausted on his feet the entire next day. For the past twenty minutes, his attention was focused on his notepad and getting down some fresh ideas on his new play. Abel was very pleased that he changed his mind about writing a novel and was now focused on a play for theater. A symphony of car horns honking broke his concentration. He looked toward the opulent Beverly Hills home. His focus centered on the large living room picture window. He could see the partiers mingling about. The four-piece band stood before the fireplace mantle performing. Food trays and champagne glasses swirled in every direction. Out of the corner of his eye, he saw a female Negro servant. Medium height and slim figure. Her curves complimented the black servant's dress that she wore. Her hair was dark black and pulled up in a bun that rested squarely off the back of her head. This time, unlike a few months back at the barbershop, he made the connection. It was her. It was Althea.

"It can't be," said Abel.

Abel quickly threw his notepad on the front

seat and made his way toward the home. The other chauffeurs stopped what they were doing to watch Abel walk across the gargantuan-sized, well-manicured front lawn just so he could stand right in front of the living room picture window. He needed a closer look. He needed confirmation that the same woman he saw in front of the barbershop three months earlier was the same woman. It was. As the other drivers gathered to watch, Abel found his face pressed tightly against the glass. His body surged with an energy—a desire to want to speak to Althea again after almost ten years. He was happy to now know that she was alive and well and away from the Alabama way of life.

"Abel! Abel!"

Ian's yelling startled Abel just long enough to snap him out of his spellbinding moment staring at Althea. He immediately recognized Ian's tone of drunken irritability, turned, and ran back to the car with haste. His chauffeur colleagues worked hard at not laughing at him in front of the boss white man.

"For goodness' sakes, what are you doing spying through the window?" asked Ian.

Abel was a few steps from the car and for his sake, Ian and Katherine did not have to wait long for him to open their car door. One minute his face is pressed against a window, being wistful about the Alabama days gone by. Placing a desire in his heart feelings that he had not felt for a woman in a very long time. The next minute, at that moment, he was praying to God that he was not about to be fired.

"Sorry, suh," replied Abel.

Ian replied, "What was happening inside that bloody house is none of your goddamn business. Your job is to sit by that car and wait. Take us to the Brown Derby."

"Sorry, suh. Yessuh."

The sounds inside the car were silent. Only Ian's drunken slurps on his flask were audible to Katherine next to him and to Abel in the front seat driving.

"Would you care for a nip, my dear?" asked Ian.

Katherine offered a headshake to say no. The silence remained. Everyone was thinking of themselves. Their own problems. Their own fears. Their own insecurities. Their own regrets. Their own hopes for the future.

All Abel could think of as he lay in his bed was what he could possibly do within his power to find Althea. He would have to ask around. Where she lived. Who she worked for. He knew nothing about Althea. No money to spread around for information or a private detective. He had no connections. He had no idea where to even start. The three hard knocks at his door diverted his attention. He knew who it was. The three knocks were a precursor to the key going into the lock. It was their little signal. The coach house door slowly opened for a moment and then closed. Abel knew it was Ian. A blend of tobacco and scotch became his signature cologne. Abel kept the lights off. Only the glow off of Ian's cigarette brightened the room. Abel positioned himself on the bed so that Ian could sit next to him. Ian showed Abel a bottle of champagne before taking a giant swig.

"I am sorry for earlier this evening. Didn't mean to embarrass you in front of the other Negro drivers," said Ian.

"I know," replied Abel.

Ian gulped one more swig off the bottle and offered it to Abel.

"No thanks."

"I am celebrating, my chocolate friend," replied Ian.

"Celebratin' what?" asked Abel.

"Celebrating getting fired by the studio. Celebrating being out of work. Celebrating the unknown. Now, move over."

23

1941. The time, the years had totaled three since Ian had procured a writing assignment or directed a studio motion picture. Three years since Ian had set foot on a studio lot. No studio wanted him. No studio wanted to read his screenplays. No studio wanted him to direct their pictures. There had been a number of near misses—some extra dialogue for a *Rin Tin Tin* picture. There was the time he went to New York for four months to aid a producer friend who needed a director for his Broadway play. That was the extent of his work experience. The Hollywood world had a saying: out of sight, out of Hollywood. Ian now found himself outside looking in. The one aspect in his life that had remained a constant was his relationship with Abel. The satisfaction and climatic exuberance that he reached being with Abel remained steadfast and a welcome diversion to his writing assignment failures and deteriorating marriage to Katherine.

The sun shone brightly through Abel's window this December morning. The window was left cracked open slightly to allow for the cool air to circulate throughout the coach house. Abel's eyes slowly opened to greet the new day. Every morning, first thing after giving thanks to God for another day, he thought about Althea. The effort, the time, the money, the frustration, and failure of not finding her have tormented him greatly. The best piece of information that he could round up was that she quit her job as a maid and moved to Oakland. That's all he had to show for his time and effort and money—a maybe. That last night, that lasting memory of Althea due to his face plastered against the windowpane of a large mansion in Hollywood Hills on a chilly evening three years ago. It was an obsession now—an everlasting hope of finding her. With each day came the realization that he may never realize that hope.

"Good morning, my chocolate friend," said Ian.

Abel heard Ian's voice, yet continued to stare upward toward the ceiling. The stroke of Ian's hand on his thigh failed to arouse him. It was enough affection to snap him out of his daydream and remind him where he was in the now—in his bed with Ian.

"You were many miles away," said Ian.

Abel replied, "I know."

Ian nestled himself into Abel's strong chiseled chest, closed his eyes, and reveled in his sunrise bliss.

"It's Sunday. I guess you have your usual golf game with Mr. Grant at the Riviera," said Abel.

Ian replied, "Yes, 2:00 tee time. Have the car out front at 1. And by the way, tell that Negro clubhouse boy to not shine my golf shoes. I prefer if you do it from now on."

Abel got out of bed to turn on the radio. It was a birthday present Ian gave him the year before. That's what happens when things go well between two people, even between an employer and his employee—you collect birthday presents. Walter Winchell's Sunday morning show was on, and as their Sunday morning custom, Ian and Abel would listen to the broadcast together. Late Saturday night to Sunday noon was their time. That was the agreement Ian and

Katherine had struck many years ago, that neither one will ever ask and neither one will ever tell. This agreement now included Ian's Saturday night walks to the rear coach house.

The radio loudly blurted out Walter Winchell's voice, loud enough to garner both Ian and Abel's attention.

"News flash! Bulletin! The Japanese have attacked the United States of America at Pearl Harbor! I wish to inform the great people of the United States of America that the Japanese have bombed our naval facility at Pearl Harbor in Hawaii."

"Stop it, Errol," insisted Katherine.

She wanted to listen to Walter Winchell's broadcast, but Errol insisted on planting kisses on the small of her back.

"Stop it, Errol. I want to listen." Katherine reached over to the radio to turn the volume up. It was a welcome diversion from the events of the past few hours for her. In between her interlude sessions with Errol were long bouts of lying on her back staring at the ceiling. Those moments of thinking of never working in Hollywood ever again brought tears to her eyes, tears Errol never saw and didn't care to see. He was in that hotel room for one reason only. Katherine would be forty next week. Already the sounds in her head calling her a "has-been" were echoing loudly. Listening to Winchell's distinctive voice telling all Americans who listened that the United States would most certainly be in the war reminded her of a director she hated with passion. She wished she was on a set listening to the blustering fool yell at her. She would give her right arm to feel the hot lights beam on her, the makeup artist fussing over her hair, and the set dresser helping her undress out of her lavish costume. Errol's tongue found Katherine's inner thighs. She fought the temptation to enjoy the pleasure and instead her eyes found the script on the nightstand. The minutes mounted as Katherine stared at the script. A script entitled *Jenny Goes Home*. RKO was offering Katherine the lead in a picture. It was a B-picture from a second-tiered studio, but she didn't care. She didn't care that it was the lead to play the mother of a rebellious teenage girl who runs away from home to join the circus. She didn't care that her future roles in motion pictures would be of mommies, aunts, and lost cousins. She didn't care. She didn't care that a teenager and a chimpanzee would be the main focus of the picture. She didn't care.

So many changes, along with so many trials and tribulations had transpired between Ian and Katherine over the years. The one constant remaining in their lives together was their affinity for lavish parties. They had garnered the reputation and moniker of "Mr. and Mrs. Entertainment of Hollywood." The war had officially begun for the United States, and Ian and Katherine began their contribution to the effort by entertaining Hollywood royalty and collecting donations for war bonds. It was all they could do. Ian failed the army physical, a paltry excuse to escape a writing and directing career that had all but dried up.

His self-delusional belief that leaving Hollywood to go become a moving target for the Japanese was a step in a forward direction that confirmed his desperateness in abundance.

"Darling, you've done a splendid job mixing these Nazi directors over here with our Commie friends," said Ian.

"Unfortunately, I invited these Prussian pricks because I desperately need to work on someone's lot," replied Katherine.

"On that note, must the musicians play Wagner? This German theme is depressing me."

"Will you forget about all of that, please? RKO tomorrow. Be on time and please be sober. Look, there is George Schaffer. I should butter him up a bit more before tomorrow."

Katherine softly kissed Ian, and with that subdued but affectionate response was their signal to mingle about to let the Hollywood world know that the McGregors were to be reckoned with as a serious acting, writing, directing team. They both circled and worked the room as though a wide-angled lens camera were watching their every step. A number of producers and directors were cordial to Katherine and Ian, but whether either one of them would ever be considered for a serious role or writing assignment again was problematic and not very likely.

"Over here, boy."

A thirsty actor of no fame or notoriety summoned Abel to bring him another glass of champagne. And as was his custom at such an affair, Abel obliged the gentleman. His job was being made difficult because of the thirsty crowd. He could not keep enough champagne glasses on his tray. Another unforeseen pit stop to the kitchen to restock became inevitable.

"Don't chu tellz m you needin' more champagne," said Mabel.

Abel replied, "'Fraid I do."

"Sho'iz a thirsty crowd out there," said Mabel.

Abel stood in a nearby corner watching Mabel prepare the tray of champagne. It was a task he had seen Mabel execute many times before. Seeing Mabel in her maid's uniform triggered visions of Althea and the last time he saw her three years ago. A vision stamped and embedded in his head.

It seemed there was always something appearing in Abel's daily routine that would trigger thoughts of Althea. The way a woman would walk down the street. How a young mother would cross her legs in the barbershop as she waited for her son to get his haircut. Even Katherine reminded Abel of Althea by the way she twirled her hair through her fingers when she was in a joking mood. It had reached a level of feeling as if he was haunted by a ghost. Just as with Heathcliff's Cathy in *Wuthering Heights*, it's an all-encompassing aura of chasing a love that may never be attained. A spirit within him, and yet her spirit was beyond his grasp. His only prayer was that he may have one more chance to love Althea again. He was convinced that if he ever saw her again, she would give him another chance. He thought about Ian. The three years they had been together. It was different with Ian. Abel was smart enough to know that. It was arousal, energy, and passion at the same time. That's all it would ever be. It would never be love. He knew he was being used for his body. A whore. A Negro whore. *What else could it be for,* Abel said to himself. A Negro possessing physical prowess went right along with his other duties: valet, chauffeur, and butler. Abel had those coveted perks and allowances the other Negro servants didn't have and didn't know about. The extra pay. The extra pay that was always in cash. His own private living quarters on the property. And for those reasons, sleeping with Ian made it all worth it to him. It wasn't forever; he never saw himself being Ian and Katherine's butler for the next twenty-five years. It was a means to an end. There were no other alternatives out there in the world for him. Back to Harlem if nothing else, and for Abel, that would never be a consideration.

Mabel broke Abel out of his trance by yelling at

him. "College boy, I sayz them champagne glasses ain't going to get served all buyze demselves."

Ian waited patiently for an opportune time to sneak outside and away from the Hollywood glitz and ass-kissing going on inside. He found the brick veranda to his liking to enjoy his cigarette. The swirling warm winds due to a brief storm had finally passed through. He failed to see a servant with a full tray of champagne passing through, so he reached for his ever-present flask filled with scotch.

"I say, you wouldn't mind if I took a swig of that?"

Ian looked around to see who was speaking. Initially, he ignored it because he didn't recognize the voice.

"Are you going to hog it all, my good man?"

This time, the voice stood a few feet behind him. He offered his flask to a handsome, dark-haired man with full eyebrows.

"My pardons," said Ian.

"Thank you. The name is Tyrone."

"I am quite aware of who you are, Mr. Power. You're a well-known man," replied Ian.

Tyrone smiled in amazement that he had been recognized as a movie star by someone other than another actor or reporter. Ian admired Tyrone's firm handshake. A well-timed glance between the two ignited an immediate chemistry. As the years transpired, Ian developed an inner sense when another man may find him attractive. Tyrone sported jet-black hair and thick eyebrows. His roguish smile made Ian feel particularly attractive. His black tux and tails provided a smooth contrast to his handsome dark features.

"You must be in the business. Which studio?" asked Tyrone.

"RKO. I'm a screenwriter," replied Ian.

Tyrone smiled and took a moment to take a long swig off of Ian's flask. The attraction between the two percolated with each passing second.

"Nice to meet a new friend who provides those special words which makes me such a big star in Hollywood," said Tyrone.

Ian replied, "I'll drink to that. To new friends."

The crowd inside the house began to plead loudly for Judy Garland to stand up and sing her rendition of an old *Show Boat* tune. The loud and happy revelry began in earnest, and for a moment, everyone at the party was trying to forget that the United States of America would be at war soon with Japan. Actors would have to enlist and actresses would join WAC. Studios would go into production making motion pictures about war stories and war heroes to keep American morale up. While the hoopla rang loud, Ian and Tyrone remained outside on the veranda sharing a cigarette and Ian's flask.

"Of course, Zanuck insisted I do my own fencing scenes like Errol did in *Captain Blood*," said Tyrone.

"You know my wife is fucking Mr. Flynn," replied Ian.

"I imagine you are okay with such an arrangement."

Out of the boisterous laughing and revelry inside the house, Katherine emerged outside looking for Ian. Her appearance was pained, aggravated, and upset. She moved closer to the veranda, pausing just long enough to finish her cigarette and extinguish it. Her eyes were able to acclimate itself to the evening glare mixed with the lighted fixtures on the veranda. Immediately, she recognized Tyrone. Everyone knew Tyrone. He was a major star and Twentieth Century Fox's number 1 box-office draw. And then she saw who Tyrone was conversing with. It was Ian. *That bastard,* she said to herself.

"Ian!" Katherine yelled. "Ian!"

Ian and Tyrone's conversation was interrupted by Katherine's yelling. They noticed her moving toward them.

"We both have our own set of arrangements," said Ian.

"My place in an hour?" asked Tyrone.

Ian nods affirmatively.

"Here comes the Mrs."

"Ian, I have an early call at the studio. I'm going home now," said Katherine.

"Very well, my darling," replied Ian.

"You're not coming with me?" asked Katherine.

Ian replied, "Tyrone and I are going to have a nightcap. I'll see you in the morning at the studio."

Katherine took a moment to allow Ian to see her disdain for his response. She turned and walked away in an angry huff. It was not the response she wanted to hear. The past six months found Ian and Katherine making a more concentrated effort in being and acting as proper spouses to each other. Katherine started coming straight home after shooting her scenes at the studio. Ian, although not working on any consistent level, was staying close to the house and cavorting less with his male lovers. That number had dwindled down considerably over the years. His promiscuity waned and the headaches had increased considerably, making it much more difficult for him to become aroused and therefore unable to satisfy in numbers as he once had. It had appeared that Ian was behaving the perfect way that Katherine always wanted him to. She knew in her heart that Ian would never completely stop loving men. But if he tried to give himself more to her, it would be enough for Katherine to sustain her love and devotion for him. And despite all that had transpired, Katherine had nary a clue that Ian's most voracious sexual appetite was reserved for the Negro man living two hundred feet away from her bedroom window in the rear yard coach house—Abel.

The clock in Abel's coach house read almost 2:00 a.m. He hated when Katherine loaned him out to friends for their own personal dinner parties. It always meant long nights and early wake-ups the next morning. He knew it would please Ian and make him happy that he wanted to make Katherine happy. It was the aftereffect of Abel's reputation as an excellent servant and butler. He was in popular demand to the Hollywood socialites. His dark and handsome features, his articulate and intelligent mannerisms, and the excellent work that he did placed him high on the bar compared to the uneducated and unsophisticated ways of his fellow Negro servants.

By now, Abel's own personal writings had taken a completely different path. He stopped writing his own book and began to keep a diary, a journal of his days, his nights, and his experiences in Hollywood and with Ian. Although feeling completely exhausted and knowing that he had to be up by 6:00 a.m. to drive Katherine to the studio, his thoughts and the pencil in his hand beckoned.

How can I think of him when I think of her?
I fear I may never see Althea again.
I want to write. To pen great words.
I desire my writings to be thought of
As Mr. Robeson's are. Enlightening.
Full of life and hope.
To keep my dream, my flame burning bright.
No one will take that from me.
Sleep, dear one.

The set crew stood around, impatiently waiting for Ian to arrive on the set. Katherine sat in her personalized chair, chain-smoking the last few cigarettes in her pack. She was already in costume—an old housewife's dress and apron while wearing domesticated and tattered shoes. Her beautiful auburn red hair fitted up tightly in a bun. Her face wore very little makeup, a deliberate effort to keep the lighting from creating spots and shadows and remove as much glamour as possible. Her role in RKO's latest picture entitled *City Life* was not what she ever envisioned, nor was it a role she truly in her heart wanted to play—the young mother and doting housewife of a growing family. The star of the picture was Marlene Dietrich, playing the role that was always Katherine's to have if ever she wanted it—the husband's mistress. The vamp, the jezebel, the voluptuous redheaded femme fatale. In this picture, Dietrich played the role of her husband's mistress. It was tearing Katherine up inside. Having to face the grim reality that her age, being the ripe young actress of forty-one, meant that she no longer would be getting the leading lady roles. Those special and coveted plums were now reserved for Ms. Dietrich, Ms. Dunne, Ms. Crawford, Ms. Shaerer, and Ms. Davis. There are those actresses who feel becoming the aging starlet is worse than death itself. Katherine was dying, in spades.

"Katherine, have you talked to Ian?" asked the director. "We are waiting for those rewrites. He hasn't shown up to the studio."

"Why no, I left home early," replied Katherine.

"Goddamnit!"

The director stormed off in an angry and impatient march. Ian was required to have rewrites for the new scenes completed and delivered to the director by the night before. He failed miserably in his duties. A no-show, not even a phone call. Katherine pulled many a string with the studio and producer of the picture to get a small but nevertheless writing work in an actual studio. And now, once more, he had failed her. Again. She dared not say that Ian never came home the night before. Her last sighting of him was witnessing Ian sharing his whiskey flask and lustful gazes at Tyrone. And just as she was about to angrily stamp out her last cigarette to the floor, Ian appeared through the sound stage door with script rewrites on hand. He found the director, handed him the rewrites, and waited patiently as the director perused his latest work. Ian received a much-wanted nod and smile of approval from the director. As he turned to head for the door, he looked over in the corner and saw Katherine. He took a couple of steps toward her. Without a sign, he stopped in his tracks. Their eyes connected. Seconds quickly converted to minutes. Anger spoke in Katherine's eyes and remorse in Ian's. It was at this very moment that Ian felt it best to turn, place his fedora on his head, and walk away, leaving Katherine to seethe.

24

This thing called love
And what is that?
So hard to find
Even harder to keep
Does he love me?
Will she find me?
What do I want?

Abel sat in the Packard outside RKO waiting for Katherine. It was taking much longer than he thought, and as always, his custom was he had his notebook and pencil handy and available to record his thoughts. His personal and unabridged diary had become his everyday companion and pet. It had been months since Ian had made his way to the coach house to spend the night with him. He was unsure as to how it was making him feel. Ambivalence with his inner feelings was all so very new to Abel. One day, missing Ian greatly, there an ache in his heart that would never dissipate. Yearning to feel his hands caress his skin. His fingertips softly digging into his inner thigh. The next moment, he sadly accepted that he was just Ian's colored stud and forcing himself to move on. *Here comes Ms. McGregor, if she only knew,* Abel said to himself. His notebook was quickly shoved into his breast pocket so he can exit the car to open the door for Katherine.

"Sunset Boulevard in Bel-Air, Abel," said Katherine.

"Yes, Ms. McGregor."

From time to time, Abel would take an occasional peak in his rearview mirror to find Katherine rummaging through the pages of her new script. A moment would arise where she would read something displeasing. A desire overcame her to run her nails, scratching the paper while creating a distorted frown as wide as a cavernous gorge.

"Everythin' okay, Ms. McGregor?" asked Abel.

Katherine did not respond to Abel's question. While she crumpled up sheets of script in the back seat, Abel kept his focus on the winding, tree-lined street of Sunset Boulevard. He loved driving through Hollywood and Pacific Palisades during the day while the sun shone, the soft blue skies helped capture its brightest glow. On the drive back to the McGregors', he thought about the question he kept asking himself over the years—What am I? Who am I? He was alone. Alone to surf and meander through his thoughts and massage his heart in. He was beginning to think that perhaps moving back to Harlem would be best for him. Start over and find a job other than butler and chauffeur. But Abel knew that he would always be a writer. He knew that this talent to express himself with pencil and paper was a blessing and that in some way his destiny.

"Abel, change in plans. Drive me to the Brown Derby," said Katherine.

"Yes, Ms. McGregor," replied Abel.

Katherine had read enough of the script. She hastily decided to skip the Bel-Air meeting with the producer for her next picture. Drowning her anger with martinis at the Brown Derby sounded like a better idea. RKO's reward for the box-office success of the Marlene Dietrich picture from five months ago was to make her play a young mother again. This time around, she'll play a young mom who must keep her teenage boy from becoming a criminal. The title of her new movie was to be *Coming Home*. Katherine, after one picture, was already tiring of RKO's insistence to typecast her as the doting housewife. RKO was a B studio making B pictures. It would never be the fertile ground to help an aging actress to recapture her A-list actress status. Katherine was also aware that all her stomping, yelling, and drinking that she had allowed herself to consume in her day and evening was never going to alter the grim reality of the direction her career was heading.

"Mr. Zanuck, I can't thank you enough for this opportunity."

Ian found himself in a place he never dreamed he would be, standing and taking up space in the large, expensively decorated office of a Hollywood studio head, feeling wanted again, and being recognized for his talent. He stood before Darryl Zanuck, shaking his hand on a contract. A contract for two years with Twentieth Century Fox. One of the screenplays he was assigned to pen starred Tyrone Power. It was Tyrone that went to the mat for Ian with Zanuck. Zanuck could get any writer he wanted. Tyrone was Fox's number 1 box office actor. With Zanuck, that rated a favor or two every now and then.

"Don't mention it, son," said Zanuck. "Welcome to the team."

The secretarial staff outside Zanuck's office bestowed Ian a look of respect as he walked past them. The whispers in and around Hollywood were that he was all washed up. His writing career consisted of one-day assignments and additional dialogue script work. Over twenty years of boozing had made him a shadow of the writer he was years ago. Everyone in Hollywood knew it. A once promising career on the decline. A life spiraling downward. There was a different cadence in his walk off the Fox Studios lot. The cigarette dangled from his mouth at the most precarious angle. Ian curled his lip just enough to keep the cigarette from falling to the ground. Cocky and confident, he was feeling like a man that had received a warden's pardon. Freedom. Another chance to show the Hollywood world that he remained one of the best.

"Sam, Tom Collins with lime," said Katherine.

"Yes, Ms. Edwards."

"Keep 'em coming," replied Katherine.

"Yes, Ms. Edwards."

Katherine found herself exactly where she wanted to be in the middle of the afternoon—parked on a barstool while drowning her sorrows with a freshly made Tom Collins every fifteen minutes and reliving those silent era days filled with nothing but fame and recognition. It is so hard, so painfully difficult to admit to yourself that the life passion you have loved doing for the past twenty-five years may be coming to an end. Certainly, moving forward, life in front of the cameras would never be the same.

Abel had become accustomed to sitting in the car waiting for Ian or Katherine to return from whatever business that they may be involved in. He started reading Alexandre Dumas' *The Man in the Iron Mask* a couple of weeks ago. He took the title of the book literally and found himself relating to the protagonist's plight, hiding and living his life behind a mask that shields his true identity. A mask fitting strong and snug around his face, serving one purpose. A mask that shielded his true identity.

I sit
I wonder
I dream
In pain
For Ian?
For Althea?
Who am I?
What am I?
What do I want
For this life?
For my life?

The past years have brought great inner conflict to Abel. Harlem was a dream of hope. To be a successful writer, performer, and orator just like his idol Paul Robson. To rekindle a relationship with his estranged brother, Isaiah. California was a dream of new beginnings. A dream of hope to be a successful and noted playwright. Never to be in the lustful eye of a down-on-his-luck Hollywood screenwriter who loves men and women. Abel sold his soul to Ian so that he may live a comfortable and secure lifestyle—a lifestyle a vast majority of Negro servants would never experience in their wildest dreams. Abel placed the book on the seat next to him. He sensed that this was the right time to sneak in a quick nap. He knew that whenever Ian or Katherine would go to a bar, it was going to be a while. It felt relaxing to lie his head and close his eyes. A quiet and subtle daydream took place in his mind. He is walking down a dirt road holding Althea's hand. The extremely hot Mississippi summer afternoon would not deter Abel and Althea from showing their affection to each other. Her kisses were soft, moist, and loving. No woman ever kissed Abel like Althea did. No woman ever made him feel as aroused as Althea. She had been the only one. As far as Abel was concerned, Althea would always be the only one.

"Sam, another," said Katherine.

Katherine had lost count on the number of Tom Collins she had consumed the past two hours. She didn't care. She wasn't keeping count. The bartender was kind enough to remove the glasses off the bar so that Katherine wouldn't have a chance to stack them.

"Well, hello, darling."

Katherine recognized the soft German accent immediately. It was Marlene, merrily making her way through, on her way out with a group of friends. Katherine and Marlene became friends during production of their film. Marlene had become the European sensation along with Greta Garbo after the Great Depression. Katherine had become the silent screen has-been. Katherine always admired Marlene for being respectful of her during shooting and never reminding Katherine that she was no longer the Queen of Hollywood.

"Marlene, I didn't see you here," said Katherine.

Marlene replied, "I was over in the corner with Werner Klaus, F.W., and Von Sternberg."

"No doubt conversing on a plot to overthrow Hitler," said Katherine.

"No, darling, but come. Everyone is heading to my place for a nightcap."

The lace curtains softly blew, allowing a cool, late-evening breeze to sift through the bedroom windows. The stillness of the night and the darkness became the backdrop to an interlude. An interlude that would begin this evening. Tyrone and Ian felt at ease with one another as though they had been lovers for years. More of an exchange of raw physical passion than a caring display of intimate caressing. Tyrone found Ian's stomach as the perfect pillow. Ian remained staring at the ceiling. He sold himself to the devil once more. A price, a debt he is paying back to Tyrone for going to bat for him with Zanuck.

"For an old man, you're pretty fit," said Tyrone.

Ian replied, "The better to ravish you with, my dear. I cannot thank you enough for getting me that writing assignment."

Ian didn't care for Tyrone's remark concerning his fitness. There was a fourteen-year difference in age, and Ian's roundish belly was no match to Tyrone's flat and toned abdominals. He needed to be nice and placate Tyrone. He was responsible for getting Ian's writing work in a major studio again.

"I wanted to help," said Tyrone.

"You already have," replied Ian. "I can never repay you for injecting some new life in my career."

"You are quite gorgeous when you are being humble," said Tyrone.

"Prove it," said Ian.

Two words aroused Tyrone and provided a motive to hold Ian in his arms and kiss him passionately. Ian felt Tyrone's passion. Intense, unrelenting, and persistent. Ian was unable to enjoy the late-night nocturnal exchange of intimate pleasantries with a Hollywood leading man due to a headache that became inexplicably sudden and unforeseen in every imaginable way. The grabbing of Tyrone's wrist so that he could squeeze tightly onto something, anything available that could divert his attention. Ian's excruciating headaches appeared once before, several weeks back, several weeks back before then, and several weeks back before then, deciding for the better part of two years to ignore those few seconds that became painful minutes.

"Ian, what's wrong?" asked Tyrone. "For God's sakes, what's the matter?"

Ian lay there, unable to speak and unable to muster a minute decibel of sound. The bedroom filled up with his loud and drawn-out moan of unbearable pain. Every effort went toward a frantic search for a pillow to cover his ears.

"My head, my bloody head," said Ian. "Make it stop! Please, damn it, make it stop!"

Abel did his best to keep himself from falling asleep. The seconds slipped by. The minutes mounted. The hours sitting in the car made his back sore. Enough time being uncomfortable forced him to get out of the car to stretch his legs. He turned just in time to see Marlene Dietrich turn out all the lights in her home. He knew all the signs. It was going to be a while before Katherine would be walking out. Abel found a reason to smile. It felt good leaning on the hood of the car with his long legs stretched out. A clear, cool night full of bright stars helped to revitalize him. There were so many of these nights where he found himself waiting for Katherine or Ian to end their evening of revelry so they could pass out in the back seat while Abel drove them home. He felt the back of his head—it was yearning to be scratched. Abel took a small pleasure scratching it. His wry smile returned. He was enjoying the direction his mind was taking him. He had his pad and pencil on hand. His thoughts charged into overdrive. He was remembering back when he and Althea would sit together on Althea's front porch. Abel would place his head on Althea's lap. She would slowly and methodically take her time running her fingers through his coarse and wooly hair, finding an occasion to find a special spot to scratch his scalp as she recited a poem that her grandmother used to serenade her with. Abel loved the poem, but he was struggling to remember all the words. He wanted to make an entry. A special entry that would remind him of Althea and those intimate moments they shared. He was desperate to hold on to anything that would keep giving him hope that he would find her. To help him believe that the time apart will be so worth the day they are reunited. *Let's see how'd it go,* Abel whispered to himself.

I am always yours
I am always the one who loves you
I am always there for you
I am who protects you
I am the one
Who you will always love

Katherine awakened. The consumed champagne continued to swirl strongly in her head. Now she remembered. She found herself sprawled on her stomach on Marlene's bed. The silk sheets encasing her body felt like velvet on her skin. The champagne tried its best to work itself through her system. There were no hints to let Katherine know how long she had been there. She smelled like Marlene's perfume—expensive and French. Her scent was all over her. She remembered very little. Their drinking, their embracing, their kissing, and Marlene's moist lips between her thighs. A hue of blur and nothing in between.

"You fell asleep, liebling," said Marlene.

It was reappearing to Katherine. She was with Marlene.

"You have never been with a woman before, have you?" asked Marlene.

Katherine replied, "Was it that obvious?"

They shared a moment to laugh together. Marlene took off her robe and returned to bed. Katherine closed her eyes to immerse herself in the enjoyment of Marlene's kisses on her body. A woman's affection felt different to her. Energy surges commenced from spots on her body that had never been explored. A woman's soft hands aroused her in a much different way. She enjoyed exploring this new frontier of her sexuality. Newness was what she needed. An aging actress on the downside of her career becomes desperate for things new and fresh and exciting.

"You have been with many women," said Katherine. "So the rumors are true."

Marlene replied, "What rumors might that be?"

"I want to know more about you."

"Now is your chance, liebling," said Marlene.

Abel moved quickly through the dining room, trying to have everything in place before Ian and Katherine came down for breakfast. The hot plates and coffee were the last items to be set out. He never knew when they would actually appear. Being told breakfast at 8:00 a.m. and when breakfast was actually served were two different things in the McGregor home. It had been a very long night. Katherine did not walk out of Marlene's until well after 3:00 a.m. Abel wasn't concerned with how tired he was feeling. It was his off day once breakfast had been served. He was going to catch a bus up to Echo Park and find a quiet place to write by the pond. He heard Katherine and Ian approaching the dining room. He ran into the kitchen to bring the coffee.

"So what's the name of the picture?" asked Katherine.

Katherine wouldn't even give Ian a chance to sit down and enjoy his coffee before grilling him about his writing assignment with Twentieth Century Fox. Ian hadn't written a full screenplay in over two years. She desperately hoped that if Ian could land plum studio writing assignments, he could use his success as leverage to land her better roles. Abel timed his arrival with the coffee to Ian and Katherine just as they sat down.

"Ian, what's the name of the picture?"

Ian replied, "Had you arrived home at a decent hour, I would have told you last night."

"Yes, well, I ran into Kay Francis and her group," said Katherine. "One hour went by and then another."

Ian ignored her response. He really didn't want to know. It was their agreement between the two of them. Don't ask who you have been with and definitely do not tell.

"Abel, I'll have three-minute eggs, toast, and jam only," said Ian.

Abel replied, "Yessuh, I'll lets Mabel know."

Abel walked into the kitchen to pass on Ian's breakfast order. Ian began burying himself in the morning paper.

"Well?" asked Katherine.

"I suppose you will keep on pestering me until I say something," said Ian.

"Smart man."

(Yelling) "Abel, bring me some aspirin too!" said Ian. "So, you know, my Kate, it is a period piece set on the high seas. A swashbuckler. *The Black Swan*."

"Who is slated to star?" asked Katherine.

Ian replied, "Tyrone Power and Maureen O'Hara. *Variety* says she will be the new Katherine Edmonds. Fox made a bloody mint on T*he Hunchback of Notre Dame*."

Abel returned with breakfast and Ian's aspirin. He took his customary position in the corner by the kitchen opening, awaiting his next instruction. He never took his eye off of Ian, not for a second. His feelings for him churned inside. His mind mixed him up with unwavering ease. Depending on the day, one moment, there was an intense desire to track down Althea. His writings were devoted to her. The next day, he desires Ian in his bed. Help him with his writing. Wash his cars. Press his slacks. Carry his golf clubs. Be his lover on call. Now, for the past decade of his life, he has done anything and everything for Ian to make him happy well beyond the scope of his job, his loyalty, and his responsibilities.

"The studio will be filming in Technicolor to accentuate Miss O'Hara's long, flowing, gorgeous red hair," said Ian. "Pity Technicolor wasn't available ten years ago for you, darling."

"Was that an attempt to be funny?" asked Katherine.

Ian took a quick glance at Abel standing in the corner. It was all the communication they needed. They learned silent signals, messages, and discreet overtures to each other when others were present over the years when those many daily moments when speaking to each other was an impossibility. Ian found Katherine's question a perfect cue to rise from his seat and walk out of the dining room.

"Of course not, my darling," said Ian. "She's a young star and you are, well, you are not. Abel, have the car out front in ten minutes, please."

25

The last seat was taken on City Metro Bus run number 2721. 2721 was the run number that traveled through the Negro section of Los Angeles. Abel sat in his usual seat, the last row by the window. Staring at the cityscape inspired him. His notepad and pencil rested comfortably on his thigh, waiting for the announcement to pounce. Without notice, the pencil played a drummer's rhythm on his thigh, feeling confident that something would inspire him to put it all down. He kept his gaze to the streets. The slow-moving cars stalled in traffic snarls. The fast-paced strolling people. The businesses that lined Washington Boulevard. The streets bustled briskly this morning, remaining spotted with mist after an all-night rain. Abel thought about sharecropping the fields in the rain. Summer rains in Alabama press hard but passed through quickly. There were no roofs and canopies off tall buildings to seek refuge under. No time to take a moment to prop open an umbrella. You toiled the fields even if it meant becoming soaked. Abel remembered stopping his plow long enough to look up and see Althea hundreds of yards away, standing on the porch. She had a dry shirt for him as soon as he finished. Now was the time for Abel's pencil to leave the starting gate.

So there you are
Standing so lovely
Within my sight
But
Not within my grasp
Many feet away
I still see the love in your eyes
As I hope for so long
You see the love in mine for you
Dearest Althea

"Washington and Centinela, next stop!"

That was Abel's stop. The bus driver yelled loudly to remind him that it was time to exit. He wanted to write more about Althea and keep reminiscing about those thunderstorm memories in Alabama. The smile painted his face, thinking about the way Althea would help him take off his drenched undershirt and help him put a dry one on. How they stood on the porch and just held hands, not even speaking a word to each other and yet thinking and knowing what the other was thinking. It was Abel and Althea's special connection. It wasn't the right time for an interruption and exit that bus just as his creative flow beckoned.

An afternoon sun began to peak itself from under an overcast sky. Abel stepped onto Washington Street, eager to absorb the cityscape ambiance and bustle. Abel's off days allowed him the time to mingle with the other Negroes every Thursday and every other Sunday. He was feeling exhilarated with the direction his writings were taking. Having to secretly work on Ian's screenplays over the years without his knowledge gave him a clearer focus as to what kind of writer he wanted to be. He loved his poetry. It was easy for him to prose his life instead of writing a novel. His passion was to turn his poems into a theater production in

Harlem. That special dream resided in his heart to one day look out in a filled-to-capacity audience and see Bill Bojangles Robinson or Paul Robeson happily applauding a production that he had written, produced, and directed.

A cement stoop in front of the barbershop caught Abel's attention. It was a place to sit. He peeked inside the barbershop and saw that his usual seat by the window was available. At that moment, he just had to sit on that stoop. He just had an inspiration to say something—words on his dreams, his hopes, his desires, and his yearnings. The swarm and buzz of pedestrians continued to saunter by, on the street. The stoop was small, not wide enough to accommodate his buttocks. Today was a great day to write. He wanted more. He needed more. It was about to happen once again.

A writer, not a writer
Until
those that read
agree
his words invoke
until
those words are on a lighted stage
for all to see
for all to applaud
for all to acknowledge me
the writer

Ian stood by the windows in the den, gazing out onto the veranda and rear yard. A blank stare rendered him pale as a ghost. Distant. He stood on top of pages and pages of balled-up pieces of paper. Discarded pages of a script so badly written that studio chief, Zanuck, would never see them. His throbbing headache appeared once more unannounced. The front of his face planed itself against the pane of glass.

"Ian?"

Ian did not hear Tyrone standing behind him. The throbbing headache pain meshed with his throbbing sense of failure as a screenwriter. He was longing for the days in the '20s, writing for theater in New York and when a director could talk to his actors while filming a scene. Talkies brought fame and fortune to many, but it brought destruction to others. Ian was in the destroyed group. The alcohol no longer masked the excruciating headaches.

"Ian!"

This time, Ian heard Tyrone standing behind him. He didn't turn around immediately. His inner pain continued to master center stage in his mind.

"I say, ol' man, are you all right?" asked Tyrone.

Ian replied, "Yes, I'm fine."

It was a hug of warmth. A hug of affection. Ian held Tyrone as he felt Tyrone's kiss on his cheek. He wanted no more and took that moment to break away to walk toward his desk. He lit two cigarettes, a second one to pass to Tyrone.

"Is that the script?" asked Tyrone.

"Yes."

Tyrone's curiosity drove him to pick the script up and began reading. He flipped through the pages, three or four at a time. Ian could see in Tyrone's eyes that his words were not invoking praise or admiration. A frown appeared on Tyrone's face, not an encouraging sign to any writer worth their salt.

"Of course it's not finished," said Ian.

Tyrone replied, "Yes, I can see that. Ian, you know Zanuck won't green-light this. Not this. What you have written so far is . . . is."

"Just an early draft, mate," said Ian.

Tyrone became immediately perturbed. Ian had insulted him. Tyrone was certainly aware what a respectable early draft of a screenplay would look like. Ian's version wasn't even close. Tyrone saw

Ian as a special friend. He felt a need to encourage and not discourage.

"I stuck my neck out, Ian. I'm counting on you," said Tyrone.

Tyrone walked out of the study, leaving Ian to himself, to return to that window, to those thoughts, and to those inner feelings that he can't shake of being finished as a writer in Hollywood. All that churning inside did not stop him from returning to the call of duty to return to his typewriter.

A compulsion overcame him to occupy that small square space area at his desk. Such a small area to inhabit when one must determine success or failure in life. The typewriter sang *ratt-taa-tatt* in succession, giving Ian a venue to divert himself from the combined physical and mental anguish his body was undergoing. One page done. He threw the page onto the floor and so quickly had a second page in the typewriter. Ian felt it slipping away with each stroke to the typewriter. Another page done, eventually finding itself on the floor. *Same old bloody bullshit,* he said to himself. *Ratt-taa-tatt.*

Abel was having one of those rare special days for a writer, those days where the words flowed freely and unencumbered. The barbershop was quieter than usual. The men were entertaining themselves, listening to a Bojangles Robinson radio show. Self-proclaimed pride of the poem he wrote about Ian. Never mentioning his name, but using one word to talk of his experiences with a man who served as boss, friend, and sometimes lover.

A man
I have seen the pain in his eyes
The fear
The hurt
The moments most vulnerable to me
Such a story

Of sadness
Shame
Willing to go to his failure
Alone

"Hey, college boy!"

Abel looked up. He recognized the voice immediately and knew what would follow. It would be some sort of question from his friend, Leroy, about women. Leroy enjoyed embarrassing Abel in front of the other patrons.

"Hey, college boy, you ever been down on a woman?" asked Leroy.

All who were present stopped with whatever they were doing to give Abel the floor to respond to Leroy's question. Abel sat silent. He wasn't certain whether to answer quickly to eliminate everyone gawking at him or to take a little longer to think up a clever response.

"You know what I'm sayin', college boy. Taste that good honey?" said Leroy.

The barbershop crowd broke out into a loud laugh. Abel managed a wry smile and a smirk. The pressure was mounting to be a braggart. Maybe throw a few names of women around to substantiate his claim. Abel knew that his words would not be true. In his mind, his only lover was Althea. He felt compelled to stick his chest out and create the biggest lie that he could think of.

"Well, college boy?" asked Leroy.

Outside, in front of the barbershop, a city bus screeched its tires to a sudden halt, narrowly missing rear-ending the car in front. The loud noise caught Abel's attention just as he was about to answer Leroy's query on his experiences with women. He paused to look outside. It was that moment he saw her—Althea. Or he thought it was Althea. She stood in front of the bus's doors, about to board. Unlike months earlier, Abel did not hesitate. He wasn't going to allow her to get away from him. He bolted from his chair and ran out of the barbershop. Just as he exited the shop, Althea boarded, the traffic light changed to green, and the bus was off, down the street. *Damn it,* Abel said to himself. Another episode of a figment of his imagination. The frustration of being so close to Althea but never reuniting with her was beginning to mount. Always close to her, but never certain. Always a momentary glimpse or a glimmer. Always seeing the back of her head. Always a quick sighting of her face. Always in his mind, but never to be forgotten.

"Why didn't you take that silly costume off at the studio?"

Katherine lay in bed watching Marlene stand before her. Their eyes gazed into each other for seemingly minutes on end. Their affair remained torrid as ever. Many nights found Katherine at Marlene's waiting for her to return after her day at the studio. Katherine had not worked on a picture in over three months.

"Darling, will you unhook me, please?" asked Marlene.

Marlene sat on the edge of the bed as Katherine unbuttoned her blouse from behind. It was a moment for Katherine to exhibit her affection, and the unbuttoning exercise also became laced with soft kisses to Marlene's back.

"You look like a true Arabian genie," said Katherine.

Marlene's and Katherine's nude figures created an alluring silhouette under the silk sheets. They had become inseparable for months. Katherine has spent more days and evenings at Marlene's than her own home with Ian. They had become close friends and lovers. Marlene's reputation was well-known around Hollywood. She would take on many lovers, men and women. Katherine was the inexperienced one when it came to female companionship. Ian was her only lover since their college days at Columbia. Ian grew up poor on the Lower East Side and had to bus restaurant tables, sell magazines door-to-door, and scrub office building floors to work his way through school and the theater. Katherine was born into a family of wealth and affluence from Park Avenue. Her father was a banker on Wall Street, survived the crash of '29, and had a seat on the board of directors at Radio City Music Hall. It all became so very easy for Katherine her entire life. Finding a man like Ian who loved her and possessed a talent to make her a better actress. Landing in Hollywood the same time as Chaplin, DeMille, Crawford, and Swanson. Young, tall, sexy, and voluptuous. The alluring smile. Twenty-five years later, she's sharing a bed with Marlene Dietrich. And as she lay there, feeling Marlene's head nestled on her bosom, it had dawned on Katherine what she had become—a forty-six-year-old has-been actress starring in B pictures and moonlighting as a bisexual whore for female stars. Katherine knew it. In a few more years, Hollywood will call her only for roles playing a mother to teenage children pictures opposite the debonair but fiftyish Clifton Webb or Walter Pidgeon. Katherine had convinced herself, perhaps ordered herself, as a call to duty that sleeping with Marlene will open up a possible leading role. A leading role as a heroine that director Josef von Sternberg was about to make with Paramount. Marlene and von Sternberg grew up together as kids in Germany. All it would take is one word from Marlene and Katherine would get the role. She didn't care how she had whored her way in a position to bolster her career. She was covering all her bases in case Ian fails in producing a great script for Twentieth Century Fox. Married to a bisexual for twenty years made it easier for her to change roles to adapt, to change so easily. In her mind, at least. There was something else. She could not deny the electric chemistry she and Marlene had. It was new. It was exciting. She had connected emotionally to Marlene. An inner renaissance to love and feeling lovable had been hatched inside her soul and her body. It felt loving to hold Marlene in her arms.

"I will talk to Josef in the morning about the lead," said Marlene.

Abel's hand softly opened the door to Ian's office. His mind vividly painted a dreadful picture of an office completely left in a destructive and tattered mess. A destructive and tattered mess that he would be required to clean at almost midnight this evening. As he stepped inside, his fears came to fruition. Hundreds of balled-up pieces of typing paper were strewn all over the floor. The lamp cracked at its base on the desk. Pieces of broken rye bottles scattered in every direction. If Abel had not known a tornado had whisked through Hollywood that day, he would have never known that after standing in Ian's office. All of that didn't matter. He was there to do his job. The reason he was hired and the reasons why he has been paid for the past ten years—Butler, chauffeur, valet, house Negro. Cleaning Ian's garbage drop called an office had been done many times before and this evening would be no different. He circled around the office, garbage can firm in hand to gather and dispose of the discarded refuse. He mumbled a tune in his head that he and Althea would share together. The tune which began in his head became a whistle from his lips.

Roses are red
To you
Violets are blue
For you

Let's share this dance
Our kiss
Forevermore

Where do I start, Abel asked himself. He decided that Ian's desk was as good a place as any. Tidy messes of paper were strewn all over in no particular order. An ashtray harbored over forty of his Chesterfield butts. The telephone was cracked and broken, dead on the floor, and off its hook. The fallen lamp on the desk beamed on Ian's screenplay entitled *The Black Swan*. It stood out, front and center. It appeared complete. Those seconds turned into a few minutes as he stared at it. The temptation to read Ian's script was becoming too much to overcome. Ten years since Ian wrote *Another Man's Poison*, the one screenplay that he won an Academy Award for, the one screenplay Abel ghostwrote for him without Ian ever knowing, and the one screenplay that saved and catapulted Ian's career in Hollywood. So much had been injected into that story by the two of them. In an aura-esque way, they worked on the story together. A burning desire remained in his heart to tell Ian that he was the sole person responsible for his success, his accolades, his notoriety, for keeping Katherine in love with him and saving their marriage, and for that Academy Award for Best Original Screenplay. Now is the time for the truth. Abel and Ian shared many moments in that rear yard coach house. He cared for Ian. He wanted to help him. It was about being a friend and helping a friend out who is down on his luck. And once he made up his mind, the script was in his hands to be read. He grabbed a pencil, furiously making notes. Abel glanced over his shoulder time and time again. He allowed his eyes to survey the office to ensure with certainty that he was alone. It all began with his first keystroke on Ian's typewriter. Abel found a portion of the second act that needed dialogue improvement.

The third act needed a more resounding sword fight scene. He had to peck on the keys slowly, one key at a time so as not to disturb anyone. Each completed sentence, each substitution of Ian's dialogue for his own exhilarated him. When a creator of words feels that elusive but special surge flowing from brain to fingertips, there is no stopping. Not now. Not when the story becomes a part of you. A part of your inner soul. A part of who you are and who you have become.

"Who do you want?" asked Marlene.

"Who do you want?" asked Ian.

"Who do you want?" asked Katherine.

"Who do you want?" asked Ian.

Marlene and Ian's voices took turns swimming throughout Katherine's dream. Their voices created turbulence in her movements. Her arms flailed as a seagull and her legs kicked in a violently rhythmic way. She looked up and saw Ian and Marlene standing at the foot of the bed, looking down, and sneering at Katherine with disdain. For those feelings of being used, Katherine saw differently. She saw desire and love in the eyes of both. She wanted to please all who care for her. More importantly than anything imaginable, advance her career in the waning years that lay ahead. The turbulence settled as quickly as it began. Her eyes opened and she woke up suddenly. *You've been dreaming,* she said to herself. She can't recall getting home without driving into a telephone pole or having a police escort. Now, without her memory helping, she was dressed in only her silk slip sprawled on top of the covers. She wanted to apply blame to the champagne as a mixer to her numerous vodka martinis, and certainly included was the insatiable sex and debauchery with Marlene. Her right hand reached over to switch on the table lamp. It made things easier for Katherine to find and light her cigarette. One second, she was staring up at her newly installed Venus de Milo ceiling and another glancing at the clock that read 2:00 a.m. Too much to think about at this hour.

Too much to think about at this hour, Abel said to himself. He was proud of what he had completed in the dead of night. Eight, nine, ten pages rewritten in one hour. His words and dialogue were cleverly woven in with Ian's script. Just a punch-up, a quick sprucing. Exactly as he had done for Ian ten years ago with *Another Man's Poison*. He read as quickly as he could. It was late. Just one friend helping out another, was Abel's rationalization.

"Just what the bloody hell do you think you're doing, mate?"

Abel recognized Ian's voice behind him. It startled him enough that he dropped the script. He was shocked beyond disbelief. *Where did he come from,* Abel asked himself. He reran in his mind the number of times his eyes had scanned across the room to make sure that he was alone. Without any time to react, Ian lunged after Abel and found his hands around his neck. It was a few short seconds before Ian had Abel on the ground, pinning his knees on Abel's chest and choking him.

"What were you doing to my script?" asked Ian.

Abel couldn't have answered Ian's question if he had wanted to. The pressure on his neck rendered him speechless. He was slowly losing consciousness. Ian was quickly losing control. The look of a homicidal maniac was in his eyes. Abel's saliva began slurring out of his mouth. And while the life was being slowly choked out of him, in his mind he had no answers to Ian's questions.

"What were you doing to my bloody script?" asked Ian.

Ian relented on his grip around Abel's neck. Ian stood over Abel while he struggled to regain his breath. There was never murder in Ian's heart, only anger and betrayal. Abel found a moment to crawl away from Ian's towering presence to regain his balance and feet.

"I didn't see you. How long you been here?" asked Abel.

Ian stumbled around the office, eventually finding what he was searching for—a half-butt cigarette and the final corner to a bottle of scotch.

"I passed out behind the door," said Ian. "You didn't even see me when you walked in. I lay in that corner for almost two hours watching you rewrite my screenplay, wondering to myself, just how does a nigger learn writing skills to be able to write a coherent piece of work? I was amazed. A genius nigger boy. It was a bloomin' freak of nature. You were like a two-headed giraffe at that typewriter, something very special."

Abel still struggled, recovering from his near-death experience. He sought relief from his scratchy and parched throat by gulping down a pitcher of Ian's water. He still had no idea what he wanted to say. He had to say something. The secret was over. It was out. Abel had to come forward and say the truth, convey his inner feelings, and bare his soul. He was about to place trust not just into Ian, but Ian the successful and respected white man.

"I like writing. Been doing it fer a while now," said Abel. "The other time I did it, I was really nervous, but not this time."

"The other time?" asked Ian. "You've rewritten my work before?"

No words, just glances. Both wanted to know the truth and speak the truth. A friendship and close personal relationship of fourteen years was to be put to the test. Many times over the years, race, status, wealth, and fame were always shoved to the side when it came down to the two of them. Ian stood inches before Abel's nose, each other's breath invaded the other.

"Have you rewritten my work before?" asked Ian.

No words, just glances. Ian saw fear in Abel's eyes. Abel's fear was real. Not for his job, but for his life.

"When?" asked Ian. *"I said when?"*

"Fer a while, 'bout ten years ago," replied Abel.

"Ten years?" asked Ian. "Which one? Which one?"

"That one called *Another Man's Poison,*" said Abel.

The mixed look of confusion on Ian's face showed surprise, anger, even a sense of betrayal. How could ten years have gone by and he had not known the secret. The secret between him and Abel. Abel, the Negro ghostwriter. There was never a moment that Abel showed Ian that he had a remote interest in writing. There was never a moment that Ian saw Abel as a writer. Ian always placed Abel in two categories: servant or his buck of a lover and occasional confidant. As always, when a crisis arose, it was the bottle that he reached for. He swapped swigs between a loud and boisterous uncontrollable laugh.

"Well, this is jolly good. Jolly good," said Ian. "I have employed a nigger who moonlights as Raymond bloody Chandler. Not only that, but he has the unmitigated gall to think he's better than me. Now, I am to believe that this nigger is responsible for the one and only Academy Award I have ever won."

"I did it for you," said Abel. "I did it to help you."

Ian replied, "You did it for your bloomin' self. You just have to prove that you're not like the other niggers. That you are so much better. Because you can read a little and write a little. Speak in the proper manner. All of those accolades and you're still a nigger. There's a bloody irony for you."

"I wanted to help you," said Abel. "I want you to do good."

Ian replied, "I took you into my employ and home. I treated you handsome and this is how you repay me. Iago! Iago! Iago!"

Ian ran to his desk and frantically reached into a drawer. A script became present in his hands, wasting little time to run back to Abel to flaunt his work.

"This is the script I am turning into Fox Studios," said Ian. "My work! My work, not yours, you arrogant nigger! Now clean up this mess and have the car out front in the morning at 7:00 a.m."

Abel replied, "Yessuh."

Abel turned his back, shamed. The loud slamming of the door triggered his thoughts, leaving him to do nothing else but clean up the mess. His feelings were smothered and buried by Ian's physical and mental cruelty toward him. He had a chance to convey, to confide to Ian that his motive was borne strictly from admiration, respect, and friendship for him. He blew that chance. Ian had never called Abel a nigger. Ever. Not once in fourteen years. That one word hurt him deeper than Ian's hands around his neck squeezing the life out of him. And knowing, knowing that by tomorrow morning, Abel's revelation and Ian's rant will become a nonexistent event. It will be as though nothing ever happened between them.

26

Ian and Katherine's Hollywood soirees at their home were famously known throughout high society circles as festive and boisterous with a dash of sexual debauchery thrown in, serving as the entertainment. Their parties were always well-attended by the reigning stars and directors, the wannabees, and the has-beens who will never be in pictures again. The years of practice made their after-five black-tie events the pinnacle that everyone wished to attain. Katherine always favored an Art Deco flavor to her rooms and furniture. She was proud of the Gauguin that hung above the marble fireplace, a prize she won as payment from Douglas Fairbanks in a poker bet.

Abel served as head waiter for these events. It had been his custom for the past fifteen years, serving, cleaning, wiping, and satisfying the evening needs of all of Ian and Katherine's guests. He had become the best in everything, and by now, Ian and Katherine had found Abel to be an invaluable commodity. The living room was filling up quickly. It was the norm for Katherine and Ian to employ additional Negro servants to handle the crowd overflow—early-evening crowd, late-evening crowd, and right-before-sun-up crowd. As he slowly circled the room with his champagne tray, Abel began to notice that tonight's crowd was a vastly different type of crowd and yet he was very sure that he had seen these faces before. There was more talking and speech making than drinking, partying, and revelry. The evening seemed to contain more of an intellectual aura mingling around than ever before.

"Good of all of you to attend this evening," said Katherine.

Katherine acted the good hostess. The guests had been there before and knew the routine: drinks, hors d'oeuvres, and lastly, political banter into the wee hours.

"We are all glad to be here," said Katherine. "There are very few of us who still believe in a Communist government. Shared beliefs and doctrines. A manifesto government that signifies equality for all and not just the rich and famous."

"How about the infamous?" asked a partygoer.

Katherine replied, "You too, Adrian."

The ongoing loud revelry and inflamed political dialogue occurring on the other side of his den door failed to deter Ian from his drinking and Camel chain-smoking party. There were moments of turning toward his typewriter to hack out a few words while allowing the ashes to drip onto his tuxedo. Ian felt hot, annoyed, and irritated. The yelling got louder outside. Back to the typing. *Clickety-clack Clickety-clack. Clickety-clack.*

Ian hated Katherine's Red Communist crowd. Every Sunday evening was "bloody Commie night," as Ian would put it. It was not that he didn't believe in its doctrines and manifesto. He knew most of that crowd from his Broadway days in New York. He simply detested Katherine's way of revitalizing her career through meetings in their home with a sort of group possessing questionable reputations with the Hollywood studio elite. They were more apt to ruin a career than enhance it. Katherine was more desperate than Ian. It was the reason she became lovers to Marlene Dietrich and Kay Francis, hoping to receive that elusive good word to the right producer and director. Ian knew that the Hollywood hierarchy would never allow writers to infiltrate Communist propaganda in any picture to be released by a major studio. He knew that his path was certain—create a well-written script. *Clickety-clack. Clickety-clack. Clickety-clack. Clickety-clack.*

The knock at the door went unheard. *Clickety-clack. Clickety-clack. Clickety-clack.* If Ian had not taken a moment to proofread his work, he would not have heard the second, third, and fourth knock.

"Yes, yes, who is it?" asked Ian.

Abel entered the den slowly and sheepishly. He was not certain how Ian would receive him. Days had passed since Ian's attack on Abel.

"Thought you might like some champagne," said Abel.

Ian replied, "And how is my literary friend doing this evening? It sounds like the Commie party continues to go strong."

"Yessuh."

Ian grabbed two glasses of champagne off of Abel's tray and downed them both in seconds. Without taking his eye off of Abel, he hurled the glasses over his shoulder and listened to the crashing sound off his wall. As always in the past, Abel became the dutiful servant and walked over to the wall to wipe the champagne up and pick up the broken glass.

"Good, bloody good," said Ian. "Do what I fucking pay you to do around here, Mr. Nigger Ghostwriter."

Abel continued his task of cleaning up, keeping his back to Ian. They both kept their backs at each other. The room slowly filled up with a Londonesque, dense air of hurt, anger, and betrayal. Ian struggled with the knowledge that his Negro butler and chauffeur also moonlighted as his script editor. For weeks, his thoughts bathed his inner self with a deep hatred for Abel. A hatred permeating both sides of the coin. An intense, inner hatred Ian had never felt before, not even when James broke his heart. The embarrassing reality that a Negro, the son of a sharecropper, penned an Academy Award-winning screenplay. The years at Yale Drama and the successes and failures on Broadway seemed meaningless. A complete waste of his time and efforts. As he watched Abel cleaning up his mess, he stared at a man, a descendant of African slaves who had become more of an accomplished writer than himself. Abel had Ian beat. One Academy Oscar to none.

"Well, of course I am right," said Katherine.

She captivated a crowd of her colleagues with her dialogue and insights on socialism and its meshing into the pictures Hollywood was making. World War II was in everyone's rearview mirror. A new Hollywood. There were pictures denouncing Communism as the next world evil. And pictures depicting cynics and the disillusioned who resort to crime, murder, and moral depravity. *Film noir* was a catchy phase among the intellectuals.

"And I want everyone to hear me when I say, it is the artists that make pictures great and put those fannies in the seats. We have an obligation to assert our First Amendment rights. Freedom of speech, and that includes inside motion pictures."

Those partygoers who happily stayed past midnight cheered and clapped loudly at Katherine's riveting socialist rant for the past hour. She was able to say all that she could and not spill one drop of champagne out of her glass. No matter the circumstance or occasion, Katherine was always the epitome of elegance.

"We have writers, directors, produces everywhere. Even at RKO," said Katherine.

Her sarcastic jab at the B-picture studio brought laughs and a boisterous cheer from the crowd. Katherine turned to see Ian standing in the corner there, watching her. His twisted smirk assured her that even Ian found her joke amusing. They walked toward each other, and at that moment, they felt a compulsion to show brief affection toward each other. Both knew that their marriage was a sham to the Hollywood elite, but not their adoring fans. They didn't care. Their love was based on a twenty-year friendship, trust, selfish motives, greed, an unquenchable desire for carnal pleasure that neither one could satisfy for the other. They got married when Katherine found out that she was pregnant. It was Ian who helped Katherine abort the fetus. Their careers meant more than future babies and a family. Nothing would get in their way toward Hollywood stardom.

"Marvelous speech, my love," said Ian

"Thank you, darling," replied Katherine. "I thought the evening has gone well. Adrian Scott and Biedermann showed up. We need other voices in the studios."

Ian snickered at Katherine's comment and rewarded her biting sense of humor by deftly performing his light-two-cigarettes-in-his-mouth trick. He slowly placed one in Katherine's mouth.

"You know, darling, I am not so certain we should be using our home for these Red parties. You cannot trust everyone you know," said Ian.

"Ian, these are our friends. We all share the same ideals and ideas on how pictures should make a statement about society," said Katherine.

Ian replied, "Until jobs become bloody scarce.

Then the piranhas will become hungry for roles and parts, then start chewing on each other's flesh."

As was the custom toward the end of an Ian and Katherine soiree, Mabel was holding court with the rest of the Negro servants in the corner of the kitchen pantry. Mabel loved sharing stories about her life growing up in Mississippi. About her first job working as a maid to Douglas Fairbanks and Mary Pickford. The time Bonnie and Clyde stopped at her folks' sharecropper home after robbing a bank and demanded they kill two chickens and fry it up for them. No one ever knew if Mabel was lying or telling the truth. No one cared. It was funny entertainment. Even Abel loved sitting in the corner listening and taking notes for a possible storyline he may want to use later.

"Tell that story 'bout the time Mr. Chaplin helped you make biscuits and gravy," said Abel.

Abel's comment brought loud laughter to the other servants. They had heard Mabel's story many times before. How a drunken Charlie Chaplin stumbled into Mabel's kitchen and demanded her recipe of fried chicken, biscuits, and hominy grits. While she captivated the other servants, Mabel's floor show jarred Abel's creative thoughts and he quickly grabbed his pad and pencil out of his servant jacket to jot down a moment he felt was compelling to his story. He was very adept at writing and listening at the same time.

"Then ol' Charley said to me, 'Ms. Mabel, can you make cucumber sandwiches?' I told him, 'Mis'er Chaplin, I can make gravy out of Mississippi mud 'n water after a summer rain.'"

His love story about two sharecroppers who want to leave Alabama for happiness and bliss in New York City had been writing itself for a number of months. Why he took that very moment to break from his hearty laugh at Mabel's joke to look up was because a Negro maid was walking out of the back door. Short height, caramel skin, petite. *Who is she?* Abel asked himself. Abel's brain did not make an immediate connection. Flashback. Pictures of her flashed through his mind by the second in photographic recall.

"Althea!"

Abel bolted out of his comfy stool and barreled through the servants so that he could quickly adhere his hands to the doorknob and thrust himself outside into the night. Left. Right. *Which way?* Abel asked himself. Down Sunset. He saw Althea standing on the corner, walking down the street.

"Althea!"

Abel ran as hard as he could to catch up to Althea. He panted heavily, finally catching up with her.

"Althea, Althea, what are you doing here?" asked Abel. "How long have you been in California?"

Althea continued walking down the street. Her pace quickened, showing no interest in what Abel had to say to her after almost seventeen years. Abel caught up to Althea.

"How are you?" asked Abel. "Purt'in near eighteen years."

Althea replied, "Abel, what do you want?"

"What'cha you doing workin' at the McGregors?" asked Abel.

Althea replied, "I was fillin' in for a friend."

A set of bright lights from down the street shone in Abel and Althea's face. The elliptical shape of the beam splashed their faces as it drew closer. Althea recognized the vehicle immediately. It was the LA city bus number 122 that rode down Sunset to Sepulveda. It was Althea's bus home. Abel and Althea's gaze at each other were two distinct and different messages. Althea wanted to leave and never see Abel again. Abel's look was that of excitement, an anticipation, a joy to see an old friend and his first lover. Who forgets their first lover?

"This is my bus," said Althea.

"I'll drive you home. Let's go get a cup of coffee."

Ian softly lay on Katherine's back. He loved kissing her creamy, fair, soft-skinned shoulders. The party revelers, studio wannabees, hangers-on, and Communist sympathizers were long gone. The wee hours brought a peaceful calm. Through the blackness of their bedroom, Ian's fingers massaged Katherine's back slowly. Intertwining passionate small love bites on the small of her back emitted the response he hoped to hear.

"Don't stop, darling," said Katherine. "Damn it, did you hear me? I said don't stop."

Ian heard Katherine's demands. He did not disappoint. Ian knew what Katherine wanted. She wanted to feel Ian's prowess from behind. She felt Ian's hands forcibly grip her hips. Her knees anchored itself into the white satin sheets. His thrusts were strong, penetrating. He yelled at Katherine about how wonderful she felt. His voice vibrated loudly in the bedroom and throughout the house. Katherine's face pressed hard on her pillow. Her breathing and panting became rhythmic. They have not been passionate to each other for almost a year. At this moment of heated passion, neither felt that way. Both were too busy with their own personal trysts to care about their intimate life together. Both were too busy trying to recapture careers gone by. Over twenty years together. No embracing of marriage vows, no children, and now, no careers. All that is left between them was their strong carnal tastes and desires for each other. Ian was finished. Katherine could always tell.

Ian groaned as though he was a Sioux chief on the warpath in the Dakota Hills.

"Always the satisfying tiger, my darling," said Katherine.

Ian replied, "Better than all of your bloody pussy cats?"

"Indescribably better, darling."

The neighbor's barking dog disturbed the peaceful night calm that surrounded the bedroom. Katherine arose from Ian's embrace to close the window. She found the same exact spot on Ian's chest still warm, still inviting, still loving.

"I often thought of poisoning that bloody mutt," said Ian.

"You've always had a flair for the melodramatic," said Katherine.

Ian replied, "Katherine, I want you to know I haven't stopped loving only you."

"You need not say, my darling. I haven't stopped loving you."

It was a moment to show their vulnerability to each other. A moment that had not presented itself in a long time. Since their days at Columbia in the 1920s, vulnerability to each other was easy for Ian and Katherine. There was always friendship between them. Trust. Love. A kismet: their destiny, their fate. For many years, Ian and Katherine thought that those were the ingredients that would bake their marriage bliss pie forever. They were both wrong. Greed, vanity, self-absorption, narcissism, conceit. Those ingredients became the substitute instead.

"Val Lewton from RKO called. They want you to write a film noir picture for Mitchum and Kirk Douglas," said Katherine.

"And?" asked Ian.

Katherine replied, "And what, darling?"

"What's in it for you?" asked Ian.

"You can be such a cad. Of course there is a

role for me if they approve the script," replied Katherine.

"Well, let's hope all goes well for the both of us, shall we?" said Ian.

Katherine replied, "Yes, for the both of us."

There was only one all-night café open in the Negro section of Los Angeles—a greasy-spoon chicken-and-waffle joint on Jefferson and Centinela called Shack Daddy's. Abel knew it well. Many nights were spent in the darkest corner that Shack Daddy's could offer so he could work on his novel. His love story set in the backwoods of Alabama. The late nights that he used to scribe pages about his deep, personal thoughts regarding his intimate affair with Ian. How painful it was to him at first. How anal pain transferred itself to intimacy awkwardness. How enjoyable it became over time that in the end, respect and friendship became the end result of it all. On recounting those many nights in Shack Daddy's, not once did he ever see Althea. Not once did he ever hear a servant speak her name. The Negro servants' community was a small one. Everybody knew everybody. It was one of very few jobs available to Negroes after the war in Southern California. There was the moment that he saw, or thought he saw, Althea that day when he was in the barbershop. That was almost five years ago. There were many nights that he lay in bed replaying that afternoon in his head, thinking of that moment, asking himself if it was her, missing her, wondering what she has been doing all these years, praying that he would see it again. This night, he got his wish.

"I've been in Oakland since I left Alabama. Just got to Los Angeles 'bout six months ago," said Althea.

"What'cha doing in Oakland?" asked Abel.

Althea took her eyes off Abel to gaze around

the restaurant. She smiled at the young mother feeding her small children in the booth across her and Abel. She listened intently to two men sitting at the counter, arguing about how many home runs Jackie Robinson would hit in his first season with the Brooklyn Dodgers.

"Sure smells good up in here," said Althea.

"Althea, what'chu doing in Oakland?" asked Abel.

"I was married. I ain't no more," said Althea.

"What happened?" asked Abel.

"Nuthin' happened," said Althea. "Nuthin' happened. Just didn't work out. Turns out he ain't the man for me."

"Closin' in ten minutes!" yelled the proprietor for all his patrons to hear.

"Guess I should be gettin' you home," said Abel.

The porch light mounted to Althea's front door was brightly lit. A blueish orange morning sky was opening up, ready to introduce the dawn of a new day. A neighborhood of quiet and peace suddenly found itself being serenaded by a stumbling drunk who decided to lay claim to a space in a street gutter. Abel and Althea walked slowly down the sidewalk. Abel's action was unpremeditated, completely spontaneous. As Abel and Althea approached the porch, Abel softly grabbed Althea's hand. She looked at him. A question of why he grabbed her hand painted her face. An affirmation of assurance painted his. They smiled at each other. A faint smile.

"I want to see you again," said Abel.

Althea replied, "Abel, it ain't gonna—"

Abel would not allow Althea to finish her sentence. He grabbed her and held her closely as he kissed her. Althea held close to the man that she always loved. She did not want to let go. The kiss stopped, just long enough to look into each other's eyes, just long enough to kiss each other again. Their passion was interrupted by the front door being opened quickly.

"Momma, what'cha doin' out here?"

Althea replied, "It's ok, son. Go back inside."

"Who's this, Momma?"

"You have a son?" asked Abel.

Althea replied, "Yes, this is my son. Go back inside."

Althea's son went back into house. The mood had changed. A romantic, early sunrise moment was abruptly interrupted with a moment of reality.

"You have a son," said Abel.

"Yes, yes I have a son," replied Althea.

"When were you going to tell me?" asked Abel.

Althea felt cornered, trapped in a maze. This was neither the time nor the place that she wanted to be forthcoming. Her head swirled. Abel looked at her with a look of betrayal. Althea felt that one twenty-five-minute sit-down at an all-night diner did not warrant a baring of her soul on what she had been up to for the past seventeen years.

"How old is your son?" asked Abel.

"Let's talk about it tomorrow," replied Althea.

"Tell me. How old is he?"

Abel grabbed Althea by the shoulders. He brought her within inches of his face. His patience dissipated with each second.

"Abel, you're hurting me," said Althea.

"How old is your son?" asked Abel. "I want to know now, Althea. How old is he?"

"He's seventeen," replied Althea.

Abel became shocked and astonished. He let go of Althea.

"Seventeen?" asked Abel. "Seventeen? Is he mine? I want to know, is that my son?"

Abel grabbed Althea by the shoulders. His vice grip on her evolved into a physical shaking. The door burst open. Althea's son appeared, running out into the porch and tackling Abel to the ground.

"Get off my momma! Keep yo' hands off my momma."

"Stop it!" yelled Althea. "Stop it! He's your father!"

Hearing those words, the wrestling match stopped.

"Abel, son, this is your father, Abel," said Althea.

27

Clackety-clack. Clackety-clack. Ding. Clackety-clack. Clackety-clack. Ding. Ian's typewriter was in frantic overdrive. He had his chance. RKO was giving Ian his last chance to be a major writer for a major studio. He stopped typing to frantically search his desk for paper and pencil. He wanted to write out a scene first before he typed it on the page, a technique he learned when he was a scenarist on Broadway. If he didn't like it, if the words didn't sit well, he could simply take his eraser and make it all disappear. The eraser was getting more of a workout than the lead tip. He gripped the notepad tighter. A sudden and excruciating headache had announced itself. Ian placed his head on the table and closed his eyes, clinging to a hope that the misery would go away. His grip on the pencil was too strong not to be snapped in two. He reached into his shirt pocket for his pain-relieving pills. His face became drowned with the pitcher of water in hopes that enough of the water will find his mouth to wash down the pills. His will took over. The importance of his screenplay took precedence over his pain. Its completion, the utmost urgency. *Clackety-clack. Clackety-clack. Ding. Clackety-clack. Clackety-clack. Ding.*

While staring up at his ceiling, Abel found

himself tracking the slow crawl of a small spider.
It had become a convenient diversion while he dealt
with an ill-timed writer's block episode regarding
the ending to his play. While he watched the spider
slowly inch along the ceiling, he thought of a
correlation between the spider and his hero. Both
wandered aimlessly with no destination, no purpose,
no vision of what will befall next. And that was
when an inspiration struck. His hero must have a
purpose and goal. A clear motive in the end. He
must go back to the love of his life and ask for
forgiveness. He must profess a love unbridled to
the only woman he has ever loved. He sat up quickly
to write everything down while it was all fresh in
his mind. He doesn't lose the love of his life. He
wins her back. A perturbed look on Abel's face took
center. It was the staff house phone. He was wanted
and needed to answer.

"Yessuh. Right away, sir."

Ian wanted Abel to bring the car around to the
front. Abel's awe-inspired ending to his play would
have to wait until he returned.

Abel stood by the Packard waiting for Ian to
exit the house. He noticed a small mud spot on
the door and felt compelled to use his coat sleeve
to buff it away. He began an impromptu inspection
of the car and stopped so he could briefly gaze
upward toward the sun-soaked, cloudless blue sky.
He closed his eyes to bask in its warmth. His years
in California aided him in appreciating this simple
pleasure. When he opened his eyes, he noticed that
the second-story bedroom window was open, with
the drapes pulled back. Katherine appeared at the
window, sipping her morning coffee, naked. Shocked,
Abel glanced at Katherine, then quickly turned his
head. He saw her and she saw him.

"Abel?" said Ian.

"Yessuh," replied Abel.

"All set?" asked Ian.

"Yessuh," replied Abel.

Abel walked around to open the door for Ian. Before entering the car, Ian looked up at his bedroom window. Katherine stood, looking down at Ian, still sipping on her coffee, still naked. She blew Ian a kiss before walking away from the window.

The road wove and curved down Sunset Boulevard, charting a path as though it was a slithering snake. A more scenic and picturesque drive instead of the meandering stop-and-go traffic through the city by Melrose Avenue. On occasion, Abel would peer through his rearview window. He saw Ian reading a script. Abel had watched Ian read hundreds of script sitting in the back while he drove him around. His thoughts were now on Althea. After seventeen years, he got his girl back. And now he is a father. A son walking the earth with the same first name as his. He was thinking about a life with his new family—starting over, moving back to Harlem, and trying to get his play produced. His trance was broken by Ian's loud boisterous laugh.

"Abel, do you know why I am laughing?"

Abel replied, "No, suh."

"I am laughing at you," said Ian. "Laughing at you, boy. That you would ever dream of being a better writer than me. I hold here my next script for RKO. A big winner, my greatest success. And I did it all without you. Big story for big stars: Mitchum, Douglas, Jane Greer. They want me, me, me! They want my story *Build My Gallows High!*"

Abel listened to Ian's ranting, ravings, and self-absorbed commentary on his writing prowess. Minutes on end, it seemed. His eyes remained on the road, but his ears were in the back seat of the Packard. It hurt Abel deeply listening to Ian go to great lengths to hoist himself up above Abel. *I reckoned he was my friend,* Abel said to himself. Abel never understood why Ian felt this impulse to insult him. Through all they had experienced together, Abel was convinced that it was more than just an employer-employee relationship. Denigrate him. After over fifteen years of working for him in his house and living in the apartment above the garage. Through all they had experienced together, Abel was convinced that it was more than just an employer-employee relationship. He spent days convincing himself that Ian was feeling betrayal from Abel. And now, Abel was feeling betrayed by Ian. The traffic light changed red. Abel braked and stopped the car. That's when reality crept in the back of his head. Abel spent many a minute of his time dismissing the notion that race was never an issue between him and Ian. Mr. Reality slapped Abel hard while he waited for the light to change green.

"Why, you're just a nigger who thinks he's a bloody Oscar Wilde," said Ian. "And while you continue to wash my cars and lay out my suits, I will write and earn my own Academy Award. On my merits and my merits alone."

"I'm not so certain why you talk like you do," said Abel.

Abel waited a few seconds for Ian's response. A still silence was being emitted from the back seat. When he looked in the rearview mirror, he saw Ian slumped over, grabbing his head in anguish. His loud shrieks of pain startled Abel. His focus remained on the winding road of Sunset.

"Everythin' ok, Mr. Ian?"

Ian remained doubled over the back seat. His right hand clenched his screenplay in a death-grip desperation. Seeing Ian in distress, Abel quickly pulled the car off to the side of the road and exited the car to hurry to Ian's aid.

"Everythin' ok, Mr. Ian?" asked Abel.

Ian replied, "Take me to my doctor's office. Dr. Sutton on Melrose."

Katherine always loved the dimly lit ambiance setting at Ming's Restaurant in Chinatown. The setting was perfect for her motive this evening. She wanted to remain unseen and unnoticed. No one in here will recognize who she was. No fan will run up to her table seeking her autograph or picture. No newspaperman, no Hedda Hopper will appear to stick a pad and pencil in her face for a story or a piece of gossip.

"Katherine, so nice to see you."

Katherine replied, "Adrian, please sit down."

The waiter appeared to set a second place mat and pour a glass of water.

"Warm sake, please, and bring the lady another of whatever she is having," said Adrian.

Katherine scanned the restaurant, making sure that she was not recognized. Her scarf and glasses proved to be an excellent camouflage for her clandestine mission.

"Now, my dear Katherine, how can I help you?" asked Adrian.

Katherine replied, "You can give me a part in that Kirk Douglas picture you're shooting in a couple of weeks. I need the work, Adrian. In case you haven't noticed, forty-five-year-old actresses are not in vogue these days."

Adrian took a long sip of his sake and noticed that Katherine had pulled a cigarette out of her case. Adrian obliged Katherine by lighting her cigarette. He paused a moment to stare at Katherine so that he may choose his next words carefully.

"There is a part. A small part," said Adrian.

"Adrian, if there is anything. I need to work."

Adrian replied, "I will talk to Jacques in the

morning. There is a part for a mother to a young girl in her twenties. Not a lot of scene time, but—"

"I'll take it," said Katherine.

"There is something you can do for me," said Adrian.

Katherine replied, "I'm all ears."

"We need Ian to be a part of us," said Adrian. "Be a part of the Party. Me and Eddie and Herbert, we're all getting pictures green-lighted with RKO. We want Ian to be a part of the team. We need you to talk to him."

"I am afraid Ian will never join the Communist Party," said Katherine. "His detestation for Stalin is equaled only to Hitler and Jack Warner."

"I need for you to try. Try hard for us," said Adrian.

Katherine slowly nodded her head in acknowledgment of Adrian's request. She was going to try her best to convince Ian. She was afraid that her part in Adrian's next picture would be predicated on recruiting Ian to join the Communist Party. Katherine was in no position to negotiate. There was a blank stare from Katherine. She was trying to read Adrian and get a clue as to whether her part in the picture was in the balance. Adrian wouldn't look up while he sipped his sake. There was no guarantee that RKO would accept Ian's screenplay for shooting. What made Katherine even more uncomfortable was the knowledge that her future in pictures was in Ian's hands. She had been in this position before. And Ian failed her before. *No repeat performance by Ian this time,* Katherine said to herself.

"I need to see you, Althea. Tonight," said Abel.

Abel listened intently while on the pay phone in front of the office building of Ian's doctor. He saw an opportunity to call and hear Althea's voice while he waited for Ian to finish his appointment.

"It's impo'tent to me, baby," said Abel.

Abel's frustration mounted while he listened to Althea. His smooth brown skin wrinkled into elongated frowns. The growing consternation with each moving second was showing its mark. The conversation does not go well.

"Please, baby, please," said Abel.

Ian stood at the window watching Abel engaging in his phone conversation. He had that wry smile on his face when he was admiring Abel's smooth chocolate brown skin. He chose this moment to close his eyes to reminisce about those evenings in the coach house. Those warm, tight embraces around Abel's strong torso.

"I'm going to write you a new prescription for your headaches," said Dr. Sutton. "You need to begin these immediately."

Ian remained at the window staring at Abel. He remained in that special daydream, happy in his special place. If Abel had not ended his phone call and returned to the car, he would still be at that window in his own dream.

"Ian, we need to talk," said Dr. Sutton.

"So?" asked Ian.

Dr. Sutton held the X-rays above his shoulder, allowing a sun-kissed room to cast a brighter image. He wanted Ian to clearly see as he talked to him. Ian's eyes slowly gazed at the X-rays, then they suddenly bulged in fear. The X-rays looked as though it covered the entire ceiling when Ian looked up at them.

"You see that white spot?" asked Dr. Sutton. "That's your brain, and this spot is a lesion, a cancer growth."

"Then cut the bugger out," said Ian.

An eerie silence and stare began between Ian and Dr. Sutton. They were communicating different messages.

"I am afraid it may not be the case," said Dr. Sutton.

Ian replied, "Look, Doctor, if I'm for it no bloody sweet bedside manner."

Dr. Sutton placed the X-rays down on his desk and walked around to the back. His bottom drawer housed a bottle of Ian's favorite scotch. He poured a double and handed Ian the glass.

"The cancer is inoperable, Ian," said Dr. Sutton. "The growth is too big. It's starting to spread to other parts of your brain. You have a few weeks, two months tops."

Ian replied, "Oh no, Doctor. Not that long."

"Darling, you are a million miles away. You are usually so responsive."

Katherine did not hear Marlene talking to her. Marlene was right, Katherine was a million miles away in her thoughts. Thoughts of fear that her life would become a great big zero. All actors and actresses want to leave a legacy, a body of work that will be remembered to the end of time. A flashback of twenty-five years in motion pictures was flipping rapidly in Katherine's mind. Not even Marlene's soft, deftly placed kisses on her bosom aroused her enough to focus.

"Liebling, what troubles you so?" asked Marlene.

Katherine replied, "Oh nothing, just a career on the downslide. Married to a husband who couldn't write dialogue for a deaf mute."

"It's 1946, liebling," said Marlene. "Studios aren't exactly making pictures starring an aging actress with a German accent."

Marlene held Katherine tightly in her arms. Now was the time for compassion and affection and not commiserating about an actress's spiraling-down career. She felt Katherine's warm tears slowly streak down her bosom. They were tears of fear.

"I'm so frightened, so terrified," said Katherine.

"My career hangs in the balance on RKO green-lighting Ian's script."

"Aren't we being a bit melodramatic, liebling?" asked Marlene.

"Am I?" replied Katherine. "They already have Daniel Mainwaring writing a backup script in case Ian falls on his face, which of course means I will fall on my face."

It was the first time Abel had ever settled into Althea's living room sofa. He scooted and squirmed so that his body would mesh into the soft fabric. Althea's roast beef, mashed potatoes, and fried okra dinner had Abel rubbing his stomach with complete satisfaction. He just wanted a moment to place his head on the pillow and close his eyes. *I could get used to this,* Abel said to himself.

"You ain't fallin' 'sleep on me, is you?" asked Althea.

Althea's voice shook Abel out of his trance. Althea stood across the room giggling at Abel like a nine-year-old girl. She always found Abel's strong-looking face as mesmerizingly angelic. Abel did not alter his gaze away from Althea's eyes from completely across the living room. The kitchen light refracted onto Althea's hazel green irises. Althea's eyes would always place Ian into a hypnotic trance.

"Come over here," said Abel.

Althea, with each step toward Abel, unbuttoned one button at a time from the front of her dress. She found Abel's lap inviting and comfortable enough to sit on.

"Sho is hot'n here," said Althea.

Abel replied, "I noticed."

A soft tender peck turned into a deep passionate kiss.

"Do you know how much I missed you?" asked Althea.

Abel replied, "Eighteen years. Seems we both have

taken a mighty long journey to get back to all of this, you and I being together again."

"I want to say somethin' to you, Abel," said Althea.

Interrupting quickly, Abel replied, "No, wait, I wanna say somethin', Althea. I'm leavin' the McGregors, getting' out of Los Angeles. I'm movin' back to New York City, back to Harlem. I have some art friends there. They want to produce my play. In Harlem, right next to the Apollo. Gonna be perfect beyond any dream I ever had. I want you and Abel Jr. to come with me."

"Just like that?" asked Althea. "What about my job?"

Abel replied, "Plenty of maid and housekeepin' jobs in New York, New Jersey too. My brother, Isaiah, has a lot of friends there that can get you work. We can do this, baby. I love you. Come with me."

"All right, Abel," said Althea.

The morning sun peered brightly through the dining room's double-hung windows. Katherine loved having breakfast with cascading sunshine throughout the room. She could only do it when she dined alone. Too many mornings Ian would need the drapes drawn because of an all-night session of heavy drinking and debauchery. She nervously pawed through her poached egg and grapefruit breakfast. Abel entered the dining room. After eighteen years serving Ian and Katherine, Abel knew when to appear to freshen Katherine's coffee.

"What time will you be taking Mr. McGregor to the studio?" asked Katherine.

"Said to bring car 'round front in ten minutes," replied Abel.

"That will be all. Bring the telephone in here, please."

"Yes, ma'am."

Katherine forgot that she already had one cigarette burning in the ashtray when she reached in her bra for another and lit that one as well. The morning article in *Variety* had captivated her attention. She decided that the cigarette in the ashtray had outlived its usefulness and only the one was left to dangle from her mouth. Her increasing consternation with each word read was too much to endure. She grabbed the phone and dialed quickly, ready to unleash a tirade of anger at whoever picked up on the other line.

"Yes, Mr. Schaeffer, please. It's Katherine Edmonds. Yes, I'll wait."

Katherine's attention returned to the *Variety* article. Such an intense look painted her face. A swirl of anger and consternation took its place around her eyes, nose, and mouth. She knocked her coffee cup over, trying to extinguish one of the two cigarettes still burning in the ashtray.

"Yes, yes, George, how are you? Katherine here. What's this story in today's *Variety* about you hiring Daniel Mainwaring for the script? But, but, I thought you had decided on Ian's script. Well, what happened? I see. I thought Mr. Tourneur was on board. Well, not much to say after that, is there? Thank you."

As she hung up the phone, Katherine knew that the beginning of the end of her acting career had started.

There he was once again, that same position he repeated several weeks back. Standing by a high-rise office window, staring out to the bustle of the street below, focusing on Abel standing by the car, reading the morning paper. A realization crawled up the back of his neck. He had been in this position before. His body felt chilly inside. An aura of fear fitted snugly around his body and made him tighten his tie around his neck.

"So what's this all about, George?" said Ian. "I thought we had a deal."

George replied, "We had a deal. Until I read your script."

"And what's that supposed to mean?" asked Ian.

George replied, "Tourneur and the producer, Sparks, want to go in another direction with the story. A bit darker. I am inclined to agree."

Ian found his way back to the window. His eyes fixed on Abel. He inherited a resolve, a deep solace watching him. He could focus on something that made him happy. Remembering all the intimate moments he had with Abel was making him happy.

"Ian, come back and sit down. Let's talk," said George.

Before he returned to the meeting, Ian wanted to absorb his moment for as long as he could. The others in the office could not see his gleam, his joy, and admiration for Abel.

"There's nothing to talk about, really," said Ian.

"Val Lewton will still head up the B-picture unit," said George. "He's going to need writers for additional dialogue from time to time."

Ian replied, "You kick me to the bloody curb, then offer me some 'don't call us, we'll call you later' offer."

The tension was building in the office. Silence was the smoky cloud that filled the room. Ian deliberately bit his lip in front of everyone. He wanted to prove that his famous Scottish temper would not win at this moment. His forehead wrinkled, stern and angry. George and the other executives wore "take it or leave it" looks on their faces. Ian got up to walk back to the window to look at Abel.

"We're offering you something no other studio has or ever will, Ian," said George. "It's a good deal."

"Not for me, mate."

Ian made sure that all his might was behind him when he slammed the door walking out. A defining and loud resonating crescendo signaled the end of his career at RKO.

Ian exited from the building and smiled brightly as he approached Abel and the car. He stopped to feel the sun.

"Home, Mr. Ian?" asked Abel.

"No, Malibu," said Ian. "I want to see the ocean."

Katherine anxiously sat. She had been in this producer's office many times before, but never for the reason she was there that day. Depression is a train that may run many tracks. It builds up speed, but unlike a locomotive, depression never derails. Katherine wanted no more depression. No more lying in bed at night staring at the vials of drugs that she could overdose on. End it. End the fear of failure. No more feeling old. No more being told that you are a box-office poison. No more watching younger and prettier actresses get the roles she held on to herself for fifteen years. No more playing a mother of teenage kids in B pictures. Finally, a starring role presented itself. *If Crawford can win for Mildred Pierce, why not me,* Katherine said to herself.

"Katherine!"

Katherine replied, "Howard, so good to see you."

"So happy we are able to work together on a picture again," said Howard.

"It has been over five years, Howard," said Katherine. "I'm so excited about this lead role. It's going to get me to the top again. I just know it."

"I could have had Bergman, Hepburn, even Rita Hayworth for this role," said Howard.

Katherine replied, "And I am evermore grateful to you, Howard."

Howard slowly moved toward Katherine and embraced

---

her with a warm hug. The temptation to kiss her was too much for him.

"Tell me, did you wear red as I asked?" said Howard.

Katherine stepped back from Howard. She was on display. Slowly, to tease, she unbuttoned and opened her trench coat. A cherry red bra and panty set was all that was to be seen.

"Very lovely figure and a very nice choice, if I may say so," said Howard.

"You may," said Katherine.

Katherine read Howard's mind perfectly. The moment to slip out of the trench coat and make her way to Howard's desk arrived.

"Leave the high heels on," said Howard.

Howard watched Katherine slowly saunter to his desk. Katherine found the corner that suited her best and bent over the corner. She became a piece of that desk. Her head rested squarely, snuggly, feeling the desk's every contour. She closed her eyes. She felt her panties being ripped down to her ankles. As she felt him over her, panting heavily, she could only think of the promise she made to herself for over twenty years. A self-imposed pact of one. Under no circumstance would she subject herself to giving her body for sex, to never allow any studio executive with power to manipulate her with their libido for a role of meaning and substance in an A picture. She swore that she never would. And now she was trapped. She had to be. Her big return as a star came with a heavy price. And she was willing to pay in spades. She sold her soul, selling off her morals, ethics, and principles like a Wall Street fire sale just to remain in the public eye. To continue being the great and lovely Katherine Edmonds. Each thrust triggered the guilt and embarrassment. Each groan of ecstasy triggered the shame. Her eyes wandered around the desk until they became fixated on a copy of the script Katherine was to play the lead in. She smiled. A wry smile of accomplishment for a job well done. A smile that washed away the guilt and embarrassment. *The leading role in a picture again,* she said to herself. It was worth it.

Ian absorbed the picturesque view that the beaches of Malibu afforded him. He took a relaxed pose, leaning on the car, enjoying it all with measured sips out of his flask and puffs off his cigarette. Seagulls flying in a single file jettisoned across the ocean beach line. Ian followed their path with intensity. Their coordinated cackling was symphonic in his ear.

Abel sat behind the wheel, staring out at the ocean. He loved the picturesque views of Malibu as much as Ian. He slipped in quickie moments to make notes on a piece of paper no larger than the palm of his hand, notes about his new play. He hunched himself over the steering wheel. He did not want Ian to see what he was doing. His mind was made up. He wasn't going to tell Ian that he was leaving to go back to Harlem. It was settled. He would simply pack and leave. No note. No phone call. No telegram. Abel, Althea, and Abel Jr. would be catching a bus next week for the cross-country trip to New York City. He always loved Harlem. Fifteen years was enough of California to last his lifetime. His brother, Isaiah, showed him so much, what it could be for him: the excitement, the bright lights, the charm and special uniqueness a neighborhood can offer. The Apollo Theater. The car-door slam made Abel sit up and quickly stuff his notes inside his jacket. A quick look in the rearview mirror confirmed that Ian had returned inside the car.

"Bloody gorgeous day," said Ian.

"Yessuh, Mr. Ian," replied Abel. "Mighty fine day."

Abel began to wonder if Ian saw him making notes. An occasional glance in the mirror found him happily sipping on his flask. He felt safe. No detection.

"Tell me something, Abel," said Ian.

Abel replied, "If I can, Mr. Ian."

"Why did you do it?" asked Ian.

"Do what, Mr. Ian?" replied Abel.

"Why did you rewrite my script that night?" asked Ian.

Abel paused. He allowed the silence to build up. He knew that he would be leaving Ian's employ. He knew in his heart that a clean break also meant to tell Ian the truth. He struggled with the words, struggled to admit something he held in his heart for over twelve years, something he never told Ian.

"I reckon I loved you," said Abel. "Ain't that why people do things?"

Abel paused. He made one more peek in the mirror. Ian smiled and nodded in agreement. He took one very long swig off his flask.

Ian replied, "That's lovely to hear. I loved you too."

Abel watched in the mirror as Ian pulled a revolver out of his pocket and stuck the gun inside his mouth. He turned to face Ian.

"No!" yelled Abel.

Bang!

Abel felt the blood splatter sprinkle his face. There was nothing to look at but Ian's slumped-over body and his once handsome face which is a bloody mess. He exited the car and jumped into the back seat. He held Ian in his arms and began to sob uncontrollably. He didn't care that Ian's blood soaked his jacket. His notes fell out of his pocket onto a pool of blood on the floor. His words dissipated slowly with each passing second the paper absorbed Ian's blood. Abel picked them up off the floor with his bloody hand. He held Ian close. Close to his beating heart for the last time.

"Goodbye, Mr. Ian."

28

―――――――

Harlem, 1951

August afternoons in Harlem were always warm and
humid. There was never an exception to this rule.
The streets on Lexington Avenue felt like hot frying
pans beneath Abel's feet. A cloudless sky permitted
the hot sun to show its might. His mission was
clear: get to the theater before he died of thirst
and exhaustion. A brisk pace was the solution.
The right hand that grasped the revisions for his
new play was soaked with perspiration, making the
pages wet. The traffic light on 127th changed to
red, and Abel became a part of the masses standing
on a small piece of hot concrete waiting for the
color green. Abel bolted across the street before
the light changed. He wanted a head start from the
pack. It worked.

His intended target was within eyesight—a massive
brick-and-sandstone block building containing
stained glass on its front façade. It was Abel's
office—the Harlem Neighborhood Theater. Abel did
not go inside right away. He wanted to look at the
small marquee mounted on top. The title of his play,
Say Amen, was depicted in bright red lettering with
black trim. Because the marquee hovered over the
sidewalk, it could be seen for the length of the

―――

entire block. *Two more weeks until opening night. Lots to do,* Abel said to himself as he walked into the theater.

"Abel, over here!"

Abel heard a familiar voice calling him over to a small corner of the theater, a space big enough to accommodate a table, four chairs, and the three men waiting to speak to Abel.

"Mr. Robeson, glad you could make it," said Abel.

"We're friends now, Abel. Call me Paul," said Paul. "I want you to meet James Baldwin and Oscar Micheaux."

"Have a seat, gentlemen." said Abel.

"James is working on his latest novel. What's it called again," asked Paul.

James replied, *"Go Tell It on the Mountain."*

"We are all here because we believe what you are doing in Harlem, Abel," said Oscar.

James replied, "Here, here to that."

Everyone's enthusiasm at the table brought a relaxed smile to Abel's face. He looked around and could see in everyone's eyes the same energy for the cause as himself. He had spent months drafting and working on a manifesto for artists in Harlem. He wanted to initiate an artist's renaissance in Harlem, a new beginning for Negro artists working in all mediums that could employ their craft and have a venue to showcase it. New York and Harlem was home for the past five years. Home for his wife, Althea, Abel Jr., and his four-year-old son, Isaiah. Home to his love as a playwright.

"Oscar, I want to hear more about your film," said Abel.

Oscar replied, "I'm excited, very excited. Shooting is complete in another month, six weeks at the most. Trying to raise more money to do Technicolor."

Everyone toasted their coffee cups. Oscar reached

into his pocket for his flask as everyone nodded that a shot of scotch in their coffee would be a welcome treat. Their toast was interrupted by the appearance of another.

"Malcolm, you made it," said Abel. "Gentlemen, I'm sure all have heard Malcolm speak around Harlem. Part of our renaissance movement is not just involving the arts and our individual craft, but an awareness for all Negroes, who we are as a people. It's not about becoming Muslim; that's not why Malcolm is here. He sees the benefit of our side of the fight too. Period."

Malcolm walked around the table to shake everyone's hand. Abel handed him a cup of coffee. No one was interested in listening to Oscar's rambling interpretation of *mise-en-scène*.

"So what are we callin' our little band of brothers?" asked Paul.

Abel replied, "We're going to call ourselves A.R.E. A.R.E. will stand for Artists for Racial Equality. Artists banding together from all mediums: writers, filmmakers, orators, musicians, playwrights, actors and actresses, painters, and sculptors. All artists. Our mission will be to make Harlem the mecca for our renaissance. Bring attention through our individual craft to spark awareness. To shine a bright light into the world through what we love most. Our work will work for us."

"No!"

Abel was irked. The stress of writing, producing, and directing his first play was building up inside of him for weeks. Rehearsals were days behind schedule. The new floodlights were not working. Part of the stage needed to be rebuilt. He had to recast three roles. Today, he felt an inner compulsion to take it out on his cast.

"Ms. Kitt, it may help the production if you could hit your mark," said Abel.

Ms. Kitt replied, "I will try my best, Abel."

"Don't try, do it," said Abel. "This is a theater production. Actors are supposed to act, wouldn't you agree?"

It was more about the production. There was also the stress and strain of producing his play. Abel was a writer, a director. He was not a businessman crunching numbers, meeting production budgets, and raising capital. The auditions, the never-ending meetings with wardrobe, lighting, publicity, and stage hands. He was feeling the pressure. It mounted his shoulders so much harder with each passing day. Hiring someone to strictly produce was not an option to Abel. He refused to relinquish any control on any level regarding *Say Amen*. It will be his creation, birth, and life's work. No one else's meddling and interference. Determination conquered all his fears. The wait of twenty years to write, produce, and direct his own stage production was over.

It was within his grasp. A dream he had slept with, wrestled with, spoiled, rewritten time after time after time.

"Once more, everybody hit their mark this time, please. Action!" said Abel.

Abel felt the side of his temples contracting, pulsating in a strong and steady rhythm. Rubbing his eyes with force and gulping black coffee was not helping. He softly lay his head down on his office desk. He had not slept for thirty-six hours. *Two more weeks,* he said to himself. His mind swirled in a confused frenzy as to what to do next. He did not hear the soft knock on his door, nor did he hear it open.

"Abel?" asked Althea.

Abel managed to open up one of his eyes so he my

see Althea. She stood before him holding a dinner tray and a small pot of coffee.

"You didn't come home for dinner again," said Althea.

Ian replied, "Sorry, suga' cake, lots to do before opening night."

Althea placed the tray on Abel's desk and began setting up his dinner.

"I fried a couple of pieces of chicken, some mashed potatoes 'n gravy, black-eyed peas," said Althea. "You gotta eat somethin'."

The alluring smell of Althea's Southern fried chicken was enough to perk Abel up to open both eyes and sit up. His fingers grappled the large drumstick as he devoured it in a matter of seconds.

"Abel, I need to talk to you 'bout somethin'," said Althea.

Abel nodded his head yes without missing his chewing and chomping cadence of Althea's fried chicken.

"So talk, baby," said Abel.

Althea had the stage. She had Abel's undivided attention. She froze. The words that resided in her mind for days could not be emitted. The silence was enough to divert Abel's attention from his chicken dinner.

"What?" asked Abel.

"It's gettin' so hard to make ends meet," said Althea. "We were late with the rent this month. Barely keepin' the lights on. Marissa needs shoes. Abel Jr. is twenty-two. He grows out of clothes so fast."

Abel replied, "I'll take care of it."

"But we can't put everythin' you make and I make cleaning houses into this theater," said Althea. "Into this play and this production."

Abel replied, "I said I'll take care of it."

"You ain't gonna let your family end up on the street because of this, is you?" asked Althea.

"I said it will be all right!"

Althea replied, "There's no reason to yell at me like that."

Abel realized the error of his ways. He had never spoken to Althea in such a harsh tone. Ever. Abel rushed his arms around Althea. A soft kiss on her cheek was planted softly.

"I'm sorry, baby," said Abel. "I promise we will be all right. Go on now, you'll be late for work."

The cast of Abel's play scurried to their positions on stage. A lighting test coincided with the madness all around. Abel stood before the stage with the latest copy of his play, feeling the clawed grasp by both hands. His pace was a brisk ten feet and turn, ten feet and turn. The strains on his face said it was not sounding in sync with his written words.

"Hold it! Hold it!" said Abel.

Abel walked up to his lead actor and stood as close as he could without touching his nose.

"I understand you are a big star now, and by the way, your debut performance on screen was magnificent. I just wonder if your inspiration for theater may have waned since *No Way Out* was released," said Abel. "I must ask, do you feel you are giving this production everything you have, Mr. Poitier?"

"I believe I am, Abel," said Mr. Poitier.

Abel replied, "You are the leader. The cast expects you to lead, Mr. Poitier. Of course if my script is unable to inspire you, there is the North American Negro Theater around the corner."

"I get the message, Abel," said Mr. Poitier

Abel replied, "Good. Shall we take it from the top?"

"You can't. Neither your father ain't neva' going to let you," said Althea.

That was not the response Abel Jr. wanted to receive. His ears creaked from the unwanted words. His body went through a series of gyrations. The sound of his mother's voice at that moment was not symphonic in any way. The speaking of his mind that he had displayed in front of his parents over the weeks bore no fruit.

"Momma, I'm twenty-two," said Abel Jr. "Ain't nuthin' here for me in Harlem. No school, no job. I ain't going to be no street hustler like uncle Isaiah either. I'm signin' up for the army."

"Momma, can I have a glass of milk?" said Marissa.

Althea turned her attention away from Abel Jr. to her five-year-old daughter, Marissa. As she walked to the icebox to pour a glass of milk, the break from her argument with Abel Jr. gave her a moment to simmer down and think about what she needed to say while waiting for Abel to arrive home.

"Thank you, Momma," said Marissa.

"You can go back to your room and play now," said Althea. "Momma will be in there in a second."

Before leaving the kitchen, little Marissa looked up at her older brother. Even the innocent eyes of a five-year-old can see pain in an older adult. Abel Jr. gave her an assuring smile. He didn't mean it. His mind was already made up. He was going to enlist in the army.

The theater was bathing in complete darkness. Abel's office door was open. The only light being emitted was from a brightly lit bulb. He wasn't writing, he wasn't reading, he wasn't studying, he wasn't creating riveting dialogue in his head. He stared out of his office window. The streetscape off 126th Street had slowed to a slow crawl of midnight pedestrians. He was just staring, not looking at anything. He didn't even hear the rapid knocking at his door.

"Abel," said Paul. "Abel?"

Paul's voice broke the trance.

"Hello, Paul," said Abel. "Rather late, isn't it?"

Paul replied, "We were at the Cotton Club. Abel, I want you to meet a close friend of mine. Alberto Gromaldi."

Abel and Mr. Gromaldi walked slowly to each other and offered a handshake gesture to each other.

"Mr. Gromaldi, Paul has said many wonderful things about you," said Abel.

"Please call me Alberto. We're all friends here," said Alberto.

Abel replied, "Have a seat."

A meeting of creative minds around a small wooden table at midnight had taken place. It's not a creative meeting or a board meeting of a large corporation. It's a business meeting. Abel saw Alberto as a way to preserve what he worked hard for.

Alberto saw increasing profit margins and a way to launder his steady stream of racketeering income. This evening, Paul was simply playing broker.

"So why are we here?" asked Abel.

Alberto replied, "Opportunity."

The truth had now been expressed to all. Opportunity was the word being branded about the table. Opportunities for success, for fame, for riches, for adoration, for professional satisfaction, for acknowledgment. All snuggled up in a warm blanket called opportunity.

"Opportunity for whom?" asked Abel

"For everyone sitting in this room," said Alberto.

"Hear him out, Abel," said Paul

It was a brief glance between Abel and Alberto.

Alberto never took his eye off Abel as he reached into his pocket for his cigarette case. Abel and Paul shared a glance toward each other. Paul wanted Abel to trust him, to hear Alberto out.

"Your theater does good business," said Alberto. "I saw your play last year. It was an excellent production. You could have made more money. You can do better."

"And you have the solution for the theater to do better?" asked Abel.

"Abel, just listen for a sec," said Paul.

"What's the pitch, Mr. Gromaldi?" asked Abel.

Alberto replied, "I want to fix up the theater. Add couple hundred seats. Bigger marquee board out front. More publicity. Get the word out on Park Avenue and not just Harlem and Morningside. Affluent whites are already coming up here and going to the Cotton Club. Your play is going to be a big success."

"For a price, Mr. Gromaldi. For a price," said Abel.

Abel got out of his chair and walked back to the window. He wanted to stare out into Harlem and listen. He wasn't sure what he would hear next. It was his way of dealing with the pending proposal.

"I get 75 percent of the profits," said Alberto. "You remain the face of the theater, complete control of all production aspects of all your plays. Your 25 percent will triple the 100 percent you are receiving now."

Abel stood, glued to the window. The seconds elapsed by leaving an indefinite term of silence and uncertainty in the room.

"Abel?" said Paul.

Abel slowly turned away from the window and walked toward Alberto.

"It's a deal, Alberto," said Abel.

Abel Jr. sat on the front porch, staring at a

midnight black sky, perfectly housing an abundance
of stars in constellation to each other. The puffs
off his cigarette were short and measured. His stare
into space resonated more than if he was speaking
to a group of his friends standing before him.

"Want some company?"

Abel Jr. didn't hear Abel entering the porch. He
grabbed the cigarette out of Abel Jr.'s hand for a
quick drag.

"Didn't know you smoked, Pops," said Abel Jr.

Abel replied, "Keep that from your momma."

The two of them sat on the ledge and watched the
people stroll the street in front of them. It was
the perfect and opportune time to finish sharing
that cigarette Abel Jr. had started.

"Your momma just told me you made up your mind
about joining the army," said Abel.

"My mind's made up, Pops," said Abel Jr. "I
leavin' for Camp Lejeune, North Carolina, next
week."

Abel signaled Abel Jr. to pass him the cigarette
for another puff. Abel found a moment to look over
his shoulder to see Althea standing in the window
looking out. He wasn't certain whether Althea was
shocked at seeing him smoke a cigarette or was that
hope in her face that Abel could convince Abel Jr.
to not enlist into the army.

"Not out here tryin' to get you to change yo'
mind, Junior," said Abel. "You a grown man now."

Abel turned once more to look at Althea. He could
not give her a sign of hope. Althea knew it. There
was no hope. Not a remote chance that Abel would
be able to sway Abel Jr. from going off to Korea
to fight. Abel shook his head "no." Althea saw what
she needed to see. She walked away from the window
as the draperies folded back to cover the window.

"Let's go inside and tell your momma her son's
gonna be a soldier," said Abel.

29

The lead actor and his leading lady held each other closely on stage, sharing a moment for endearing words of sentiment and love. Words of commitment. A warm embrace was followed by the end of the play. The curtain slowly fell as every single ticket holder rose to their feet in adulation and applause. Abel joined the cast onstage for an encore bow. The roars of applause reached a deafening pitch. Abel's smile was wide, wide as the stage itself. He was proud. An achievement of one's dream will do that. His eyes watered while his tears slowly cascaded down his cheek. A myriad of memories. Twenty years since his first days in California. Reuniting with Althea and finding out that he had a son. The years working for the McGregors. The moments with Ian, the Ian who made him cry, the Ian who made him laugh, the Ian who listened to him, the Ian who made love to him, the Ian who hurt him. The hours on end watching him drink until he passed out. Washing and waxing Ian's cars. Laying Ian's suits neatly on his bed. And in the very end, he became Ian's closest friend. Allowing someone to witness your own suicide was very personal. Everyone who surrounded Abel on stage thought it was the overwhelming emotions of the huge success of his play. Quick and vivid flashbacks through the years of pain, hurt, creative breakthrough, disappointment, an awakening and acceptance of your sexuality, and finally receiving accolades for your creative work made you feel your world, your life, had come full circle.

Althea and his children, Abel Jr. and Marissa, stood in the front row beaming with pride. Abel caught a glimpse of Althea blowing him a kiss. He gave her the widest smile he could ever create. The standing ovation had now exceeded three minutes. The throng bellowed as strongly as it had begun. He was an artist. Whether the medium was film, theater, painting any art, dreams and visions of accolades by the throngs who view their work was the ultimate in satisfaction. To be known for one's expressive vision was everything an artist craved. That was and will always be the ultimate reward.

Abel held his entire family in a loving hug. Four members of a family, embracing each other lovingly and celebrating the career and family success of one.

"When you comin' home?" asked Althea.

Abel replied, "Soon. Have to shake a few more hands. You'all go on home. I won't be long."

One last hug and kiss for all before the door closed. For the first time all day, Abel was to benefit from a few months alone to absorb everything that happened earlier in the evening . . . . He always knew he could write. He always knew he wanted to write and produce his own plays, a desire that burned deep into his soul. *As you dream, dream big,* he would tell himself for many years. He glanced over to his desk and saw a copy of the script for his next play. A very faint smile painted Abel's face for he knew that with the success of *Say Amen,* a long run of the play was at hand and his next project would be delayed. A very soft knock was heard. Abel rose to answer.

"Hello, Abel," said Katherine.

The immediate shock of seeing Katherine ignited his flashback memory. Five years. Five years since she had seen Katherine at Ian's funeral. Five years since he watched Ian spray his brains all over him and the inside upholstery of Ian's car.

"Ms. Katherine," said Abel.

"May I come in?" asked Katherine.

Abel replied, "Yes, ma'am, of course."

Abel opened the door fully to allow Katherine in. He hurried to his chair to move the newspapers and scripts stacked, one on top of the other. He motioned to Katherine to have a seat.

"It's been a long time," said Katherine.

Abel replied, "Yessum, lotta water has run through the creek."

"I loved your play," said Katherine. "I had no idea you were such a talented writer. It was quite an accident that I found you in Harlem writing and directing. I was always so impressed by your manner. Your obvious higher literacy and education than the other Negroes has always impressed me. I understand Ian, well, why he liked you so much."

Abel reached into his drawer for his bottle of scotch and two glasses. He motioned to Katherine if she was interested. Katherine nodded in approval.

"Thank you," said Katherine. "To your success, Abel."

"What brings you to New York?" asked Abel.

Katherine replied, "Actually, I am in a production myself on Forty-second. A small part. I play the oldest sibling in a family. One of my acting colleagues recommended I come up to Harlem to see this wonderful play. She could not stop talking about it. When I saw your name and picture in the playbill, standing on that stage, taking bows. You have come a long way, Abel."

Abel smiled and gave Katherine a warm nod in

appreciation. He sensed that Katherine was ready for another shot to her glass.

"You ain't actin' in Hollywood no more, Ms. Katherine?" asked Abel.

Katherine replied, "No, I'm afraid Hollywood is done with me. I have been what you called blacklisted. For my past Communist point of views. My well-attended Red parties, as Hedda Hopper has penned. Just glad Ian is not alive to live through all of this."

"Sorry you on hard times, Ms. Katherine," said Abel.

Katherine needed a break. A short swig out of her glass. She found the paintings, pictures, and sketches hanging on Abel's wall attractive, as if she entered a museum gallery. Her head rotated around the office as if on a swivel. And then one photograph caught her attention. She rose from her seat and walked to the wall to stare at this one photograph. A photograph of Abel standing by Ian's Packard as Ian exited the car. Abel watched Katherine for minutes until she turned around and walked toward him.

"Where did you get that picture?" asked Katherine.

"From Mr. Ian," said Abel.

Katherine replied, "Yes, I know how close you and Ian were."

"Beggin' yo' pardon, Ms. Katherine?" asked Abel.

Katherine replied, "My marriage to Ian was like being married to a chameleon. It took on many colors, many hues. But there were never any secrets between him and I. Never."

"No, ma'am, no secrets," said Abel.

"I've taken enough of your time. You probably want to get home to that nice family of yours. It was good to see you, Abel. Good luck."

Katherine opened the door softly and walked out of Abel's office. Abel stood for a moment to stare at the door, trying to absorb what had just happened. He turned and walked to the wall where the picture of him and Ian hung. He began to do something that he had done every day for the past four years—stare at that picture.

Everyone always had a place to go in a train station. Everyone scurried with a specific destination at the front of their mind. Grand Central Station, being the main culprit of this large city phenomenon, displayed behemoth masses of people circling every angle within sight on a warm Indian summer morning.

"Your momma's hopin' you understand why she didn't come down with us," said Abel.

"Yeah, I know why, Pops," said Abel Jr.

"Too painful for her to see you go. Maybe you won't come back."

Abel Jr. replied, "Don't worry, Pops, I'll be back."

A father hugged his son. A son who was grown. A son about to do a grown-up thing and join the army, go off to Korea if needed be. Abel wanted it to be a hug of "see you son," but there was pain in his heart in fear of loss. His fear grew as his embrace tightened. He missed out on the first sixteen years of Abel Jr.'s life. He didn't blame Althea. Those were the circumstances of his life he had no control over. You can't get to know a young man in only six years, then see him leave, perhaps for the final time. Perhaps that's why Abel held on him so tightly. Having his son in his life with him was a gift. The gift was saying goodbye.

"Sweetie, pass the butter to your Pops, please."

Marissa complied with Abel's wishes. The dinner table of four is now a dinner table of three.

"Momma," said Marissa.

Althea replied, "Yes, baby."

Abel knew the dinner conversation would turn to

Abel Jr. A young child will never understand why a family member, a loving older brother, would leave home for a faraway land. Abel and Althea shared a glance, knowing between each other what was to become would be the inevitable. As a signal to Althea that she had been nominated to conduct the conversation with their daughter, Abel buried his head in the evening dinner.

"Why did Junior leave?" asked Marissa. "I thought he loved us."

Abel picked and prodded the food in his plate. Never on cue like one of his plays, he kept looking over at Abel Jr.'s empty seat at the family table.

"Junior did love us, sweetie pie," said Althea.

Marissa replied, "Then why did he go to the army?"

It became time for Althea and Abel to exchange stares.

Althea silently pleaded with Abel to take over the conversation.

"Sweetie, your brother is almost twenty-three," said Abel. "He's a grown man. It's his choice to go to the army. When you are twenty-one, your momma and I won't be tellin' you what to do either."

"I wish he would come back home tomorrow," said Marissa.

A piece of balled-up paper hit the floor and nestled itself next to other nine pieces of paper . . . Abel sat at his office desk scrawling out dialogue as best and as fast as he could. Writing . . . Writing . . . Writing . . . He stopped suddenly to rip up, bawl, and discard another piece of paper . . . He kept writing through the knocks at his door.

"Not now!" yelled Abel.

Abel continued writing. The knocks continued on the door.

"Not now, I said!" yelled Abel.

The door slowly creaked open. Abel's costume designer sheepishly slid her head inside the door.

"I am sorry, Abel," said MaryAnne.

Abel replied, "Now that you're in, what is it, MaryAnne?"

Abel placed his script to the side as MaryAnne walked with a number of dresses in her hand.

"These are the dinner dresses for the third act," said MaryAnne.

Abel remained seated while MaryAnne held each dress up to her for Abel's approval or disapproval. He stood up and walked around MaryAnne to absorb every angle the dress could be seen on stage during the performance.

"Take the black dress, put the white lace around the V-neck opening in the front. Classy and sexy at the same time."

MaryAnne replied, "Yes, sir."

MaryAnne turned toward the door only not to be able to exit right. Alberto appeared, stood in the doorway, allowing MaryAnne to exit before he stepped into the office.

"Bonjourno, Abel," said Alberto

Abel replied, "Alberto, what can I do for you?"

"Business," said Alberto.

"Business?" asked Abel.

"Things are going well with your play," said Alberto. "Look at you, already working on the next one. The next one, we raise ticket prices. The next one, I get a bigger cut."

Over the years, Abel picked up one of Ian's myriad of habits—a daily habit of drinking scotch. He walked over to his desk to pour a deep shot.

"You drive a hard bargain," said Abel.

Alberto replied, "What'cha talkin', huh? You makin' a what, thousand a week clear? Why until

I came around wasn't no niggers from Harlem or anywhere coming into this rathole."

Abel poured a shot of scotch and hoisted his glass toward Alberto for a toast.

"Here's to a better-lookin' rathole".

The tall, gray, drab limestone walls of Sing Sing Prison surrounded Abel on all four sides. The sun-kissed sky was long gone. The strong gust of wind had picked up in the last few minutes, the need to turn his coat collar up and place his hands in his pocket . . . He had forgotten that he had stuck every letter Isaiah had returned to him over the past twenty years. They counted ten. Abel pulled them out of his pocket. The letter on top was the latest one he wrote six months ago. Every letter written to Isaiah had been returned to him unopened. Isaiah had yet to be processed and released. Abel decided to pass the time by reading one of the letters he had written to Isaiah. Twenty-three years served out of a twenty-five-year sentence for murder. For murdering Flo. Abel clutched the envelope in one hand as he held the letter.

My Brother Isaiah,

You do not know how happy I am to be writing this letter to you, brother. I know it will be my last one. In six months, you will be a free man. I have dreamed and prayed that this day would come. To not see each other for almost twenty-three years has broken my heart. I do not know what happened that night I left Flo. I wanted to explain to you my side of everything. For so long, I had wished you had written me back. Told me what happened . . . told me that you forgave me for betraying you. I have said I am so sorry for hurtin' you, brother, so many times . . . the guilt I have felt . . . I am responsible for your being there . . . I pray

*there will be some sort of way that you will forgive
me . . . and that I can somehow make it up to you.*
  Your loving brother, Abel

The letter was softly rolled and placed back into
Abel's pocket. Abel's eyes squinted. The blustery
winds had him grappling for his coat collar. The
sound of an iron gate could be heard behind him.
Once Abel could turn around and see, it was Isaiah's
walk. His gait. It was Isaiah.

Abel and Isaiah slowly walked to each other. They
stood before each other. Their embrace was much more
than an embrace. It was a strong grip between two
people, two brothers who haven't seen each other in
twenty-five years. The energies of emotion surged
through the both of them. The times growing up in
Alabama. The times spent in New York. And now, an
unknown as to what the future may bring.

"Hello, brother," said Abel. "You're lookin'
good."

Isaiah replied, "You're lookin' a little betta."

They couldn't resist, and so they gave in to
temptation. Another warm, tightly clutched hug
between the two of them.

"Gimmie that bag," said Abel. "Althea got dinner
waitin' for us."

Abel and Althea quickly found it comfortable
with Isaiah occupying the dinner table seat
that once belonged to Abel Jr. It was good to
have someone, a family member, seated instead of
relegating themselves to stare at an empty chair
every evening. Every evening, their minds navigated
down a winding road of fear, anxiety, and doubt,
unable to understand a subject matter beyond their
grasp. Something they had no control of what was
occurring thousands of miles away in Korea . . .

"Is there any more chicken?" asked Isaiah.

"I knew you might be extra hungry and I just

happened to fry up some extra pieces," said Althea. "Left 'em in the kitchen. Be right back," said Althea.

"And how old you, Marissa?" asked Isaiah.

Marissa replied, "Seven."

"So cute," said Isaiah. "You certainly gonna be Daddy's little girl."

"She sure will be," said Abel.

Althea returned with a basket full of fried chicken. She circled the table serving food and collecting dirty dishes at the same time, and finding a quick moment and pass a signal to Marissa to hurry and finish her meal.

"Althea Motley, my, my, my," said Isaiah. "How long has it been?"

Althea replied, "Don't righty know. Abel left round 1928, so you were gone 'bout four years 'fore then."

"That's right," said Isaiah. "It was summer of '25."

"Say good night to your uncle Isaiah," said Althea.

Marissa replied, "Good night, Uncle Isaiah."

"Good night, baby gurl," said Isaiah

Isaiah watched Althea and Marissa leave the dining room. He enjoyed a smile that he had not enjoyed for over twenty years. His little brother, his baby brother, Abel, found a way to make him smile with great pride . . .

"You gotta mighty nice family, baby brother," said Isaiah.

Abel nodded in appreciation and pulled out a pack of cigarettes out of his pocket.

"Gimmie one of those," said Isaiah.

Abel obliged Isaiah. He lit his cigarette after his.

"What are your plans?" asked Abel.

Isaiah replied, "Ain't got no plans."

"It's all settled. You gonna come work for me," said Abel. "I need a janitor and building manager for the theater."

"Got plenty practice sweepin' and moppin' in Sing Sing," said Isaiah.

"Those days are behind you," said Abel.

Isaiah turned his head away from Abel. He looked up and stared at the ceiling, taking a couple of long drags on his cigarette.

"Why did you do it?" asked Isaiah.

Abel replied, "Do what?"

"Come on, man. I gotta yell it out for the whole goddamn house to hear?" asked Isaiah. "Why did you fuck Flo?"

"Isaiah, I . . . I . . . I," said Abel.

Abel was not giving Isaiah the response he waited twenty-five years for. He wanted an answer. He wanted a confession. He wanted to hear humility and repentance from Abel. It was the time to hurl his plate of food against the wall. Althea's voice could be heard yelling on the other side of the wall asking Abel what was going on.

"It's okay, baby!" said Abel. "Go back to sleep!"

"I went to jail because of what you did," said Isaiah. "Twenty-five motherfuckin' years."

"I'm sorry, I'm sorry, Isaiah. But I ain't the one who pulled the trigga. You went to jail for what you did to Flo. I didn't mean for it to happen. It happened. I would have stayed. Flo told me to get up on out of there. She said she would take care of things. I was young. I was stupid. Next thing I know, I'm outta New York and workin' the trains in California."

"And I'm doing twenty-five for killin' a no-good bitch who was fuckin' my baby brotha'."

"I can't change the past, Isaiah. I know you were savin' me from being a witness to those two killins.

That policeman you shot. I know you were protectin' me. I let you down."

"No, you didn't. It was Flo who let me down," said Isaiah.

"I'm sorry," said Abel.

Isaiah replied, "Well, like you said, I can't change the past. What time do you need me for work at the theater tomorrow?"

30

His face was buried deep on top of his chipped and dinged wooden desk. Abel's typewriter had ceased clicking and clacking hours earlier. The perspiration spot under his arms blotted the entire shirt sleeve on both arms. The enveloping cloud of his writer's block had become unbearable. His new play, *Undercurrent,* was weeks behind, and opening night was scheduled to start in two months. There was this moment occurring. Abel glanced upward to stare at the mounted photo of him and Ian. He was trying to remember the hundreds of times he would enter Ian's office to clean up while Ian slept off his latest drunken stupor. Ian's voice was ringing in Abel's head.

"Look at you on your bloody own."

He raised his head off the desk. The fatigue had nestled in his eyes and the rubbing of them made his eyes feel better.

"The great Negro writer," said Ian.

Abel placed his hands over his ears. He believed that by doing this, it would keep Ian's voice out of his head. *Don't look at the picture,* he said to himself. He grabbed his latest version of the script and ran out of the office.

"Okay, everybody, gather around," said Abel.

The actors circled around Abel, with the script

being held in everyone's hand. That was a special requirement. When Abel spoke in an impromptu fashion before his cast, everyone had to have their copy of the script with them.

"Look, everyone, the pace for the first act is not quick enough," said Abel. "Now, I know everyone is still tryin' to learn their new lines, but we have to pick up the pace. It's too long. Carl, step it up. Mary and Alex, make your kisses mean something. This is a damn play. Act like you are in love. Now, let's get it right."

The actors took their marks on stage. Everyone was prepared, set to move, eager to make Abel happy.

"Action!"

While the actors scurried around the stage reciting their lines, Abel became what he is best at—a jack of all trades, the mega producer. Double-checking the dialogue, inspecting the lighting, ensuring the blocking on stage was exactly the way he wanted it. He was in full-blown creative fury.

"Cut!"

Connie, please tell me you are acting as though you are in love with this man," said Abel.

Connie replied, "I thought I was."

Is that how you look into a man's eyes when you are about to kiss him?" asked Abel. "Is that how you signal to a man you want him to make love to you? Because if it is, Ms. Connie, you must be a pretty lonely young woman."

The cast including Connie chuckled in unison. Abel's tongue-in-cheek humor was easily recognized, and everyone knew he was not being derisive or hurtful. It served as a relaxation technique while delivering a message that he was not happy with how the production was going.

"Okay, everyone, I believe Connie is ready to be an actress," said Abel. "Places, please! Action!"

Firmly entrenched in his customary place in the rear of the theater, Isaiah swept and mopped up the garbage and filth left behind by the theater inhabitants. He stopped and looked toward the stage every time Abel would direct his cast. Isaiah felt an irony surging through his body. How him and Abel have taken two different life paths, two different roads. Isaiah wished he had furthered his education and taken the same path as Abel. He knew had he done so, he wouldn't be slinging a mop and picking up garbage and also killing the occasional rat.

"Cut!" said Abel. "Ok, better. Not great. Ms. Dandridge, if you would please stick to the blocking. Poor Reggie is getting dizzy walking in circles. Once again, on second thought, that's it for tonight. See you, everyone, tomorrow at eleven. Eleven!"

Abel kept his head buried in his script as the actors and actresses walked by him. He learned the lesson many years ago that a writer is always a writer all the time. Abel turned over his shoulder and saw Isaiah walking toward him.

"Just need to get the trash out," said Isaiah.

Abel replied, "Meet'cha by front door."

Lennox Avenue rang boisterously with everyone walking and filling the sidewalks and everyone driving and filling the streets. A Harlem that bustled. A Harlem that lived.

"How come you never answered any of my letters?" asked Abel.

Isaiah replied, "What fo'? Didn't make no fuckin' difference if I had or not."

"Would have made a difference to me," said Abel.

Isaiah replied, "If that wasn't so fuckin' funny, I'd laugh."

As Isaiah stopped to drop his cigarette butt to the ground to extinguish it, he looked up to see a dirty, shabbily dressed hobo sitting in the corner of a dilapidated brownstone building. Isaiah did not move for seconds. He was just staring at the man.

"Isaiah, what's wrong?" asked Abel.

Isaiah replied, "I know that fella. He was at Sing Sing with me. The fuck he doing over there?"

Abel and Isaiah walked over to the hobo and stood over him, just staring. The hobo, cuddled up in a ball, slowly opened up his eyes, recognizing no one.

"You're Patch Jenkins, ain'tu?" asked Isaiah.

The hobo took a few seconds to divert his attention from his fifth of bourbon to give Abel and Isaiah another look.

"Who the fuck are you?" asked Patch.

"Isaiah," said Isaiah. "I was in cellblock next to yours at Sing Sing."

Patch was unable to place Isaiah's face. Too much time had passed. Too many blurred faces meshing with the downed liquor.

"Leave him be," said Abel.

"Gimme two dollas," said Isaiah.

Abel reached into his pocket and handed Isaiah two dollars. Isaiah held the two singles close to Patch's eyes.

"Got get you somethin' to eat," said Isaiah.

The swell of people quickly surrounded Abel and Isaiah as they continued their walk.

"Who was that?" asked Abel.

Isaiah replied, "Patch Jenkins. He was in the cell next to mine at Sing Sing. He took a shiv meant fo' me one day in the chow line. Nigga came at me, sayin' I cheated him rollin' dice. Pulled out a shank and went at me wit it. Patch jumped in front of me and got slashed. Took eleven stitches. And one more thang, he gave that nigga a whuppin within a inch of his life. He never fucked wit me again."

"Why did he do all of that for you?" asked Abel.

Isaiah replied, "It was a kind of a payback."

"Payback?" asked Abel.

Isaiah replied, "It was a long time ago. You were still in Alabama. Patch is Flo's younger brother. He got into some trouble, and I took care of the problem for him. Permanently, as in fo' good."

"No!" yelled Abel. "We worked on the blocking for this over fifty times. Maurice, your shoulders must be turned like so. It's critical to the lighting. Again, please."

The actors took their marks and proceeded to enact the scene on stage. They are unaware that Abel pranced around them like a panther sniffing out his prey from thirty feet away. There's a moment he approved of what he saw and heard. His words sang a song his ears wanted to dance to, flowing in a melodic way while the actors correctly took their blocking. One nod of approval followed the other.

"Abel Johnson?"

Startled, Abel turned around to face a middle-aged white man dressed in a suit and fedora.

"Abel Johnson?"

Abel replied, "Yes, that's me."

The man reached into his breast pocket to hand Abel a document. Abel stuck his hand out to accept it.

"This is for you," said the man. His final task was to turn and walk out of the theater.

Abel held the document in his hand, folded up neatly with a blue outer cover. He was not certain what it was, yet fearful that bad news was about to be unveiled.

"Let's take lunch now. Ninety minutes. Back here by two o'clock."

Abel sprinted out of the theater. A short burst in the following seconds found him outside joining the walking throng along Madison Avenue. His pace was brisk, barreling down the street in a perfectly straight line. His efforts into trying not to bump into anyone failed more often than he ever intended. The grip on the documents delivered to him by the process server became tighter with each forward, moving step. Abel stopped walking for a moment. He had lost his breath. He bent over in hopes that his panting would subside. He looked up to see that his destination, Momma Sassy's Restaurant, was down the street on the corner.

Abel entered the restaurant and stopped at the entrance door. He knew who he was looking for. He ate and socialized every day at the same time. His head rotated around, staring at every booth and at every person seated at the counter. His ears peeled back, wide open, to hear his most distinguishable voice. He found him sitting in a corner booth, enjoying a glass of his favorite Merlot. As he made his way toward the booth, Abel's eyes and his friend Paul's lock onto each other.

"Paul," said Abel.

Paul replied, "Abel, have a seat."

Abel sat across from Paul. A waitress walked over to the booth to lay a placemat before him.

"Just coffee," said Abel.

"It's been a while my friend," said Paul. "How's the play moving along since those rewrites?"

Abel reached inside his pocket, pulled out the document, and slid it over to Paul.

"Do you know what this is?" asked Abel.

Paul replied, "It appears to be a subpoena. I have one of those too."

"How did they get my name?" asked Abel

Paul replied, "Don't matter how. They got it."

"Who is this House of Un-American Activities?" asked Abel. "What do they want with me? I don't know nuthin'. Nuthin' that would interest them."

Paul replied, "You were there, Abel, servin' food 'n drinks to all of those Red Commies the McGregors had in their home. You know names, you know dates.

You know who, you know where. They want names. Even if it comes from a Negro servant."

"I ain't gonna do it, are you?" asked Abel.

Paul replied, "I'm not a sellout, Abel. I'm not going to be responsible for betraying the confidences of friends and colleagues that I have had the great fortune of talking to, creating next to, performing with over these many years. White folk. Black folk. All folk."

"What'cha going to do, Paul?" asked Abel.

Paul replied, "I have a plan."

"A plan?" asked Abel. "What's your plan?"

"England," replied Paul. "The London stage. I've been offered to produce *Show Boat* with James Whale on the West End. I want you to write the play and direct it."

"I can't just pack up and leave my family for England," said Abel.

"You don't have a choice," said Paul. "If you don't honor the subpoena and testify, they could put you in jail for contempt. Niggas in jail stay in jail. Just ask your brother."

The evening brought quiet and solace as Abel and Althea cuddled warmly in their bed. Abel stared at the ceiling as Althea found a new spot on Abel's chest to nestle in. Abel did not have any answers. He didn't have a solution. All he did have was fear. Fear of ending up incarcerated like his brother, Isaiah. Fear that Althea will refuse to move herself and their daughter to England. Fear that he would have to give up a career that was his life's desire.

"You asleep?" asked Abel.

Althea replied, "Why, you want me to wake you up?"

Abel closed his eyes. He was the only one who could sense his trepidation with what he had to say. The minutes transpired and the quietness surrounding the bedroom remained steadfast.

"What's the matter?" asked Althea.

Abel replied, "I dunno where to start, baby. I've been told by a judge I have to give some people certain names of all the people I saw when I was workin' at Mr. Ian and Ms. Katherine's parties."

Althea replied, "Judge? What'chu done got yo'self into, Abel?"

"Nuthin' more than being in the wrong place at the wrong time. Now, if I don't testify, they could throw me in jail," said Abel.

"Jail?" asked Althea. "You can't go to jail, baby. What about us? What'cha gonna do?"

Abel replied, "There's a way I won't have to."

"Tell me, baby," said Althea.

Abel replied, "We'll have to move to England. Live in London. I've been offered a job to write and direct a play."

"London?" asked Althea. "But we don't know nuthin' 'bout livin' over there."

Abel replied, "Baby, we ain't got a whole lotta choices in the matter."

Althea softly held Abel's hand as he brought her close to his body. The seconds of silence allowed them to hold each other close, a loving embrace to mask their fears and trepidation of leaving America, with a distinct possibility that it may be forever, never to return. Althea's tears slowly fell onto Abel's chest as he stared at the ceiling. The ceiling fan turned slowly, and with each revolution, both knew what the right decision had to be.

"We're a family and we stay together," said Althea.

Abel replied, "Start packing tomorrow. I need to go see a friend to help us with our passports."

The curtain rang down after another outstanding performance by cast and crew. The last performance of Abel's play, *Undercurrent,* had left the present, and now the memories were about to begin. *The* sold-out crowd rose to their feet to douse the theater with a deafening round of applause. It would be for the last time, the last Abel Johnson production the theater will ever see.

"I want to thank everyone who has been involved these past five years for making our theater a great success in Harlem." said Abel. "Harlem is alive, vibrant, and we are a part of that. This success is never about one person, one writer, one actor, one dress designer, one producer. It is about, quite simply, all for one and one for all. That and only that is what makes a production a success, what makes people attend your production, what makes me stand here and bask in everyone's applause. The theater will continue to produce plays of meaning, of significance, of promoting the Negro art. Let's all vow to make sure that our vision relishes forward. From my heart, I say thank you all."

Autumn days in Central Park evolved into a blending of bright hues of orange, brown, and yellow. Distinct aromas of peanuts, popcorn, and hot dogs swirled between a parade of people scurrying in every direction. Abel always found Central Park as his tranquil getaway from Harlem, from the grind of the theater. He could think, pray, reminisce, long for, and relax. This afternoon, it was business. His head was buried in the new script he was writing for Paul for the London production once he arrived. He didn't see Katherine standing before him.

"A new script?" asked Katherine.

That was the moment Abel looked up to a recognizable voice. His business reason had finally appeared.

"As a matter of fact, it is," replied Abel.

"Does it have a name?" asked Katherine.

Abel replied, "Call it working title for now."

"Quite," said Katherine. "Would you like to tell me why we are meeting?"

"I need your help," said Abel. I'm moving to London, taking my family with me. Negroes can't get passports. I need for you to say you are traveling to England and that my wife and I are your domestics for visas.

"I am flattered, but why England?" asked Katherine.

Abel replied, "For the same reasons as you. I am not going to stand before a bunch of white folks and tell them what I saw and who I may know at all them parties. I never knew those people walkin' round you and Mr. Ian's house. I ain't got no reason to ruin lives. For what? I ain't gonna to be no Hollywood director. No Hollywood actor. I ain't gonna be no Hollywood writer either. I can write and produce my plays over in England."

"I see," said Katherine. "I paid a big price. I've been blacklisted. No studio will have me because of my political beliefs. And you know what? I am ok with that. I've done many distasteful things to save my career from ending. I wasn't going to betray trust and friendships like the others. And I know Ian would have done the same as I. We seem to have more in common than meets the eye, Abel."

"So, you will help me?" asked Abel.

Katherine replied, "Yes, I'll have the tickets day after tomorrow. *Queen Mary* is at Pier 62. I will board with you then leave before the ship sails. I will cable a very good friend of mine in London who has some connections and will meet your ship when it arrives."

"Thank you, Ms. Katherine," said Abel.

Katherine replied, "No, Abel, thank you."

Abel looked around his tightly cramped office to allow his eyes to entertain itself for one final gaze. The leather chair with the rip down the middle. The painted garbage can that was more damaged than painted. The hole in the baseboard,

laughingly remembering the kinship he had formed
with that little gray mouse. Late at night as the
wee hours beckoned, trying to rewrite something
that was never good to begin with. Eye-to-eye with
a small gray rodent standing twenty feet away. A
one-rodent audience waiting for Abel to create
something wonderful and inspiring to all who will
one evening be present to experience it inside his
theater.

His moments of gazing and whimsical flashbacks
ended. Abel stopped looking. It was the picture of
him and Ian that had his full attention. He walked
over and slowly took it down. He grasped it tightly
in his arms as though it was a masterpiece hanging
in the Louvre. As he returned to his desk, he
carefully placed it inside his valise.

"A friend of yours?" asked Alberto Gromaldi.

The question was enough to get Abel to return to
the business at hand. A final transaction that will
free him of all responsibilities to the theater. A
clean and final break.

"Yes, a friend of mine. He was my boss when I was
in California. Let's finish business," said Abel.
"Do you have the money?"

Alberto placed his large valise on top of Abel's
desk. He opened it slowly to allow Abel to see the
treasure of cash inside.

"Fifty grand, the agreed buyout price for you,
my friend," said Alberto. "Wanna count it?"

Abel smiled at the prospect, but shook his head
no. Looking intently into the valise was enough
satisfaction for him. Abel snapped the valise close
and, as a warm gesture, stuck his hand out to
Alberto to shake.

"Abbiamo un accord, amico mio?" asked Alberto.
"Do we have a deal, my friend?"

"My brother, Isaiah, gets promoted to manager

of the theater, and his cut of the house is 10 percent," said Abel.

Alberto replied, "Un accord."

The handshake turned into a warm embrace as Abel and Alberto walked out of Abel's office for the last time. Alberto waved goodbye, walking into the darkness of the theater. The hallway light flickered. Isaiah stood on a ladder changing a lightbulb as Abel watched him. Once the hallway returned to its yellow glow, Isaiah stepped down the ladder and walked over to Abel.

"And then there was light," said Abel.

Isaiah replied, "Somethin' like that."

Abel reached into his valise and pulled out ten thousand dollars.

"Here, take this. It's ten thousand dollars," said Abel.

Isaiah replied, "Look, man, you ain't owe me nuthin'. Go out the game you came in."

"Too late for that, brother. Take it."

Isaiah slowly took the money from Abel and placed it in his pocket.

"I can't never pay you back for the twenty-three years of your life you lost in prison," said Abel. "You're manager of the theater now, so hire a new janitor. Make that first thing on your list. You get 10 percent of the house take too. Grimaldi is your paymaster. He's good people. He's gonna make sure you get paid. I just wanna say, I just wanna say, I just wanna say."

"Then say it," said Isaiah.

Abel replied, "Take care of yo'self, brother."

It was the warmest hug Abel and Isaiah shared with each other in many years. Each one of their shoulders felt the moistness of tears running down each other's cheek. It would never be known if it is an embrace of "see you later" or "goodbye forever, brotha." It was an embrace of well-wishes and uncertainty of what the future holds for the both of them in their separate lives.

"Go on now, get," said Isaiah. "You got a boat to catch first thing."

The moment Abel stepped out into the deck of the *Queen Mary*, the late-afternoon sun emerged from behind a blanket of white puffy clouds. Abel basked, allowing the warm rays to douse his face. He kept his eyes closed and ran a series of flashback moments pertaining to the last twenty-four years of his life. Alabama, Momma, Sonny the chicken, Harlem, being responsible for Isaiah going to prison, Hollywood, Ian, getting Althea back in his life, finding out he has a son, family, and now a new home in England.

The New York City skyline became smaller with each passing moment. A signal for Abel to say "goodbye" was under way. It was time to think about what would be ahead. What life experiences would unfold before him. Living in a foreign land in a foreign city with a myriad of new hopes, new dreams, new challenges, and new prejudices. A place where the sight of an American Negro will not be common. The stares and the whispers he and his family would have to endure. There's that sun reappearing again, washing Abel's face with a newfound hope. The waters swathing the bow below him soothed his fears and trepidations. He had come to a conclusion—he was doing the right thing for everyone concerned. And that is when Abel smiled the brightest. He felt Althea's and Marissa's arms wrapping around him from behind.

"What'cha doing out here, Abel?" asked Althea.

Abel replied, "Sayin' goodbye."

Finish

Printed in the United States
by Baker & Taylor Publisher Services